THE
PRINCE
OF
RISK

ALSO BY CHRISTOPHER REICH

Rules of Betrayal

Rules of Vengeance

Rules of Deception

The Patriots Club

The Devil's Banker

The First Billion

The Runner

Numbered Account

CHRISTOPHER
REICH

THE
PRINCE
OF
RISK

DOUBLEDAY

New York   London   Toronto   Sydney   Auckland

Copyright © 2013 by Christopher Reich

All rights reserved. Published in the United States by Doubleday, a
division of Random House LLC, New York, and in Canada by Random
House of Canada Limited, Toronto, Penguin Random House Companies.

www.doubleday.com

DOUBLEDAY and the portrayal of an anchor with a dolphin are
registered trademarks of Random House LLC.

Book design by Michael Collica
Jacket design by John Fontana
Jacket illustrations: man © Veer/michaeldb;
vortex © Elenasz/Shutterstock

Library of Congress Cataloging-in-Publication Data
Reich, Christopher, 1961–
The Prince of Risk : a novel / Christopher Reich.—First Edition.
pages cm
1. International finance—Fiction. 2. Terrorism—Fiction.
3. Suspense fiction. I. Title.
PS3568.E476284P75 2013
813'.54—dc23
2012041924

ISBN 978-0-385-53506-9

MANUFACTURED IN THE UNITED STATES OF AMERICA

3 5 7 9 10 8 6 4 2

First Edition

To Joseph C. Raible III,
in memory

THE
PRINCE
OF
RISK

PROLOGUE

United States Federal Reserve Board Room, Eccles Building, Washington, D.C. Sunday, July 28, 10:50 p.m.

The three men sat at the head of the conference table, graying lions hunched over a kill.

"If only half of what this damn thing claims is true, we're in trouble," whispered one.

"And if all of it is?"

"We're royally—"

The door opened and a Secret Service agent stepped inside. "Excuse me, sir," he said. "We're standing by when you need us."

A domed chandelier hung above the long table, filling the cavernous room with a dim, funereal light.

"Give us a moment," said Secretary of the Treasury Martin Gelman. "Shouldn't be too much longer." Gelman waited for the Secret Service agent to leave, then tapped a finger on the dossier. "How many people on your end know about this?"

"Just my assistant," replied Edward Astor, chief executive of the New York Stock Exchange.

"No one else?"

Astor shook his head, staring at the treasury secretary and the man seated beside him, Charles Hughes, chairman of the Federal Reserve. No two men exerted more power over the economy of the United States. "I had my suspicions when I commissioned the report," said Astor.

"And who provided those?" demanded the chairman of the Federal Reserve.

"The firm that wrote it. It brought the matter to my attention in the first place."

Martin Gelman pushed his glasses higher on the bridge of his nose as he studied the dossier's cover. "Never heard of 'em. What the hell's that name supposed to mean?"

"Illumination," said Astor. "Apparently it's a Sanskrit word."

"Great," said Charles Hughes, who at seventy years of age was the youngest present. "Leave it to a bunch of Indian mystics to tell the United States that we're up a creek without a paddle."

"I believe they're American," said Astor. "At least as American as any of us."

"And who, or *what*, exactly are these folks?" inquired Gelman.

"Spooks. Seers. Savants. I'm not sure what you'd call them."

"Private sector?" asked Hughes.

"Any more private and they'd be invisible," said Astor. There was more, but he left it at that.

"If word gets out . . ."

"That's why it's just the three of us at eleven o'clock on a Sunday night," said Astor.

Silence echoed through the chamber. Astor stared at the Great Seal of the United States high on the wall and thought about the decisions made at this very table, some responsible for rescuing the country from financial catastrophe, an equal number for precipitating catastrophe in the first place.

And now one more.

Martin Gelman pulled his cell phone from his jacket. "I'll have to tell the president."

Astor clamped a hand on his arm. "Not with your phone."

"What the hell, Ed!"

"What about the report didn't you understand?" Astor relaxed his hold. "I suggest we inform the president *personally*."

It was Hughes's turn to protest. "At this time of night?"

"I'm sure the president will forgive the intrusion."

Hughes nodded unsurely. "It's just that it all seems rather impossible."

"Quite the opposite," stated Astor, with enough certainty for both of them. "Ask me, we practically begged them to do it. For ten years we've known or suspected. All those reports from the FBI, the CIA, even the Brits, telling us to be careful not to give away too much. In all that time, we've done nothing. We might as well have sent out an engraved invitation and put a welcome mat by the front door."

Hughes shook his head. "How did we allow this to happen?"

"Greed. Naïveté. We're all responsible."

Hughes brought his fist down on the table. "I'm just so damned angry."

"So am I, Charlie, but we still have time." Astor opened the report to the conclusion. "'. . . and though there is no question about the extent to which critical national systems have been penetrated, the aggressor cannot use TEP to trigger a modal system-wide default at his primary target until a source code is introduced.'"

"What does that mean in English?" interrupted Hughes.

"It means they've got the house wired top to bottom with C4, but they can't set off the charges. At least, not yet."

"Why the hell not? They've managed everything else."

"They don't have the fuse," said Gelman. "Without that, the house can't go bang."

"There's still one more step," said Astor. "They need to find a way in."

"Any idea how?" demanded Hughes.

"A few," said Astor.

"So how much time do we have?"

"Difficult to say. We have to assume that they have their eyes on an entry point and that their plan includes the probability of detection."

"Meaning sooner rather than later," said Hughes.

Astor nodded. "That's a safe assumption."

"Well, then." Gelman shot from his chair, scooping up the dossier and shoving it into his satchel. "It's four blocks to 1600 Pennsylvania Avenue. Time to roust the commander in chief out of bed."

Minutes later, the three men were seated in the back of an armored Chevrolet Suburban speeding down Constitution Avenue. Given the time of night and the impromptu nature of the meeting, the security detail numbered two agents. Both rode in front. No car followed. Astor had been adamant that they not attract undue attention.

"Take the State entry," said Gelman, referring to the security gate located at State Place, off 17th Street past the Ellipse. "We'll park in the West Wing lot."

Edward Astor glanced out the window. Ahead, the Washington Monument rose into the night sky. Beyond, bathed in light at the far end of the Mall, stood the Capitol. He was an immigrant's son, and the sights stirred his love for his country. His father had come to America eighty years before with an unpronounceable name and little more than the clothes on his back. In the space of twenty years, he had advanced from skinning cowhides for women's gloves to owning the glove factory itself. He worked tirelessly. He acquired a rich man's name. He saved to send his son to the best schools, and later helped him secure a job as a ticket runner on the floor of the New York Stock Exchange. Edward Astor liked to think he had done the rest on his own, but he never forgot his debt to his father and to the country.

"Only in America," his father used to say in the Czech accent he was never able to erase.

Astor looked at the report sitting on his lap. He'd be damned if he let someone steal what belonged to the country. *His country.*

The engine revved angrily, jarring Astor from his reverie. The vehicle surged, throwing him and his fellow passengers against their seats. Frightened, Astor grasped the armrest. The car swerved, then regained its lane. "Everything all right?" he asked.

As suddenly, the revving died and the engine slowed.

"I'm sorry, sir," answered the driver. "I must have hit the pedal a little hard."

Astor clutched the report to his chest. He said nothing, but his heart was racing.

The vehicle passed the Organization of American States and swung left onto 17th Street. Oak trees lined the road. Through branches swollen with summer leaves, he could make out the White House.

"Sir, I'd like to radio ahead," said the Secret Service agent in charge of the detail. "We don't like surprises."

"Absolutely not," said Astor, louder than he'd wanted.

"You heard him," added Secretary Gelman. "Pull up nice and slow. They'll know the car."

Astor turned in his seat. "To make sure, did either of you tell anyone we were meeting?"

"Not a soul," said Gelman. "The wife knows better than to ask."

"Don't have a wife," said Charles Hughes. "May have said a word to the vice chairman, though."

"Did you or didn't you?" asked Astor.

"Guess I did. We work closely on all matters. I don't hide anything from him."

"Wasn't he our ambassador out there prior to coming aboard?" asked Gelman.

"That was six years ago," protested Hughes. "You have no reason not to trust him."

"It's not a question of trust," retorted Astor. A terrible thought came to him. A shaking hand drew his phone from his jacket and scrolled through his address book. He stopped at a name he knew as well as his own. Years had passed since they had last spoken. Years filled with rancor and acrimony. Still, Astor did not hesitate. There was no one he trusted more.

In the dark, his thumbs struggled to find the correct keys.

"P–A–L," he began to text.

The Chevrolet slowed and turned into the State Place entrance. A guard belonging to the uniformed division of the Secret Service stepped from his booth. A Delta barrier blocked the road ahead.

Secretary Gelman rolled down his window. "Good evening, sergeant. You know who I am. The chairman of the Federal Reserve, Mr. Hughes, is with me, as is Mr. Astor, from the New York Stock Exchange. We're here to see the president."

"I don't have you on the list, sir."

"It's an emergency."

The guard demanded their identification, then stepped into his booth.

Astor continued typing. "A–N–"

The guard handed back the pieces of identification. "The president asks that you go to the West Wing portico."

The gates opened and the vehicle advanced slowly. In front of them, the Delta barrier lowered into the ground. The engine revved again and Astor braced himself but this time it was just the driver easing the car into drive. The Suburban advanced a few yards, then halted as a mirror was run beneath the chassis to check for explosives. The all clear was given and the car advanced to the next barrier. The blockade disappeared into the ground. The Chevrolet shuddered as it drove over the steel plate.

"Have you met the president?" Gelman asked.

"No," said Astor. "Different political persuasion."

"He's a good man, though he'll be none too pleased."

The car made a sharp left onto West Executive Avenue. The lane continued for 50 yards, passing the White House swimming pool on its right and widening into a parking lot for West Wing staffers.

"As long as he listens," said Astor.

"I'm sure he will. He's a—"

The Chevrolet surged forward, forcing the passengers against their seats. The engine revved more loudly than before. The car quickly gathered speed and in seconds was barreling down the lane.

"What the hell?" said Gelman.

"Slow this thing down," shouted Astor.

"My foot's on the brake," said the driver. "It's not doing a thing."

Directly ahead, a third Delta barrier blocked the way.

"Watch it!" cried Charles Hughes.

The driver yanked the car to the right, hopping the curb and hurtling onto the lawn. Astor bounced in his seat, striking his head on the roof. The phone tumbled from his grasp and fell to the floor.

"Shift into neutral," said the agent in charge, riding in the passenger seat.

"Driveshaft's locked."

The Chevrolet continued to gain speed, the needle on the speedometer passing 50 miles per hour, the car rocking over the uneven terrain. The driver steered between trees, as branches slapped the windshield, obscuring his view. Then the branches were gone and the vehicle was bounding across the South Lawn. Thirty yards of open grass separated them from the White House.

"Yankee Blue, this is Sierra Six," radioed the agent in charge. "We have an emergency. Vehicle out of control."

"Commo's dead, skipper," said the driver.

Ahead, the South Portico loomed. Astor grasped the seatback. "Stop this thing," he shouted again.

"Sir, I do not have control of the vehicle," answered the driver with unnerving calm.

And then Astor knew that everything in the dossier was true. The car was under someone else's control. Not an individual, but something far more frightening. And the driver was powerless to stop it.

Secret Service agents emerged from the trees, taking up position on all sides of them. Astor counted four men standing on the terrace of the South Portico. All were holding machine guns and had their weapons raised.

A tire exploded and the car listed violently.

"God help us," said the driver.

And then the night erupted. Orange and yellow blooms lit up the darkness. Bullets struck every section of the vehicle, a deafening, percussive rain. The windshield cracked, then splintered.

Seeing his phone, Astor dropped to his knees and grasped it. Hand shaking with fear, he entered the last few letters.

"T–I–"

A second tire exploded. The car lifted into the air and landed on its side. Astor's head slammed the window. He tumbled against the door, the phone falling from his grip again. Chairman Hughes landed on top of him, and Astor felt his shoulder pop. His arm went limp and he screamed.

For an endless moment the car skidded across the lawn. All gunfire ceased. The vehicle slowed and, in an act of capitulation, rolled onto its roof.

Hughes slid off him. The Fed chairman was unconscious. Gelman sprawled close by, eyes open in terror.

Astor lay on his back, trying to control his breathing. He was aware of the engine ticking down and of voices shouting instructions to remain inside the vehicle. He turned his head. The phone lay a few inches away. He read the letters typed on the screen. "P–A–L–A–N–T–I–"

One was missing.

Astor forced his good arm above and around his head until his fingers clutched the phone. With his thumb, he typed the final letter.

"You okay?" The driver was bleeding from his forehead.

"Yes," said Astor. "I'm fine. But my shoulder is—"

Edward Astor never finished the sentence. At that moment the fuel tank, filled to capacity with 25 gallons of gasoline, exploded. A blast of infernal heat lifted him, enveloping him, cauterizing his every sense and sensation.

And in the instant before he died, his fingers curled around the phone, as an infant clutches his mother's hand, and whether on purpose or accidentally, he pressed Send.

1

"Jump!"

Bobby Astor curled his toes over the lip of the chimney and looked down at the pool 20 feet below. It was a big pool with plenty of room to land. Even so, his knees were shaking and it required his last measure of courage to stand up straight. The problem wasn't just the height. It was the leap. He had to carry a good 6 feet of flagstone to make it to the water. Call it 8 feet to the safety zone. Anything shy and he'd get a mouthful of cement.

It was not the smartest bet he'd ever accepted.

"Two mil," came another voice. "You can do it!"

"Come on, Bobby. We don't have all night."

The $2 million wasn't a bet exactly, but more like a pledge. All Astor had to do was jump from the chimney into the pool and the money would go to charity. Last year he had brought in a million seven walking across a bed of hot coals. The year before he'd parachuted out of a chopper onto the beach. It dawned on him that the stunts were growing increasingly dangerous. It might be better to skip next year altogether and just write a check.

"Hold your horses," said Astor, with a bravado he had no right to claim. "Let me enjoy the view."

Afternoon thundershowers had left the sky clear. Stars glittered across the evening canopy. Up the coast, the lights of Amagansett on the eastern shore of Long Island glowed invitingly. Closer, the breakers fizzed like seltzer on the black sea. Along Further Lane, his neighbors' homes were dark.

Astor steadied himself and studied the water. It was midnight and the pool lights were on, and the water had that spooky aquamarine translucence he'd marveled at off the coast of Phuket and in the ocean grottoes beneath the cliffs of Capri. Twenty feet didn't sound like much, but when you were perched on a piece of rock the size of a phone book, it was high enough. The wise, cautious part of him urged him to bend down, take hold of the brick, and lower himself onto the roof. He couldn't, of course. There was the bet. And there was the other thing. The other thing was his pride. Bobby Astor always kept his word.

"Come on, Bobby! Don't be a pussy! Jump!"

"Here, kitty, kitty!"

Astor raised a hand above his head to show that he was ready. At forty-one, he was lean and fit and stood a few inches under six feet. At prep school and college, he'd played football and lacrosse and earned the nickname "the Hammer" because of the crushing hits he laid on his opponents. He still had an athlete's build: broad shoulders, flat stomach, muscled legs. He also had an athlete's knees, with long, ugly scars crisscrossing both, evidence of the nearly dozen operations he'd undergone.

His hair was dark and short and receding faster than the polar ice cap. His eyes were brown and serious, keen to meet life's challenges. His smile could win over his bitterest rival. His scowl meant war. If anything, he was too thin. Over the past month he'd lost ten pounds, and his board shorts hung low on his hips. He never ate when he had a big bet on the market.

Someone turned off the music and the guests quieted. Two hundred sweaty, sun-reddened faces peered up at him. He looked among them, counting his friends. He stopped at three, then cut the number to two. His enemies were more numerous, and easier to spot. But it was the weekend, and hostilities were suspended until the market opened in the morning. Until then, he'd consider them his business associates like the rest, men and women he worked with on the Street. Brokers, traders, fund managers, salesmen, and, of course, his employees. Good people for the most part. Hardworking, intelligent, nearly honest.

It was July 28, and the seventh annual Comstock Clambake was lurching to a loud, boozy halt. Comstock came from Comstock Partners, Astor's company, and Comstock Partners was an investment firm that managed a little more than $5 billion of very wealthy people's money. More commonly, it was referred to as a hedge fund.

As always, the clambake was a ritzy affair. There were clams, of course, but also lobster, sushi, Wagyu beef, and so on and so forth. There was an open bar and bottle service and plenty of servers wandering around the patio to make certain everyone got their fill. The band had stopped an hour earlier, and a DJ from one of the trendier clubs in the city was on until midnight. To cap things off, every guest received a gift in parting—a Gucci handbag for the ladies and an engraved Dunhill lighter for the men.

All in all, the clambake ran to a cool half million. Astor had been poor enough once to know the value of every one of those greenbacks. Though born to money, he'd had the silver spoon yanked out of his mouth when he was sixteen. What he'd called pride, his father had called defiance. Astor decided he liked his definition better. The decision left him an emancipated minor living on his own. Not exactly penniless, but as close as he ever wanted to come.

Astor lived in another world now. In this world, parties cost $500,000 and guests received ungodly expensive purses for showing up. He knew it was crazy and he scolded himself for buying into the entire scene. But in the end, buy he did. And as with everything he committed to, he did it in a big way. *The Astor way.* He knew enough about luck and risk and the wicked whim of fate to feel privileged to be able to pony up and pay.

Anyway, it had been a good year.

"Come on, Bobby! You da man!"

"Jump!"

"He'll never do it," shouted a Brooklyn-born voice. "All talk and no show." It was Marv Shank, Comstock's vice chairman and head trader, and until that outburst Astor's best friend.

"Says you," called Astor. "You're coming up here next."

"Not in a million years," said Shank, waving him off amid a flurry of expletives.

"Ladies and gentlemen," said Astor. "Your attention. As most of you know, it's our tradition at the clambake to give back a little of the good fortune we who work in this industry have been so lucky to have. A few years back, Marv convinced me that instead of just asking, I ought to do something crazy to help convince you to donate your hard-earned money to an organization I started, Helping Hands, which does a great job with kids in our fine city who didn't get the fairest shake in life. This year I'm pleased to announce that you nice folks have come up with a cool two million dollars, which I will happily make you pay if and when I gather the courage to jump."

"You can do it, Bobby," shouted a woman.

"So," Astor continued, "before I give this a shot, I just want to say thank you for coming out and making this night special for me—and for the kids. Drum roll, please."

It was then that a gust blew in off the ocean. Umbrellas swayed on the deck. A woman shrieked as her cap skittered across the flagstones and into the pool. The wind hit Astor like a baseball bat. One foot lifted off the chimney, and for a moment he swayed perilously. He threw his arms out for balance. Teetering, he landed a heel on a barb protruding from the ember grate. He bit his lip, burying a yelp, then quickly waved to show everyone he was all right. He even managed a smile. A smattering of applause broke out. Someone whistled, and with a bold step he retook his position at the edge of the chimney.

Marv Shank glared at him from the far side of the pool. He was a short, barrel-chested man, a grind in the office and out, argumentative by default. He was as white as a ghost, and his pale stomach bulged obscenely over the waistline of his madras shorts. Shank shook his head, and Astor could read his mind: one more dangerous situation the boss had gotten himself into.

Because, of course, it hadn't been Shank's idea to do the stunt each year.

It had been Astor's.

Shank cupped hands to his mouth and shouted, "Swan dive!"

"Not a chance!" Astor shook his head furiously, and Shank repeated his demand.

A current of excitement rolled across the crowd.

Astor let it build. Shank's request was no random demand. When it came to Helping Hands, Astor was zealous in his efforts to separate his guests' money from their wallets. "How much you give me?"

"Twenty grand," said Shank.

"Make it fifty."

"Fifty."

"Deal," said Astor. "Any other takers?" He called out a few of his wealthier guests and they graciously agreed to chip in, taking the total to $2,250,000.

Shank turned to his fellow guests and raised his arms in the air, exhorting them to join him. In a moment the entire crowd was chanting, "Dive! Dive!"

Over the heads of his guests, Astor caught a pair of headlights turning onto Further Lane a half mile up the road. It wasn't a BMW or a

Mercedes or even a Lexus. The car had its brights illuminated and was moving fast. He followed it up the road until he recognized it as a Dodge Charger. Black. He knew the car's stats by heart: 5.7 liter V8 Hemi engine. Dual Flowmaster exhausts. Eibach shocks. This one even came with an assault shotgun under the driver's seat, a 3,000-lumen floodlight, and a light stick of red and blue strobes.

What was she doing out here at this time of night?

"Dive! Dive!"

Astor squared his shoulders and raised his chin. He knew it was too far, and that if he had any brains at all, he'd jump feet first and take his lumps afterward.

But that was out of the question. A bet was a bet.

And after all, Bobby Astor was invincible.

He dove.

2

Astor gazed at the tall, athletic brunette standing in the doorway. "Hello, Alex. A little past work hours, even for you."

"Did you make it?" she asked, taking in his dripping shorts, the towel wrapped around his shoulders.

"More or less." Reflexively, he pulled the towel tighter. He didn't want her to see the red, inflamed skin where his back had struck the water.

"Showing off again?"

"Raised two million and change."

"Next time write them a check. It's safer."

"You care."

"Your daughter cares."

The woman wore jeans and a navy T-shirt with three yellow letters stenciled above the breast. Her eyes were hazel, her skin olive and taut, lines forming at the corners of her eyes like cracks in an Old Master's painting. She'd pulled her thick, glossy hair into a ponytail, which showcased the angles of her face, the high cheekbones, the sharp Roman nose. As was her custom, she wore no makeup. Mascara didn't go with the Glock she carried on her belt. Against his every wish, he felt something tighten in his stomach, a desire he thought was long quelled, a longing even. The Federal Bureau of Investigation had chosen wisely when they'd admitted this one to the academy. Her name was Alessandra Ambrosiani Forza, but she went by Alex, not Alessandra, and never Astor. For eighteen years she had been his wife.

"If you're coming for the clambake," said Astor, "you're late."

"I got the invitation. Sorry. I was busy."

"You still knocking down front doors and rousting homegrown bin Ladens out of their beds in Queens and Rockaway?"

"I'm still at CT-26, if that's what you mean. I'm running it now."

"So I heard," said Astor. "Congrats."

"Speaking of front doors, you want to ask me in?"

Astor threw back an arm. "Won't you come in?"

Alex brushed past him, and he noted that her cheeks were flushed, her eyes too puffy for just another long day. "This isn't about Katie?" he asked worriedly.

"Katie's fine."

Astor was wary of his ex's civil response. Habit made him jump back to offensive. "And home alone, I take it."

"She's sixteen."

"That's two years shy of being an adult last time I looked."

"Not in Manhattan."

"When I was sixteen, I was—"

"Drinking fog cutters at Trader Vic's while you were playing hooky from Choate," retorted Alex. "Or whatever rich boy's academy you were getting kicked out of that year."

"It was Deerfield and Kent."

"Stop!" she said. "I'm here about your father."

Astor took a step back. He swallowed, his throat tightening. "What about him?"

Alex placed a hand on his arm. "I'm sorry, Bobby. Your father's dead."

For a moment Astor didn't respond. He was aware of the music blaring, of several men shouting, and knew that some kind of fracas had started out by the pool. He had been expecting the news since spotting the Dodge. He had not been able to think of another reason that would bring her so far from home so late at night.

Dad was dead.

He had not loved the man. The two shared a long adversarial history. More Hatfield and McCoy than father and son. Years had passed since they'd spoken. And so it was a fright when he felt the roiling in his gut, the prickly warmth at the corners of his eyes, the geyser of loss and emotion welling inside him with an uncontrollable and overwhelming rapidity.

"Bobby . . . are you all right?"

"Fine," he said woodenly. "I . . . I saw him at the Four Seasons last week. He looked . . . good. He looked healthy. What happened?"

"Can we go to the study?" asked Alex. "It's a little loud."

"Sure." Astor led the way up the stairs. He was thankful for the respite. With each step he tamped down his recalcitrant emotions, much as a man uses a carpet to beat down a stubborn flame. He reminded himself that Edward Astor had no claims on his feelings. The father had ceded those long ago, and it was his fault, not the son's.

The black belt.

The memory came to Astor like a thunderclap. In an instant his stomach calmed. His eyes dried. By the time he reached the top of the stairs, he'd stuffed any feelings he had for his father back inside the impregnable vault where he'd kept them locked away for thirty years.

The study was small and airy, with bookshelves lining the walls and traditional furniture. Astor closed the door behind them and the noise from the party dissipated. "What happened?" he said. "Heart attack? Car accident? I'd have heard if he had cancer."

Alex stood facing him, hands hanging by her sides. "This evening at eleven p.m., your father, Charles Hughes, and Martin Gelman were driving together to visit the president," she began. "Something went wrong with their car after they entered the White House grounds. I don't have the details, but apparently it left the road and drove across the South Lawn. The Secret Service thought the car was headed directly for the White House and posed a threat. They opened fire. A bullet punctured the gas tank. There was an explosion."

"All of them . . . dead?"

"Yes."

Astor considered this, the enormity of the event dawning on him. "Let me get this right. The chairman of the Federal Reserve, the treasury secretary, and the head of the New York Stock Exchange were traveling together at eleven o'clock on a Sunday night to see the president. What's going on?"

"I don't know."

Astor opened a cabinet in the bookshelf that housed a television and searched for the remote. "The markets must be going apeshit."

Alex grabbed his arm. "What are you doing? Who cares about the markets?"

"He would have."

"You're not him."

"If there's more to it, I need to know. My god, the president must be in his bunker in Maryland by now."

"Bobby!"

"Okay. You win." Astor put down the remote. He had people working for him who were better placed to respond to a crisis like this. If anything happened to materially affect the firm, they'd let him know.

"I cared for him," she said.

"I know you did," he said, not unkindly.

"So I take it you never reached out?"

"It was up to him."

"How does that matter now?"

"Edward Astor died tonight, and I'm sorry for that. But my father passed away a long time ago."

Alex shook her head. "But it was just business. A stupid argument about money."

"No, Alex. It was never about business." That had been the excuse. A business disagreement was the easiest scapegoat. Astor wanted to say more. He wanted to say that he'd picked up the phone a thousand times to call and put it right back down. That she might know Edward Astor as a kind and respectful father-in-law, as the affectionate grandfather to their daughter, but she didn't know him as he did. If she asked him right then, he'd tell her.

But Alex shrugged and looked away. She walked to the window and straightened her shoulders, and when she turned around, the woman he'd married was gone. The beast that was the Federal Bureau of Investigation had retaken control of her. "You'll receive a formal notification any minute," she said. "You can call the Secret Service to fill you in. They can provide you with more information. I have to go."

Astor stepped closer to her, placing a hand on her shoulder. "Allie, stop. Come on. What do you want? Tears? You know how it was between us."

She knocked his hand away. "Don't call me that. You don't have the right."

"Come on," he said. "It's me."

"We're divorced. Get that through your head. I came here as a courtesy. Nothing more."

"Just doing your job, right?" Astor peeled back a curtain and looked down into the forecourt. A strapping blond man stood next to the passenger door of the Dodge. Like her, he was dressed in jeans and a T-shirt. Astor recognized him as one of her "young lions," the name she gave to her stable of capable, motivated, exclusively male subordinates.

"All this went down on the White House lawn?" he said, returning his attention to his ex-wife. The mood between them had swung back to its old bluff and battery-acid self.

"It's going to be a big one," said Alex.

Astor could see the spark in his wife's eye, that ember of excitement that only her job could provide. Two years after they'd separated, and a full ten months since their divorce had been finalized, it still upset him. "If I were you, I'd get on a plane to D.C. first thing," he said. "Take the G4. I'll call and get it fueled up, see that a crew's there in an hour."

"It's not my case."

"Might want to put in for a transfer. There're going to be a lot of headlines for whoever heads this thing up. Could be your chance to get to D.C. I know how much you want that deputy director's slot."

"That's not fair."

"I'm just saying," Astor went on. "Your career cost us our marriage. Might as well get your money's worth."

"This from a man who didn't set foot inside his house before nine on weeknights and didn't bother coming home at all on weekends."

"Look what it got us."

Alex approached, her face an inch from his. The spark in her eye was still there, but it was caused by anger, not excitement. "Yeah," she said. "I'm looking. Not a whole helluva lot, from where I stand."

She pushed past him and left the study. Astor followed her down the stairs. "What were you doing out here anyway? You said my father was killed an hour ago. No way you could have made it out from the city that fast."

Alex stopped at the front door. "Let me know when the funeral is. Katie and I would like to pay our respects."

Astor looked at her attire again—the jeans, the T-shirt, the hair pulled back. He observed that she was wearing her work boots, too. He had his answer.

"Hey," he called. "Be careful."

But Alex was already in the driver's seat, slamming the door.

3

Outside, Astor snaked through the crush of guests to the bar. "Vodka," he said to the bartender. "Make it a double."

"Any brand in mind?"

"The kind that's eighty proof."

The bartender filled a glass with ice, poured in a few fingers of vodka, then placed the bottle next to it. Astor picked up the glass and walked toward the guest villa. Several people approached to congratulate him on the dive. He ignored them. He was done talking for the night.

Inside the guest villa, he changed back into his clothes. He picked up his phone and saw that it was already filling with voice mail. First was a text message from a number he didn't recognize. Astor was careful about his privacy. He gave his number only to friends whose own numbers he catalogued. The text was from a local area code. Something about the number rang a bell. He opened the message.

One word.

PALANTIR.

It meant nothing to him.

The message had arrived at 11:07, more than an hour earlier. He placed his thumb on the Delete key, then changed his mind. Alex had said that his father had died around eleven. He called the number. After seven rings, the call went to voice mail.

A smoky, bourbon-aged baritone spoke. He had not heard the voice in five years. Even so, it took only a syllable to make the hair on his arms stand to attention and send a current of undistilled dread from head to toe.

"You've reached Edward Astor. Leave a message."

Astor picked up the glass of vodka, walked to the pool, and poured it in.

"Hey!" he shouted as he jumped onto the diving board and walked to the end. "Everyone, listen up."

No one paid him any attention. He stuck his pinkie and index finger into his mouth and whistled. The music skidded to a halt. The guests turned his way.

"Party's over."

4

Two thousand miles to the northeast, the sun was rising on a desolate, windswept plain guarded on three sides by the youngest mountains on the planet. Heather and scrub rose in scattered stands. Vapor from sulfur hot springs seeped into the air. It was a land that time had forgotten. The region was known as Aska and it lay in the center of the North Atlantic island nation of Iceland.

Until a year ago, Aska had been the exclusive domain of ecotourists and wilderness enthusiasts. Visitors to the island flocked to the famed Ring of Fire, the scenic road that skirted the country's dramatic coastline. Locals preferred the southern coast, where temperatures could be counted on to be a few degrees warmer than inland. With the nearest road a three-day walk, only the hardiest men and women ventured so far into the island's interior.

All that changed when an international investment group purchased a 200-square-kilometer tract in the region and announced its intention to build an upscale eco-resort. Pictures of the planned resort were printed in the *Morgunbladid,* the nation's oldest newspaper. Opposition was vocal and immediate. Icelanders had a long history of distrusting foreigners. It was not the resort itself they minded. It was what lay below it. Ceding valuable gas and mineral rights to a group whose allegiance was unknown would be imprudent at best.

More immediate concerns won the day. The global banking crisis of 2008 had devastated Iceland's economy, wiping out the country's banks and saddling its citizens with a whopping debt of 60,000 euros per person. A project that would inject hard currency into the economy was a godsend. Prudence be damned.

Questions about the investors' origins were answered perfunctorily. The group was domiciled in the Cayman Islands and maintained executive offices in New York and Singapore. The primary shareholders were impressively capitalized corporations with lofty-sounding names like Excelsior Holdings and Sterling Partners. The sole executive to visit the island was a tall, dark-haired man named Magnus Lee.

Lee was a mystery from the start. From afar, he appeared Asian. He had an Asian's black hair and a certain nimbleness about his step. But there was nothing Asian about his size and the breadth of his shoulders. Close up, one couldn't help but stare at his blue eyes, which one smitten woman likened to her country's glaciers. He spoke English like the Queen, and was heard speaking the czar's Russian to a fishing executive from St. Petersburg. Talk about his nationality was short-lived. Icelanders knew a gentleman when they saw one. Most important, he had money. Barrels and barrels of money.

One year later, the first phase of the resort was complete. A road had been built. Grounds had been cleared. A billboard showing a color representation of the finished structures held pride of place atop a rise of the razor-sharp pumice. An iron fence topped with concertina wire encircled the building site. Yet of the hotel itself there was no sign. Inside the fence was only a single low-slung, windowless concrete edifice. And next to it (and far more impressive) a freestanding satellite dish.

Construction would end there.

Mr. Magnus Lee did not intend to build an upscale resort, eco or otherwise. He had purchased the land to listen. From the remote plains of Aska, he could maintain the clearest contact with a network of surveillance satellites positioned in geosynchronous orbit above the Northern Hemisphere.

At 3:07 local time, a chime had sounded on the console of the lone technician working at the site. The chime indicated an intercept of a communications device under surveillance and graded urgent. In this instance, the device was a cellular phone. The number appeared on the screen, followed by its designation, Target Alpha. Procedure required the technician to notify his master at once.

"Target Alpha made a transmission."

Halfway around the world, Magnus Lee answered at once. "A call?"

"No, sir. A text."

"Go on."

"It was a single word. We might have pulled down jibberish."

"What was it?"

"Palantir." The technician enunciated each syllable as if it were its own word. *Pal-an-teer.*

Lee blinked several times in rapid succession. He always did when he received disturbing news. "I see. And who was the recipient?"

"We don't know who uses the phone, only that it's registered to an American company. Comstock Partners, Ltd., with an address at 221 Broad Street, New York. The owner is Robert Astor."

Lee knew the name, of course. "Place a tag on the number. Initiate surveillance. Grade it 'urgent.'"

"Yes, sir."

"Keep up the good work and I'll see to it that you receive a transfer home by year end."

Afterward, Magnus Lee strode to the window. From his living room on the eightieth floor of the city's newest and most sought-after residence, he enjoyed an unmatched view over a prosperous metropolis. Sparkling new skyscrapers, towering edifices of glass and steel, carved up the skyline, engineering marvels all. In between them stood more construction cranes than a man could count. He saw streets filled with new cars and an ocean crisscrossed with the wakes of a hundred freighters and ferries.

Everywhere he looked, he saw the future, and the future was money.

A last transmission.

PALANTIR.

Lee blinked rapidly again. He thought of the years of planning, the enormous investment, the hard work. Mostly, though, he thought of himself. His rise to power could not be stopped. Not now. Not when all was so close to fruition.

He regarded the name of the company he had written down and its owner.

Comstock Partners.
Robert Astor.

Lee drew a deep breath and held it inside him, seeking his center.

He had a vision of a pebble striking a placid pond. As it sank, ripples spread outward toward the shore. Concentric circles expanding one after another.

The pebble had struck the water.

The ripples must not be allowed to reach the shore.

5

"How'd he take it?"

Alex kept her eyes on the dash as she buckled her seat belt. "I don't know."

"He wasn't upset?" asked Special Agent Jim Malloy. Malloy was thirty, a three-year man who'd come to the Bureau after putting in six years with the navy, first as a diver, then as a SEAL, with two deployments under his belt.

"Oh, he's upset. He'll just never let you see it." Alex checked her BlackBerry. "Anything go down while I was inside?"

"Nada. Place is silent as the grave."

The "place" was 1254 Windermere Street in Inwood, Long Island, site of a surveillance operation Alex had mounted to look into the activities of a possible arms smuggler—or worse.

"Two days," she said. "He's got to come back soon."

"Maybe he's on vacation."

"He might be gone, but he ain't on vacation. You saw the pictures. He's got to come back sometime. And when he does, we'll be waiting to speak with him. All right, then—*andiamo.*"

Alex spun the car in a tight circle and pumped the accelerator to scatter some expensive Italian gravel as she left the driveway. She turned right on Further Lane toward the ocean and had the Charger doing sixty in six seconds. The estate faded from view. In the rearview, it looked like a dollhouse all lit up. Alex couldn't get away fast enough.

Malloy caught her looking. "You really didn't get any of it?" he asked.

Alex dropped her eyes from the mirror. "Of what?"

"It. The money. Word is you didn't take a penny in the settlement."

"Word is correct."

"Nothing?"

"Nada."

"But look at it . . . It's . . . it's . . ."

"Yes, it is a beautiful home with a beautiful view and beautiful polished gravel that he imported from a beautiful quarry in Carrara, Italy."

"He's a billionaire," protested Malloy. "No one walks away from that."

Alex laughed to herself. Her ex—the billionaire. People used the word in the same tone as *messiah*. "He's no billionaire. Don't believe everything you read."

"But close?"

"Closer than me."

"And so?"

Alex looked at Malloy. He was a new father with infant twin daughters at home. It was no wonder that money was a concern. "Don't worry about me, Jimmy. I'm doing okay."

"On a buck and a quarter a year?"

"A buck fifty. I'm an SSA now."

"That and a dime will buy you a double latte. It's Manhattan."

"He takes care of Katie. School, sports, vacations, all of it. The apartment in the city's in her name."

"Still . . . how could you let that go?"

"Easy. I don't want anything to do with him. Don't you see? I take a cent of his money, I'm still Mrs. Robert Astor. That's over, Jimmy. I'm Supervisory Special Agent Alex Forza."

"That's an expensive name."

"Worth every fuckin' penny."

Malloy laughed, but she could see that he didn't get it. Money. Alex hated everything about it. Extending an arm, she activated the GPS and looked at the directions to Inwood. "Forty minutes. I say we make it in thirty."

Malloy grasped the armrest. "Shit."

"Twenty-nine minutes, forty seconds," said Alex later as she guided the Dodge off the Long Island Expressway and onto the broad, potholed boulevards of Inwood.

In the passenger seat, Malloy had turned an interesting shade of green. "Must be a record."

"Thought you SEALs were used to this kind of thing."

"I didn't like the helo flights either," said Malloy. "But at least I could take Dramamine."

"Fresh out."

Alex drove up Atlantic Avenue and turned onto Windermere Street, slowing as she approached the rendezvous point. It was a street of single-family clapboard houses. Waist-high chain-link fences enclosed front and back yards. She lowered the window. The bracing scent of fresh salt air was gone, replaced by those of jet fuel and brackish water. Inwood was a shithole and it had the smell to go with it. She pulled to the curb behind a van parked a block up.

The time was 12:50. She waited, letting the engine tick down, her eyes running up and down the road. No late-night dog walkers. Sparse traffic. A few lights burned in upstairs windows. Except for a police siren a few streets over, the neighborhood was asleep.

She left the car, walked to the van, and knocked twice on the window. "And so?" she asked when it had rolled down.

"Nothing," said the driver. "I'm telling you the guy has flown the coop."

"Maybe," she said. She thought of the picture. Of the olive green crate with the yellow markings and the foreign alphabet. She thought of what was inside.

"What do you want to do?" asked the driver.

"We wait," she said.

6

Monday morning traffic was a bitch.

Bobby Astor surveyed the line in front of him and shook his head. The Hamptons were done. Ten years ago, he could zip out to the house on a Friday afternoon without breaking a sweat and leave early Monday morning to be back in the office by eight. No more. Fridays worked fine, but the return leg was a bear. This morning was a perfect example. After a straight shot out of Amagansett, past Southampton, and across Long Island, he'd been stuck on the far side of the East River, circling, for twenty minutes.

"How much longer they keeping us in the pattern?" he asked.

"We're next in line. Just waiting for the pad to clear."

Astor loosened his shoulder harness. It was a gorgeous day, with blue sky as far as the eye could see. Looking south, he enjoyed a clear view to Atlantic City. Through the Perspex canopy of the Aérospatiale AS350 "Squirrel," he counted four helicopters circling the Downtown Manhattan Heliport.

Astor shot a glance at the tablet in his lap displaying a summary of world financial markets. Europe was off 2 percent on fears that the incident in Washington had been a terrorist attack. In Hong Kong, the Hang Seng had dropped 4 percent before rebounding. China had its own problems, and the deaths of three American financial luminaries would have no effect, either positively or negatively, on them. Futures on the New York Stock Exchange, NASDAQ, and the S&P 500 were sharply lower.

Astor brought up a list of his open positions. One column tallied his profits and losses, the sum total shown in bold numerals at the bottom. The figure was black, but not by much. His eye fixed on a single symbol. Next to it stood the nominal value of his investment: $2,000,000,000. It represented a bet on the value of a currency. All summer the number had not fluctuated more than half a percent up or down. The currency had steadfastly guarded its value against the dollar.

Sometime in the next few days, all that was going to change.

Astor slipped the tablet into the satchel at his side. Away to the west, he watched a chopper lift from the pad and head up the East River. He was thinking how his father had hated helicopters and how he had refused to join him for the flight into the city even when they had been getting along. It wasn't the helicopter so much as that his son owned one, and that he'd defied Graham and Dodd's every precept to earn it. There was no wrath like that of a value investor scorned.

Astor took out his phone and brought up the message from his father.

PALANTIR.

A search on the web had offered a definition meaning "illumination" and nothing more. If the news had accurately reported the time of his father's death, the message counted as his father's last words. Or at least his last message. Regardless, it was to be taken seriously.

The phone rang. Astor saw it was the office calling. "Yeah, Marv, be there in ten," he said.

No one replied. The earpiece filled with white noise.

"Marv . . . you there? Marv?"

Astor checked the screen and saw that he had four bars of reception. Still, he could not hear his partner. He hung up and called back, but the call didn't go through. Phone reception in Manhattan was a work in progress. He didn't worry about it. Marv could wait.

Astor looked again at the text message. He'd spent the night glued to the wall of monitors, switching from program to program, hoping to glean some piece of information he might have missed, anything that might help him understand what had happened to his father, and, more important, why.

By dawn the analysts had broken down the incident into four questions: Why had Hughes, Gelman, and Astor's father demanded to see the president so late on a Sunday night? And why had they been meeting in the first place? Why had the Secret Service agent, a twenty-five-year veteran with a family of four, left the paved road and driven across the South Lawn of the White House? And why had the agents on the grounds seen fit to blow to kingdom come the Chevrolet Suburban in which they all were traveling?

Answers to the first two boiled down to an unknown threat to the nation's financial system. Most of the talking heads were in agreement that it was Edward Astor's presence with the nation's two highest-ranking economic officials that offered the most clues. Yet as to the nature of the threat, no one had an answer. The only other person who appeared to have known about the meeting was the vice chairman of the Federal Reserve, who confirmed that the three men had convened at the Eccles Building at 9 p.m. As to who had asked for the meeting, he did not know if it was the treasury secretary or the chief executive of the New York Stock Exchange. It was not, however, the chairman of the Fed.

The third question involved more fertile ground for conspiracy theorists. Answers bandied about ran from the driver of the vehicle being a homegrown extremist to Hughes, Gelman, or Astor being a latter-day Manchurian candidate, a sleeper spy brainwashed by a foreign power to assassinate the president. No one could offer a credible response.

Only the fourth question merited a quick reply. The Secret Service agents charged with guarding the White House grounds had deemed that the vehicle carrying Hughes, Gelman, and Astor posed a clear and present danger to the president's safety and the safety of others inside the White House and had acted accordingly.

"Q E friggin' D," said Astor. It was short for *Quod erat demonstrandum*, which was about the only Latin he remembered. Give or take, it meant "No shit, Sherlock."

But not once had he heard the word *Palantir*.

Astor shifted in his seat. He was made uncomfortable by the notion that in his final moments, his father had reached out to him. Astor had no brothers or sisters. His mother had died of cancer when he was ten. There had been no valiant struggle. She did not "fight cancer." She never had the chance to be a "survivor." She was diagnosed. She went to the hospital. A few weeks after that, she died. It was over, beginning to end, in three months. It was summer, too, he remembered. A sweltering July spent inside Sloan-Kettering hospital waiting for his mother to die. It was the smell that stayed with him most. Ammonia, disinfectant, and a lemon cleaner used to polish the floors. Somehow it still hadn't been enough to camouflage the odor of death. He had sworn never to go to a hospital to die.

After that, it was just father and son. Astor went off to prep school in seventh grade and never really returned home again. He saw his father on vacations, but briefly, in segmented, scheduled bursts, never more than three or four days at a time. These included a few days at the beginning and end of summer, wedged in between ten-week stays at sleep-away camp in Maine. Thanksgiving, Christmas, and spring break involved travel to resorts in places such as Vail, St. Moritz, and Bermuda where outdoor activities served to maintain a respectful separation between the two.

It was better that way.

The trouble began at fourteen. Astor was expelled from his first school in ninth grade, his second in tenth, and his third in eleventh. It was never a question of intelligence. When he applied himself, he received top marks. And of course there was the question of the PSAT, on which he earned a perfect score, and the fact that he was named a National Merit Finalist. The problem, his teachers agreed, was motivation, or rather the lack of it.

Astor begged to differ, but he was in no mood to share his family secrets with strangers.

It required the intercession of his father and a considerable donation to the school fund to find him a place for senior year. He made it all of two weeks before being dismissed for "unbecoming conduct," namely running a sports book out of his dorm room. Alcohol and marijuana were also found. The fact that ten teachers, including the school's chaplain, were his largest clients was not brought up at his adjudication.

And so that was the end. At seventeen, Astor asked to be declared an emancipated minor. Broke and free of all family ties, he graduated from a public school in western New Hampshire, where he lived with the family of a close friend.

So why me? he wondered, staring at the message. If his father had no other immediate family, he had many close friends, most of whom held positions of considerable power. Surely they were better placed to find out what *Palantir* meant. Why reach out to a son he hadn't spoken to in five years?

The question stayed with him as the helicopter banked and the sapphire surface of the Atlantic Ocean enveloped the windscreen. The radio squawked and the air traffic controller gave them clearance to land.

"I have the stick," said Astor.

"The stick is yours," said his pilot.

Astor lifted the collective and brought the chopper over the landing pad, nose up, and the wheels touched down firmly.

7

Marv Shank was waiting by the elevators when Astor arrived. "Hey, Bobby. Half day? I didn't get the memo."

Astor checked his watch. The time was eight-thirty, but Shank looked as if he'd been at work for hours. His shirt was untucked, his tie askew, his face moist with perspiration. Astor patted him on the shoulder. "I knew I could count on you not to bring up my father."

"You hated the guy. What's to bring up?" said Shank, hurrying to keep up. "Wanted to make sure I grabbed you before anyone else. Press conference at nine-fifteen from Shanghai. U.S. trade representative."

"Know what he's talking about?"

"Not a clue. That's what makes me nervous."

"Any change in the position?"

"Nada."

"Then why are you so nervous?"

"It's my job to be nervous."

"If you didn't get nervous," said Astor, "we wouldn't make any money."

"But this time . . ."

Astor stopped and turned to face his friend. "This time what?"

"It's a little rich for my taste."

"Show a little faith. Have I been wrong on something this big before?"

Shank pulled open the glass door leading into the office. "The market," he said, "doesn't care about before."

Astor walked inside. "Comstock Partners" was written in gold block lettering on a bleached maple divider behind the reception desk. He rapped his knuckles on the counter as he passed through the reception area. "Hello, ladies," he said, addressing the receptionists, both young and male and hoping for a shot at the trading desk. "Bring me the usual. This time make sure it's hot."

"The usual" was a double espresso with a lemon rind on the side, some biscotti, and a shot of wheatgrass, in case he felt so inspired. In fact, the espresso was always piping hot, but he felt it his duty to keep the newbies on their toes. Lesson one: in this business, you couldn't be careful enough.

Not breaking stride, Astor continued down a corridor housing administrative offices—accounting, legal, IT. "What about my fifty grand?"

"Check's on your desk," said Shank. "That was some dive. Your back okay?"

"Don't remind me."

"You could have heard that flop in the next county. Great party, though. I'm just sorry it had to end on a sour note."

"I thought you weren't going to bring that up."

"It just slipped." Shank took hold of Astor's arm and stopped his progress, guiding him against a wall. Astor stood still, Shank's compendious belly pressing against him. "Marv, what are you going to do? Give me a kiss?"

"Really, Bobby, you doing okay? We're talking about your father here. You can talk to me."

Astor looked Shank straight in the eye. "I'm fine, Marv. Really."

"You're sure?"

"Do you want me to pinkie swear?"

"Screw you," said Shank, dismissing Astor with a shove down the hall. "Shows what I get for caring."

"If you want a friend . . ." began Astor.

"Buy a dog," the two men said in unison. Astor raised his hand and Shank high-fived him.

"Thought you were getting soft on me," said Astor.

"Thought you had a heartbeat."

"Never."

The trading floor was a long open space, a floor-to-ceiling window that looked over Ground Zero and past Wall Street to the East River making up the outer wall. A desk ran the length of the room. Fourteen traders sat across from one another at uneven intervals. A host of flat-screen monitors demarcated each post. Workspaces varied from immaculate to chaotic. He counted three boxes of Pepcid, two containers of Tums, and a bottle of Maalox. Pro ball players got concussions. Traders got ulcers. If you weren't playing injured, you weren't playing hard enough.

Aware that the room had gone silent at his arrival, Astor stopped and addressed his team. "Okay, everyone, listen up. I know you've all heard about my father. I have no more idea what happened than any of you. If I find out anything, I'll announce it over the hoot-and-holler. Your condolences are appreciated, but as most of you know, we had a falling-out a while back. Don't expect me to hide in my office while I get over it. I'm going to be out here on the desk riding your ass like any other day. So get to work and make some money."

Astor waited, but no one made a move. He clapped his hands. "That means now."

The room came back to life.

Astor continued to his office. He had founded Comstock Partners fifteen years earlier, at the age of twenty-six. The firm's name was a lie from the beginning. There were no partners. There was just Robert Astor, sole owner and principal investor. In the world of finance, Comstock was technically classified as a hedge fund. *Hedge fund* was one of those funny terms that meant everything and nothing all at once. Simply defined, a hedge fund was "a private partnership that invested in publicly traded securities or financial derivatives." That meant he bought and sold stocks, bonds, commodities, currencies, and just about anything you could legally speculate on with a view toward making a profit. But that was only a beginning.

Most hedge funds had four things in common. First and most important was *fee structure*, since traders, Astor included, cared about only one thing, and that was making money. Comstock, like the majority of its competitors, used something called a "two and twenty model." Comstock kept 20 percent—a full one-fifth—of all profits for itself. On top of the 20 percent, it charged a management fee of 2 percent on all funds invested with Comstock, win or lose. In this last regard, Astor was a gentleman. He charged the 2 percent only on the funds actually invested in his positions. Any money sitting in a bank got off scot-free. He even credited his investors the interest.

The other three things hedge funds had in common had to do with the way they invested the money entrusted to them. As the name implied, Astor often hedged his investments, meaning that if he bet that one stock might go up, he bet another might go down. The idea was to guard against swings in the market. Hedging might limit your returns, but it provided the investor with a margin of safety. It was never smart to put all your chips on red or black.

Next, Astor used something called "leverage" to jack up the value of his bets. Leveraging just meant borrowing to increase the size of your bet. Back in the day, an investor would buy stock "on margin," which meant he used the value of the stock he had bought to double-down and buy some more. That was old school. These days an investor leveraged. Astor borrowed billions of dollars to amplify his bet on anything: stocks, bonds, oil, wheat, pork bellies, and especially currencies.

The last element was freedom. Hedge funds like Comstock operated in a nether region where regulation held little sway. When an investor signed a disclosure agreement and transferred his money into a hedge fund, he was giving Astor his trust to make money the best way he saw fit.

And that's why Astor loved the business. Hedge funds were a license to bet—and to bet big—without Big Brother looking over your shoulder telling you what to do and how to do it, and, worse, demanding an outsized share of your profits when you won. God bless the U.S.A.

Astor continued to the end of the desk. Though it was summer, most of the traders wore fleecies and sweatshirts. Astor kept the room chilled to a brisk sixty-two degrees. He liked his boys and girls alert. Many of their sweatshirts bore names of alma maters. There were more Stony Brooks than Whartons. Astor couldn't care less where someone had gone to college. (After all, he hadn't managed to get a degree anywhere.) He cared about smarts. He'd cherry-picked the twelve men and two women who worked for him from the best firms in the world. He had two Brits, a few Indians, a gal from Shanghai, an Israeli, even a few Americans. They ran the gamut in personalities from extroverted jerks to introverted jerks. Talented traders were not renowned for their people skills. Or, as Alex had often commented, "It takes one to know one."

Astor's office occupied a corner of the building adjacent to the trading desk. The door stood open and he was greeted by a view south across Battery Park to the Statue of Liberty, Staten Island, and New Jersey.

New York City. The center of the universe.

Astor set down his satchel and dropped into his chair. An electronically tinted glass wall allowed him to look onto the floor. This morning the wall was opaque. His first order of business was a check of the markets. He spun to face the panoply of monitors that took up half his desk.

Futures showed that the market would open strongly on the down-side, a bit more than a 3 percent drop. European markets were mixed. Asian markets had closed down a percent. The fall in the U.S. market was a knee-jerk response, and the market would bounce back in a day or two.

Viewing the numbers, Astor experienced an immediate and visceral thrill. With $5 billion in the game, he wasn't merely an observer but an integral, albeit tiny, part of a bigger, immensely powerful and efficient machine. A vast, seething highway of ever-changing, ever-evolving information. Some people got off on scaling granite cliffs or jumping out of airplanes. Astor got his thrills in this chair. It was a game of intellect and daring, with chance in the guise of unforeseen events always dangling above your shoulder. A Damocles sword fashioned of gold and greed. Sit down. Buckle up. And plug in. He'd been doing it for fifteen years, and it never got old.

Astor skipped past the futures to the one symbol that concerned him most.

The position.

"Six-thirty," he said, looking over his shoulder at Shank, who hovered nearby. "No worries."

"I still want to look at the press conference."

Astor punched a button and a slim screen emerged from a credenza situated against the wall. "Bloomberg, right?"

Shank said, "Yes."

Astor opened his drawer and began digging through the contents. There were small orange prescription bottles of Lipitor, Xanax, Imodium, Ambien. He settled for a box of Altoids and popped three into his mouth. Another screen showed his morning schedule.

At nine there was a meeting with Septimus Reventlow, who managed the Reventlow family office. *Family office* was the term used to describe money passed down from generation to generation and managed on behalf of the heirs. Think Rockefellers, Rothschilds, or even Astor's namesake. When he'd first started in the business, family offices invariably involved "old money," money earned fifty to a hundred years before by a long-dead tycoon. These days it was the opposite. Family offices handled the billions earned by private equity mavens, software billionaires, and Internet entrepreneurs, all of whom were still very much alive.

At ten he had a meeting with Pacific Ventures, a private equity firm that managed about $10 billion. Pacific Ventures' main game was buying up companies, restructuring them (trimming the deadwood and invigorating what was left), and selling them for a profit several years down the road. It also invested in hedge funds like Comstock. Astor punched in the account and saw that as of this morning Pacific Ventures had just over $100 million invested in his Astor fund. Pacific Ventures was a good client.

Comstock operated four funds. Comstock Alpha was a long/short fund. This was the classical hedge fund, which didn't seek to demolish the market return but was satisfied to beat the major indexes—the Dow, NASDAQ, and S&P—by a few percentage points.

The team that traded the Alpha fund lived life glued to their monitors. When the market got frothy on the upside or fell through the floor, they couldn't afford to leave their desks for a moment, not even to use the john. People liked to joke that they kept a motorman's caddy at the ready. As for the other thing, they'd fart it out. True on both counts. No one said a trading floor was a nice place to work.

Comstock Risk was an arb fund, and arb funds invested in two areas, company takeovers—both announced and rumored—and currency plays. It used leverage to double the bets, maybe triple them, but never more than that.

Comstock Newton was a quantitative fund. Frankly, Astor had no idea what its team did, except that they did it with lots of math and sophisticated algorithms that predicted whether stocks or gold or oil, or whatever you might want to bet on, would go up or down. Much of their work involved high-frequency trading, which meant buying and selling stocks hundreds of times an hour. Competition among high-frequency traders to see who got their orders in first had become so intense that the New York Stock Exchange even allowed firms to position their computers in the same building as the Exchange's, a prisonlike facility in the wilds of New Jersey. Even a delay of a millionth of a second could mean significant losses.

Astor's quant team didn't work in Manhattan but in a locked-down bunker in Greenwich, Connecticut, where they could bang out code day and night. Rumor was that from time to time they threw geek orgies, which involved drinking the latest microbrew, gobbling Slim

Jims, and formulating new and ever more sophisticated algorithms. All math, all the time.

Together, these three funds managed $2 billion. Quant was doing best this year, boasting a 27 percent return. The Risk fund was faring poorest, returning only 4 percent.

And then there was Comstock Astor, the fund that Astor managed himself. Comstock Astor was a macro fund, which meant that it bet on the bigger picture, specifically the direction of currencies. Since currencies didn't move very much, the Astor fund relied on leverage to amplify its bets. Borrow enough and a 2 percent move up or down meant a 20 percent gain or loss. Keep borrowing and the gain could become 200 percent. Leverage was a drug. The more you used, the more you wanted to use. Making money . . . up your leverage and hit a home run. Losing money . . . borrow more and make your money back.

Traders were never wrong . . . *until they were.*

The Astor fund managed $3 billion on its own. As of this morning $1 billion was invested in "the position."

Finally, at eleven o'clock, there was the weekly Monday review, when Astor's managers met to discuss the status of their funds, what had gone up, what had gone down, to bitch about the market if things were going badly, and to brag if things were going well.

"Time for the conference to start," said Shank.

Astor checked the screen. A news feed ran across the bottom: *Press conference rescheduled to 0800 Chinese time.* "Looks like we're out of luck."

"What?" Shank shuffled over and read the banner. "Oh eight hundred Chinese time, that's nine tonight our time. I'll have to catch that at—" Shank ended his words midsentence. "Holy crap."

"What is it?"

Shank stood transfixed in front of the currency monitor. "The position."

"What about it?"

"6.295," said Shank. "6.292. The fucker is strengthening."

Astor rolled his chair closer to the screen. "It can't move that fast."

"It" was the Chinese currency, officially named the renminbi but better known as the yuan. And the 6.292 referred to how many yuan it took to buy one American greenback. If the number went down, the yuan was said to be strengthening versus the dollar. Fewer yuan were needed to buy one dollar. (Conversely, the dollar was weakening.) If the number went up, the yuan was weakening. More yuan were needed to buy one dollar. (And conversely, the dollar was strengthening.)

Another screen broadcast the value of Comstock Astor's investment in the position. One minute earlier, the digits had blazed a healthy black and showed a $50 million gain. The digits were red now. All nine of them.

"Are we down a hundred million?" said Astor.

"Looks like it," said Shank.

Bobby Astor was betting that the yuan would weaken against the dollar. He was sure that soon it would require more yuan to purchase one dollar. He wanted the number to increase. He had bet $2 billion of his fund's money that he was right.

And then, before Astor could say another word, before he could blink, the digits turned black again.

6.30.

"We're back in the black."

Shank looked at the screen as if it had bit him in the ass. "What just happened?"

"No idea," said Astor. "But I'm guessing it has to do with why the trade representative rescheduled the press conference."

"Jeez—ya think?" said Shank.

For the past ten years, China had been allowing the value of the yuan to appreciate versus the dollar. The movements were slow and steady, just 1 or 2 percent a year. Five years ago, it had taken seven yuan to buy one dollar. Today it was only six and a third. This "revaluing" or appreciation of the yuan made Chinese exports more expensive and U.S. imports cheaper. The United States liked this. China did not.

"You want to give your guy a ring?" asked Shank. "Ask him what he thinks."

"No," said Astor. "I don't need to bother him with this. He's busy."

"He's the expert on these things."

"We're good." Astor called his assistant. "Barb," he said when she answered. "Push my meetings to this afternoon."

"Septimus Reventlow is already here. Reception just announced him."

"Marv can take him."

"Me?" said Shank. "What am I supposed to say?"

"Tell him we don't need his money right now. We're fully invested. If that bothers him, he'll have an opportunity to withdraw his funds after the next accounting period. I think that's September thirtieth."

"He won't like that."

"I imagine he won't."

"Too late, anyway," said Shank.

"Why's that?" Astor looked out the window and saw a tall, narrow-shouldered man in a three-piece suit crossing the trading floor. Septimus Reventlow spotted him and lifted a hand in greeting.

Shank shot Astor a look. "Hot money's here."

8

S eptimus, a pleasure."

A soft hand, white as snow, gripped Astor's. "Bobby, so nice to see you. Though I wish it were under happier circumstances. Have you learned anything more?"

"Only what I hear on the television."

"The police haven't contacted you?" asked Reventlow. "Or is the Secret Service heading up things?"

"I wouldn't know. No one's called yet. My father and I weren't close. I'm the last person who could help."

"What a shame. Family is precious. When's the last time you spoke?"

"Actually, he—" Astor began, only to cut himself off. His personal affairs were none of Reventlow's business. "It's been years. Like I said, we weren't close."

Astor showed Reventlow to a chair in the corner of his office. Astor flew fixed-wing aircraft as well as helicopters, and the room had a sleek aeronautical feel to it. Stainless steel surfaces, a titanium-colored carpet, even a vintage poster for Pan American Airways.

"Marv's bringing in a printout of your portfolio," began Astor. "He'll go over the positions and show you where we stand."

"That won't be necessary," said Reventlow. "I'd prefer to speak with you. My family has decided that we would like to increase our holdings in Comstock."

"I heard that. I appreciate your vote of confidence. If I'm not mistaken, you have one hundred million in the Astor fund. Are you looking to invest in one of the others? Our quant fund is having a spectacular year."

"Actually, we'd prefer to stay in the fund you manage personally."

Septimus Reventlow was a reed of a man. He had sharp cheekbones and dark hooded eyes, and his thinning black hair was meticulously combed and swept off his forehead with a generous dollop of pomade. He was impeccably dressed in a black suit, a bold checked shirt, and a maroon tie that he had knotted loosely, almost casually. He wore his wealth like a birthright, the lord to the manor born, and it never failed to rub Astor the wrong way.

"The Astor fund?"

Reventlow nodded.

"That's a tough one. We've closed that fund. We're a hundred percent invested as it is. Not much we can do."

"We were hoping to deposit three hundred million dollars."

Astor smiled inwardly. Three hundred million dollars was big money. There was a time not so long ago when he would have begged, beaten, and killed for half that amount. "As I said, Septimus, we're not taking any more investors in that particular fund. It's nothing personal. There's no way I can add to my position for the time being. It's more administrative than anything else. I'd be happy to revisit the issue in a few months."

Astor's excuse was not entirely truthful. In fact the reason was personal. Reventlow's was a little different from other family offices. The source of his money was always a bit hazy. Reventlow claimed it hailed from a German industrial dynasty dating to the era of Bismarck and the first kaiser. Astor knew about the Krupps, the Thyssens, and the German branch of the Rothschilds, but he'd never heard of a Reventlow, except for an obscure count who'd married Barbara Hutton, the heiress to the Woolworth fortune. And of course there was the question of the man's looks. It was not that he didn't look German so much as that he didn't look anything. He was some kind of strange Eurasian mongrel.

In the end, Astor couldn't really care less where the money came from. It was Reventlow's reputation as an investor who expected quick returns and who pulled his money if he didn't get them that bothered him. The hedge fund business had a term for people like Septimus Reventlow: *hot money*. It was not a compliment.

"We're set on investing now," said Reventlow. "We sold some of our interests in the Far East and enjoyed a rather significant financial event. We don't like our capital to lie fallow."

And that was the problem with hot money, thought Astor. It was always chasing the highest returns, moving in and out of funds like some horny teenager rushing from bar to bar chatting up the girl with the blondest hair and the biggest boobs. If he got lucky in ten minutes, he stayed. If not, he moved on to the next one.

One stellar quarter did not a track record make.

Hedge fund managers liked continuity. They sought to build assets quarter after quarter, year after year. They preferred clients who shared their investment philosophy and were with them for the long term (barring a nuclear meltdown or the equivalent, say a loss of 10 percent or more in any one year). Reventlow was as rich as a Rockefeller, but he invested like a riverboat gambler.

"Look," said Astor. "I understand your not wanting your money to sit around earning money market rates. I'm sure we can find an arrangement. All of my other funds would welcome your investment. I can get our managers in here in two minutes. I think it would be worth your time to hear what they have to say."

"The Astor fund," said Reventlow, as if stating a decree. "And yes, I'm sure we can find an arrangement."

Astor smiled, if only to keep from punching Reventlow in the teeth. There was a method to his madness. Increasing his position in the yuan was not simply a matter of calling up his broker and buying another ten or twenty thousand contracts. Comstock Astor currently held $3 billion in its coffers, give or take. Of that, Astor had a billion down against the yuan, or had shorted it, meaning that he was betting it would depreciate in value versus the dollar.

Here's how the math worked. To speculate on currency, you bought contracts that stipulated what that currency might be worth thirty, sixty, or ninety days in the future. One contract controlled $1,000 worth of the currency. Astor had purchased 200,000 contracts, giving him control of $20 billion worth of the currency, or around 126 billion yuan. But Astor didn't have to put down the entire $20 billion. According to the margin requirements as set forth by the Chicago Board Options Exchange (CBOE), the organization that looked after currency trading, he needed to deposit only 10 percent of the contracts' value, in this case $2 billion. Astor put in a billion himself. He borrowed the other billion from banks that specialized in this kind of thing, thus leveraging his position twofold.

If he took $300 million from Reventlow, he would have to go to all his lenders and renegotiate his agreements.

"No," said Astor. "We can't."

"Excuse me?"

Astor stood and made a point of looking at his watch. "We can't find an arrangement. Fund closed. Is there anything else?"

Reventlow's brow tightened, and red arrows fired in his cheeks. "We are both talking about three hundred million dollars?"

"Three hundred million or three billion, it's all the same."

"But—"

"I'm sure you'll be pleased with our returns this quarter, however. We're expecting a major event ourselves in our primary position. Now, if there's anything else . . ."

"You can't turn me down. I have to—we have to—invest this money."

Astor moved toward the door. "Goodbye, Septimus."

Septimus Reventlow rose from his chair, his pale face paler, his calm demeanor ruffled, a man in the first stages of shock. Clearly, no one had ever told him to take $300 million and shove it up his ass.

Astor allowed Reventlow to walk himself out of the office. Returning to his desk, he opened his drawer and popped a Zantac. It was barely ten o'clock and his stomach was already acting up. He wasn't sure what was going on inside his gut, only that it felt like Vesuvius getting ready to blow.

Reventlow.

Hot money always did that to him.

Astor passed Shank on the way out.

"What's up?" said Shank. "You can't just skip out."

"I have something I need to do."

"Like?"

"I'll tell you later."

"What about the position?"

Astor stopped at the door. "What about it? Everything's fine. Just a blip."

"Exactly," said Shank. "But blips never happen with the yuan."

Astor didn't answer. He was already moving across the trading floor. Shank was right. Blips never did happen with the yuan. Unlike other currencies, the yuan was not freely floating. The Chinese government maintained a strong hand on its daily ebb and flow. It was only recently that the government had allowed the currency to be traded by foreigners at all. The sudden move made him anxious. Maybe that's what was causing his stomach to go haywire. Either way, he'd worry about the position later. Right now he had another priority.

9

Halfway across the globe, someone else was worried about the blip. "Good afternoon, gentlemen," said Magnus Lee, chairman of the China Investment Corporation, or CIC. "And lady. We have a full agenda. I suggest we begin."

Lee stood at the head of a conference table on the twentieth floor of the New Poly Plaza building in Beijing. It was the last Monday of the month, and as such, time for a meeting of the investment committee.

Created in 2007, the China Investment Corporation's sole purpose was to invest the country's vast foreign exchange reserves. For decades China had exported far more goods and services than it had imported. The result was a cumulative surplus of $3.5 trillion, an amount equal to the annual gross domestic product of the Federal Republic of Germany and less only than those of Japan, China itself, and the United States of America. Three-quarters of that money was placed in the safest, most conservative financial instrument on the planet: United States Treasury bonds. But one quarter was allowed to seek out more attractive returns. The money allocated for investments in equities, corporate bonds, real estate, and what financiers enjoyed calling "special situations" was placed into what was called a "sovereign wealth fund." It was this money that the committee had met to discuss.

Lee had established the fund with a stake of $200 billion. Since then he had run the money up to $900 billion. He liked to think of himself as the richest man in the world. Still, $900 billion was only a small portion of his country's total reserves. Like most rich men, he was congenitally greedy. He wanted more.

From his place at the head of the table, Lee silently greeted each committee member with a smile and a look from his glacier-blue eyes. The meeting followed a strict agenda. Each director stood and offered a succinct report of his or her department's recent activities. Lee began with the director in charge of North American equities. "Please, Mr. Ping, go ahead."

"I'm pleased to announce that we have increased our stake in Morgan Stanley to twelve percent. This is our first significant share purchase in the company since our original investment in 2007. Clearly the moment was not ideal."

"But Mr. Ping," said Magnus Lee, "even the loveliest rose cannot bloom in poor soil."

Ping beamed, publicly absolved of his poor timing. "During the last month," he went on, "we purchased an eight percent stake in Noble Energy Group for $900 million, a seven percent stake in Boeing for $5 billion, and a four percent stake in Intel for $5 billion. To date, we hold stakes in eighty-nine U.S. corporations valued at $400 billion. Sixty-seven of them are Fortune 500 corporations. Twenty-five are Fortune 100 corporations. Marked to market, our investments show an increase of two hundred percent."

It was CIC policy to take only minority stakes in foreign corporations and never to influence company policy. It was also CIC policy to invest in a spectrum of industries: energy, consumer products, finance, airlines, automobiles, and of course technology.

Finally, the director of North American equities stated that he had just completed negotiations to purchase a sizable stake in one of the financial service industry's most prestigious companies, American Express.

Lee clapped, and the entire table quickly followed suit. "Impressive," he said. "Perhaps we will all receive platinum cards."

"Ah, but Mr. Lee, surely a vice premier deserves the Black Card."

The table again clapped to show their support. In a country that worshipped status, the Black Card, issued only to those who spent over $100,000 a year, was the ultimate symbol of wealth.

Lee shook his head in false modesty while waving an admonishing finger. "No, no, Mr. Ping. Such a position is surely beyond my capabilities. There are many candidates far more qualified than I."

Lee was lying, and everyone in the room knew it. Face demanded that he not appear too convinced of his election. In four days the members of the Chinese Communist Party would gather for a once-in-a-decade congress to choose the country's next leaders. Besides the president, the party would select the ten-member Standing Committee to head up the more important ministries. It had been Lee's fervent dream to be appointed vice premier of finance one day. Every action he had taken in the past ten years had been directed to this end. Some, like the creation of the China Investment Corporation, were known to all and formed the basis of his public record. Others were more impressive but known to only a few. The few, however, sat at the pinnacle of the government and ruled over the army, the Ministry of State Security, and of course the Ministry of Finance. It was these actions, not his stellar investment returns, that would guarantee he achieved his long-desired goal.

"And besides," Lee went on, "where would I have enough money for such a card?"

The meeting continued. The next man discussed investments with U.S. private equity firms and hedge funds. Again the returns were impressive, as were the CIC's investments in corporate bonds.

The CIC's investments were not only made for financial gain. Each held strategic considerations as well. Companies who counted the CIC, the investment firm, as an important shareholder tended to support policies beneficial to China, the country. Such policies included favorable tariffs on Chinese imports; support, or at least silence, on the issue of reunification with Taiwan; and a steadying hand on the issue of revaluation of the Chinese yuan.

This last issue was especially important to Magnus Lee. He had been shocked by the trade representative's announcement that the country would continue following a policy of currency appreciation. China was currently suffering a severe slowdown in economic activity. While officially it was announced that the economy was growing at over 9 percent per annum, he knew better. The undoctored reports showed the economy puttering along at an anemic 7 percent, a disastrous figure in a land where over 100,000 people joined the workforce each day. As a trained economist, he knew that only by boosting the sagging export sector could his country reinvigorate its fortunes. And to do that it must make its goods more attractive to foreign markets. There was only one solution: depreciate.

Lee had another reason. Like all government officials, he had personal interests in the private sector, namely real estate development. Everyone knew the bottom had fallen out of the housing market. No one better than he. Until the economy picked up, he would have no buyers for his many luxury projects. There was far more to it than that, but Lee forced himself not to think about it. All would be better in a matter of days.

The last director rose and spoke for ten minutes about the council's ambitious forays into real estate. The most recent land deals included purchases of 200,000 acres of prime farmland in Colombia, 50,000 acres in Peru, a million acres in Chile, a gold mine in South Africa, a silver mine in Australia, a diamond mine in the Congo, and a parcel rich with uranium in Australia. There were also purchases in Namibia and Pakistan, and even in the United States of America.

"I must report some bad news," announced the director of real estate and natural resources. "I am sad to say that two of our esteemed country managers were killed in Zambia during the past week. On a visit to one of our gold mines, the men were trapped by miners demanding an increase in pay from four to six dollars a day and a decrease in weekly hours from eighty to sixty. Naturally, our managers refused. The miners beat them to death with their pickaxes."

"Savages," said Lee.

With that, he declared the meeting adjourned. As he shook hands and wished his directors a good day, he reviewed the meeting's highlights. Ever larger stakes in ever more companies in the U.S. and Europe. Ever more purchases of mineral-rich land in countries around the globe. Ever more bond purchases of U.S. Treasuries, increasing America's reliance on China. Each year his country was growing stronger and the rest of the world weaker.

It was only the beginning.

10

The New York Stock Exchange stood at the corner of Wall Street and Broad in Lower Manhattan. Built in 1903, the building hearkened back to the Parthenon, with six Corinthian capitals (or columns) supporting a broad marble pediment. Since 9/11, it had been customary to drape an American flag over the breadth of the building's façade. Astor's father had worked here for six years. In that period Astor had visited the floor a dozen times, but never once had he thought to contact him. Setting eyes on the building, he considered how easy it would have been to give him a call, to say hello and suggest they meet for a drink around the corner at Bobby Van's.

How very easy . . .

Astor slowed his pace, then stopped altogether. A rueful smile crossed his lips. No, he reminded himself, it wouldn't have been easy at all. His father had never liked unannounced visits.

"Robert, is that you?"

Astor took another step into the room and tried to stand taller. The year was 1987, early October. He was fifteen and five feet, eight inches tall and prayed nightly that he would keep growing. His father's birthday present was wrapped and tucked under his arm. He was dressed in his school uniform—blue blazer, gray trousers, white shirt, and striped tie—and it dawned on him that he had made a mistake in wearing it.

"Hey, Dad. Happy birthday."

Fifty or so well-dressed, rosy-cheeked men and women crowded the three tables in 21's private upstairs dining room. Though not acquainted with most of them, he recognized many of the faces. He saw the mayor and the chief of police and a famous newscaster. There were several prominent executives from Wall Street. He spotted the head of a big investment bank and, seated at a table across from him, the man he had replaced a year earlier. As one, the faces turned toward him. The women smiled. The men waited for their cue.

"I brought something for you," said Astor, clutching the gift. "To help you celebrate."

Edward Astor stood up laboriously, making no move to approach and welcome him. "Today is Thursday, is it not?"

"October fifteenth," said Bobby Astor. "At least, I hope." A few guests chuckled. He chuckled, too, pleased to have broken the ice, his eyes flitting nervously from face to face, marshaling support.

"Still at Deerfield, young man?" It was the mayor. Astor recalled hearing his father denounce him in terms that would make a marine blush. Yet here he was, seated at his father's side and somehow aware that Astor had attended Deerfield Academy. Astor saw his father's eyes flash. The mayor could not have asked a worse question.

"No, sir," answered Astor. "I didn't—"

"He was kicked out," Edward Astor stated, in the same stentorian baritone. "My son the pyromaniac."

Astor tried to grin. The effort was painful. "It was just a paper fire . . . in my trash can . . . bad grade on a test."

"A paper fire that enveloped the curtains and severely burned one of your fellow students."

"Just his hands. Only second-degree. He's fine."

A silence fell on the room. All the bonhomie and goodwill present when he'd entered had vanished as if sucked out through a pressure grate. The smiles vanished, too.

"My son attends the Kent School at present," said Edward Astor.

Astor tucked the birthday gift back under his arm. It didn't matter what he had brought. It wouldn't be enough. "For the moment, at least," he added sheepishly, hoping to win back the crowd. "I'm getting a math test back tomorrow."

There was a guffaw and a few chuckles. His father cleared his voice and the laughter stopped. "Speaking of tomorrow, there is school?"

"Yes, sir."

"Pray tell, Robert, how did you get leave to join us this Thursday at nine o'clock in the evening?"

Astor hadn't expected the question. Or if he had, he'd expected it man-to-man, when he could make up a bullshit story about getting permission *from the dean of students. He was a good liar, but he was punching above his weight with the chief of the New York City Police Department staring at him. He looked at his father, standing there like a statue in a three-piece suit, hands tucked into his waistband, eyes boring into him as if he'd been caught stealing someone's wallet.*

"I . . . uh . . ." Astor considered leaving. The door was right behind him. A rapid about-face and he could be gone before anyone could say a word. His pride might be tarnished, but he'd have time to stop at Trader Vic's in the Plaza for a mai tai and still make the 11:04 to Westport.

"We are waiting," declared his father, a judge demanding a confession.

It would be the truth, then.

"I bribed my proctor," said Astor.

"Ex—excuse me?"

It was the closest to a stammer Astor had ever heard come out of his father's mouth.

"My house proctor," he went on. "I took him for fifty bucks playing poker before football practice. I knew he needed the money to take out his girl-friend this weekend. I told him I'd forget about the dough if he'd let me come into New York for the night."

"And he agreed?"

"He wants to get laid, doesn't he?"

At that, the entire room burst out laughing. The chief of police covered his mouth and looked away, but he was smiling. So was the mayor. Astor waited long enough to see his father's eyes narrow, his jaw set, then added, "I explained that it was your birthday, of course."

Edward Astor waited until the room quieted. "Very amusing, Robert, as always. I'm sure we'll all be equally amused when you are expelled for leaving campus without permission."

"Don't worry, Dad, I'm going now. I just wanted to bring you this." Astor made his way between the tables and handed his father his present. It was slim and the size of a sheet of paper.

Edward Astor dropped it on the table.

"Don't you want to open it?"

"The only present I want from you is a decent report card," said his father. "Hopefully without an F."

Astor came closer so that they were face-to-face and could speak without the entire room overhearing them. "It's a paper I wrote for school. It's about the stock market. You see, I think that something's going to happen—"

"Do you? I'm glad. Something always happens in the market."

"I mean, I think there's a bubble. Prices are too high, given earnings."

"And what would you know about any of this?"

"I've been doing some trading. Not real, just on paper . . . you know, at school."

"Trading or gambling? There is a difference."

"Yes, sir. I know that."

"You can't bullshit the market, Robert."

"I've been doing well. Trading. Like you taught me."

"A rising tide lifts all boats."

"I don't think it's going to continue. In fact, I think something bad is going to happen. Like a crash. And soon."

Edward Astor turned from him and spread his arms to the guests. "My son the fortune-teller. Not content to play hooky from school and embarrass me in front of my dearest friends, he's now giving me advice on the market."

"Dad, just let me finish . . ."

"You just did."

Astor stared into his father's eyes, wondering how he could have come from this man, how he could share any part of him. Without another word, he made his way from the room and continued downstairs to the cloakroom. He looked at his watch and saw that the time was coming up on ten. He knew the doorman at the Limelight. He forgot all about the 11:04 and school tomorrow and the consequences that his absence would unleash.

"Young man, wait a moment."

Astor turned. It was the head of the famous investment bank. "Yes, sir?"

"What was your hand?"

"Excuse me?"

"When you were playing poker this afternoon and you beat your proctor, what were you holding?"

Astor put on his overcoat. "Me? Nothing. I was bluffing."

11

The sound of a truck grinding to a halt nearby returned Astor to the present. Fifty yards away, a large van with NYPD markings stopped at the entry to Exchange Place, the pedestrians-only square fronting the Exchange. A dozen men clad in black assault gear—helmets, vests, boots—jumped from the van, machine guns cradled to their chests. He recognized them as members of the NYPD's elite Hercules detachment. The Stock Exchange building was one of the city's prime "hard targets." Nothing better represented all that was good and bad about America's brand of capitalism. Living in Manhattan made everyone at least a little bit of an expert in counterterrorism.

Astor presented himself to the uniformed guard at the 2 Broad checkpoint. A blond, ruddy-cheeked man dressed in a blue suit stood a few steps away. Hearing Astor's name, he came forward. "Sloan Thomasson," he said, extending a hand. "My condolences. I handled security for your father. Come with me."

Thomasson led the way into the building. Astor cleared the metal detector, and the two continued to a bank of elevators. "Have you visited before?" asked Thomasson.

"Only the floor."

"Your father's office is in 11 Wall. The Exchange complex comprises eight buildings that take up the entire block. It's a real labyrinth."

The elevator arrived and Thomasson pressed the button for the seventeenth floor.

Astor waited for the doors to close, then asked, "Did you know my father was planning on going to D.C. this weekend?"

"No, sir, I did not. I'm only required to provide security here at the Exchange and for official trips. I spoke with your father Friday morning as he was leaving the office. He told me he was spending the weekend at his home in Oyster Bay."

"Taking off on a Friday morning? That doesn't sound like him. Did he seem preoccupied with anything? In any way out of sorts?"

"It's not my place to say, but as far as I could see, no. We had a trip planned to Atlanta early in the week. Your father didn't much like dealing with the new owners. Nothing special about that. But preoccupied? No."

In December 2012, the New York Stock Exchange had been purchased by IntercontinentalExchange, or ICE, a giant multinational concern active in the trading of futures and derivatives. Astor didn't think the new owners were the problem. It was his father's arrogance. Edward Astor didn't like reporting to anyone but himself.

The elevator slowed. The doors opened. Thomasson zigged and zagged down a series of corridors. Astor stayed at his shoulder. It was his first time in the executive quarters of the Exchange and he was feeling like a rat navigating a maze. Thomasson was right to refer to it as a labyrinth. The corridor emptied into a large, high-ceilinged anteroom with blue carpeting and photographs depicting the Exchange's history.

"Here we are," said Thomasson. "Your father's office is inside. Mrs. Kennedy, his secretary, is expecting you."

"Thank you." Astor shook hands. "Tell me something, what did you do before taking this job?"

"Twenty-five years in the Secret Service. My last post was heading up the PPD—the presidential protective detail."

"Still have friends in the service?"

"Lots."

"You know what went down last night. What happened?"

"Word is that the driver lost control of the vehicle."

"The car was making a run across the South Lawn. That's a little more than jumping a curb and running into a tree."

"Yes, sir, it is."

Astor thought Thomasson knew more than he was letting on. "Well?"

Thomasson leaned in closer, as if vouchsafing a secret. "When I said 'lost control,' I didn't mean that he was driving too fast or that it was in any way his mistake. I meant that the driver was no longer able to control the vehicle in any way, shape, or fashion."

"Then who was?"

Astor waited for an explanation, but Thomasson said nothing more. Before Astor was able to press him, a petite, birdlike woman emerged from her office, walked directly to him, and hugged him. "I'm so sorry for your loss," she said.

Astor returned the hug gently. He could feel her sobbing and he held her until she stopped.

"Please, excuse me," she said, stepping back and wiping her eyes. "I'm Dolores Kennedy. I worked with your father for the past five years."

Kennedy was a kindly-looking brunette with short hair and a schoolmarm's inquisitive gaze.

"I'm afraid we weren't close," said Astor.

"Oh, I know," she said, as if the estrangement pained her. "But he talked about you."

Astor didn't comment. He didn't think he'd like to learn what his father had had to say. He thanked Thomasson, then followed Dolores Kennedy into a large suite of offices. "May I look around?"

"The FBI phoned first thing. They requested that none of his belongings be disturbed until their team arrives."

"I won't touch anything."

The secretary shot a glance over his shoulder. Thomasson nodded. "Very well," she said. "Right in here."

The office was palatial, with high molded ceilings, dark carpeting, and a desk that would have done a robber baron proud. Photographs of his father ringing the opening bell with various businessmen, entertainers, athletes, and political figures crowded the credenza, vying for space with Lucite blocks announcing the latest companies to list their shares.

The New York Stock Exchange was a business like any other, and its first priority was to turn a profit. It made money in several ways. First, and most important, it charged a fee on every share of stock bought and sold. The amount had plummeted over the years, from dimes to nickels and then lower. These days the Exchange charged fractions of a penny per share traded. It wasn't a high-margin business. On the other hand, the volume of shares traded had skyrocketed. A normal day saw well over a billion shares change hands.

The Exchange charged a far larger amount to companies that wanted their shares listed, or available for trading. The four thousand listed companies paid annual fees as high as $250,000, earning the Exchange more than $800 million a year. IBM, Caterpillar, Alcoa: they all had to pony up. The NYSE was a very large enterprise indeed.

"If I might be so bold," said Mrs. Kennedy, "I'm a little surprised to see you."

Astor responded earnestly but not altogether honestly. "I'm surprised to be here. My father sent me a note last night shortly before the accident occurred. It was the first time in years he tried to contact me. I think he had an idea something bad was going to happen. I wanted to ask you some questions to see if you could shed a little light on what he'd been doing lately."

"He was a busy man. When he wasn't traveling, he was hosting guests here at the Exchange or going to meetings."

"No doubt he was," agreed Astor. "Can you tell me if he ever mentioned something called Palantir?"

Mrs. Kennedy pursed her lips. Behind her rimless glasses, her eyes were alert and perceptive. "Never heard that word."

"Never?"

The woman shook her head emphatically.

Astor walked behind his father's desk. The surface was neat and uncluttered. In and out trays set side by side were empty. He wondered if his father had straightened up, knowing that he might not be back.

"Was he working on anything out of the ordinary?" asked Astor.

"He was seeing Miss Evans quite a bit," replied Mrs. Kennedy. "She's his executive assistant. She handles many of his day-to-day assignments—correspondence with our partners, issues with the listed companies and those wishing to list, just about everything."

"Sharp gal," added Thomasson, still standing in the doorway. "English. She worked for one of the big banks for a few years. She's been with us fourteen months."

"May I speak with her?"

"She's not in yet," said Dolores Kennedy.

Astor checked his wristwatch and saw that it was nearly eleven o'clock. "Is she sick?"

Kennedy shot the security agent, Thomasson, a worried glance before returning her attention to him. "She isn't answering her phone."

"Do you mind if I try to contact her?"

"I'm not permitted to give you that information."

"Please, Dolores. It would mean the world."

She looked back at Thomasson, who nodded. "All right, then," she said. "Stay right here. I'll print up her phone and address."

Kennedy left the room and Thomasson stepped away to answer

a call. Suddenly alone, Astor spotted his chance. Moving quickly, he made a reconnaissance of his father's desk. He opened the top drawer. A leather-bound agenda with the current year stenciled in gold print lay inside. He reached for it, his fingers brushing the cover. The agenda would be considered evidence. Taking it would constitute obstruction of justice, an offense that he knew from his ex-wife counted as a felony. The doorway remained clear. This was hardly the time to worry about the law. Astor snatched the agenda and tucked it into the rear of his trousers, taking care to arrange his jacket over it.

Hardly a second later, Dolores Kennedy returned. "She lives at 1133 Elm Street, Greenwich," she said, waving a flap of paper. "I'll give you both her numbers, too."

Astor stepped away from the desk. The drawer remained open an inch. There was nothing he could do about it now. He crossed the room to the doorway and took the paper with Penelope Evans's information. "Thank you, Dolores."

"No, thank you," the secretary replied. "It would make your father happy to know that you cared."

"How did you—" Astor cut himself off. "Thanks again."

"How did you know?"

November 1987. One month after Black Monday, the crash that had seen the Dow Jones Industrial Average lose more than 20 percent of its value in a single day, Bobby Astor sat at a table in the Grill Room of the Four Seasons at 52nd and Park. He had not left school surreptitiously this time. He had come by invitation. A lunch in the city between father and son. The head of school was happy to sign his day pass.

"So you read my paper?" asked Bobby.

"Of course I read it. So did all of my partners. We're impressed. In fact, we're more than that. Half of them want you to quit school and come to work for us right now."

Bobby smiled, his cheeks flushing with pride.

Edward Astor leaned closer. "The other half want to know who you copied your work from."

The waiter arrived. Edward Astor ordered an old-fashioned. "And give the boy a beer. He thinks he's an adult anyway."

The waiter nodded and left the table. The Four Seasons existed in a parallel universe where mortals' laws held no sway.

"I wrote it," said Bobby.

"Then tell me. How'd you know?"

"Like I said in the paper. Prices were too high, given earnings. Not just that, they'd risen too fast. Not just in the States but everywhere. It was all in the numbers. Something had to give."

"Everyone reads the same numbers. Everyone knew P/Es were too high. Your timing was specific. 'Sell everything now.'"

"The market felt frothy. It just seemed like it was about to give."

"You're fifteen," Edward Astor said. "How do you know what frothy means?"

"Things were out of kilter, that's all."

"And this is how you spend your spare time? Studying the market?"

"Pretty much. And playing poker."

"You're still not answering my question. How did you know the crash was imminent?"

Bobby looked into his lap, then lifted his chin and met his father's gaze. "It's like this, Dad. When I study the numbers and the charts, I get lost in all that data. It's like I'm swimming in it. All that information becomes part of me. Like in Star Wars. *The numbers create some kind of force and I can feel it."*

"You can feel the force?"

"Yeah, I can." Bobby shrugged. "So how did I know the crash was going to happen soon? I just knew."

Anger flashed behind Edward Astor's eyes. His mouth tightened and he rose in his seat. Bobby knew that intuition went against everything his father stood for as an investor. As quickly, his father sat down again. A look of understanding brightened his features. Before he could reply, a diminutive, curly-haired man slid into the booth next to him. The two men spoke quietly for a few minutes. As the man stood to leave, Edward Astor motioned toward Bobby. "Henry," he said. "This is my son, Robert. Robert, meet Henry Kravis."

Bobby shook hands and smiled uncertainly.

Edward Astor looked into his son's eyes. "You'll want to remember him, Henry. The boy's a genius. One day he's either going to be richer than any of us or broke and in the poorhouse."

Sloan Thomasson was waiting in the antechamber. "Leaving already?"

"I've got what I needed," said Astor. "Can you help me find my way out of here? I'll never get back to the elevator. You're right. It's like a maze."

"No need to go back. There's an express elevator that goes down to the ground floor. Normally it's just for the CEO and his guests. If you don't mind exiting on Broadway, we can take that."

"That would be fine," said Astor. The agenda cut a crease into his lower back. It was difficult to walk without wincing.

Thomasson showed him to the elevator. "Exit at one," he said.

Astor shook hands and thanked him. The ride to the ground floor required less than ten seconds. He rushed out the door and onto the pavement beyond.

The felon was happy to escape the building.

12

Each day before beginning work, Supervisory Special Agent Alex Forza bowed her head and prayed.

"Dear Father, I ask your blessing that I meet today's challenges with intelligence, courage, and fortitude, that I give no quarter, now or ever, to enemies of this country, and that I perform my duties to your highest standards and in a manner that will bring credit to the Bureau."

She kept her eyes closed a moment longer, allowing the words to resonate, then lifted her head and gazed at the photograph behind her desk. It was a portrait of a ruthless, cynical, manipulative middle-aged man. At fifty, he looked seventy. His hairline was receding, his jowls flabby, his eyes bulging, and he was well along the way to acquiring the toadlike stare of his later years. He was not an attractive man. Yet there was no mistaking the purpose in his forthright gaze, the single-minded and holy commitment to duty that was the cornerstone of his life and that, God-like, he had transferred to the Bureau.

"And Father," Alex added in closing, whispering because this was a private matter between the two of them, "no matter what, do not let me fuck up."

J. Edgar Hoover stared back mutely.

Alex took a seat at her desk and began sifting through the incident reports that had come in the night before. The stack was thicker than usual for a weekend, and she suspected that many of the calls were false alarms, or what she called "Al Qaeda alarms." The first report validated her suspicion. A passenger riding in a taxi complained that the cabdriver had made derogatory comments about the United States and was, in his estimation, "a friggin' terrorist." The time of the call was 1:30 a.m. The caller left his name as well as the cabbie's and the taxi medallion number. Alex classified the report as "nonurgent" and started a pile to the right. When time allowed, one of her investigators would call and interview the complainant. She felt confident that the city would be safe until then.

Alex headed CT-26, the Bureau's threat assessment squad tasked with investigating claims of suspicious activities pertaining to acts of terror on United States soil. "See something, say something" was the watchword of the day, and the citizens of New York had taken it to heart. The hotline received north of fifty calls a day, and it was up to Alex and her team of twenty-six investigators to separate the chaff from the grain.

Alex had been given command six months earlier in an effort to provide the squad with a more aggressive stance. She'd made a name for herself in the bank robbery squad and child crimes before joining the CT pool five years back. There were agents who had more arrests, but none could match her take-no-prisoners attitude. No one gave the Bureau more than Alex Forza.

One glance at her office testified to that commitment. There was no couch, no coffee table, and no chairs for visitors to sit in while they were shooting the shit. Meetings were conducted standing up and face-to-face. Other than the photograph of J. Edgar Hoover, the walls were bare. The only furniture was her desk, her chair, and a bookcase, all standard issue. She was not, however, without a flair for decoration. A handheld battering ram lay against one wall. Her prized Benelli twelve-gauge assault shotgun stood in a corner next to it, along with her Kevlar vest. The office was everything she'd ever wanted.

Alex powered through a dozen incident reports, finding none to be urgent. An hour had passed when Jim Malloy popped his head in the door. "Hey, Alex, you already here? Thought you'd sleep in and get some rest."

"I'm the boss," she answered. "I ask those questions. Why aren't you grabbing forty winks?"

Malloy stifled a yawn as he entered the office. "Me? You kidding? I got home just in time to wake up my little cherubs. Guess who gave them breakfast and looked after them while his wife slept an extra hour?"

Alex frowned. "So you show up at work tired and your wife is fresh as a daisy. Bad decision."

Malloy's disposition soured. "I'll remember that."

Alex pointed to the photo of Hoover. "You think he came to work tired so he could let his wife sleep?"

"He wasn't married."

"Not officially, at least." Alex cracked a smile to show that the boss was human.

Malloy wandered over to the corner and picked up the battering ram. "This the thirty-five-pounder?"

"Little Bess." Little Bess weighed thirty-five pounds. Big Bess weighed fifty. As the first woman to make the FBI's SWAT team, Alex had been rewarded by being allowed to carry Little Bess up five flights of stairs every other Saturday when the team met to train. She didn't mind one bit.

Malloy dropped the battering ram. "We get the warrant for Windermere yet?"

"Not enough to go on. No way to tell if the picture is real or fake. Plus no imminent threat. We wait another day. If our guy doesn't show, I'll call the judge."

"Fair enough. Still, I wonder what—"

Alex's phone rang and she raised a hand to interrupt Malloy. "Yeah?"

It was Jason Mara, one of her squad members, calling from Inwood. "Our guy just came home."

"You're kidding me, right?" said Alex, but she was already snatching her blazer off her chair, burying an arm in one sleeve and lunging for her vest. "When did he show?"

"A minute ago," said Mara.

"What took you so long to call?"

"You serious?"

"Shut up and listen. Get that place locked down. He is not to leave the premises under any conditions. Do I make myself clear?"

"Yes."

"Who's out there with you?"

"DiRienzo."

"Good. I'll be there in forty minutes."

Alex hung up and looked at Malloy. "Let's go earn a beer."

13

The call had come in three days earlier.

A woman in Long Island phoned the hotline claiming to have witnessed her neighbor unloading crates of military hardware from his car at three in the morning. The report was verified and a written copy forwarded to CT-26, where it landed on Alex's desk.

The mention of military hardware graded the call "urgent." Alex vetted the source herself. The woman was named Irene Turner and lived in Inwood, a scruffy lower-middle-class neighborhood on the southern tip of Long Island. Inwood had plenty of temporary residents, some organized crime, and a significant foreign-born population, but it was the town's proximity to John F. Kennedy International Airport, a major international freight hub, that piqued her curiosity and made the hackles on the back of her neck stand up.

"I saw guns," the woman named Irene Turner explained.

"Really? What kind?"

"Well, actually boxes full of guns."

"Boxes of guns?"

"They were really crates with markings on them. I'm Russian. The writing was Cyrillic."

Alex hadn't caught an accent. "Have you lived here long?"

"Since I was four. My parents were refuseniks. We emigrated in 1982. I have my American passport."

Alex's interest ratcheted up a notch. "Please go on."

"It was past three in the morning. I don't sleep. I was downstairs in the kitchen making coffee. From my window, I can see into his garage. Of course, he doesn't know this. Otherwise he would think I'm some kind of crazy for watching him so much."

"Do you know your neighbor's name?"

"Oh, no. We don't speak. He moved in a couple of months back, but I don't see him much. He's nice-looking. About thirty. Tall. Fit." She giggled. "He has a nice behind."

Alex began to get a picture of Irene Turner. Thirty-five years old. Single. Lonely. A life lived looking through windows. "About the guns . . ."

"Yesterday night he came home late. He opened the back of his truck and that's when I saw them. The crates. Green with rope handles . . ."

"And Cyrillic writing on the side."

"It said *Kalashnikov.*"

"Excuse me, Ms. Turner, I don't mean to be rude, but how can you see that far?"

"The writing on the side was yellow. It was easy to read. I took a picture."

"A picture?" Alex smiled to herself. The technology these days. Every man a spy.

"With my phone."

Alex asked her to send the photograph to her own phone. Fifteen seconds later she had it.

The picture was terrible. It was dark and out of focus and of course taken from 50 feet away. Still, there was no mistaking the olive-drab crate with rope handles and some kind of yellow writing on the sides.

Alex considered this. Wooden crates with rope handles. Cyrillic writing. Whatever was inside the box—Kalashnikovs or Tokarevs or little wooden matryoshkas—it sounded as if it were military issue and a resident of Nassau County should not be in possession of it.

Alex ended the call after confirming Turner's address and that of her neighbor and extracting a promise from Turner to come to the FBI's office in Chelsea for an interview the following day. After that, she walked into the bullpen and waited until all her young lions raised their heads and gave her their attention.

"Gentlemen and gentlemen," she announced, with the theatricality she reserved for promising leads, "we have a live one."

14

A lex stood beside Jim Malloy at the door of 1254 Windermere. "Ready to go?"

Malloy nodded. "Let's do it."

Alex rapped twice on the door, then stepped back so that the keyholder could see her. She pushed her shoulders back and lifted her chin. She liked this moment best. The moment before the real job began. She never knew what she might find out, what crime she might discover, what threat she might mitigate. Too much of her job involved waiting, analyzing, convincing, and cajoling. This is what she had joined the Bureau for. Catching bad guys.

The house was a two-story clapboard with a shingle roof built in the early '40s. A fringe of lawn out front needed mowing. An American flag hung limply next to the door. The owner was one Maxim Ustinov, an immigrant from Russia like Irene Turner, the neighbor who had called in the report, but Ustinov was just the landlord. The tenant, or in FBI parlance "the keyholder," was a thirty-one-year-old male named Randall Shepherd. According to the owner, Shepherd was a model tenant. He had moved in on June 1 on a twelve-month lease. A cashier's check in the amount of $9,000 had covered the security deposit as well as the first three months' rent.

Alex had established twenty-four-hour watch on the house two days earlier. During that time there had been no sightings of Shepherd coming or going. To verify that no one was inside, she'd conducted a pretext, sending Malloy and Mara to the front door, posing as activists canvassing the area for signatures. No one had answered, and readings from the infrared scanner programmed to detect warmth emitted by human beings came back negative.

She was raising her hand to knock again when the door swung open.

"Hello." The man was tall and fit, with dark hair cut to the scalp. He wore a white T-shirt and loose-fitting jeans. His eyes were blue and

steady. Alex couldn't tell if he had a nice behind or not. He did, how-
ever, have arms like a weightlifter, his biceps bursting from the sleeves.
Alex felt a pinch between her shoulder blades, a twinge, nothing more.
It was her sixth sense, and it said, "Trouble."

"Mr. Randall Shepherd?"

"Yes?" The response was tentative, as the man looked at the two
agents, both attired in dark suits, both wearing sunglasses.

Alex badged him. "I'm Special Agent Forza with the FBI. This is
Special Agent Malloy. We were wondering if we might have a word."

"Am I in trouble?"

"Not yet." Alex smiled as she removed her sunglasses. "May we
come in?"

"I'm happy to answer any questions out here."

Alex detected a hint of a foreign accent. The *h* in *happy* was too
soft, more *'appy*. A background search on Shepherd had come up close
to empty. He had no credit cards, didn't subscribe to cable TV, and
neither the IRS nor Social Security had heard from him in years. The
Texas driver's license number he'd given on his rental application was
valid, though she hadn't been able to pull up the picture. And of course
there was the matter of the cashier's check. No one paid three months'
rent in advance. To Alex's eye, he was a straw man.

"We'd prefer to come inside," said Malloy. "We can get a warrant if
you'd like."

Shepherd shrugged and his blue eyes softened. "Come in, then. The
place is a mess. Don't want to give the FBI the wrong impression."

Shepherd swung open the door. Alex followed Malloy inside. The
home was cheaply furnished and smelled of smoke and stale beer. There
was a sagging couch, a beat-up armchair, and a coffee table scarred with
cigarette burns. Copies of *New York*, *Time Out*, *This Week in New York*,
and, more interestingly, *Guns and Ammo* lay arranged messily on one
end. At the other, Alex noted a residue of spilled coffee or tea, not in a
puddle but shaped very clearly at a right angle, as if it had been spilled
next to a magazine. A magazine that had been hastily hidden.

"You like guns?" she asked.

"I'm from Texas," Shepherd volunteered. "I hunt."

"Whereabouts?" asked Malloy.

"Where do I come from or where do I hunt?"

"Both," said Alex.

"I come from Houston, but we used to hunt in East Texas. A place called Nacogdoches, near the Louisiana border."

"Where in Houston?" asked Malloy. "I'm from Dallas myself."

Alex said nothing. Malloy was born and raised in Seattle, but she liked his tactic to keep the pressure on Shepherd.

"Sugarland."

Malloy nodded, then asked offhandedly, "Who's mayor down there?"

"No idea," said Shepherd. "I haven't lived there in years. Who's the mayor of Dallas?"

Malloy stumbled and Alex picked up the baton. "You don't sound like you're from Houston," she said. "Are you in this country illegally?"

It was Alex's practice to go at a suspect head-on. She believed that confrontation yielded the greatest results, both immediate and in the long term. You had to shake the tree to see if any fruit might drop to the ground. She liked to shake it hard.

"I'm American," said Shepherd. "Last I checked, that gives me the right to be here."

"Do you have a passport?"

"Okay, enough," said Shepherd, holding up his hands. "Can you please tell me what this is about?"

"I'm sure you know."

Shepherd didn't respond, and Alex saw his eyes narrow, a current of anger rustle the calm façade.

"We want to know where you are keeping the machine guns," she added.

"Pardon me?"

"I believe they are AK-47s."

Shepherd's eyes widened, and he laughed as if a great weight had lifted off his shoulders. "AK-47s? Here? You're serious? At least now I know you're at the wrong house. You had me worried."

Alex assessed Shepherd's body language. His arms hung loosely at his sides. His eyes held hers. The laugh was rich and easy. There was no fidgeting, no playing with his hands, no delaying or prevaricating or any of the giveaways typically found in a person who had something to hide. Everything indicated that he was telling the truth. The twinge had lessened, but it was still there.

"We had a report that you were unloading a crate with Russian markings at three a.m. a few days ago," she said.

"That?" Shepherd chuckled, showing a set of straight white teeth: just a big ole Texas boy. "Can you stay here a second? I show you."

I show you. Odd, thought Alex. "We'd rather come with you."

"Suit yourself." Shepherd led the way through the kitchen and into the attached garage, where a late-model Ford pickup was parked. He skirted the truck and stopped, pointing at the ground. "There's your crate," he said. "I like to play paintball. That's our ammo."

Alex rifled through the crate, sifting the bags of paint balls. Malloy picked up a bag, then dropped it, disappointed. He looked at Alex and sighed. Case over. One more false alarm. Alex couldn't read Cyrillic, but she could make out *AK-47* well enough. She ran a hand inside the crate; her fingers came away slick with paint. She rose, and the three walked back through the kitchen.

"That's some load of groceries," said Alex. "Expecting someone?"

"Family," said Shepherd. "Barbecue tonight."

"They in from Texas?"

"All over, actually," said Shepherd. "You're welcome to stop by and see for yourself. We're firing up the grill around seven."

"That won't be necessary," said Malloy.

Alex slowed, eyeing the groceries on the counter. There was milk and orange juice, bread and peanut butter, and bags of beef jerky. To one side were amassed a dozen small bottles of five-hour energy drink. Above the fridge sat two cartons of Marlboro Reds, but she knew Shepherd didn't smoke. His fingers were clean, with no nicotine stains between the index and middle fingers. And there were those white teeth. She didn't see any chicken or steaks or ground beef: staples of a summer barbecue. Of course, he could have already put it away. She looked at the refrigerator, then thought better of it.

She and Malloy stopped at the front door. "Thank you for your cooperation, Mr. Shepherd," she said. "We're sorry to have intruded on your day."

"It is no problem."

Alex smiled as the twinge in her back turned into a dagger. There it was again. The clumsy syntax. The faintest of accents, turning *it* into *eet*. She didn't know exactly where he was from, but it wasn't Houston, Texas.

She rubbed her fingers together and found them as slippery as a few minutes before. Not paint but grease. The kind of grease that keeps rust from gun barrels. And all the while she kept her eyes locked on Mr. Randall Shepherd.

You bastard, she thought. *You goddamned, Oscar-winning bastard.*

Shepherd stared back, eyes steady, unblinking. He ran a hand over his scalp, and Alex observed two rivulets of sweat at his temple beginning to roll toward his jaw.

"Au revoir," she said, as lightly as her thundering heart would permit.

"Au revoir," said Shepherd. The response was immediate and unrehearsed. It was *French* French, not her clumsy American variant. She knew it, and he knew she knew it. Shepherd shook his head, chuckling to himself. *"Mais merde."*

"Hands against the wall," said Alex. "You're under arrest."

"What is it?" asked Malloy. "Did I miss something?"

But by then the man who called himself Randall Shepherd was bringing a large semiautomatic pistol to bear and Alex was pushing Malloy aside as she cleared her Glock.

"Drop it!"

She was a second late.

15

The first bullet struck her in the chest. She wasn't sure where, only that she felt as if she'd been flattened by a truck. The second hit her in the same place, and even as she tumbled backward and her head hammered the doorframe, she knew that he was a professional. What kind of professional, she wasn't sure, because by then she'd hit the ground and she couldn't breathe, and even though her eyes were open, all she could see were skyrocketing colors.

Alex tried to raise her head, but nothing happened. The thought came to her that she was wearing her vest so the bullet couldn't have penetrated the Kevlar plates and injured her spine. She tried again, with only a marginally better result. She didn't like slackers, or anyone else who refused her orders, and the same went for herself. Angered, she ordered her fingers to curl, but for all her efforts, she remained as immobile as a petrified rock.

Gunfire battered the air, the bangs and concussions so loud that her ears hurt worse than her chest. There was a thud on the floor beside her, and like that, she could see again. Malloy was lying next to her. Blood spurted from his neck in messy arrhythmic geysers. *He's a goner,* she thought. *No one can lose that much blood.* She knew this was a terrible thing, and that later she was going to be heartbroken. But for now she was too stunned to feel anything.

The floorboards shuddered beneath her. Feeling rushed back into her limbs. She raised her head in time to see Shepherd running up the stairs. He stopped halfway and fired his pistol. The shot sounded louder than the others and brought her back to her senses. More gunshots followed. She was in a shooting gallery at Coney Island, if every shot made you wince and rattled your insides. Jason Mara came out of the kitchen, firing across the room at Shepherd. He and DiRienzo had taken the back door to insure against Shepherd's pulling a runner. Mara's head snapped back. Blood splattered the wall behind him. He fell. She knew he was dead.

Shepherd continued up the stairs. Alex aimed her pistol and fired. And fired again and again. Filaments of plaster and wallpaper erupted around him. He twisted and pointed his pistol at her. He was 20 feet away, but she felt close enough to count the grooves in the barrel. He had her dead to rights. The muzzle flash blinded her. Wood splintered an inch from her ear. All this time, she kept firing. Sixteen rounds, she told herself, though she had no idea how many times she'd pulled the trigger. Her hand was sore from squeezing so hard, and her wrist was shaky. She paused for a second—less, even—trained the sights on Shepherd's chest, then fired three times in succession. Shepherd appeared to hurl himself against the wall, rebounded, and flipped forward over the balustrade. His head struck the floor first, cracking the rotting planking. He didn't move after that.

The silence was louder than the gunfire.

Alex struggled to a knee and turned her attention to Malloy. "Hang in there, Jimmy," she said. "I'll get help."

Malloy's eyes beseeched her. His mouth hung open, lips trembling. He was speaking, but the words were incomprehensible. He repeated himself and she understood. "My girls," he was saying. ". . . love them."

"Stay still, baby. It's going to be okay."

Alex avoided his eyes. She had to find his carotid artery. Her fingers probed inside the gaping wound, but there was too much blood and half his goddamned neck was no longer there. Malloy's hand shot up and grasped her arm, his fingers digging into her flesh. Slowly the pressure relaxed. The hand fell back to the floor.

"Jimmy," she said.

Malloy stared lifelessly past her.

Alex stood. A pall of smoke drifted across the room, the cordite so thick it burned her eyes. Mara was dead, too. She already knew that. DiRienzo lay a few feet away. He had a hole in his cheek and the back of his head resembled a savaged pomegranate.

She crossed the room. Randall Shepherd lay on his stomach, his head swallowed by the old, termite-eaten floorboards. She kicked him and he did not respond. She kicked him again, because he was an asshole. Kneeling, she put two fingers to his neck, but she could find no pulse. She could see into the space beneath the house. An olive-drab crate with yellow Cyrillic writing sat inches from her feet. She still had no idea what the writing said. It didn't matter. There were numbers, too.

She could make out AK-47 just fine.

16

Bobby Astor stepped to the curb and raised a hand in the air. A steel-gray Audi SUV swerved into the right lane and pulled to a halt in front of him. Astor jumped into the back seat. "Good morning, Sully. You will kindly refrain from any mention of my father. I've been taking condolences for two hours now and I'm fed up with it."

"Screw you, too," said Detective First Grade (retired) John Sullivan, turning in his seat and fixing Astor with his watery blue eyes. He was sixty-seven, stout, and ruddy, very much in fighting trim. Since retiring from the force two years earlier, he'd worked as Astor's official chauffeur and unofficial bodyguard. "My condolences on the passing of your father."

"Condolences accepted," said Astor. "Get me to midtown."

Sullivan guided the car into traffic. "Jesus, Mary, and Joseph, what a shitty day. First your dad and then this thing out on Long Island."

"What thing is that?" Astor asked, only half interested. He freed the agenda from his back and set it on his lap, eager to study his father's business dealings for a clue as to what *Palantir* might mean.

"In Inwood, near JFK. Three FBI agents were killed in some kind of operation. It's all over the news."

Astor looked up from the agenda. "Did they give any names?"

Sullivan's blue eyes peered at him in the rearview. "Not yet. You know—have to contact the relatives first. Why?"

"Alex was on a raid last night."

"Long Island?"

"I think so." Astor speed-dialed his ex. He tapped his foot, waiting for her to answer.

"You're an hour late," said Alex when she picked up. "And yes, I'm all right."

Astor was more relieved than he cared to admit at hearing her voice. "Was it Jimmy?"

"He, Jason Mara, and Terry DiRienzo."

"I'm sorry, Alex."

"Yeah, well."

"What happened?"

"You know I can't discuss it. Listen, I'm busy right now. We can talk later."

Astor hung up, shaken, feeling somehow as if he were the one who had dodged a bullet.

"She okay?" asked Sullivan.

"Same as ever. Her partner was killed. Jim Malloy. Good guy."

"God bless," said Sullivan.

"Yeah. God bless," said Astor. "What the hell was she doing out there?"

Sullivan didn't answer. There was a time when he'd worked with Alex. The two didn't get along. He called her a maverick and thought she was too keen on taking risks, too eager to put herself and her team into the line of fire. Astor had no grounds to argue with him. Alex was Alex. She knew only one direction: forward. And always at top speed. Astor was the same. He often thought it was their similarities that had drawn them together, each seeing his or her own best traits in the other. It had made for a torrid romance. But narcissism, in whatever form, wasn't a good recipe for a long-term relationship.

Astor's phone buzzed. He checked the number. "What is it, Marv?"

Shank's voice rattled the car's speakers. "We got problems. Some of our guys called. They saw what happened earlier. They're nervous about the position."

By "guys," Shank meant the banks that had lent Astor the money to finance his bet on the yuan. Astor checked the monitor built into the rear seat. The yuan was holding steady at 6.30. "We're good. What are they complaining about?"

"Afraid it might happen again. They're talking about upping our margin deposit."

"They can screw themselves. A deal's a deal."

"Tell that to our lenders. If you've got a minute, you might want to stop by and boost their spirits."

Astor knew this was an order, not a request. "Who?"

"Brad Zarek."

Zarek was a senior VP who ran the prime direct brokerage department at Standard Financial. Not Astor's favorite guy. "How much are we into them?"

"Four hundred million."

Four hundred million was a substantial sum. Zarek had every right to be calling. "Listen, Marv, any other day I'd be there in a heartbeat. I've got something else going."

"This isn't any other day. If Standard Financial sneezes, all the other guys will get the flu."

"Yeah, all right. Call Zarek and tell him I'll be over. Listen, I gotta go."

"Head over there now. The sooner we nip this in the bud, the better. You coming back in, after?"

"Maybe."

"Maybe, my ass. It's not just the banks that are calling. I'm fielding calls left, right, and center from our clients. People are scared. They don't want to talk to a schmuck like me. They want the schmuck whose name is on the fund."

"That would be me."

"That would be you, schmuck."

"Yeah, okay . . . I'll see what I can do."

And the hits keep coming, thought Astor. He leaned forward and told Sullivan to take him to Standard Financial's headquarters at 45th and Sixth. Astor patted his driver on the shoulder. "Hey, Sully, sorry I barked at you like that earlier."

"Don't sweat it, chief. I've gotten worse."

John Sullivan had first pinned on a badge in 1966 at the age of twenty. He'd seen all the hot spots: narcotics, vice, homicide. Somewhere in there he'd been shot. Word was he'd pulled the bullet out himself and chased down the bad guy. Astor met him when Sullivan was working with Alex on the Joint Terrorism Task Force, better known as the JTTF, the force within a force run together with the FBI and a multitude of smaller agencies.

Astor didn't need a full-time bodyguard, but he didn't mind having someone licensed to carry a firearm drive him around town. There was an additional upside to hiring a cop as a chauffeur. When necessary, Sullivan could drive as fast as needed, run every red light in the city, and park where his heart desired, or rather, where Astor told him to.

No detective first grade, retired or otherwise, ever got a traffic violation in New York City.

Astor turned his attention to the agenda. He opened to the month of July and began reading. It was apparent that Edward Astor kept a meticulous record of his activities. A check of the past Monday showed a 7 a.m. breakfast with the CEO of a prominent social networking company about to do its IPO, or initial public offering. At nine there was a meeting with Sloan Thomasson to review the itinerary of the Germany trip. Nine-fifteen brought "P. Evans" for an "update." By 9:30 he was expected on the floor to ring the opening bell with a United States marine who had been awarded the Medal of Honor. And so the day continued—meeting upon meeting—until 7 p.m., when he departed.

The days afterward had been equally busy. Edward Astor arrived before seven in the morning and never departed before seven at night. Twelve-hour days were the norm, fourteen and fifteen hours all too common. Astor saw where he'd acquired his own work habits. He was reminded of the saying apropos of those who chose a career on Wall Street: "You won't know your children, but you'll be best friends with your grandchildren."

Astor turned to the past Friday, his father's last day in the office. The day started with a breakfast, this time with the chairman of the floor traders' association, followed by a meeting with "P. Evans." Astor thumbed back through the past ten days. It appeared that his father had had no fewer than twenty meetings with "P. Evans" during that time, and that didn't count the times they'd breakfasted and lunched.

Astor returned to the most recent Friday. At 9:15, the notation listed "Update on Special Project—P. Evans," whatever the "special project" was. The day ended there. He noted a diagonal line drawn through all meetings scheduled after 10 a.m., along with the word *canceled*.

Why? Astor wondered. Sloan Thomasson had felt certain that nothing had been bothering his father that morning. He was not sick. So what had forced Edward Astor to cancel all his appointments?

Astor's thumb returned to the entry for 9:15. "Update on Special Project—P. Evans."

He suspected that Penelope Evans might be the one to tell him.

17

Astor's first call was to Penelope Evans's home phone. After six rings, the call went to voice mail.

"You've reached the home of Penelope Evans. If you'd be so kind as to leave a message, I'll get back to you promptly. Toodles."

An Englishwoman. Cool, resolute, educated, with a royal's plummy upper-class accent. A snob if ever there was one. And then the chirpy "Toodles," Miss Evans thumbing her nose at herself and merry old England. A good sport, then.

Astor placed the second call to her cell. Six rings and counting. As he prepared to hang up, someone picked up. He waited for a greeting, but no one spoke. "Hello?" he said.

Silence. Astor pressed the phone to his ear, unsure if he heard a person's rushed breathing. "Miss Evans?" He added hurriedly, "This is Robert Astor—Edward Astor's son. Are you there?"

"I'm here."

"Yes, hello. As I said, this is Robert Astor. I just left my father's office. I was wondering if I might speak to you for a few minutes."

"What about?"

"What happened in Washington last night. I was wondering if you had an idea why he might have gone down there."

"Why would I?" asked Penelope Evans quickly, defensively.

Astor turned the pages of the agenda, his eye landing on Penelope Evans's name time and time again. "Mrs. Kennedy said that you and my father worked together on a number of projects," he replied. "I thought that he might have mentioned something to you."

"My work involved targeting new customers for the Exchange, updating software on our trading platforms, and writing research reports."

"According to her, you helped my father with everything."

"I did my job."

"She was very complimentary of your efforts," said Astor. "Were you working together on any projects for the government?"

"No."

"So you wouldn't have an idea why he had to rush down to D.C. to see Martin Gelman and Charles Hughes?"

"No."

"And you and he never worked on any project that might be considered . . ." Astor searched for the word. "Perilous?"

"I already said no." She was no longer just defensive but downright bitchy.

Astor held his temper. It was apparent that the woman's skill set did not include lying. There must not be a course in it at Oxford or wherever she'd gone to university. He was done with the kid gloves.

"Listen, Miss Evans," he began again. "Penelope . . . I can tell you're upset. Scared, even. I would be, too, if my boss got himself killed trying to deliver an urgent message to the president. I know you were working closely with my father, and I know it wasn't just targeting new clients and updating trading software. So let's cut the song and dance, shall we? On Friday morning at nine-thirty, immediately after meeting with you to discuss some kind of special project, my father canceled all his meetings for the rest of the day and got the hell out of Dodge. Something was up. I'm asking you again, what were you working on?"

"Why are you calling me, Mr. Astor? You haven't been a part of your father's life for years."

"Because he contacted me last night."

"Edward phoned you?"

Astor paused. He wasn't sure if it was surprise or jealousy he heard in her voice. He knew only that the tone belonged to a woman who had cared for his father.

"For the first time in five years. I think he was in the car on the way to the White House. He knew something was wrong—that he was in some kind of danger. Anyway, he texted me. Just one word. Can you guess what it was?"

Penelope Evans did not reply. Astor didn't hurry her. Finally she said, "They hear everything. That's why he went to Washington. He had to tell them."

"Who's 'they'? Palantir?"

"Palantir's the source. He told us about them. Of course, we suspected—at least, your father did. Edward didn't trust anyone. He was smart." Evans sniffed, and Astor could imagine her drawing herself up straight, gathering herself. "They're listening now," she went on. "They'll have keyed on the text your father sent you. Your phone will be in their system. It was one of their acquisitions. They hear everything we say."

"Who's 'they'?" Astor repeated.

"I've said enough, Mr. Astor. You don't need to be any more involved in this matter than you already are."

"My father thought differently." There was a pause. He could hear the woman breathing rapidly. "Please."

"Not over the phone."

"I'm free now. Where can we meet?"

"Do you know Morse code, Mr. Astor?"

"No. Why should I?"

"I do," said Sullivan, who could hear the call on the speaker system. "She can spell it out and I'll do my best."

A tap for a dot. A "Shh" for a dash.

There followed an excruciating two minutes of cat and mouse with Sullivan doing his best to decipher the series of dots and dashes. "Got it," he said afterward.

"Sure?" asked Astor.

"I was an Eagle Scout, wasn't I?"

"How quickly can you meet me?" asked Penelope Evans.

"An hour," said Sullivan.

"Please hurry."

18

Three seconds after Bobby Astor hung up with Penelope Evans, a transcript of the call landed in the technician's inbox in Iceland, already translated into his native language and ready for forwarding to his master halfway around the world. The technician did not read the transcript. He had no interest in the affairs of the men and women on whom his master spied. There were far too many people to keep up with any one.

At last count, the satellite was programmed to intercept the communications of over 57,000 individuals. One slow evening he had perused the names listed next to the phone numbers. Some he recognized. Some he did not. But in general the names fell into two categories: government officials and corporate chieftains. There were presidents and prime ministers, senators and delegates from nearly every country on the globe, including plenty from his own. There were bankers and industrialists, chief executives of this corporation, chairmen of that. There were lawyers in Berlin and magistrates in Bulgaria. After an hour he abandoned his task. One thing was clear. Sooner or later, every influential individual in the world ended up on the list.

The technician tapped his keyboard, forwarding the message to his master's private mailbox. His duty done, he swiveled in his chair and gazed out the window. It was midday and the sun blazed high in the sky. Crystals embedded in the fields of pumice sparkled like diamonds on a stormy velvet sea. He considered his position, working alone in such a solitary, isolated corner of the world. He daydreamed often about achieving a higher rank, of bettering his job and earning more money. He was a young man, bright, hardworking, obedient. Anything was possible.

The technician decided he was happy where he was. There were more important things than being influential. He did not want to end up on the list. When he talked to his girlfriend, he didn't want anyone to be listening.

19

Magnus Lee, chairman of the China Investment Corporation, exited from the elevator at the twentieth floor. He checked the direction markers and set off to his right, toward offices 2050–2075. With its industrial carpeting, fluorescent lights, and wood veneer doors, it could be any corridor in any corporate office in the world. Though it was nearly midnight, a steady stream of men and women walked past. They were smartly dressed, well coiffed, purposeful of step, every bit the equal of their Western counterparts.

As he walked, he passed beneath signs hanging from the ceiling adjacent to each office door. Written in English and Chinese, the signs read GENERAL MOTORS, IBM, MICROSOFT, EXXON. He was currently on the twentieth floor of building F-100. He was not twenty floors above the earth's surface. He was twenty floors beneath it.

F-100 stood for "Fortune 100." And building F-100 was one of six interconnected structures in the sprawling subterranean complex that made up the Institute for Investment Initiative, or i3. Buildings F-200 to F-500 housed companies ranked 101 to 500. A sixth building, known only as T, was reserved for special projects and companies that possessed products, technology, or intellectual property deemed to have the highest strategic value for the state.

The CIC was the tip of the iceberg, the portion above water, impressive to behold but benign. i3 was the remaining three-quarters of the iceberg, the enormous mass that remained below the surface, hidden from view, and possessing an infinite capacity for danger.

Lee had founded i3 a year after taking the reins at the China Investment Corporation. It was not enough to invest in foreign companies. Investment provided an attractive monetary return, but it was the corporations that truly benefited. The infusion of capital enabled them to hire more workers, develop new products, and expand market share in their respective industries. If China was to compete, it must develop its own industry. It must make its own automobiles and airplanes, its own computers and software, its own everything. In short, it must assemble an economic and industrial infrastructure of the highest order that not only rivaled the West's but surpassed it.

It was a daunting task . . . *without help.*

And so he had suggested an idea to his colleagues in the Ministry of State Security.

Industrial espionage as a state-sponsored covert policy.

An aggressive campaign of systematic, targeted thefts of any and all corporate knowledge, with the goal of copying, implementing, and improving said knowledge for the benefit of Chinese business.

Five years later, Lee's idea could be judged a success by any measure. China was able to compete with the most technologically advanced companies in America, Europe, and Japan across a wide swath of industries: automobiles, computers, microchips, even satellites and rocketry. All had made use of pirated technology to achieve their gargantuan leap forward.

For his work, he had been awarded a commission in the People's Liberation Army and given the rank of major general in the Intelligence Division. In a few days he would learn whether he would receive a more coveted title, that of vice premier for finance, one of ten men to serve on the Standing Committee.

One of ten to rule more than 1 billion.

It took Lee another minute to reach his destination. The sign above the entry to office 2062 read CISCO SYSTEMS and was printed exactly as you might find on the cover of the company's annual report. Lee was a stickler for detail.

Cisco Systems (No. 62), with revenues of $45 billion, was a San Jose–based manufacturer of computer hardware and software, notably routers and switches, the components that built the Internet's backbone and speeded traffic along the information highway. It was estimated that 99 percent of all Net activity passed through at least one Cisco device.

Lee walked past row after row of executives seated at workstations. A large overhead picture of Cisco corporate headquarters occupied one wall. The company's name was emblazoned in large block Lucite letters on another. The room's furnishings were identical to those found at the main Cisco campus, and each worker wore a Cisco personnel badge around his neck with a genuine neck strap. The men and women seated at their terminals were even working on projects similar to those of their counterparts in California. Some were engaged in designing new routers, others in updating existing switches, and still others in keeping up with current customer orders.

But the Cisco Systems office in building F-100 was no official subsidiary. It was a clone or, more precisely, a parasite latched onto its host, copying its DNA project by project, department by department, division by division via a web of hacked e-mail servers, mirrored hard drives, tapped phone exchanges, and concealed surveillance devices in hardware, software, and physical plants. There was even a micro audiovisual transmitter in the chief executive's office. All these devices gave Lee and his team access to 80 percent of the company's daily business activity.

"General Lee, an honor to have you with us," said the office director. The man had a PhD from Stanford and had logged eight years working at Cisco headquarters, including two years as assistant to the chief executive. As he approached, he held out a rectangular black unit the size of a car stereo. "I wanted you to be the first to see it. The Nexus 2000. An exact copy of Cisco's latest and most advanced router. We'll manufacture it under our own Bluefire label and have it ready for delivery to customers six months before Cisco."

"Price?"

"Twenty percent below the American model."

"Impressive." Lee felt his cell phone vibrate and checked the screen. *Urgent: An intercept from STS-1 in Iceland.* "Would you excuse me?"

Lee left the room and read the transcript of a conversation that had taken place minutes earlier between Robert Astor and a woman named Penelope Evans, who he quickly gathered was Edward Astor's personal assistant. It seemed that Edward Astor had had a partner in his investigation, and now the son was intent on speaking with her.

For a moment Lee was taken back to a day a few years earlier. Construction on the i3 complex was complete. Every month he and his team were siphoning more information from their rivals. He was at his desk when the door opened and a familiar figure entered. Lee stood at once, both thrilled and frightened.

"Copying is no longer enough," said the premier, the most powerful man in China. "Our policy of state-sponsored industrial espionage can take us only so far. It is not enough that we succeed. The West must be seen to lose."

Lee nodded.

"Can you do more to help us?"

"Yes," said Lee. "I can." For he had been harboring the same thoughts and had spent long hours thinking about how to help his country. And so he told the premier his plan, and the premier gave him his blessing.

On that day Troy was born.

Magnus Lee reread the intercept, biting his lip. It could not have come at a worse time. He had not yet revealed to anyone that Edward Astor had contacted his son about Palantir, or that there was any kind of possible breach whatsoever. And now the son was taking up his father's crusade.

The ripples were closing in on the shore.

Troy was at risk.

Lee found a quiet corner and placed a call to New York State.

"Hello, brother," came the strong, familiar voice.

"Hello, Shifu," said Lee, using the respectful title for "master." "How quickly can you find someone for me?"

20

The FBI's New York office for counterterrorism was housed on the upper floors of a red-brick building on Tenth Avenue in Chelsea. The Bureau shared space with several fashion designers, a software startup, and a law firm. Two restaurants occupied the ground floor. One belonged to a television chef famed for his bald pate and brusque manner. The other had recently received three stars in the *Times* and boasted a bone-in rib-eye steak priced at $135. Both eateries were beyond the reach of the dedicated men and women earning government salaries who passed by every day.

Alex exited from the elevator on the eighth floor. She passed through the biometric security station—thumb plus six-digit personal entry code—and headed to her office. Word of the shootings had spread through the office. Friends and enemies approached to offer their sympathy. She acknowledged each without breaking stride. If she stopped for a second, she was finished. Her carefully constructed façade would crumble to the ground. She had to keep moving. Work was the disease and the cure.

Alex's office sat in a lonely corner of the building off the bullpen that housed her squad. Dr. Gail Lemon was waiting inside when she opened the door.

"I'm surprised to see you," said Lemon. "You're required to take a few days off."

Alex continued past her to her desk. "And you're required to have the courtesy to wait for me to arrive before barging in."

Lemon was the New York field office's staff psychologist. She was petite and prim and looked as if Alex's battering ram outweighed her by 10 pounds. "You've suffered a traumatic loss," she said, with a beatific smile. "I understand you're upset."

"You don't understand squat."

"There's no need to be hostile."

"That wasn't hostile. You're still standing and I don't see any blood."

The smile faltered. "Now, Alex—"

"It's Special Agent Forza . . . and remind me, Dr. Lemon, do you carry a badge?"

"Of course not. I didn't go to the academy."

"And you've never spent a day in the field?"

"Not exactly . . . but if you—"

"Then get out of my office."

Lemon stood her ground, arms crossed. "Alex—I mean, Special Agent Forza—you're required to seek help."

"You want me to talk to a shrink, send someone who knows what it feels like to lose three men. They were family."

A half-dozen people gathered by the door, drawn by her raised voice. "It's okay, everybody," she said, speaking over Lemon's head. "Dr. Lemon was just heading out."

"Three days' leave," stated Lemon through gritted teeth. "Those are the rules for agent-involved shootings."

Alex held the door. "I have work to do."

Still Lemon wouldn't leave. She turned a half-circle, taking in the barren room—the metal desk, the half-empty bookcase, the battering ram, and of course the picture on the wall. Her mouth twisted as if she'd tasted something putrid. "Something is wrong with you, Special Agent Forza. You're a sad, hostile person. I'm going to have a word with the assistant director."

Alex shooed Lemon out of the room. "Make sure you say hello from me. She's the one who gave me this job. Have a pleasant day."

Dr. Gail Lemon's response was unrepeatable. The beatific smile had left the building.

Alex shut the door and blew out a sad, hostile breath. One more word and she would have struck the woman. Her gaze shot to the photograph of J. Edgar Hoover on the wall behind her desk.

"Father," she said, "I promise you that I am going to catch the sons of bitches who did this to my boys. And then . . ."

Alex left the last words unspoken. What she had in mind did not conform to the highest ideals of the FBI.

21

There was a knock on the door and a head poked around the corner. "Boss," came a squeaky voice. "Got a sec?"

Alex looked up from her paperwork. "Get in here, Mintz."

Special Agent Barry Mintz shuffled into the office. He was forty going on fourteen. Tall, gangly, with thinning red hair, trusting blue eyes, and an Adam's apple to rival Ichabod Crane's, Mintz was the lone holdover from her predecessor's team at CT-26. Those who hadn't transferred out voluntarily, she'd pushed out herself. All except Mintz. He wasn't brash, bold, or confident, which was how she liked her agents on the threat response squad. In manner and bearing, he was the opposite. He was quiet, self-effacing, and polite. Mintz was the guy in the corner no one noticed. And yet Mintz got things done. He was a six-foot-three-inch package of administrative whup-ass. When he entered the room asking if she had "a sec," Alex knew enough to put down whatever she was working on and pay attention.

"Got a call from Windermere," said Mintz. "Guys found something at the scene."

Alex tapped her pen impatiently. "Yeah?"

"There's not just machine guns under the floor," Mintz continued. "Looks like they turned up a lot more."

"How much more?"

"Don't know. But I think he used the words 'a fuckin' arsenal.'"

Alex dropped the pen. A second later she was up, throwing on her blazer, and coming around her desk. "Mind if I drive?"

"Sure . . . um . . . do you have to?"

"Attaboy." Alex patted Mintz on the shoulder and led the charge to the elevators.

She remembered that there was only one thing that she didn't like about Mintz. On the shooting range, he qualified last among all her charges on every occasion. His nickname was Deadeye.

In recent years, events in the Bureau's history had come to have their own names, one- or two-word monikers that not only brought to mind the crime but somehow encapsulated the entire event: the criminal act, the investigation, and the aftereffect on the Bureau. WTC referred to the first bombing of the World Trade Center, in '93. Oklahoma City, to the bombing of the Alfred P. Murrah Federal Building by the homegrown radicals Timothy McVeigh and Terry Nichols. Waco referred to the bloody and botched standoff between the federal authorities and the Branch Davidians led by David Koresh. There was Ruby Ridge and Flight 800 and the *Cole* and of course 9/11. With three officers killed in the space of a few minutes, Windermere was set to join that black pantheon.

It was this thought that filled Alex's mind as she drove the Charger across Manhattan. She was under no illusions. Her career was history. There would be no formal reprimand. No mention of fault would be scribbled into her personnel file. Nonetheless, she was done. Within a month she would receive a transfer to a less visible and less important post. Or maybe a letter from headquarters offering early retirement, with a coyly worded suggestion that she would be wise to accept. They might even throw in free airfare to the retirees' job fair held every January and June in D.C. But never again would she receive a promotion. Alex Forza had topped out at supervisory special agent, and all her privately held dreams of one day serving as the Bureau's first female deputy director had been killed as dead as Jimmy Malloy.

Still, she refused to be sad. She was allergic to self-pity. She was pissed. Somebody was going to pay.

Windermere Street was cordoned off at both ends of the block. Alex flashed her badge to get through the line. Police vehicles clogged the street. She double-parked next to a blue-and-white and slipped her badge into an ID pocket and hung it around her neck.

The shooting was classified as a multiple homicide. The crime scene belonged to the NYPD. Normally a detective first grade would run the scene, but the deaths of three federal agents bumped things up the chain of command. She introduced herself to the lieutenant running the show, then passed under the police tape and entered the house.

Inside, the forensics teams were finishing up. A half-dozen men and women in white Tyvek "bunny suits" passed her on their way out. No one had cleaned up the spot where Jimmy Malloy had died, and the blood had coagulated into a crusty black pool as thick as mud. She halted, unable to keep herself from staring.

"Um, boss." Mintz tapped her on the shoulder.

"Yeah, sorry." Alex skirted the hole in the floor where Shepherd had fallen, ducking her head so no one would see her wipe away a tear. "Who's running things for us?"

"I am," said Bill Barnes from the top of the stairs. "Come on up. I want to show you something."

Barnes was the ASAC for intel, and nominally Alex's boss. He was a TV agent: tall, fit, a little too good-looking, hair too perfect, with a groomed mustache and twinkling brown eyes. He was wearing jeans and a white polo shirt with the New York CT logo on the breast pocket.

Alex hustled up the stairs and shook Barnes's hand. "Hello, Bill."

"Knew you'd be back," said Barnes, not happily.

"For once, you were right." Alex looked over the railing. "I thought all the stuff was downstairs."

"We'll take a look in a second. I think you'll want to see this first."

Barnes walked to the end of the corridor and gestured toward the last room on the left. Alex looked inside. Six cots sat at right angles to the wall, three to each side, in the manner of a very small dormitory. Each cot was fitted with a top sheet and a gray woolen blanket. Each was made to perfection.

Barnes took a quarter from his pocket and bounced it on the nearest cot. The quarter rebounded and he snatched it out of the air. "Mommy doesn't teach you how to make a bed like that."

"Looks like Mr. Shepherd was expecting guests."

"Looks that way," agreed Barnes.

The three FBI agents descended the stairs and made their way through the kitchen and into the garage.

"We found a passage cut into the drywall behind a filing cabinet," said Barnes.

"Mintz said something about an arsenal."

Barnes tossed her a Maglite. "See for yourself. And keep your head down. Especially you, Deadeye."

Alex followed Barnes into the passage, turning on the Maglite as she entered. A set of tracks laid into the ground allowed a trolley to roll back and forth, she guessed, to facilitate moving the heavy crates.

Ten steps in, the ground fell away to either side, excavated to create rectangular moats 4 feet deep, 20 feet long, and 10 feet wide. Crates stacked as neatly as in any armory—some the same olive drab as those that held the machine guns, others plain pine or painted black—filled the depressions.

"Done an inventory?" asked Alex.

"Preliminary," said Barnes. "It'll scare the shit out of you."

He hopped off the raised dirt path into the storage pit to his left. Light shone from the hole in the floor where the assailant had fallen onto the crates of machine guns. Alex jumped down, then turned and offered a hand to help Mintz. The three walked among the wooden boxes. The first markings read *Antipersonnel Grenades*.

Oh yeah, thought Alex, she had put her foot in it.

For the next two hours she helped Barnes, Mintz, and several members of the JTTF haul the weaponry out of the garage so it could be tagged as evidence and examined. The tally included two crates of AK-47s, count 8; two crates of 7.62mm ammunition, count 1,000 rounds; one crate of antipersonnel grenades, count 20; one crate of white phosphorus grenades, count 20; one crate of Sig Sauer 9mm pistols, count 8; and four rocket-propelled grenade launchers with sixteen grenades.

"There's enough here to start a war," said Alex when they'd cleared everything out.

"A small war," said Barnes.

"War doesn't need an adjective in front of it."

Four unmarked crates remained to be opened. Alex slipped a crowbar under the lid of the first and pried it open. Communications equipment. Kneeling, she removed a transparent bag holding one complete multiband radio set—receiver, headset, lithium batteries, and belt pack. The items had been removed from their original packaging, assembled as a unit, and repackaged.

"Eight sets total," she said, handing one bag to Mintz. "I want a trace on all these items. Someone bought them somewhere. I want to know where and when."

By now Barnes was working on the next crate. With a crack, the wood splintered and the cover fell to the ground. "Vests," he said, removing a navy-blue protective vest.

"Why not?" said Alex. "They have everything else." She picked up a vest. It carried two 4-pound plates in front and an 8-pound plate in the back. "Twenty pounds before your commo gear, your ammo, your rifle, and your helmet."

"Whoever wears one of these had better be in shape if he wants to keep moving for more than ten minutes," remarked Barnes.

"Someone who makes a bed you can bounce a quarter off." Alex noted a slim band of white plastic peeking from a breast pocket. Deftly she slid out a folded rectangular booklet. The title on the cover read *Walker's Map of Manhattan*. The numeral 1 was written in royal-blue Sharpie on the top corner. She showed it to Barnes and Mintz. "Check and see if all the vests have one of these."

"Roger that," said Barnes, as one after another the maps were discovered.

Alex looked at Mintz. "How many vests?"

"Eight."

"All with maps?"

"Yes."

"All numbered?"

"Yes."

"So we're looking for eight shooters," said Barnes.

Alex gathered the maps and read the numbers from each corner. What had been a bad day got considerably worse. "We're not looking for eight," she said.

"What do you mean?" said Barnes.

"Take a look." Alex handed him maps numbered 1–4.

"Yeah—so?"

And then she handed him maps numbered 21–24. "We're looking for twenty-four."

Barnes held the maps, saying nothing. Mintz winced and said, "But . . ."

"Hey, boss," shouted one of the uniformed policemen who had been helping them remove all the crates. "Found one more. Almost didn't see it way in the back."

The policeman dropped the crate at Alex's feet. It was small and slim, no more than 3 feet by 2 feet and as thick as a phone book. The markings on it were Cyrillic with numerals scattered here and there.

Alex took up the crowbar and pried open the box. Inside was a single metal tube, drab green, looking like nothing more than a plumbing fixture. She knew better. Gripping the tube at one end, she gave a yank and it telescoped to twice its length. Lifting it to her shoulder, she unlatched the vertical sight and put her eye to the crosshairs.

"That what I think it is?" asked Mintz, with equal measures fright and disbelief.

Alex spun and pointed the TOW antitank weapon directly at him. "Ka-boom."

22

Astor left the elevators on the sixtieth floor of the Standard Financial building to find Bradley Zarek waiting. "Bobby. Great to see you. Thanks for coming so quickly."

"I was in the neighborhood," said Astor.

"I know it's a tough day. We're all in shock about what happened last night. If I could have waited on this, I would have. But . . ." Zarek splayed his hands to show that events had overtaken them both. The market was their master. "Come on down to my office. Let's chat."

Zarek was a senior vice president in the bank's prime direct brokerage division. Prime direct was a little-known but extremely profitable branch of banking, set up to deal with very high net worth individuals, private equity firms (or "sponsors," as they were known in the business), and hedge funds like Comstock. In effect, prime direct was a bank for other bankers and traders. When Astor needed to borrow money, he went to Zarek or one of his clones at any of the banks where Comstock did business.

Zarek showed him into his office and shut the door. Investment banks place a premium on space, and even a big shot like Zarek commanded a glassed-in cubicle barely larger than Astor's guest bathroom. From the memorabilia crowding the shelves and credenza, it was apparent that Zarek was one of the last Mets fans in the city. Astor picked up a worn mitt, slipped it on, and gave the pocket a few good thumps with his fist.

"That was Tom Seaver's," said Zarek nervously as he sat down at his desk. "He pitched with it in the '69 World Series."

"Some year."

"Oh, yeah," said Zarek, brightening as if he had lived it. He was chubby, average height, with a five o'clock shadow at 2 p.m. and a scrub of curly black hair. He was maybe forty years old, which meant he had been just a twinkle in his parents' eyes when the Mets had made their miracle run. "They came from nine down in mid-August and won thirty-nine of their last fifty games to take the division. Looks like you've gotten yourself into the same kind of jam."

Astor examined the glove, then leveled his gaze at the banker. "Way I see it, we're favorites to win the Series."

Zarek chuckled uncomfortably. "That's not quite how we see it."

Astor took a step toward Zarek. "Oh? How do you see it?" He had no intention of making Zarek's job easier. For years Comstock had been one of Zarek's best customers. When Comstock borrowed to leverage up a position, Astor could count on getting a call from Zarek and his cronies, asking much too politely if they might get a piece of the action. As a rule, Astor only accepted investments starting at $25 million (and preferably $100 million). He went further, limiting his clients to other hedge funds, sponsors, family offices, and sovereign wealth funds. But Astor knew how the game was played, and he always set aside a few scraps for Zarek and his fellow remoras.

"Look, Bobby, we know you have a track record—"

"That track record put your kids through elementary school."

Zarek smiled even more uncomfortably than he had a minute before. "And I'm grateful. But you're a little over your skis on this one."

Astor punched the sacred mitt a few more times just to see Zarek wince. "Says who?"

"No one thinks the Chinese are going to devalue. Not when they've been letting the yuan increase for the past five years. The RMB is up thirty-one percent since 2006."

RMB for renminbi.

"So?"

"So . . ." Zarek's face creased into a single fold of disbelief. "What makes you think it's going to change?"

Astor slammed his balled fist into the mitt again. "Tell you what, Brad. You want, I can still let you in on the fund."

Zarek's eyes widened like a virgin's in a strip club. He rose a few inches out of his chair, only to sink back. "Not this time, Bobby. But if you'd like to tell me something you know about the currency that I can share with the loan committee . . ."

Astor was hardly about to reveal his investment strategy to Bradley Zarek. Zarek was a drone—a highly paid, expensively educated, whip-smart, hardworking drone, but a drone nonetheless. Astor shot him the mitt with a little mustard on it. "Okay, Brad, let me have it. What gives?"

Using both hands, Zarek gingerly replaced the mitt on his shelf, repositioning it several times until it was just so. Satisfied, he turned his attention to his monitor, then spun it around so Astor could see. "We've lent you four hundred million."

"All collateralized."

"When the market moved against you, you were down the eighty million and then some."

"It came back."

"Today. What if it happens tomorrow?"

"It's called leverage. You were okay with the position going in."

"You left leverage behind when you jacked up your bet to twenty times what you put down. As it is, you're shooting craps."

"Actually, Brad, I'd like to borrow some more."

Zarek blinked as if he hadn't heard correctly. "We don't allow customers to leverage up above twenty times."

"I'd like another hundred million."

"Another hundred million dollars? You're serious?"

Astor nodded.

"Without additional collateral?"

"You heard me."

"We were thinking more along the lines of your either increasing your collateral or cutting your position."

"You don't think I can cover it?"

"It doesn't matter what I think, Bobby. It is what it is. There are rules. It's not 2008 anymore."

"How much more collateral are we talking about?"

"If you could just transfer a hundred million, we'd all be more comfortable."

"A hundred million?"

Zarek nodded. "Just a hundred."

"That's all?"

"Cash, or just pledge some equities, if you'd like. We'll make sure word gets out. Look at it as a vote of confidence. It will calm a lot of nerves." Zarek leaned forward. There was no mistaking the gleam in his eye. It was the gleam a man gets when he's about to shove a dagger into another man's gut and give it a nice, vicious twist for good measure. "Within twenty-four hours."

Astor shrugged complacently, as if he were on board with the suggestion. "Hey, Brad, tell you what."

"Yeah, Bobby?"

"Fuck you."

"Excuse me?"

Astor approached the desk. He had a gleam in his eye, too. It was the kind he got when he was fighting his corner. "What? You need a hearing aid to go along with the balls you're missing? You guys make me sick. Offer me an umbrella when the sun's shining and want it back when it starts to rain. Typical." Astor rapped the desk with his knuckles. "What's my track record?"

"Stellar, Bobby. No one is disputing that."

"I asked you, what is my track record?"

"You've been up over eight percent ten years running."

"And three of those years we were up over twenty. Right?"

"Right," said Zarek, backpedaling furiously. "Look, Bobby, the bank wants to be in business with you."

"Really? Because it sounds to me like you want to put me out of business."

"Nothing could be further from the truth."

"Then give me another hundred million."

"Impossible," said Zarek, shaking his head adamantly. "Not going to happen. Be reasonable."

"All right, all right," said Astor, hands raised in a calming gesture. "I hear you. Fair enough." He returned to his chair, shot his cuffs, composed himself. "Tell you what. Because I respect you and I respect Standard Financial, I can do twenty-five million."

"You want me to lose my job?" Zarek shuddered, as if physically repulsed by the offer. "I can make seventy-five work."

Astor considered this. He nodded, his eyes narrowed as if it just might work. Then abruptly he shook his head, a man coming to his senses in the nick of time. "Twenty-five."

"Sixty."

"Forty."

"Fifty."

"By end of business today?"

"Done."

Zarek extended a hand. Astor grabbed it and shook. "Deal."

Astor left before Zarek could change his mind.

Outside, Astor called Marv Shank. "Transfer fifty to Standard Financial."

"Out of petty cash?"

"Very funny."

"I've got to check with finance and see if we have that kind of cash."

"We've got it."

"If we do, it won't be by much."

"Just do it."

"You talk to our guy?"

"Not yet."

"What are you waiting for?"

"Don't want to abuse the privilege. I'll ask if and when I think we're in trouble."

"Then why the blip?"

"Calm down and transfer the money."

"You sure there isn't anything else wrong?"

"What do you mean?"

"I knew Zarek was going to hit you up for some dough. He mentioned a hundred mil."

"Yeah, and I got him down to fifty."

"That's why I'm worried. Any other day, you wouldn't have paid him a cent over twenty-five."

Astor hung up. Suddenly his victory felt hollow. Shank was right. He'd given in much too early.

He looked up the street for Sully. There was no sign of the Audi. He checked his watch and calculated the time overseas. He slipped out his phone and brought up his old friend's number. He thought of what he might ask and imagined his friend's wonderful erudite voice telling him to stay calm. "Nothing has changed, Robert, has it? There is only one possible outcome."

Astor spotted Sully barreling around the corner. Half the afternoon was already shot. He hoped the traffic to Greenwich wouldn't be too bad. Astor forgot all about making the call to his friend. He wanted to talk to Penelope Evans.

23

So what are we looking at?" asked Janet McVeigh, ADIC of the New York office, before sipping her mug of coffee.

It was three in the afternoon. Alex sat across the table in the eighth-floor conference room. Bill Barnes sat next to her. He'd changed out of his jeans and polo shirt into a freshly pressed navy suit, white shirt, and blood-red tie. Naturally, there was an American flag pin in his lapel. She noticed that Barnes's hair was combed as neatly as if he'd just stepped out of the barber's chair. She caught the faint reflection of herself in the window. She'd been too busy prepping for the meeting to think about getting cleaned up. Her hair was a mess, and she had rings under her eyes that would do a raccoon proud. She sat straighter and tucked her blouse into her pants. Only then did she notice that she had an American flag in her lapel, too. Take that, Hollywood Harry.

"Here's the final tally of the arms found at Windermere." Alex slid a paper across the table, then gave another copy to Barnes. "I sent e-copies to both your mailboxes. As you can see, we have a major haul: machine guns, hand grenades, ammu—"

"And an antitank weapon," said Barnes. "We've got serial numbers from the machine guns and pistols, as well as batch numbers and shipment information from some of the crates. We're doing a back-check now."

"How soon can we expect to hear anything?" McVeigh was a compact, pretty blond woman in her early fifties. Even after twenty years with the Bureau, she liked to keep her nails longer than practical, buffed and polished in the French style, and was never seen without her makeup just so. Her attractive looks and feminine demeanor hid an interior every bit as steely as Alex's.

"The manufacturers are based in Europe," said Barnes. "We'll start calling at eight a.m. their time." He looked sidelong at Alex. "Pardon me—I didn't mean to cut in."

Alex went on. "Besides the weapons, there were cots for six persons and a fully stocked kitchen. However, I don't think we're looking at seven bad guys. Based on the numbering found on the communications gear, we can assume there are twenty-four."

"Twenty-four? So there may be more safe houses?" asked McVeigh.

"Yes, I think—"

Again Barnes interrupted. "And more weapons. Only eight machine guns were found at the scene. That contrasts with the number of vests and, as Alex said, the numbering on the communications gear."

"Have you alerted Port Authority?" asked McVeigh. "It's probable that most of this stuff came through JFK or one of the container terminals at Newark, Baltimore, or Philly. We don't want that guy bringing in any more."

"Done," said Barnes.

McVeigh made a note on her pad. "What do you know about the shooter?"

"Shepherd? Not enough," said Alex. "His wallet held a Texas driver's license that we're still checking out, a few debit cards he could have purchased at any supermarket, and fifty dollars."

"Phone?"

"He was smart. He destroyed his SIM card before we entered the house. We did find a passport. Portuguese. Name of Henrique Manuel Lopes Gregorio. Picture matches. I'm guessing it's a fake or a stolen blank."

"I didn't know you were an expert on phony travel documents," said Barnes.

Alex ignored the jibe. "I put in a call to the Portuguese embassy in D.C. They're checking out the number. The ambassador promised to have an answer for us by morning."

McVeigh consulted the inventory of evidence found at the scene. "I like what I'm hearing. We're moving on a lot of fronts. All the same, this is looking pretty scary."

"I want to know more about the shooter," said Alex. "I'd like your go-ahead to visit the morgue and take a look at the body."

"The morgue?" said Barnes. "What for?"

"Our man was a pro. He shot accurately and he maintained his composure. I'm guessing he's a soldier. If that's the case, he'll most probably have tattoos. We might see something that will give us a clue who he served with. We have his fingerprints. It would make identification that much easier if we knew where to send them."

Barnes swiveled his chair to face her. "Look, Alex, we appreciate your help, but it's been a long day. You're suffering from emotional trauma. I can handle this from here on out. You're just not—"

"I'm fine, Bill."

"As evidenced by your earlier outburst at Dr. Lemon."

"I said I'm fine. I'm sitting right next to you. If you want to know how I feel, ask me."

Barnes returned his attention to McVeigh. "Be that as it may, this is no longer Alex's bailiwick."

"'Bailiwick'?" said Alex. "Who are you? Sherlock fuckin' Holmes?"

"Alex," cautioned McVeigh.

"Screw that, Jan. I'm not going to sit here and let Hollywood Harry patronize me. I'm staying on this case and that's that."

"The hell you are," Barnes retorted. "This is a domestic CT matter now. One of my teams will head this up. Get that through your thick skull."

"Cool it, Bill," said McVeigh.

"She's always sticking her nose into everyone's business. Miss Friggin' Know-It-All. I'm sick of it." Barnes smoothed his tie and settled back in his chair. "Jan, you and I agreed that Alex isn't heading up this investigation. I mean, calling the Portuguese embassy on your own is a little above an SSA's pay grade. I'll assign a team from CT-3."

"And I'll be on it," said Alex.

"Let's all of us calm down," said McVeigh. "We can get back to who's running what later on."

"Jan—"

"Can it, Bill." McVeigh studied her notepad, then drew a breath and directed her attention to Alex. "That's a smart idea to check if our shooter has tattoos, but Bill will handle it." She smiled in a patronizing way, and Alex knew she was about to get the coup de grâce. "Bill is right," McVeigh went on. "This is nothing for CT-26. Given the nature of the threat, I've made the decision to set up a task force, and I'm asking Bill to head it up."

"But this is my deal—"

"Not anymore it's not. I want you to take a few days and get some rest. You've been through a lot. You need to process this, and you can't do it working twenty-four hours a day."

"We don't have a few days," said Alex.

"Is there something you're not telling us?"

Alex grabbed the sheaf of paper listing everything that had been found at Windermere. "Check the inventory. Page three—the list of all the food. I broke it down into meals. Three meals a day. Seven opera-tives, each eating a minimum of twenty-five hundred calories. There's enough food for three days."

"Guesswork," said Barnes.

"Damn right it's guesswork," said Alex, putting a fist to the table. "That's what they pay us to do. You want to call it a guess. I call it a plausible theory. The stuff in that fridge was fresh and perishable. The way I see it, the people who were going to occupy those beds are due in today or tomorrow. I don't see them hanging around to visit the Statue of Liberty. Not with all that gear hidden in the house. They're profes-sionals. That clock starts ticking once they hit U.S. soil."

"If they're still coming," said Barnes.

"Why wouldn't they be? Think of the planning required to smuggle those weapons into the country. This isn't some mom-and-pop job. This is top-drawer. They've got an entire network set up. Our killing one of their team and uncovering a cache of weapons isn't going to stop them. If anything, it's going to light a fire under their butts. Wake up. This is happening now."

"What exactly do you think 'this' is?" asked McVeigh.

"They're taking a building, a plane, a school—hell, I don't know. Give me your worst-case scenario and multiply it times ten. What do twenty-four trained terrorists armed to the teeth with everything from AK-47s to antitank weapons go after?"

"Worse than storming a building or a hostage situation?" asked Barnes. "Stop being such an alarmist."

Alex looked at McVeigh. "What if they're taking Manhattan?"

"You mean a Mumbai scenario?"

Alex nodded. "That's exactly what I mean. Mumbai."

24

At nine o'clock at night on November 26, 2008, twelve relatively untrained terrorists landed at the port of Mumbai, India, in rigid rubber-hulled motorboats. The men broke into four teams. Every man carried a machine gun, two hundred rounds of ammunition, hand grenades, and a store-bought cell phone with which to speak to the others. No one had a Kevlar vest. No one had state-of-the-art communications gear, and no one carried an antitank weapon. By any measure, it was a rudimentary martyrdom operation.

One team attacked the famed Taj Mahal Palace Hotel; another, the nearby Oberoi Trident; another, Mumbai's central railway station; and yet another, Nariman House, a Jewish Chabad-Lubavitch center. For the next thirty-six hours, the entire city of Mumbai, population 16 million, was effectively paralyzed. Business ground to a halt as the city shut down and all economic activity ceased. The only people more poorly trained than the terrorists were the police. Their ineptness peaked when the police chief and his motorcade drove directly into a terrorist ambush and he was shot dead in the back seat of his car.

In the end, nearly two hundred people were dead, including more than thirty Western tourists and Jewish émigrés. The Taj Mahal Palace suffered a major fire. Worse was the economic cost to India, in both the short and the long term. Twelve young men armed only with machine guns and grenades and the will to give their lives caused over $5 billion in economic damage and brought one of the world's most important financial capitals to its knees. The attack coined a new phrase, *shoot and scoot*, and brought a startling new tactic to the world of international terrorism.

"Twenty-four people . . . take Manhattan?" Barnes shook his head. "Come on. Not going to happen."

"Look what twelve did to Mumbai," said McVeigh.

"That what you think this is?" asked Barnes. "A shoot and scoot?"

"Too soon to say. Whatever it is, lots of people are going to die."

"I'm not fighting you on this," said Barnes, raising his hands in a gesture of surrender. "Just trying to be prudent. We don't want to run off half-cocked."

"Half-cocked? That sounds like your problem, Bill."

Barnes colored and rose in his chair.

"Hold on, Alex. We're with you," said McVeigh. "This is a chance to stop something before it happens. In the past, we've arrived late to the ball every time. We're not going to mess this one up. But Bill's correct in saying that we're going to do things the right way. Calmly, efficiently, and professionally."

Consensus building. Mediation. All that diplomatic crap. Alex rubbed her eyes, thinking she'd been foolish ever to dream of getting to D.C. That was for people like McVeigh. "Okay, then," she said. "We're clear."

McVeigh smiled at her like a kindly aunt. "You can't operate at the level we need going on no sleep for thirty-six hours. I want you to take a couple of days and rest up. We'll talk Wednesday afternoon, see how you're doing."

"Jan—"

"That's it, Alex. Two days on the bricks. No discussion. Give Bill everything you've got. If we need anything, we know where to find you. I'll make sure Barry Mintz keeps you in the loop."

"And what about the shooter's fingerprints?"

"We're putting them through the system. If we get anything, we'll let you know."

"But—"

Jan McVeigh stood. "We're done here. Go home. Get some rest."

"Yes, ma'am."

Alex left the room. She'd be damned if she'd take two days off.

Didn't they understand?

This was happening now.

25

It was past four when Astor reached Greenwich.

The Audi Q7 drove rapidly along the two-lane road, climbing rolling hills, accelerating through forest so dense the sun threatened to disappear. Astor rolled down the window and a blast of warm air, thick with the scent of cut grass, invaded the car. The town of Greenwich, Connecticut, was a forty-minute drive north of Manhattan and a hundred light-years away.

Penelope Evans lived at 1133 Elm, a two-story Colonial set well back from the road. A circular drive led down a slope to the house. A Range Rover was parked near the front door. A flagpole stood in the center of a broad lawn. On this fine day, no flags were hoisted.

"Looks like she's home," said Astor.

"Give her another call," said Sullivan.

For the past ten minutes, Astor had been calling to alert Evans of their impending arrival. She had not answered. He was worried. Sullivan drew the Audi up behind the parked car and killed the engine. Astor opened the door. "Wait here."

"Sorry, boss, you got no say in this one." Sullivan climbed out of the car, moving like a man twenty years younger. The two men walked to the front door. A welcome mat said "Keep Calm and Drink Scotch." Astor had been right about the sense of humor. He knocked and met Sullivan's gaze as they listened for a response inside the home. He knocked again. No one came to the door.

"What do you think?"

"Nothing good," said Sullivan.

Astor retreated down the walk and approached the Range Rover. He noted a parking sticker for 12 Broad on the windshield. "It's her car," he said. He looked back at the house. The silence he'd remarked upon earlier no longer pleased him. To his ear, it wasn't quiet. It was deadly still. "I think the case could be made for us to assume that Miss Evans is in danger. Isn't there some law allowing us to . . ."

"Break in?" suggested Sullivan.

"Gain access to administer aid."

"She could be at a friend's house or taking a walk. Maybe she has two cars."

"Bullshit, bullshit, and bullshit," said Astor. "She knew we were coming."

"I'm just making you aware of the situation before we do anything we might regret."

Astor crossed the lawn and tramped through a flowerbed fronting a bay window. The curtains were not drawn, and he had a clear view into Evans's living room and past it, into the foyer. The house appeared clean and orderly. There was no sign of activity within. He placed his ear to the glass. He caught a distant rumble that might be voices.

"Anything?" asked Sullivan.

"Maybe something from upstairs. TV or radio."

Astor continued around the side of the house, opening a latched gate and sliding past the garbage cans, then walking another few feet to the back yard. A portable sprinkler attached to a garden hose irrigated the lawn. The grass was waterlogged and soggy. Water spurted from a leak at the head of the hose, flooding a 10-square-foot expanse of lawn.

"Someone isn't worried about their water bill," said Sullivan.

Astor jumped onto the red-brick veranda at the rear of the house. The sliding doors opened easily. "Hello," he called, sticking his head inside. "Miss Evans?"

Sullivan pushed past him, his service pistol drawn and held at the ready. "Stay behind me," he commanded. "And don't touch a thing."

"Whatever you say, detective."

Sullivan passed through the dining room and into the foyer. The air inside the house was warm and close. Clipped voices drifted from upstairs.

"Miss Evans? Penelope? This is Robert Astor. Are you home?"

No one replied.

Sullivan started up the stairs, the pistol held stiff-armed in front of him. Astor followed at his shoulder. It was the television that Astor had heard through the window. With every step, the voice of a news commentator grew louder. The master bedroom was situated across a landing at the top of the stairs. The wood floor groaned beneath their steps.

Sullivan halted at the doorway. "Oh boy."

Astor looked into the room and immediately turned away.

Ten steps away, a woman with long brown hair lay on the floor next to the bed, eyes wide open. She wore only panties and a brassiere. A thin line of blood trickled from a knife wound to her chest.

"Is she . . . ?" asked Astor.

Sullivan knelt down and felt her neck. He nodded, then looked more closely at the wound. "Whoever did this was some kind of pro."

"What do you mean?"

"Look. There's relatively little blood. This guy managed to get the knife into her and puncture her heart so quickly it instantly stopped pumping. That takes practice."

"What do we do?"

"Stay put." Sullivan checked the bathroom and closets, then ducked into the hall. "No one here."

Astor stepped inside the bedroom. An open suitcase sat on the bed, half filled with clothing. He looked at the television and noted that it was tuned to CNBC. A magazine lay half hidden beneath the bed covers. He tugged at the corner and saw that it was a professional journal titled *Information Technology Today*. The journal was opened to an article about something called "application software frameworks in the energy management sector": "Our platforms allow for building and managing complex monitoring, control, and automation solutions . . ."

Astor put down the journal, uninterested. He returned his gaze to the dead woman. "Is it her?"

Sullivan picked up a framed photograph on the dresser and compared the radiantly smiling woman to the corpse. "Yes."

"When?"

Sullivan took hold of Penelope Evans's body, feeling her arms and neck. "She's still warm. Less than an hour."

"We could've gotten here."

"And it could have been us lying there beside her. Whoever did this was good. He got into the house, came upstairs, and killed her without her even knowing he was here. You heard those floorboards. They squeak if an ant walks over them. This guy is a phantom. He *floated* in here." Sullivan headed to the door. "We should go."

Astor grabbed him by the arm. "I think you mean we should call the police."

"It's too late to do her any good. I'll make a call from the city."

"We can't just walk away. She deserves better."

"She's dead. She doesn't deserve anything except us trying to find who did this."

Astor released his grip. "I'm sure we can explain things . . ."

"You don't have time for that. Mr. Shank needs you back in the office. Call the Greenwich PD and you'll be lucky to be home by midnight. There's a bounty on rich assholes like you these days."

"You can't be serious."

"You think anyone would holler if you spent a few days in the cooler?" Sullivan leaned closer, and when he spoke, it was with the tempered voice of experience. "I spent my whole life as a cop. I know what cops can do. You take this to the police, you're going to be the lead story on the national evening news. Tomorrow morning your picture's going to be on the front page of the *Post* with some kind of headline making it look like you're the prime suspect. It'll make you nostalgic for that last gem they ran in the *Post* about you and your girlfriends at the beach. You want press like that? You want it now?"

Astor gave Sullivan a hard look. He was pretty smart for a dumb cop. "I'm not naive. If I explain that we're looking into my father's death . . ."

"Look at her. Look!" Sullivan forced Astor to step closer and gaze at the body. "She's hardly wearing a scrap of clothing. One of those cops you have so much faith in is going to pocket a couple of C-notes and allow a photographer to get a shot of her. This stuff sells papers."

"Even so, we need to stay."

Sullivan looked at his watch. "From what you've told me, I think we can assume that whoever killed your father had a hand in killing this woman. You want to help both of them, start looking around for clues. You can't do anyone any good from inside a police station, can you?"

Astor considered this. "No, I don't suppose I can."

"You got ten minutes."

26

Concealed in a grove of birch trees on a hilltop across the road, the monk watched the house.

He'd known that Astor and Sullivan were coming. He had been listening as they drove from the city. He was listening now. He could hear them speaking, though their voices were muffled and at times indistinct. This was to be expected, as Astor carried his phone in his pocket.

Wind rustled the branches and made the sound of a flowing river. For a moment he knew serenity. The feeling took him back to his years at the temple. He was there again, a shaven-headed boy running barefoot across the cold stone floors, bowing before his masters, waiting for his commands.

He had arrived at age six, a thin, weak boy. The master had asked him one question: "Are you prepared to eat bitter?"

"Yes," he responded. And so the training had begun.

For twelve years he rose at dawn and went to bed at midnight. He studied and meditated. He did as he was told. But mostly he trained. Three hours of calisthenics and physical exercise every morning. Four hours of wushu, or martial arts, in the afternoon. His discipline was Baji kung fu, the most rigorous of the schools. He trained until his fists bled and his legs would not carry him. He suffered. He did not complain. He ate bitter.

And in the end, he was awarded the monk's orange robe.

But that was not to last.

For he had desires that life in a temple could not satisfy. Desires not appropriate for a man or a monk. Not even a warrior monk.

"Ten minutes," he heard someone inside the house say. It was the older man, with white hair and red face.

He considered his instructions. It would be so easy to return to the home and finish the business. He knew the value of cleaning one's trail. He saw himself moving up the stairs, his bare feet caressing the warped wooden floorboards, moving effortlessly, silently. *Floating.* He loved the feel of the knife in his hand, its weight, its promise of death quickly delivered.

At the temple they had taught him the way of the fist and the staff and, later, of more exotic instruments: nunchakus, swords, pikes, and lances. In countless shows and exhibitions, he had thrilled audiences with his mastery of them all. No one moved more quickly, more elegantly, more forcefully. But exhibitions were not enough. The warrior monk had wished to put his skills to more practical use.

It had started when he was sixteen and his blood ran hot for the first time. He would leave the temple at midnight. Even then, he walked so quietly the master could not hear him. He would roam the hills and pass through surrounding villages. He would peer into homes until he found a suitable choice, inevitably a girl, young, innocent, unsuspecting. He would enter and stand beside her. He would wait until his heartbeat matched her own and he knew serenity.

He was invisible.

He was silent.

He was death.

The warrior monk stared at the home. Fingers that could crush a larynx caressed the knife's handle. It would be so easy. They would not know he was among them until it was too late.

It was not to be.

Above all, he was an obedient brother.

The warrior monk called 911.

"Hello," he said, in an English an American would swear was his own. "I'm walking my dog and I saw some men breaking into the house at 1133 Elm."

He hung up before they could ask his name.

Five minutes later, he heard the sirens approaching.

He turned and retraced his path up the hill through the birch trees. He walked as he had been taught so many years before. His feet touched the leaves but left no track.

He did not make a sound.

He floated.

27

Astor stepped over Penelope Evans and leaned onto the bed to pick up the magazine.

"Hey!" shouted Sullivan. "What did I say about not touching anything? Use a handkerchief, or better yet, just leave things be."

Astor pulled a handkerchief from his pocket and used it to retrieve the magazine. *Information Technology Today* was not exactly what he figured a thirty-five-year-old woman read in her spare time. The magazine lay open to an article titled "Next-Generation Solutions for Connecting Devices." The first paragraph discussed a company in Reston, Virginia, called Britium. It began, "This cutting-edge software has fundamentally changed the way devices and systems connect, integrate, and interoperate with each other and the enterprise." It got worse from there. He skimmed the remaining pages with an eye toward one word: *Palantir.* He put down the magazine disappointed.

A stack of paperbacks was piled high on the night table. Most were crime fiction by best-selling authors. The books confirmed his first thought. She did not read *Information Technology Today* for fun.

Astor poked his head into the bathroom. He saw nothing of interest and retreated through the bedroom and turned into the hall. He found Penelope Evans's office on the opposite side of the corridor. Thick curtains stifled the daylight. A lamp burned on the desk, illuminating a raft of papers. In the room, it was still night.

Astor approached the desk cautiously, keeping in mind Sullivan's admonition not to touch anything. He had never been arrested, but as a registered representative of the New York Stock Exchange and a principal of the National Association of Security Dealers, his fingerprints were on file and easily retrievable. Again he wrapped his fingers before thumbing through the stacks. There were articles downloaded from a variety of newspapers and periodicals, the subjects ranging from the latest batch of Silicon Valley startups to the growing influence of sovereign wealth funds on Wall Street to local concern over the sale of a chunk of Icelandic soil to foreign buyers.

Iceland?

Astor sorted through a stack of annual reports perched on the corner of the desk. The first few came from high-tech companies listed on the NASDAQ. There was a manufacturer of silicon wafers, a provider of routers and switches—something that would be classified as "Net infrastructure"—and an aerospace company involved in the manufacture and launch of communications satellites. He thumbed through the first few pages of each. Again he was unable to find any mention of Palantir. Nor did he find anything that struck him as sinister or alarming, or that in any way might be related to his father's murder. In fact, the reports had nothing in common except the fact that they all concerned newly listed companies, the oldest having gone public a year earlier.

Thinking this might be the thread, he checked to see if all shared a common underwriter. They did not. A dozen different banks had participated in bringing the companies to market. He knew the underwriters to be upstanding firms.

Astor continued checking the annual reports, if less studiously. The emphasis was on technology, but there were more traditional industries as well, and these companies were not exclusively American. There was a South African mining company, an Australian maker of heavy equipment—tractors, trucks, backhoes, and the like—and a well-known German manufacturer of electronic components, primarily high-fidelity audio and communications equipment. It was only as he replaced these that he noted that the reports dated back several years. The most recent came from 2008.

He looked again at the German electronics company's report and remembered that the organization had been taken private by a well-known private equity firm several years back. Other than that, nothing.

A laptop sat open on the desk. Astor clicked the mouse and the screen blossomed to life. Another article, not about "next-generation connecting devices" but a piece from the *Financial Times* about the Flash Crash of May 2010, which occurred when a breakdown in the orderly matching of buy and sell orders caused the Dow Jones Industrial Average to plummet a thousand points in minutes, only to regain two-thirds of the loss minutes later.

"The cause of the sudden precipitous decline had been thought to be a single faulty sell order that in turn triggered computer-driven programs to rush thousands of sell orders to market. A new analysis suggests that the cause might have stemmed not from the first massive sell order but from an error in the New York Stock Exchange's proprietary trading platform . . ."

Astor consulted the laptop's History panel, scouring the list of websites Evans had most recently visited. Not annual reports this time, but corporate websites. A manufacturer of silicon wafers and another of microchips, both stalwarts of Silicon Valley. A petroleum company. An American glass manufacturer with ties to the computer industry. They might be a crosscut of the NASDAQ. Tech heavy, to be sure, but not exclusively.

Still no mention of Palantir. Still no common thread.

Sullivan poked his head into the room. "Time's up."

"That wasn't ten minutes," said Astor.

"Who cares about ten minutes? Don't you got ears?"

It was then that Astor heard the siren. The wail came and went, still far away.

"Who called?"

"My guess? The killer. He's watching the house."

"But why?"

"That's a no-brainer. He doesn't want us to find anything."

"I need a second," said Astor.

"We don't have a second," said Sullivan, taking hold of his arm and yanking him away from the desk.

Astor wrested free and returned to gather up the annual reports as well as the articles Evans had printed out. "You said look for clues. These are clues."

"I said look. Not steal. That's obstruction."

"I'll let you explain once we're arrested."

Astor brushed past the detective and continued down the hall to Evans's bedroom. Something in the first few paragraphs of the article Evans had been reading had stuck in Astor's mind. He wasn't sure what had caught his attention, only that it might be important. "Get that magazine on the bed," he said. "My hands are full."

Sullivan stood frozen in the doorway, as if nailed to the floor. "We don't have time."

"Just do it."

"But—"

"I need it."

Sullivan swore under his breath, then pried his feet loose and retrieved the magazine.

The sirens were louder now. Not one but two police cars.

Astor stopped at the bottom of the stairs, frightened, unsure whether to leave the house the same way they'd come. Sullivan nearly knocked him to the ground in his rush for the front door. "Forget the back," he said. "Move."

Astor slammed the front door behind him. As he ran to the car, he realized that he had dropped the handkerchief somewhere inside the house. He climbed into the passenger seat as Sullivan started the engine. In a burst of acceleration, the Audi crested the driveway and turned onto the street. Astor twisted in his seat to look over his shoulder. He caught sight of the first police car, but only for a second. The next, the Audi slid around a curve, and an army of trees blocked the road behind them from view. He remained in that position, watching, waiting, expecting at any moment to see the police car round the bend, lights blazing, siren going full-force. No one followed.

Astor put on the safety belt. He sat still, gazing straight ahead, saying nothing as he played back the last seconds in the house: the rushed theft of the annual reports, the mad scramble down the stairs and out the front door. He did not know where he'd dropped the handkerchief.

Sullivan looked shaken. "Take my word, Bobby. We did the smart thing."

Astor didn't respond. It wasn't the handkerchief that bothered him. It was plain and white and lacking any monogram. It was something else. Something worse.

"What is it, kid? What's wrong?" asked Sullivan, patting his leg in a fatherly manner. "Had enough of playing cop for one day?"

Astor looked away. In his mind's eye, he was replaying the moment when, in his hurry to leave the house, he'd placed his bare left hand flat against the inside of Penelope Evans's front door.

He could still feel the door's smooth texture beneath his fingertips.

28

Alex stood with her back against the front door of her apartment. She didn't want to be here. She had work to do.

She entered the kitchen and threw her jacket over the back of a chair. She ran a hand over her forehead and cheeks. Her fingers came away veneered with dirt and grime. She needed a shower and sleep. Janet McVeigh was right. She couldn't perform at the top of her game as she was. But first she needed a drink.

Alex opened the fridge. In contrast to the stuffed refrigerator at Windermere, her own was sadly understocked. There was milk and juice and Katie's energy drinks, plenty of condiments, and some cheese and yogurt, but not much to make a meal with. With a twinge of guilt, she recalled the platters of leftover spaghetti, lasagna, and veal, the neatly wrapped trays of cannolis, the brimming bowls of antipasto that occupied every inch of her mother's refrigerator. True, her family owned a trattoria in Little Italy. It made sense that there was always lots of food. But being an FBI agent didn't absolve her of the responsibility to feed her daughter.

Alex took a bottle of chardonnay off the shelf and poured a glass. She took a sip, then crossed to the sink and dumped the rest out. She was in no mood for ice-cold, slightly sour wine. She walked into the dining room, knelt to open the liquor cabinet, and selected a bottle of Patrón. She poured three fingers into a highball glass and drank it all. The tequila carved a blazing path to the pit of her stomach. She walked into the living room and made a slow, loving examination of the framed photographs that decorated the shelves. Pictures of summer vacations and Christmas holidays, of school pageants and family birthdays. Pictures of dogs and cats and the longest-living goldfish in Christendom. Pictures and more pictures. All of them just smoke and mirrors to disguise the truth that Mom hadn't been around.

Alex poured herself another shot of tequila, this one smaller, and wandered down the hall to Katie's room. The door was open and she entered. As usual, the room was in perfect order. The bed was nicely made, throw pillows arranged just so. The desk was clear. There wasn't a drawer that wasn't pushed all the way in. Alex wondered if it was normal for a teenager to be so neat or if it might represent some failing on her own part.

With a sigh, she sat down on the bed. She looked at the old cat clock on the wall, watching the eyes go back and forth ticking the seconds. Nostalgia filled her. The clock had belonged to her as a child and had held a similar place in her bedroom. She stood and noticed a piece of her daughter's stationery on the night table.

A note.

> Hi Mom,
>
>   I appreciate you letting me go to the lake. Ali and I can take care of ourselves. You don't have to worry about me. I'm so sad about Grandpa Edward, but I'd be sadder just staying and hearing everyone tell me how sorry they are. I'm more worried about you. Try and do something for yourself while I'm gone. Go see a movie or even a show to take your mind off things. (Daddy always gets the best tickets—maybe you and he could go together. He might need cheering up, too.) Just don't work all the time. Gotham will survive a day or two without you. And please, please, please tell me if you hear anything about what really happened to Grandpa Edward.
>
>   We'll all be okay.
>
>   Love you tons,
>
>   K

Alex reread the note, then folded it and held it tightly in her hand. She was crying. A reflex made her peer over her shoulder to make sure no one was watching.

Her Katie, the strong one. She was a straight-A student, president of Model UN, and captain of the field hockey team at her high school. She made curfew without fail, and despite her sometimes snotty attitude toward her mother, she was never less than a polite, well-mannered, respectful young lady to others.

Her relationship with her grandfather had been loving, if distant. The two had been close when Katie was a little girl, but the demands of his job combined with the equally strenuous demands of being a teenage girl in New York City conspired to limit their contact to the usual holidays—Thanksgiving, Christmas, Easter—and even then, one or the other was often away. Over time, he had slowly drifted out of their lives.

Alex went to the window. The view was to the southeast, and the sun shot darts off the Chrysler Building's steel carapace. She put her hand to the glass. It was warm and comforting. She thought of Malloy and Mara. She would visit the families when she could. But not now. She couldn't grieve yet. She was too close to it. Too fragile. She could feel a fissure forming inside her. She couldn't allow it to split open. Not yet. There was too much to do. She could not allow emotion to interrupt her work.

She left the bedroom and headed to her own room. The guest bedroom merited a glance along the way. Bobby had slept there for two years before the divorce. The marriage had ended the day he left their bedroom. It seemed so obvious now.

Inside her bathroom, she undressed, throwing her blouse and slacks into the dry-cleaning pile. She started the shower while her mind continued on its tour of her failings. Wife, mother, and now, the role she would never admit to anyone else that she held most dear, FBI agent.

Windermere had been her fault. Malloy's death her fault. Mara's death, too, and DiRienzo's. Time and again she ran over her preparations for the job. She had followed procedure to the letter, but procedure wasn't enough. It never was. Instinct won the day and she'd failed to obey her own. Never again.

Two days on the bricks.

The idea angered Alex, and as she stepped into the shower and let the hot water wash over her, her anger hardened into resolve.

Two days on the bricks.

Not a chance.

She had failed as a wife. She was a lousy mother. The job was all she had left.

She already knew her next move, and the next move was tonight.

29

Astor walked tiredly down the street toward Battery Park. A hot, humid breeze skipped off the East River, snapping his cheeks. The wind smelled oily and foul, and he hated it, hated the day, hated his predicament. He checked over his shoulder and watched as Sully drove away. At some point on the ride back into town, he had told the former detective about his gaffe inside Evans's home.

"It'll take 'em a day to dust the place for prints and another day to start feeding what they got into the system," Sullivan had explained. "And that's with all the heat this case is going to get, and believe you me, it will get plenty. The FBI will be out there and so will the Secret Service. They'll go slow and methodical. Even so, I wouldn't bank on them IDing you. Who knows how many people visited that house? There could be a hundred different prints on that door. All depends on what they're able to lift. This is real life, not some TV show. You're lucky if you get one perfect print."

"I put my hand flat on the door," said Astor.

"We already established you're a numskull. Let's not belabor the point."

"How long before we know?" Astor had asked.

"You got forty-eight hours until you have to start worrying," said Sullivan. "Then it's a crapshoot. You feelin' lucky?"

Astor kept his answer to himself.

That was an hour ago.

He had forty-seven to go.

Assured of his privacy, Astor jogged across the pavement, loosening a button on his shirt as he cursed the heat. He'd told Sullivan he needed some space, a little time to think things through. There were some things best kept private.

Reaching Battery Park, he continued to the tourist telescopes. He paused, looking up and down for a lean, compact man, always impeccably dressed. There was no one who matched the description. Astor glanced at his watch, then stepped closer to the railing.

"Hey."

A hand tapped him on the shoulder, and Astor jumped out of his shoes.

"Take it easy," said the sandpaper voice.

Astor spun and looked into Michael Grillo's wizened brown eyes. "You scared the crap out of me."

"I told you I'd meet you here."

"I expected you in front of me. Not sneaking up on me like a . . . a . . ."

"A spook?" Grillo tightened his lips, which was what passed for a smile. "Habit. Too many years making sure I saw people before they saw me."

Astor shook Grillo's hand. "Good to see you, Mike."

"Likewise." Michael Grillo was small and leathery, a retired jockey in a $3,000 suit. His hair was gray and close-cropped, his skin taut, craggy, tanned a permanent brown by the sun of hellholes the world over. He had the usual résumé: Army Ranger, Delta Force, tours in Iraq (both wars) and Afghanistan. He also had a Wharton MBA. That was not so usual. He called himself a "corporate security analyst." No company. Just a crisp linen-stock business card with a single phone number, a promise of utmost secrecy, and an unrivaled skill set he brought from his former profession. Mike Grillo got things done. Astor knew better than to ask how, but the size of his fees suggested some shadowy dealings. Shadowy, as in dark black.

"You look like shit," said Grillo.

"Tough day."

Grillo took this in. He was a man who knew when to ask questions and when not to. "This about your dad?"

"Good guess."

Grillo lit a slim black cigarette. He was the last man in Manhattan to smoke Nat Sherman 100s. "What can I do for you?"

"Palantir."

"What's that?"

"Let's walk." Astor headed north out of the park. He went over what had happened the night before in Washington, sharing the message he'd received from his father and his belief that the word was a clue about who was responsible for the attack. "My father was working on a secret project at the Exchange," he added, handing over the stolen agenda. "It's all here. See for yourself."

Astor didn't go into what had transpired at Penelope Evans's home in Greenwich. Grillo was an employee, not a friend. Astor was quick to draw that line, though there was more to it than that. Sharing that information would make Grillo an accessory. Grillo wouldn't want that.

They crossed State Street and walked up Broadway. Grillo, an expert in all matters security, was unable to envision any scenario that would engender a Secret Service agent driving his vehicle onto the South Lawn. Astor brought up Sloan Thomasson's suggestion that the driver had forfeited control of his vehicle. Grillo scoffed at the idea, then seemed to take it more seriously. "Forfeited how?" he asked. "You mean like someone else was driving the car for him?"

"Something like that," said Astor. "I don't know. Just spitballing here."

"I think we need to take a step back," said Grillo. "It's not what happened on the lawn. It's what happened before. You said he texted you a minute before he was killed?"

"Yeah."

"That means he had an idea something bad was going to happen. He knew they were onto him—whoever 'they' are. We have to find out what those three big shots were going to tell the president."

The men stopped at Trinity Church.

"That word . . . Palantir," said Grillo. "Might ring a bell. When do you need something?"

"Yesterday."

"I need some information about your pop: phones, credit cards, Social Security number."

"How soon?"

"Yesterday."

Astor shook hands with Grillo. "I'll e-mail you what I have."

"Do that."

30

The Office of the Chief Medical Examiner was located in a six-story government building on the corner of First Avenue and 30th Street adjacent to NYU Langone Medical Center, where Alex had given birth to Katie and, in the years after, had recovered from two miscarriages. She parked in the red zone across the street, throwing her law enforcement shield on the dashboard.

Inside the building, the air conditioning was fighting a losing battle against the heat of the day. Alex crossed to the security desk, upset that the morgue assistant hadn't come up to meet her as promised. She badged the young woman and waited as she called down to the body shop—the refrigerated storage locker where corpses were kept pending autopsy or burial. The morgue assistant appeared five minutes later. He was a short, bearded, unattractive man, slovenly in appearance as well as in manners.

"NYPD was already here," he said as he led her to the elevator and they descended to the basement. "Got prints, DNA, took some pics—the whole nine yards."

"I got the memo," said Alex. "I still need to see the body."

The attendant opened the door to the storage room and walked in ahead of her. Alex waited as he located the body and transferred it to an examining table. "Take your time," he said. "He ain't goin' nowhere."

Alex approached the table without hesitation. A Catholic childhood and its attendant visitations and open-casket funerals had robbed her of any fear of the dead. Her job had done the rest. She stood over the assailant, Randall Shepherd, true name unknown. The body had been washed. Hours in refrigeration had turned it the complexion of a fish belly.

Three entry wounds decorated the torso. Two were spaced an inch apart just above the liver. The third defined an immaculate circle directly above his heart. Alex shot 40-caliber hollow-points designed to explode on impact and spend their energy within inches of entering a body. In layman's terms, they went in small and came out big, and in between wreaked havoc on bone, arteries, and organs.

The hatred provoked by the sight of this lifeless, inert form astounded her. A will to violence rose up inside her. She dug her fingers into the seams of her pants to stop herself from striking the body. Death wasn't enough. He deserved worse.

Three hits and thirteen misses.

If one of those misses had struck him earlier, Mara and DiRienzo might still be alive. The thought would haunt her for a long time. Alex released her grip on her slacks. She was not angry at Shepherd. She was angry at herself.

But she hadn't come to the morgue to critique her marksmanship. She had come to confirm her hunch that the assailant was a professional soldier. It was not simply the perfect barracks corners on the beds. It was how Shepherd had handled his weapon. How he had fired in crisp three-shot bursts. How he had kept his cool under fire, holding his position and concentrating first on one target and then on another. She had no doubt that the assailant had been in a gun battle before, more likely more than once.

Alex had come because soldiers have tattoos.

At first glance she spotted three. A Samoan war band around the left arm and a series of tribal stripes running up the shoulder. The design was standard and told her nothing about the shooter. A second tattoo was more promising. Below the shoulder on the right arm, a striking cobra was inked, and below it the Roman numerals III.III.V and the words *Vincere aut Mori*, which she took to be Latin for "Conquer or Die."

Alex snapped a photograph of the tattoo with her phone.

A third tattoo, on his right breast, showed an inverted isosceles triangle inside which a small, comical black owl sat staring straight ahead. A parachute filled the space behind the owl. In one corner was a red 1^0. In another, a green *2 REP*. A single Latin word was written along the exterior of each of the triangle's legs: *Legio. Patria. Nostra.* She knew the tattoo signified membership in a military organization. The question was which one.

Again she took a picture.

On a hunch, she lifted the right arm. She saw it at once and some small part of her felt assuaged. There on the fleshy underside of his torso were the letters *AB*.

AB for the soldier's blood group.

Not just a soldier, she told herself. A commando.

And most probably a mercenary.

31

A gentle breeze rustled the palms surrounding Simón Bolívar International Airport in Caracas, Venezuela. It was dusk and the thermometer registered a mild 75 degrees. A veil of mist decorated the crown of the El Ávila, the mountain that divided the city and stood as an imposing guard to the airport's west.

Inside the terminal, 110 passengers crowded the waiting area at Gate 16, anxious to board Mexicana Flight 388 with service to Mexico City. Departure had been delayed two hours owing to a cell of thunderstorms passing to the north. Children pressed their faces to the glass, eager to spot a bolt of lightning streaking across the sky. They returned to their parents disappointed. The sky was cloudless. Not one of them had seen so much as the spark from a firefly. Parents shook their heads. Faulty weather forecasts were the least of Venezuela's problems.

No one paid attention to the chartered bus that crossed the tarmac a little after 6 p.m. and pulled up to the rear of the aircraft. Nor did anyone notice the twenty-three men and women who alighted from the bus and climbed the mobile staircase onto the plane, having bypassed normal airline check-in procedures, security checkpoints, and passport control. When boarding was announced, the passengers sighed and filed onto the aircraft. No one said a word about the gringos already seated in the cabin. Nor did anyone comment when the plane landed in Mexico City and they were asked to remain in their seats while the gringos exited before them.

Two men waited for the twenty-three inside Benito Juárez International Airport. One was tall and broad-shouldered and wore the uniform of the Guardia Nacional. The other was short and dumpy and wore a wrinkled suit and expensive sunglasses. The soldier smiled and spoke loudly as he welcomed the group to Mexico. He had wonderful teeth. The short, fat man in the rumpled suit told him to shut up and get moving. The soldier clamped his square jaw shut and led the twenty-three to a door across the hall from Immigration Control.

Another uniformed official waited inside a large, unremarkable room. He asked the visitors to line up and have their passports ready. One by one, he examined the travel documents. All were new Portuguese passports that had never been stamped. The official had worked in immigration for many years. He knew that citizens of the European Union required a visa to visit Venezuela. He also knew better than to point out this discrepancy. One by one, he returned the passports to their owners. He did not, as was his custom, stamp each. Nor did he pass any through the optical scanner that recorded a person's entry and read the biometric magnetic strip containing the visitor's personal statistics. The official was a smart man and possessed a remarkable memory. It did not require significant effort to memorize two of the passport numbers and the names written inside. The official had many masters.

Thirty minutes after setting foot on Mexican soil, the twenty-three boarded a private bus and were driven to a respectable hotel on the outskirts of the city. Here they showered, changed clothes, and enjoyed a traditional Mexican dinner of carnitas, tortillas, and frijoles. Each was allowed one beer.

At 11 p.m., the first of three vans pulled into the hotel's forecourt. Eight individuals—six men and two women—climbed aboard. All were trim and fit and in high spirits. They did not speak Portuguese but a mixture of German, French, and English. The van drove them to a private airstrip north of the city. A Pilatus P-3 waited on the asphalt runway. The eight stowed their bags and mounted the staircase. At midnight, the Pilatus took off and pointed its nose north for the five-hour flight to its destination.

Team One was airborne.

The second van collected a group of seven, six men and one woman. Again, all were fit to look at, impressively so. In contrast to the plain van that had picked up Team One, this one was painted sleek black and was as shiny as if it had been driven directly from the car wash. Two golden interlocking S's adorned the doors on either side. The van drove west across the city to a private airport that catered to the city's wealthiest citizens—industrialists, oilmen, ranking officials, and the landed gentry who counted as Mexico's aristocrats. Tonight, however, the armed guards manning the main gate waved the van past without even a cursory inspection.

The van continued to the western end of the 6,000-foot runway where a Cessna Citation business jet waited, stairs lowered, navigation lights flashing, a uniformed steward standing by to help his passengers board. Like the van, the jet had the symbol of interlocking S's painted on its fuselage.

At 1 a.m. the Citation radioed "wheels up" to the control tower. Its flight plan called for a first leg northwest to the city of Puerto Vallarta before it turned due north, crossed the United States border at El Centro, and continued on to its destination, San Francisco. Somewhere over the Sierra Madre mountain range, the pilot dipped the nose and descended to 6,000 feet. He plugged new coordinates into the plane's navigation system. Moments later, the wings banked and the needle on the plane's compass swung to east by northeast. The pilot was pleased to note that the fuel needle had barely strayed from full an hour after takeoff. His passengers were going to need every mile he could get if they hoped to reach their destination.

Team Two was en route.

A third van collected the final group of eight. The van drove all night east through the jungles of eastern Mexico. At 5 a.m. they arrived at the port city of Vera Cruz. The eight did not board a ship, however. Instead, they proceeded to a private airstrip owned by one of the multinational oil corporations based there and boarded a Bombardier business jet for the two-hour flight up the coast to Tampico. In Tampico they exchanged the jet for a CH-53 helicopter, formerly in the service of the United States Marine Corps but purchased recently by Noble Energy Corporation. The helicopter was spacious inside and fitted for another class of able-bodied men and women: roughnecks.

At dawn, they took off for the short flight to Tamondo.

Tamondo was not a city. It was the name of Noble Energy's newest oil rig located in the Kaskida Field, 250 miles southwest of New Orleans.

Team Three was under way.

32

D innertime at Comstock.
    As Astor pushed through the doors to his firm and hurried down the corridor toward his office, he was assaulted by a barrage of scents. Teriyaki chicken battled with microwave bean burrito. Someone was having lamb curry and someone else an Italian dish with enough garlic to make his eyes water. He might as well be in the cafeteria of the United Nations building.

The time was a few minutes past seven, and the trading desk was nearly as full as when he'd left that morning. The market had closed two and a half hours earlier, but only the parents left before six. The diehards stayed till nine. Two of the quants from the arb fund were throwing a Nerf football. Astor intercepted a pass and drilled a bullet right back. "That's how you throw a spiral," he said.

The trader raised his hands and said, "Touchdown, Astor."

Astor smiled and patted him on the back. The boss didn't mind a little ass-kissing now and again.

Marv Shank rounded the far corner with a sheaf of paper in his hands and a giant, dripping hamburger in the other. "The prodigal son returns."

Astor waited at the entry to his office and extended a hand to show Shank inside.

"Where were you all day?" asked Shank, collapsing into a chair with a huff.

"Private business." Astor sat down and scanned the market indices. The position was solid. The yuan hadn't moved a tick since the disturbance that morning.

"Enough with the top-secret bullshit," said Shank. "I've got twenty big bills in the fund. Call me cheap, but I consider that a lot of dough. If you're not here on a bat-shit day, I deserve to know the reason why."

"Yeah, yeah, all right then," said Astor. "Just give me a minute to decompress, and while you're at it, put a napkin under that burger.

You're making a mess. I mean, come on." He hit a button under his desk to shut the office door, then obscured the window so no one could see in. "This goes nowhere."

"Schtum," said Shank, zipping his lips closed.

"Schtum."

And so Astor told him. He told him about getting his father's text and about stealing the agenda out of his desk at the Stock Exchange. He told him about speaking to Penelope Evans and the shock of discovering her body. Here Shank stopped him. "You broke into her house, found her dead, and then did what?"

"We looked around for clues that might help us figure out who did it."

"And you never called the police?"

"Sully and I decided it would be better for the firm not to."

Shank nodded, satisfied for the moment. "Go on."

Astor described the disparate materials found in her house and asked if Shank could make something of it. Shank mulled this over but ultimately said he couldn't. Astor did not tell him about Mike Grillo. It was a sound rule of thumb never to tell someone everything, even your best friend.

"So that's where I was today," concluded Astor.

Shank sat stone-faced, saying nothing.

"It's okay to talk," said Astor. "*Schtum* doesn't mean you're suddenly mute."

"I'm the Jew here," said Shank. "I know what *schtum* means. And I'm not being mute. I'm being absolutely fucking speechless. Tough titty if you find my language offensive. Or maybe I should say it like you Upper East Side Episcopalians—'Pardon me, Robert, but I'm a bit tongue-tied.'"

"It's a mess, all right."

"A mess?" Shank shook his head. "A mess is when you don't clean up your room or you forget to pay the electric bill three months running or you have two girlfriends and you made a date with both of them on the same night. That's a mess. This is . . . it's . . . well, I don't know what this is, except that it's wrong."

"I know," said Astor. "We should have called the police."

"I couldn't care less about the police. You shouldn't have left the office to begin with." Shank eyed Astor from beneath a frustrated brow. "Just as long as it ends here."

"What do you mean?"

"I mean, you're done. Finished. Over. Who do you think you are, Harry Bosch?"

"Look, I was just doing what any son would."

"Really? 'Cause I got a dad, too, and I'll tell you what this son would have done. I would have gotten on the horn with the FBI or the Secret Service lickety-split and I'd have told them all this stuff. They're professionals. You're a two-bit stock picker. What do you know about murder?" Shank frowned in disgust. "You tell Alex yet?"

"No."

Shank picked up the phone and shoved it at Astor. "What are you waiting for?"

"Not gonna happen."

"Now."

Astor calmly took the phone and equally calmly replaced it in its cradle. "N–O."

"Unbelievable," said Shank. "Or maybe I should say 'typical.' You actually think that you can do a better job than the friggin' FBI. Believe it or not, Bobby, there are other competent people out there. Some even more competent than you."

"Doubtful." Seeing Shank's eyes narrow, he added at once, "Kidding, Marv. Really."

"Sure you are. You're a piece of work, know that?" Shank sank back in his chair and rubbed his scalp viciously with both hands, teeth clenched, issuing a brief, angry groan. "Worst of all, you blew off Reventlow. You let three hundred million walk out the door."

"Come on, Marv. Calm down. Reventlow's hot money. That's not our style."

"Since when do we have style?"

"Leave it alone, okay? It is what it is."

Shank laughed humorlessly. "Who the fuck uses the word *decompress*?"

"I know *schtum*."

"The last goyim. Detective Robert Astor. I should feel blessed."

"Marv . . . on your chin . . . there."

Shank rushed to wipe away an errant gob of mustard.

Astor felt a rush of affection for his business partner, colleague, and friend. Running a fund together was similar to being in a marriage. The job demanded the utmost in confidence, loyalty, and trust. The pressures were immense and unyielding. Probably the hardest part was just being able to remain in close proximity with someone else for twelve hours each day, week in, week out, year after year, without crushing his skull with a sledgehammer. Fifteen years and counting. Astor knew more about Marv Shank than anyone on the earth.

"So what's up?" he asked.

"There's a lot of scared Injuns out there," said Shank.

"Anyone pulling out?"

"Too soon for that, but don't be surprised when it starts."

"It was a momentary blip. The entire episode lasted five minutes. How does anyone even know about it?"

"Because everyone knows everything."

Astor knew this to be true. The Street ran on gossip, rumor, and innuendo. Traders spent their days on the phone to clients and colleagues passing along the latest news, be it true, false, or unverified. The reasoning was twofold. They needed to prove they were in the loop and thus "connected," and if on occasion they were correct, they could claim to have brought "value added." Anything to get a leg up on the competition.

"And you? Scared, too?"

"Nah," said Shank. "When have you ever been wrong on something this big?"

"Exactly." Astor brought up his appointments on the monitor. He was penciled in for a cocktail party at the New York Public Library, an opening at Gagosian's gallery uptown, and a speech on the growing government debt at the Peterson Institute. It was Monday night. The week only got busier. There was only one entry for 8:30: "HH—Brooklyn."

Astor stood.

"Where you going?" asked Shank. "The news conference in China starts in fifteen minutes."

"Getting changed. I've got a thing at Helping Hands in Brooklyn. New vocational building. Why don't you come along? We can watch the press conference in the Sprinter."

"I live in Westchester. Why the hell would I want to go to Brooklyn?"

Astor shrugged. "Peter Luger after?"

"You think I give two shits about a steak right now?"

"Porterhouse? Onion strings?" The porterhouse at the Peter Luger Steak House in Brooklyn was acknowledged to be one of the biggest, juiciest, tenderest cuts of red meat on the planet and was always impeccably prepared. Astor looked at him askance. "Come on, Marv. It's you. You can't say no."

Shank studied what remained of his hamburger. "Split it?"

"You on a diet?"

"Very funny," said Shank, loosening up, the tension easing from his shoulders. "Deal. But you're buying."

"It'll be a pleasure for the fearless man with twenty big bills in my fund. Give me a minute."

Astor walked down the hall and entered a suite of rooms housing a private apartment. Finding the remote, he turned on the TV. He was interested not in Bloomberg but in local news coverage. Impatiently he flipped from channel to channel, seeing if he could spot any mention of Penelope Evans's murder. As yet there was nothing.

He showered and traded in his suit for jeans, chukka boots, and a chambray shirt. Dressing, he noted that his eyes were tired, his face drawn. He tried to smile, but for once he could not. He told himself to buck up, that everything would be all right. It was no good. Things were spinning out of control. He feared his best efforts might do little to affect them.

"The market doesn't care about before."

He put his head against the mirror. His breathing was fast and shallow. One thing at a time. One evolution, then the next. He knew better than to think too far ahead, but the events of the day overwhelmed him. He saw Penelope Evans's corpse in his mind and bit a finger to keep from crying out. Shank was dead on. He should have called the FBI, or at least contacted his ex-wife.

And now they were talking about steaks at Peter Luger?

Astor opened his eyes and stared deep into himself.

One thing at a time.

One evolution, then the next.

His breathing calmed.

He managed a smile.

He stood tall.

The eyes were still tired, the face just as drawn, but the veneer was back in place. There was no problem that the mature, confident man in the mirror could not overcome. He had to fool himself before he could fool everyone else.

As Astor left, he noted that his jeans were loose. He tightened his belt to the fourth notch. He made a note to order the porterhouse for himself and to eat every bite.

33

The Sprinter was a Mercedes-Benz passenger van on steroids. Painted a sleek jet black with no windows apart from the windscreen, the vehicle measured 24 feet in length and 7 in width and was tall enough for Astor to stand to his full height inside. The standard diesel V-6 had been replaced with a turbocharged V-12. Heavy-duty shocks cushioned the ride. The vehicle had been armored from top to bottom in case of armed insurrection. Boasting a fully fueled street weight of three and a half tons, the Sprinter required just six seconds to reach 60 miles per hour.

But the real improvements were in the interior.

Astor slid the door closed and took a seat in one of three Recaro leather lounge chairs. A 60-inch high-definition screen formed the wall separating the driving compartment. There was a sleek wood table, a Sub-Zero refrigerator, a Bang & Olufsen sound system, and an iMac built into one sidewall. A couch in the back extended into a bed. There were enough bells and whistles to raise the final sales price to a lick over three hundred grand. Astor had nicknamed the vehicle the Imperial Destroyer, after Lord Vader's ship. A hedge fund manager wasn't officially on the dark side, but he wasn't too far off.

"Turn on the tube," said Shank, cracking open a beer. "I'm counting on some good news to salvage a piss-poor day."

Astor hit the remote and the large screen came to life. It showed the same backdrop as that morning, a navy proscenium with American and Chinese flags and a wooden dais in the center. At precisely 8:15, the U.S. trade representative took the stage in the company of a diminutive Chinese technocrat.

Astor punched up the volume as the trade representative began to speak.

"After three days of full and frank discussions, I am pleased to announce that the Chinese government remains committed to its policy of allowing the yuan to slowly but steadily appreciate against the dollar."

"What the . . . ?" said Shank.

"Quiet."

"And that it is the government's stated desire to stimulate the growth of its domestic consumer market by allowing the importation of cheaper foreign products. It is the government's decision to allow the yuan to appreciate a further three percent by the end of this year."

Astor killed the volume as the Chinese official began to speak.

"Three percent," said Shank. "Did he say three percent?"

"Yeah," said Astor. "That's what he said."

"We're toast. French fried with maple syrup."

"Cool it, Marv. It's all misdirection. See? Rates are holding steady."

Shank looked at one of the flat screens built into the cabinetry. The yuan/dollar rate remained stable at 6.30. "Three percent. Market's going to factor that in."

"Over time. We can sell our contracts tomorrow."

"About those rates," said Shank. "You might want to take a gander."

Astor watched in horror as the exchange rate flashed and the yuan continued to appreciate: 6.28 . . . 6.275. . . . 6.255.

"The markets will rebound. Just wait—it's an aberration. The Chinese bank still controls the rate of appreciation. They never allow it to move so much in one day. They like things slow and orderly."

"You better call our guy."

"If he says they're going to depreciate, they're going to depreciate."

"Since when do you believe everything someone tells you?"

"He knows what he's talking about."

"So does our trade rep. Get on the horn this second."

"Maybe later, Marv. Let me think on it."

By the time the Sprinter reached Brooklyn twenty minutes later, the yuan had stabilized at 6.175, an enormous 2 percent increase in value versus the dollar and a loss in Astor's position of $400 million.

"We're going to have a cash problem tomorrow," said Shank. "After wiring out that fifty million to Zarek, we're running on fumes."

"We have plenty of equities in the fund we can sell."

"It'll be a fire sale. Count on a significant loss."

"It's one day. Things will change."

"We don't have time. Those margin calls are going to be coming fast and furious tomorrow afternoon. There's blood in the water."

"I'll raise more money."

"How?"

"There's a way."

"Hot money? As I recall, you sent him packing with his tail between his legs."

"Even I can make a mistake," Astor admitted.

"You? The almighty Astor? On something this big?"

Astor looked away.

The Sprinter rolled up Albany Avenue in Lefferts Park and stopped at the corner of Rutland Road. There were balloons and lots of youngsters in red Helping Hands T-shirts. Astor spotted a famous councilman whom he hated and who he knew hated him even worse. He looked at his partner for moral support and got only another scowl.

"We still going to Peter Luger after?" asked Marv Shank.

34

Michael Grillo sat at his customary table at the rear of Balthazar, the French brasserie in SoHo that did double duty as his private office. It was 9 p.m. and the joint was packed. The appetizing scents of roast chicken and French onion soup drifted from the kitchen. Grillo sipped his Campari and soda and reread the message he'd received earlier from Bobby Astor giving Edward Astor's mobile phone number as well as his Social Security number. Taking a pencil from his coat, he transferred both to a notepad. For a man of Grillo's talent, the two were more than enough information to unlock a trove of personal information, information he hoped would shed light on Astor's activities and help his client discover who or what Palantir was and how it had played a role in Edward Astor's death.

Grillo sent the message to his personal server. Immediately afterward, he deleted it from his phone. He knew about the vulnerability of cellular technology. He made his living exploiting it. Below the two numbers he wrote the word *Palantir*. The name was familiar, though he wasn't sure why, or where he might have heard it before. His instinct told him to be wary. Grillo paid his instinct close mind. It had kept him alive through three wars.

His first call was to the private number of a highly placed executive at the nation's largest phone carrier. A woman answered on the second ring. "Hello, Mike."

"Hello yourself. Got a sec?"

"For you, always."

Grillo smiled his prim, menacing, gambler's smile. "Have a pen?"

He read off Edward Astor's cell number and the woman asked him to hold. She returned to the line thirty seconds later. Grillo could tell that she had moved to a quieter location, and when she spoke the warmth had bled from her voice. "You know whose number this is?"

"I do."

"The FBI already called."

"They're upping their game." Grillo kept his eyes on the door. A gaggle of tourists—he guessed Spanish by their coloring and dress—entered and approached the maitre d'. "Is it yours?" he asked, meaning did the number belong to the carrier?

"It's ours."

"If it makes any difference, I'm working with the family."

"I'll sleep more soundly tonight."

"I'm pleased."

"How far back do you need?"

"Two billing cycles. Sixty days should do the trick. I'm most interested in the last week. Calls to and from. If you can get names and addresses, it would help."

"I'll see what I can do."

A rough-looking man stood outside the restaurant peering through the plate-glass window. Six feet, jeans, black T, chiseled arms. Grillo took out his lighter and flicked the cover open and closed. It was a stainless silver Zippo. He'd carried it into battle on three continents, and his father had carried it before him in Korea.

"If you can give me a head start," he suggested, "I'd appreciate it."

"That's a big if."

"It carries four zeroes."

"I'm sure your client can afford it."

"Impress me." Grillo hung up. The hard type with the black T-shirt was coming through the front door. A little girl with pigtails held his hand. He picked her up and asked a waitress for a restroom. Grillo put away the lighter. It came to him what he'd heard about Palantir. Something about a firm that did security work for the NSA. Cutting-edge stuff.

Well, thought Grillo, it had to be. Everyone acknowledged that the National Security Agency was pretty much the smartest guy in the room. Twenty thousand souls locked away inside a compound in the rolling hills outside of Washington, D.C., scouring the world's communications traffic for any and all things sinister and threatening to the security of the United States of America and its allies. On the record, the NSA admitted to pulling down twenty petabytes of raw data a day from the world's digital traffic: phones, Internet, satellites, all of it. That was enough information to fill the Library of Congress a hundred times. The NSA was as secret as secret got. Doing security work for it was like being a bodyguard for the marines.

He looked at the word on his notepad.

Palantir.

Bobby Astor had no business putting his nose into this kind of stuff.

Grillo walked outside and smoked a cigarette. The night was hot and sticky, but he kept his jacket on. He disliked walking around in shirtsleeves and a necktie. A uniform was a uniform. Ten years back it was cammies and combat boots. These days it was Tom Ford and Ferragamos. For the first time in a long while, he wasn't sure which was more dangerous.

Inside the brasserie, the staff had wiped down his table and refilled the coffee. He sat, careful to adjust his trousers and jacket. His next call was to a small but respected credit advisory bureau. He read off Edward Astor's Social Security number and requested a list of all credit cards in Astor's name. His contact promised an answer by tomorrow afternoon. Grillo told him he wanted it by noon and hung up.

The daily specials were pot-au-feu, grilled trout, and cuisses de grenouille.

"The usual," he told the server. "And remember, *bleu.*"

"*Bien sûr, monsieur.*"

Grillo started playing with his Zippo again. It was all coming back now. He remembered the man who'd mentioned the name. The recollection did little to boost his spirits. A man from the murkiest depths of the secret world.

The server arrived with Grillo's steak. "*Voilà. Votre steak frites.*"

"*Bleu?*" Grillo asked with friendly disbelief.

"*Comme vous l'aimez.*"

Grillo cut into the steak. The center was dark red, essentially untouched by heat.

"*Eh bien?*" asked the waiter.

"*Parfait,*" said Grillo.

Content, the server bowed and left.

Grillo cut himself a piece of meat. Strangely, he could not bring himself to take a bite. He had lost his appetite.

35

A stor needed a drink.

He needed a drink to get over his father's death. He needed
a drink to deal with the meltdown of the position. He needed a drink
to soothe his conscience for failing to report Penelope Evans's death.
Mostly he needed a drink because he needed a drink. Having a drink
meant he was in control. When he put the glass to his lips and let the
liquor flow into his mouth and down his throat and felt the wonderful, healing warmth spread through his limbs, the first joyous step to
oblivion, he knew that he, Robert Astor, was in charge, and the world
was no longer a threatening place, and if everyone would please just
give him a little time, if they would just back off and chill, he would
fix everything.

"Lights."

Astor stepped off the elevator directly into the foyer of his home
as the overhead lights came to life. His primary residence in the city
was a two-level penthouse on Tenth Avenue in Chelsea, just across the
street from the High Line and no more than a mile from Alex's office.
He walked into the kitchen and selected a bottle of mineral water and
a large lime from the refrigerator. He cut the lime and dropped it into a
highball glass, then poured the mineral water. The glass had to be stout
and heavy, the lime fresh, and the mineral water carbonated and with a
dash of salt. Those were the rules. He grasped the glass in his fist, took
a long sip, and the craving vanished.

He was safe.

Astor gazed across the living room. Not 20 feet away stood a fully
stocked bar. He could see it now, the bottles of Stolichnaya and Bulleit
and Grey Goose and all the others glittering like forbidden treasure.
The bar was his jailkeeper. He had made himself a promise a year ago,
when Alex had confronted him and threatened to bar him from seeing Katie. If he ever cracked a bottle, he would go away. He would
do his time at a facility. His colleagues would know and the Street

would know. Alex would know and Katie would know. And finally, he would know.

Astor lugged his satchel upstairs and set it on the floor of his bedroom. "Music," he said. "Sinatra. *In the Wee Small Hours.*"

A moment later the rich, melancholy horns of the Nelson Riddle Orchestra drifted from the concealed speakers.

Astor took off his jacket and hung it on the back of a chair. The house was wired top to bottom. Lights, climate control, appliances, entertainment system, security: all could be controlled by voice or remotely, either from the Net or from his phone.

"Softer."

Sinatra began singing "Mood Indigo." Astor dug the annual reports he'd taken from Penelope Evans's home out of the satchel, then kicked off his chukka boots and lay down on his bed, arranging the pillows to ensure he sat up straight. Windows made up two of the walls, and he looked across the Hudson River toward the lights of northern New Jersey.

"Air conditioning. Sixty-eight degrees."

Astor began with the journal titled *Information Technology Today* that he'd found on Evans's bed.

Our configurable software frameworks extend connectivity, integration, and interoperability to the millions of devices deployed in the market today and empower manufacturers to develop intelligent equipment systems and smart devices that enable collaboration and communication between the enterprise and edge assets. Our platforms allow for building and managing complex monitoring, control, and automation solutions, including applications for building control, facility management, industrial automation, medical equipment, physical security, energy information systems, telecommunications, smart homes, M2M, and smart services.

Penelope Evans had been the executive assistant to the CEO of the New York Stock Exchange, and as far as Astor knew, "managing complex monitoring, control, and automation solutions" was not in her purview. Nor could he find any connection between such a technology and his father's murder. Edward Astor had sought out the counsel of the chairman of the Federal Reserve and the secretary of the treasury, not the secretary of defense and the chairman of the Joint Chiefs of Staff.

Again he keyed on the mention of the firm leading the drive in this field. The company, Britium, based in Reston, Virginia, was in talks with two private equity firms for an imminent sale. The firms were named Watersmark and Oak Leaf Ventures.

Astor shifted his attention to the annual reports. He set the stack beside him on the bed and divided them into two piles, one for the firms that had recently been taken public and one for the firms that were no longer publicly traded. He began with the publicly traded firms.

Silicon Solutions was a Palo Alto–based designer and manufacturer of routers and servers that formed the core of the Internet backbone.

"Net. Google. Silicon Solutions."

A flat-screen monitor rose out of the credenza facing the bed. The screen came to life, showing the Google home page. The company name appeared in the search bar. A blink and a list of relevant pages appeared. He spent a few minutes reading articles about the company, then continued on to the next company in the pile. As he worked, he made notes, analyzing the companies by industry, revenue, country, and currency.

There was a large provider of IT services, including data storage and Internet service providers. There was a company that designed and built machines that fabricated microchips. To round out the high-tech sector, there was a manufacturer of microchips, too.

There was a French company that built and launched communications satellites and a Japanese multinational corporation that built high-speed rail systems and the trains that ran on them as well as elevators, electronic security systems, and home electronics. There was a renowned American engineering company that was the world leader in building power plants, both nuclear- and coal-fueled. There was an Australian mining corporation with operations in twenty countries around the world, from India to Iceland. And a large supermarket chain named Pecos active in the southwestern United States.

An hour later Astor had educated himself about all seven companies that had warranted Penelope Evans's attention. The result was a picture-perfect risk-diversified portfolio. He could find nothing to link them to one another, nothing that suggested the slightest impropriety. Maybe he was wrong. Maybe Penelope Evans's research into these diverse firms was simply part of her normal assignments. Maybe these companies had nothing to do with his father's death.

Or maybe not.

Astor grabbed the report for Silicon Solutions and started rereading it. There had to be a connection between the firms, as disparate as they appeared. There was a reason Penelope Evans was studying the reports even after his father had been killed. Somewhere inside these pages was a clue, and he was determined to find it. He turned to the financial statements. A footnote to the balance sheet stated that the company had been owned by a private equity firm. Britium, the company mentioned in the *ITT* article, was also the object of attention from a private equity firm.

Astor scrambled to a sitting position and combed through the reports again. Each firm, he noted, had had dealings with a sponsor at some point in its corporate history. Either the company had been purchased by a sponsor and subsequently taken public, or it was currently a publicly traded company soon to be taken private.

"Memo," he said aloud.

A blank page appeared on the screen. Astor read the names of the nine private equity firms involved. All were known and respected. He counted acquaintances at all of them. But the pattern he sought eluded him. Only one of the firms was listed in more than one transaction.

"Save. Send to office."

Astor felt vexed. He knew that the presence of the private equity firms in all the companies' histories was no coincidence, but the trail ended there.

He picked up the reports and articles and carried them to his desk. He stared out across the river. He was tired, overanxious, and frightened. He imagined the police technicians lifting an immaculate set of his fingerprints from Penelope Evans's door. Sooner or later they would make a match and he would be called on the carpet and asked to explain what he had been doing at Evans's house. He had no worries about being falsely accused. Not in the long run. He did not own a gun. He could prove he was not present at the time of death. (Sullivan was his alibi.) He had no motive. It was the short run that posed a problem. Today and tomorrow and the day after, days crucial to Comstock's survival. Besides, as John Maynard Keynes had said, in the long run he'd be dead.

"Bloomberg. Foreign exchange cross rates. Yuan–dollar."

Astor stepped in front of the screen. The rate was stable at 6.175. The position was still underwater. Snatching a notepad, he listed investors he might approach to shore up his fund if he received a margin call at the end of business the next day. He stopped after four names. It was not a promising beginning.

He threw the notepad onto his desk. It missed and landed in the trash can. *Touchdown, Astor.* As he bent to pick it up, he inadvertently knocked a few of the annual reports to the floor. Something fell from the pages and floated to the carpet. It was a piece of sky-blue stationery with a navy border. Two words printed in copperplate ran across the top: *Cherry Hill.*

Astor carefully replaced the annual reports before picking up the paper. Cherry Hill was the name of the family estate in Oyster Bay, his boyhood home. Someone had written on it—a woman's feminine, looping script.

Cassandra99

Before he could study it more closely, the phone rang. The caller's name and number appeared on the screen. "Donald Costanza. Doorman."

"Phone," he said. Then: "Yeah, Don, what is it?"

"There's a problem with your car. Can you come downstairs and take a look?"

"What? The Ferrari? Are you kidding me? It's after eleven."

"There's a problem with your car. Can you come downstairs and take a look?"

"I heard you the first time. Be right there."

Astor hustled downstairs and dug a keychain with a black stallion rampant on a yellow background out of the key drawer. The car in question was a 1972 Ferrari Daytona. The last time he'd checked, it was valued at just over $7 million. He did not drive it frequently in the city.

"Elevator."

Astor walked to the entry alcove and waited. If Don the doorman was calling at this time of night about the Ferrari, it meant that something bad had happened. Astor housed the car in a separate bay and kept it covered with an apron 24/7. He had no idea how any harm might have come to it. Unless . . .

Visions of Don the doorman taking the $7 million machine out for a joyride, hurtling down the scarred, potholed streets of Manhattan, filled his mind. He thought of the pummeling given to the rebuilt Koni shocks, the wear and tear on the tires, the damage to the undercarriage.

The elevator arrived.

Astor stepped inside.

But the elevator was not there.

Astor stared into the bottomless shaft. One foot dangled in the abyss as his momentum propelled him forward. Frantically he threw his arms out. He twisted, looking for something, anything, to grab hold of. His hand skidded off the wall. The other flailed at empty space.

And then he saw the cable hanging in the darkness.

He lunged, and caught it with both hands.

He swung back and forth, quickly coming to a halt. He tried to wrap a foot around the cable, but the tension was too strong. The cable did not bend. He slipped a few inches. A ladder ran up the wall. He kicked a leg out. His heel struck a rung. Notching his toes beneath it, he pulled himself closer until he could grasp the ladder with his hands.

The door to his apartment closed.

Darkness.

Astor let go of the cable and took hold of the ladder. Below, a faint light shone through the roof of the elevator, stationary on the ground floor. Somewhere in the shaft a machine engaged. It was the pleasant, efficient whir of the elevator rising. He looked past his feet and saw the tiny light coming toward him, growing larger, brighter.

He tilted his head back. The dark was impenetrable. The shaft ended at the sixth floor. He did not think there was room for him and the elevator. His only hope was to jump on top of the rising elevator and pray that he would not be crushed.

The elevator drew closer. It no longer sounded pleasant or efficient. To Astor's ears, the elevator sounded like a table saw. He was stuck. He could only wait.

The elevator approached. He could see it clearly now. As it came near, he extended a foot, threw himself onto the roof, and made himself as flat as possible. The car continued to rise, and he felt the cold cement of the shaft around him. The light from inside the elevator illuminated the top of the shaft. Four feet became three . . .

The elevator stopped.

Astor found the handle for the emergency exit and forced it upward. The hatch opened grudgingly. He maneuvered around the elevator's roof, finally slipping his feet through the opening and lowering himself into the elevator. He pushed the Door Open button and stepped back inside his home.

He stood still for a moment. His knees shook. His breath came in gasps. The elevator door closed. He staggered and threw a hand against the wall for support. Slowly, his breathing returned to normal. He stood upright and walked into the kitchen.

He needed a drink.

36

L *egio. Patria. Nostra.*

Alone in her study, Alex typed the words into the laptop's search bar. Her phone lay on the desk beside her, its screen illuminated with a picture of the colorful symbol inked on Randall Shepherd's chest. She knew the tattoo signified membership in a military organization, but which?

She tapped the Enter key, and her response appeared immediately. "Our Country's Legion."

It was the motto of the French Foreign Legion, or Légion Étrangère.

Alex searched for tattoos associated with the Foreign Legion. She found one similar, but not identical, on the second search page. The *1°* stood for "first company." The *2 REP* for second regiment.

It was a solid start, but Alex wasn't finished.

She examined the other noteworthy tattoo inked on Shepherd's arm. It showed the Roman numerals III.III.V and beneath them the words *Vincere aut Mori.* "Conquer or Die." She performed a search combining the numerals and the Latin phrase. Fewer than a dozen pages appeared. None offered a further clue to Shepherd's true identity.

Alex reasoned that the roman numerals represented a date. III.III.V translated to March 3, 2005. She was rewarded with 2 million hits. She added "Win or Die" and the number fell to 200,000. No help there.

Alex retreated a few steps. Several of her young lions had served in the marines, and each had body art to remind him of a difficult campaign—Fallujah in Iraq, Helmand Province in Afghanistan. Perhaps the tattoo was to commemorate an operation or a battle won or lost. Diligently she culled through accounts of the Foreign Legion's recent engagements. There were deployments to the Middle East and Kosovo, as well as less publicized actions in Africa and Asia. Nowhere, however, did she find a mention of a specific battle or operation that had taken place on March 3, 2005. She could not validate her supposition that the roman numerals signified a date.

Alex slid back the chair and padded into the kitchen. The clock read 11:30. She realized that she hadn't eaten since early that afternoon. Her stomach informed her in no uncertain terms that she was starving. She opened the fridge and found a piece of Gruyère and an apple. Slim pickings. She had a memory of sneaking into the kitchen with Bobby late one night after making love, finding a giant bowl of leftover spaghetti carbonara in the fridge, and sitting together at the table, toes touching, wordlessly scarfing it down. It was too bad they got along only when they didn't talk to each other. The carbonara sounded delicious right about now.

Bobby was a wonderful cook.

Alex sat lost in her thoughts until the minute hand reached twelve. Rising, she returned to her office and at 12:03 placed a call to Paris, France, where the day was just beginning.

"Allo?" said a sleepy voice.

"Jean. It's Alex Forza in New York. We have a situation."

Jean Eyraud, deputy director of the French DGSE—the Direction Générale de la Sécurité Extérieure, France's national counterterrorism organization—snapped to attention. "How can I help?"

"I have some fingerprints I need you to run. He's one of your guys. Former Légion Étrangère."

"Send them over. I'll see to it immediately."

"And Jean . . . vite."

37

It was not an accident.

Elevator doors do not open by themselves when the elevator itself is six floors below, Astor told himself as he stood in his kitchen, stunned, unsure why he was still alive, part of him not quite believing what had happened.

It was not an accident.

Not when the elevator belongs to someone looking into his father's murder and the murder involved a vehicle inexplicably careening across the White House lawn. And not when the dead man's assistant is murdered by a pinpoint knife-thrust to the heart by a person or persons able to float through a home without making a noise.

It was not an accident.

Still, if it were only his febrile mind desperately seeking a means to connect these events in the wake of narrowly escaping his own death, he might be able to posit a modicum of doubt. He might be able to argue that he was mistaken, that strange as it may seem, elevators sometimes do malfunction, and like it or not, this was one of those times.

But that was not the case.

He had proof.

Astor hurried from the kitchen and stumbled upstairs, falling half-way to the top, then raising himself, urging himself onward, carrying himself like the secret drunk he used to be. Inside his bedroom, he made a beeline for the desk, his hands sorting through the annual reports, examining the covers, discarding them one by one until he found what he was looking for.

The Sonichi Corporation of Japan.

He sat down on the floor cross-legged and thumbed the pages. He saw the heading and stopped. It was on page 23. "Industrial Products Division." It read, "Last year the company extended its market line in its elevator business, branching laterally from the commercial sector to the residential sector with the introduction of two models, the Express 2111 and the Express 2122."

Astor chucked the report aside and ran back downstairs. He punched the elevator call button. Seconds later the door opened. A brightly lit elevator car beckoned. Boldly, he stepped inside. The name was proudly stamped above the call buttons. *Sonichi Express 2122.*

There was one last matter.

Leaving the elevator, he placed a call from his cell.

"Yessir, Mr. Astor. How may I help?"

"Hello, Don, just wanted to check if you called me about five minutes ago."

"Excuse me, sir?"

"Something about my car. You asked me to come downstairs and take a look."

"Your car is just fine, sir. Checked it myself when I came on shift." Don the doorman laughed wryly. "You goofing on me, Mr. A?" Read as, "You back on the sauce again, Mr. A?"

Astor paused. "No, Don. I must have misunderstood. Don't worry about it. Good night."

Astor ended the call.

It was not an accident.

It was attempted murder.

Later, after he had reported the malfunction to the building superintendent and the inspector and repairmen had come and gone and pronounced the system in perfect working order, and they had scratched their heads because no one could find anything wrong anywhere, and they had all smiled politely, not quite hiding their opinion that the man on the sixth floor might not be operating with a full deck, Astor retreated to his bedroom. He did not bother with the reports strewn about the floor. Instead he walked to his night table and picked up the slip of pale blue stationery with the words *Cherry Hill* embossed across the top that had fallen from one of the reports.

Cassandra99

He did not know what the word meant, but for now, that didn't matter. The stationery told him other things. The feminine script confirmed the tremor in Penelope Evans's voice earlier that day and confirmed that she and his father had been working together on a secret project at the Astor estate in Oyster Bay.

Palantir.

Astor realized that he hadn't thought of the word since meeting with Mike Grillo earlier that evening.

He looked at his phone and scrolled through to Alex's number. The sight of her name was enough to scratch any idea he had of contacting her. With Alex it was all or nothing. If he called, he would have to tell her the whole story from A to Z. She would not be interested in hearing about the elevator until he explained why he had had the temerity (she would use a different word) to leave Penelope Evans's home without calling the police. It would not suffice to blame Sullivan. There would also be the matter of the stolen agenda, and no doubt a dozen other failings on his part.

He could not call Alex.

It was then that Astor took a second, longer, and altogether darker look at his smartphone. It had been acting up since that morning, when he'd had trouble getting a clear line to the office while flying in. He thought about the timing of Penelope Evans's death. Sullivan had stated that she had been killed less than an hour before they arrived. If he had not stopped to see Brad Zarek at Standard Financial to discuss the terms of the loan, he and Sullivan would have arrived in Greenwich at the same time as the killer. Did that mean that the killer knew about Evans only after he did? That somehow Astor's interest in her had alerted him? If so, how?

Astor turned the phone over in his hand. Smooth, elegant, much too powerful. A necessary tool. But was it also a weapon?

And then there was the matter of Don the doorman's call.

Astor accessed his voice mail and searched among the deleted messages. There were over a hundred, and he patiently scrolled through them all until he found what he was looking for. A message from three weeks earlier.

"Yeah, Mr. A. It's Don. You might want to come down and take a look at your car. Don't worry. There's no problem, but it looks like the tires could use some air. That's it."

Astor listened again and again. He didn't quite remember what Don had said earlier, but he was relatively certain the words were close to the same. They had simply been rearranged.

Calmly he walked downstairs and set the phone on the kitchen counter. He found the tool basket in the pantry. He chose a hammer—heavy, rubber-gripped, barely used—and returned to the kitchen. He stood before the counter, took careful aim, and brought it down squarely on the phone. And then he hit it again and again.

Not a weapon, thought Astor. A necessary tool.

For his enemies.

38

I t was a dream.

Randall Shepherd said, "I'm going to shoot you and then I'm going to shoot your partner and there's nothing you can do about it."

Alex stared back at the killer. She saw him pulling the pistol from his waistband and immediately started for her own weapon. She'd always been a fast draw, but this time something was wrong. Her arms refused her commands. She stood immobile, her hands stuck by her sides, her entire body as stiff as a slab of petrified wood. She could only watch and wait as Shepherd raised the pistol and pointed it at her forehead.

"You won't stop us," he said.

I will, said Alex, but now her speech failed her too. She could utter no words as she watched his finger tighten on the trigger.

But then Shepherd turned the gun away and pointed it at Jimmy Malloy. And now Alex could scream, but she still could not move, and so she was condemned to stand still and watch helplessly as Shepherd shot Jimmy in the head. She was screaming, the gunshot loud in her ears, when her phone rang, waking her.

"Forza."

"Alex, this is Jean Eyraud in Paris. It's my turn to wake you."

Alex threw off the sheets and sat up. "Did you get a match?"

"Quite an exceptional person you decided to kill. You should count yourself lucky to be alive. His name is Luc Lambert, thirty-five years of age, nine years in the Légion Étrangère, a sergeant. He fought in Africa and the Middle East. Decorations for valor and bravery. For fun, I ran his name through all our databases. We like to keep track of these guys. Someone like Lambert, with that kind of record, has to have a reason to leave the *légion* before putting in his twenty."

"Shoot."

"Ever hear of an outfit called Executive Outcomes, based in London?"

Alex searched for a notepad and a pen, then scribbled the name and underlined it several times. "Can't say I have."

"Professional soldiers. Mercenaries. Recruiters for that kind of thing."

"Nice guys."

"The nicest, if you get my drift. It seems they put together a team a few years back to overthrow the government of Comoros, a small oil-rich nation off the southeast coast of Africa, in order to get their hands on sizable offshore reserves. The coup was led by a mercenary named Trevor Manning and was backed by a group of international businessmen."

"When was that exactly?"

"Two thousand five."

"March?"

"March third," said Eyraud, surprised. "You know it?"

"Lambert had a tattoo on his arm with that date. I figured it stood for something."

"The coup was a failure. Everyone knew they were coming before they even set foot in the country. Manning and his team were arrested as they landed to refuel in Zimbabwe. The lot was flown to Comoros and put on trial. Most of them were released after a month or two, but Lambert did a full year. In the trial, it was revealed that he was Trevor Manning's right-hand man."

"A year doesn't sound long for that kind of thing. I'd have thought they'd have been taken out at dawn and shot."

"It took a lot of strings to get them out. One of the sponsors was the son of a former English PM. We all know about him." Eyraud gave a cynical chuckle.

"I'm afraid you'll have to fill me in."

"He was a front for your boys, of course."

"What do you mean, 'our boys'?"

"The CIA. Who do you think?"

"Are you saying that Lambert worked for the CIA?"

"I'm not saying anything. You can connect the dots yourself."

Alex stood and paced the bedroom. Eyraud's revelations, true or not, had turned the investigation on its ear. The mere possibility that Luc Lambert, an experienced and battle-tested mercenary who had been involved in an operation backed by the CIA, was assembling a team on U.S. soil elevated the threat level by an order of magnitude.

"By the way, Alex, you didn't tell me what Lambert was doing in your part of the world."

"Getting ready to put his skills to use." Alex explained about the raid at Windermere, the deaths of Malloy and the others, and the trove of weapons discovered beneath the house.

"I don't like the sound of it," said Jean Eyraud. "Any idea where or when?"

"We found maps of Manhattan. There was fresh food in the refrigerator for Lambert and a half-dozen accomplices. I'd say sooner rather than later. Days. A week at most. We're frightened that we may be looking at a Mumbai-style attack."

"Not good."

No, thought Alex, definitely not good. If what Eyraud said about the CIA's being involved in any way with the failed coup was true, they would have managed it through the directorate of operations or, more likely, a shadow organization funded off the books that did not officially exist. Knowledge of the affair would have been compartmentalized at the highest levels of the Agency. Sadly, Alex knew no one with access to such information.

"Jean," she began uncertainly, "you mentioned something about a recruiter for mercenaries based in London."

"Executive Outcomes."

"They still around?"

"I haven't seen their name recently, but you never know."

"London, eh?"

"Yes, London."

"*Merci*, Jean. We will keep you in the loop on this one."

"Before you go, Alex, may I tell you something? I served alongside many legionnaires when I was in the army. Men like Lambert. Tough. Smart. Maybe a little crazy. Some even work for me today."

"What are you trying to say, Jean?"

"These men are not terrorists. This guy Lambert, he didn't want to die. Whatever he was planning to do, he was planning on getting out of it alive."

39

The Pilatus P-3 landed at sunrise.

At Matamoros Airport on the southernmost tip of the Texas border with Mexico, the temperature on the ground was a balmy 88 degrees. Three black Chevrolet Suburbans waited on the tarmac. The members of Team One deplaned and were at once overcome by the scent of mesquite and yucca. Requiring no instruction, they divided themselves into groups and climbed into the vehicles.

The convoy left the airport by a restricted gate at the east end of the field, one mile from the main terminal, and traveled north on Highway 101 until reaching the Zona Industrial, a swath of warehouses and factories situated a stone's throw from the American border. Matamoros was a center of *maquiladora* manufacturing, and the Zona Industrial was home to many of the world's most famous corporations, including General Electric, Walmart, and Sony, to name a few.

In the cars, the six men and two women were given breakfasts high in carbohydrates, energy drinks, and snacks to sustain them in the hours ahead. The next leg of their journey would not be as comfortable. Most busied themselves as they ate, studying maps, memorizing radio frequencies, mentally repeating the tasks they would be asked to perform during the coming crucible. All were professionals, and they knew how to use the time remaining to them wisely.

After thirty minutes the vehicles pulled up to a gate at the rear of an unmarked warehouse as large as two football fields laid end to end. The gate rolled back on its tracks and the vehicles entered a loading zone running the breadth of the building. They drove past three eighteen-wheelers lined up at the docks, bays open, an army of men and machines filling each with pallets of finished goods bound for export to the United States.

A fourth rig sat alone at the far end of the loading zone. The three SUVs parked beside it. The team members climbed out and stretched their legs. Several recognized the name of a large American chain of supermarkets painted on the side: *Pecos Supermarkets*. Atop the cabin was a refrigeration unit designed to chill the truck's interior to 32 degrees Fahrenheit. The rig was a meat hauler used to transport freshly slaughtered beef and poultry from industrial farms in northern Mexico to stores in the United States.

At 7 a.m., a lean, mustachioed Mexican wearing a white straw Stetson and mirrored aviators emerged from the factory. The leader of Team One was expecting him. The two men shook hands but did not exchange names.

"You have something for me?" asked the Mexican.

The leader of Team One was blond and compact and tanned. He had served for ten years in the South African Army, where he'd earned the nickname Skinner. He handed the Mexican a plastic freezer bag containing the passports used to pass through Mexican immigration control. From here on out, no one would carry any form of identification, false or otherwise.

"Eight. All accounted for."

"*Excelente*," said the Mexican.

The Mexican led the members of Team One to a dressing room adjacent to the loading platform. To one side hung row upon row of jumpsuits; to the other, fur-lined parkas. Gloves were piled into a rack in one corner. Insulated boots occupied another. The men and women moved from one garment to the next, selecting those that fit. They emerged ten minutes later looking as if they were bound for the Arctic Circle.

The Mexican accompanied them into the rig. A concealed door at the rear of the cargo area opened into a narrow compartment. There was no room to sit. The team filed in and took their places shoulder-to-shoulder. The Mexican closed the door. A short time later, the refrigeration unit rattled into operation. The compartment grew colder. Frost crusted eyebrows and eyelashes.

The manifest called for the rig to haul five tons of beef carcasses to a meat processing plant in Harlingen, Texas. Loading began promptly at seven-thirty and ended one hour later. The truck left the Zona Industrial at 9 a.m. The stop at the border was short and uneventful. The supermarket chain was too large to be suspected of smuggling illegal immigrants. A company such as that did not break the law.

At 10 a.m., the truck arrived at the meat processing plant. The team waited patiently, shivering in the cold. No one complained. They were earning too much money to let a chill bother them. Unloading the carcasses was a slow affair. It was not until one in the afternoon that the rig was emptied and the Mexican with the white Stetson and mirror aviators opened the door.

"Bienvenidos a los Estados Unidos."

Team One had arrived on American soil.

40

Astor left home at 5 a.m. The office was 3 miles away. It was too early to wake Sully, and he didn't want to drive the Ferrari or the Benz or even the Ford Fusion. For that matter, he didn't want to get into anything with a motor. A brisk anonymous walk was his safest option. He took the stairs to the ground floor and said good morning to Don the doorman, who was eyeing him with suspicion, as if trying to figure out which Mr. Astor it was this time: the serious model of the last year or so, cordial, polite, in bed at eleven and up at five, or the ungoverned model of yore, back to his boozy, licentious ways.

"You waiting on Mr. Sullivan?"

"I'm walking it today."

Don motioned at the rectangular package wrapped in thick brown paper that Astor carried under his left arm. "Sure you don't need a radio car? That looks kind of heavy."

"I think I can handle it."

Outside, the morning was cool and crisp. Astor hesitated at the curb, looking up and down for anything suspicious. He stopped after a few seconds. He wouldn't be able to spot a hit man if one walked up to him with a gun in his hand. He set out nervously, but his anxieties left him after a few blocks. The sun crested the horizon and its soft rays cleansed all they touched: the cobblestones fronting the corner café, the grime-encrusted grille protecting the liquor store across the street, even the brick walls layered with graffiti. All were colored shiny and new and radiated the promise that was the city's greatest strength.

He headed south on Tenth Avenue for a few blocks before cutting over to Washington and making his way through SoHo and the Village. He had donned his usual outfit: navy suit, white shirt, lace-ups, with a necktie tucked into his pocket for emergencies. There was a good chance it would see some use today. He looked at every street corner, the familiar storefronts and restaurants, with a kind eye. He knew he'd been granted a second lease on life, maybe even a reprieve. At some point he'd come to believe that things happened for a reason. He wasn't sure if there was a purpose to life, and if there was, what his might be. He was not so presumptuous as to guess why these things happened or to assume that a higher power was involved. He just knew in some inchoate but unshakeable way that life gave you signs and it was up to you to spot them and, more important, to act on them.

And so he knew that there was a reason he had not stepped straight into the elevator shaft and fallen to his death. He did not believe the reason was that he could go right back to work and continue devoting his energies to making as much money as possible. There was a bigger reason, and that reason was to find out what had happened to his father.

Astor kept it as simple as that. It wasn't exactly a road-to-Damascus moment, but whatever—he wasn't a saint. Just thinking about it made him uncomfortable.

Astor happened to glance up at a street sign.

Church Street.

"Coincidence," he said aloud.

He kept walking.

"What are you doing here so early?"

"Couldn't sleep."

"Me neither."

"We're in it deep and stinky, boss."

Marv Shank peered from his desk. It was just past six and already his shirt was rumpled, his necktie askew, his cheeks dark with stubble that had eluded his razor. *If I look half as bad as that,* thought Astor, *we are in trouble.*

"Come on down to my office. We'll see how we can get our boots clear of this."

"They're still going to smell."

Astor put his hand on Shank's shoulder as they walked the length of the office. "Ye of little faith."

The trading floor was deserted. A stuttering fluorescent bulb lit the room, giving it the melancholy, abandoned feel of a ballroom after the fest. In an hour, thirty of the smartest men and women on the planet would be patrolling the area, people of seething ambition and robust intellect, plotting strategies, marshaling facts, placing bets on the most efficient marketplace in human history, filling the room with enough energy to light the island of Manhattan and the other boroughs of New York. For now, though, it was just the two of them up against it.

Inside his office, Astor switched on the light and set the package down against the side of his desk.

"What's that you got?" asked Shank.

"That?" Astor settled into his chair, swiveling to study his price screens. "Insurance."

Shank picked up the package, felt the edges, then set it back down. "Is that what I think it is?"

"Yup."

"And you just put it in your car and carried it here?"

"Actually, I walked it over. Didn't want to wake Sully so early. We had a rough day yesterday."

Shank turned paler than he'd been a minute before. "You walked it over?"

"It's only three miles from my place to here. Who's going to hassle me at five in the morning? Lots of people out and about that early. Safest time of day."

"Yeah, I saw some of them loitering by the bridge, having their morning constitutional on my way in. Real safe."

"No worries. I run that route all the time."

"Now I'm feeling better. For a second there, I thought I was working with a raving lunatic."

Astor considered this. "Not raving." He squinted to read the numerals on the screen. "So what you got?"

"Same as yesterday. Rock-steady at 6.175."

"So we're looking at a six-hundred-million-dollar margin call at closing if this sticks. What do we have in the till?"

"After the fifty we wired to Zarek yesterday?"

"After that."

"Comstock Astor has another thirty free. The rest is in equities."

"Only thirty? Who allowed me to commit forty percent of the fund to one position?"

"That would be you, sir."

Astor stood. "Loans from banks are out. No one is going to give us a cent until we get our head above water. That leaves two options."

"Reventlow?"

"Or someone else smart enough to realize that our bet is correct and that sometime in the next seventy-two hours, when our man is elected to the Standing Committee, the yuan will start to lose value like air from a punctured tire and they will stand to make a heap of money."

"That investor would also have to be smart enough to believe that you, a New Yorker whose entire personal knowledge of China comes from a six-month visit when you were twenty years old, knows more about the economic policies to be enacted than a ranking government official who just got off the tube promising that his country would continue to allow its currency to appreciate versus the dollar."

"Precisely."

Shank ran a hand over his mouth, a poor bid to conceal his skepticism. "What's the second option?"

"You know what it is."

Shank's eyes had never been darker. "The Hindenburg."

"Liquidate the fund. Sell off everything we have in Comstock Astor. Pay the margin call."

"Shutter the firm."

Astor nodded. "Who entrusts their money to a man who just lost two billion dollars?"

"I'm not coming up with too many names." Shank sniffed and pointed at the rectangular package. "How much?"

"Not enough."

"Anything else?"

"The house in the Hamptons. Cabin in Aspen. Cattle ranch in Wyoming."

"I'll buy the Ferrari from you."

"Thanks, Marv. You're a lifesaver."

"Even if it added up to four hundred million—which it doesn't—we couldn't get the cash anywhere near in time. You know the rules. Twenty-four hours to pay up after the margin call is issued."

"You can get 'em to stretch it?"

"Maybe. Maybe not. Either way, it would be all over the Street like wildfire."

"So we're looking at option one."

Astor saw a light go on at the far end of the trading floor. He stepped out of his office in time to see a small, ratlike figure scurry down the corridor.

"What is it?" asked Shank.

"Ivan. I need to speak to him." Astor came back into the office. "Oh, and Marv. Set up a meeting with the China team at eight."

"Those guys usually don't get in till later."

"Eight. I have to leave right after."

Shank shrank back, his brow furrowed in disbelief. "Not again. I told you to keep out of it."

"It's not your call."

"You're damn right it's my call. You have no business deserting the office today. And for what? To go on some wild-goose chase. Get real. If you don't contact Alex and tell her about this, I'm going to."

Astor had a fistful of Shank's shirt and tie before he knew it. "You're not going to contact anyone. Do you understand?"

Shank blinked madly, his hands raised, unsure of what had just happened, what his best friend was doing. "What the hell?"

Astor released him. He was surprised at his action, but he did not regret it. "Hey, Marv . . ."

"Yeah?"

"Mind your own business."

41

"Ivan. I need you for a second."

"Everything all right? None of the platforms are off?" Dr. Ivan Davidoff jumped from his desk and began scanning the array of monitors and screens that made up his office.

"Everything's fine," said Astor. "Relax. Unless of course, you've come up with a way to make the numbers only go up."

Ivan looked at him nervously, as if the thought had crossed his mind. "No . . . not yet."

Ivan was thin and pale with a three-day stubble, a shaved head, and dark eyes that looked as if he'd just gotten 30,000 volts. He had a PhD from Rensselaer Polytechnic Institute in upstate New York and had spent three or four years out west at Apple doing cutting-edge stuff he still refused to talk about. It was the stress that had done him in. Ivan wasn't built for fifteen-hour days and the relentless, deadline-driven world of Silicon Valley. He was built to design and oversee the sophisticated trading platforms that powered Comstock's daily business and to work in a quiet, orderly environment that he could control.

"I wanted to ask you a few questions. Just stuff for my own curiosity."

"What about?"

Astor closed the door and pulled a chair up to Ivan's desk. "I'm not sure how to put it. I guess about controlling things. Like at my home. I can turn the lights on and off by voice command. And I can program the heat and air conditioning and the TV through my phone."

"That's old technology. Very simple. If you'd like, I can explain."

Astor stopped him before he could get started. "Not necessary. Just listen to what I have to say."

Calmly and with as much objectivity as he could muster, he related the events of the past evening, leaving out a few salient details—for example, how he'd fallen into the elevator shaft and nearly been killed. Ivan took in the information blankly, registering no surprise even when

Astor explained how the elevator doors had opened without the elevator's being there.

"The first part is simple," said Ivan. "Someone hacked your phone, accessed your voice mail and manipulated the data, then resent it to you."

"How can they do that?"

"Depends. You ever leave your phone anyplace that people can get it without you looking?"

"My office, maybe. Home. But I always keep it close. Why?"

"Someone could have cloned it. Takes about ten seconds."

"What's that—cloning?"

"Copy your SIM card. Get all the information from it. Numbers, contacts, texts, and passwords. Or they could have installed spyware. I can check. Give me your phone."

"Actually, I don't have it."

"You leave it in your office?"

"I crushed it."

"Excuse me?"

"Last night. With a hammer. I was kind of pissed off."

Ivan looked at him with a newfound respect. "They can access it other ways," he went on. "Get into your voice mail. Or through social engineering, you know, contacting someone at your phone company and convincing that person to give them the passwords for your accounts or to reset everything to factory defaults. You'd be surprised how many people at those big carriers are on the take."

Astor thought about Mike Grillo and his contacts at those very same big carriers. Point taken. "And the elevator? I mean, you can't tell an elevator what to do."

"Why not? A computer controls it. You control the computer."

"But it's inside the building. I mean, who would know how to reach it?"

Ivan smiled and began rocking in his chair, and Astor could practically read his mind. *Welcome to my world, homey.*

"Nothing is inside anything," said Ivan. "Elevators are like computers themselves. They have software that tells them how fast to go up and how fast to go down. How long to keep a door open and how quickly to close it. But someone has to be able to control the elevator itself, and that someone is probably not always on the premises."

"How do they do that?"

"By connecting the elevator to a remote operating platform that is hooked up to the Net. The platform probably controls everything in the building: heat, security, lights. Hack the platform and you can take control of the elevator. For the elevator doors to open without the elevator's actually being there, someone had to break into the platform and issue an override command."

"So it's possible?"

"For an outsider with little knowledge of the system, it would be very, very difficult," said Ivan. "But if he worked for the elevator manufacturer, easy-peasy."

"Thanks, Ivan. That should cover it."

"You sure I can't help you with something else?"

"You've been more than helpful."

Astor left the office and headed across the trading floor. Halfway there, he stopped. A thought came to him, as clean and white-hot as a bolt of lightning.

Page 23. Sonichi annual report. The Sonichi Express 2122.

Whoever wanted to hurt Astor didn't work for the company.

He owned it.

Astor slammed the door to his office and turned on the whiteboard.

"Memo. Private equity investors in Evans's companies."

The names of the private equity companies that had invested in those firms whose annual reports he'd found at Penelope Evans's home appeared on the board. One by one, he called up their websites and scrolled through the contents until he found a list of companies the equity firms had invested in, past and present. He was not sure what he was looking for. He was only hoping that if there was a pattern, he could sniff it out and make sense of it.

"Watersmark."

Astor paid particular attention to the sponsor that had been involved with the Sonichi Corporation. He noted that Watersmark had purchased Sonichi seven years earlier and taken it private for $6 billion. There was no mention about how Watersmark had restructured Sonichi, only that Sonichi had recently achieved record earnings and was set to go public again in the fourth quarter of the present year. Watersmark could count on making a hefty profit. Chalk up one for the good guys.

The other companies in Watersmark's portfolio included Pecos, a large supermarket chain based in Texas and with operations in the southwestern United States; Silicon Solutions, a microelectronics company out of Canada; and a mining company in Australia.

Astor tried to imagine a connection between them. What might an industrial engineering firm whose smallest division manufactured elevators have in common with a supermarket chain or a mining company or a maker of specialized microchips? He could think of nothing. Nor could he link them to the bigger question: How might products manufactured by any of these companies allow someone to take control of an automobile?

Astor dug out the sheet of blue stationery from his father's home that he'd found at Penelope Evans's. Cassandra99. Still the word meant nothing.

She was there with my father, thought Astor. *In our home. A home I swore never to set foot in again.*

The answer was in Oyster Bay.

"Boss, the China boys are ready." Marv Shank stood in the doorway, coffee in one hand, daily breakfast burrito in the other. "You good?"

"Be right there," said Astor.

Whether he was good or not was another question entirely.

42

There were four of them, and they sat at opposite sides of the table. Astor and Shank, and Longfellow and Goodchild. Longfellow was his China hand. Goodchild was his currency man. There was no chit-chat. No mention of his father's death. No banter about the Yankees or the Mets or who had screwed which pretty young thing over the weekend in the Hamptons. Goodchild and Longfellow had Bloombergs on their desks, too. They knew the score. If anything, the conference room was colder than the trading floor.

"So," said Astor, when he'd stared at them long enough. "What the hell's going on?"

Goodchild was blond and lanky and English, with a narrow, pock-marked face. He splayed his forearms on the table and leaned forward. "Posturing," he said, eyes darting from face to face as if sharing a secret. "They're afraid the cracks are beginning to show."

Longfellow nodded in agreement. "Like a bully puffing up his chest. All show."

"Really," said Astor, a very pissed-off devil's advocate. "What's the flash PMI?"

"Forty-eight." Shank responded without taking his eyes off the two traders.

The flash PMI, or purchasing managers' index, measured economic activity as defined by demand for raw materials and industrial goods. Figures above fifty indicated an expansion of economic activity; below fifty signaled contraction.

A reading of forty-eight spelled catastrophe.

"And GDP is still forecast at nine percent?" said Astor.

"Nine point two, actually," said Goodchild. "But it's a sham. Things have only gotten worse since we made our evaluation three months ago."

"So they put their deputy minister for trade on TV to confirm their policy of allowing the yuan to appreciate to fake us out?"

"No choice," said Longfellow.

"Yeah, I know," said Astor. "The cracks are beginning to show."

"Precisely," responded Goodchild, as if he were back debating at the Oxford Union.

"The only change," said Longfellow, "is the increased pressure the Treasury Department is putting on the Chinese to revalue."

Longfellow was a Scot, a graduate of Fettes and St. Paul's before he took a PhD in astrophysics from Stanford. He was tall and fat, with messy red hair, beady eyes, and a constant sweat that dampened his cheeks and forehead. At some point in his career he'd spent two years in the Chinese hinterlands—Sichuan Province, to be exact—teaching English to schoolchildren (though with his nearly incomprehensible brogue, Astor wondered just what kind of English his students had ended up speaking).

"It appears to be working," said Astor.

"Not for long," retorted Longfellow. "It can't. The Chinese have to devalue."

"That means telling the U.S. government to go screw itself."

"Indeed," said Longfellow.

"We're betting a boatload of money on that opinion."

"It's not an opinion," blared the Scot. "It's fact."

Astor slammed an open palm on the table. The three other men snapped to attention. But when Astor spoke, his voice was a whisper. "We're down four hundred million bucks," he said. "That's the only fact that concerns me."

China. The Middle Kingdom. In just over thirty years, the country of 1.4 billion inhabitants had undergone the most titanic economic transformation the world had seen since the Japanese had welcomed Commodore Perry to Tokyo Harbor in 1854 and ushered in the Meiji Restoration.

The basis of the remarkable leap forward was the creation and development of an export-based economy. Cheap Chinese labor lured foreign corporations to manufacture products at an advantageous price. These corporations invested in factories and exported their products to the rest of the world. Housing, primarily in the form of towering apartment complexes, was built to provide lodging for the hundreds of thousands of peasants fleeing the countryside to earn a living wage. Roads were laid to transport raw materials to the factories and finished goods to market. Ports were expanded to enable more and larger ships to take on merchandise. New airports followed. Power plants were constructed to generate and distribute electricity to the rapidly expanding industrial base. Cities like Guangzhou, Shenzhen, and Chongqing exploded, moving from forgotten backwaters to industrial dynamos.

As the country prospered, its citizens enjoyed a rising level of income. In financial terms, per capita income skyrocketed from $300 per year in 1987 to $3,000 in 2012. Gross domestic product, a measure of the country's economic might, increased 330 percent, at an annual rate of more than 12 percent. (In contrast, over the same period, America's GDP increased a mere 60 percent.) The populations of Shanghai and Beijing doubled. By 2012 there were 160 cities boasting more than 1 million inhabitants, 35 cities with over 3 million, and 9 urban conglomerations counting more than 5 million people. Shanghai and its suburbs alone were home to 23 million souls.

But instead of spending freely and buying consumer goods—and as a consequence building domestic demand for their own products— the Chinese saved. The Chinese had always demonstrated a maniacal desire to own property and gold. These savings were held in the form of gold coins and bullion or invested in residential real estate. The government stopped being the principal builder of housing. The private sector took over.

The pace of construction accelerated. Banks flush with cash generated by the country's burgeoning export industry could not make loans quickly enough. Regulation over lending practices was scant, and more often than not overlooked. Speculation was a national pastime. Apartments were purchased as soon as they were built. Investors, many of whom had been farmers or peasants a few years before, flipped properties at a dizzying rate. Values skyrocketed. Simple apartment complexes gave way to larger residential developments, and finally to entire spec cities. By 2012 these "ghost cities," urban conglomerations complete with homes, parks, storefronts, roads, sewage, even fiber-optic cable to deliver phone, television, and Internet services, could be found all over the country. In short, they had everything but living, breathing human beings.

And still the Chinese built.

The scale of the country's growth was so enormous as to be unimaginable.

Easier to admire were China's engineering marvels. There was the free economic zone of Guangzhou and Shenzhen, where hundreds of thirty-story apartment buildings stood as close to one another as soldiers on a parade ground on land that until twenty years before had been rice paddies. There was the Three Gorges Dam, the creation of which had formed a 50-mile lake and which counted itself as the world's largest hydroelectric power plant. (Little was said of the more than 5 million peasants forcibly relocated with little or no compensation.) There was the Bird's Nest Stadium, built for the 2008 Olympic Games in Beijing to herald to one and all the arrival of a glittering, technologically advanced, and thoroughly modern China. And the strangely futuristic Pudong district of Shanghai, with its weird skyscrapers topped by gigantic globes.

China's most recent obsession was the drive to construct a high-speed rail network connecting the nation's largest cities. In one frenzied year, the Chinese succeeded in laying 800 miles of rail between Beijing and Shanghai, reducing travel time from nearly a day to five hours. By 2015 a national high-speed rail system running the length of the eastern seaboard from Guangzhou to Dalian, with spurs to the mammoth and largely forgotten cities of the inland, would be complete.

But as Longfellow declared, there were cracks.

For every benefit of prosperity, there was a cost. Smog and pollution were rampant. Beijing laid claim to having the world's worst air quality. On a recent day, the particulate count had risen to ten times the maximum level deemed safe for human respiration. Visibility routinely dropped to 200 yards, with the sun hidden behind a dense yellow cloud of muck. It was not uncommon for five hundred people to drop dead from respiratory distress in a single day. In Hong Kong, one of the world's most scenic harbors, pollution from coal-fueled power plants to the north cloaked the island in a noxious cloud so thick it was impossible to see Hong Kong Island from Tsim Sha Tsui, only 500 yards across the water.

It was not only air quality that was abysmal. The rivers were fouled. The Yangtze, the country's primary tributary, was a repository of industrial waste, raw sewage, dead animals, and toxic chemicals. To put it more colorfully, the river was a stinky, brown, slow-moving,

3,000-mile-long cesspool. Deforestation in the mountain districts caused landslides and erosion. Strip mining denuded thousands of square miles of land. Toxic runoff poisoned water tables. There were no environmental laws to govern such practices.

And, worst, there was corruption. Power rested in the hands of appointed officials at every level of government. A village mayor's power was absolute. The police chief's power was absolute. A district governor's power was absolute. Each had a fiefdom, and tribute must be paid.

On top of this creaky mountain sat the provincial mayor. Mayors of megalopolises like Chongqing (25 million), Shanghai (27 million), and Beijing (30 million) acted as de facto warlords: all-knowing, all-powerful, all ruthless. The federal government had no sway.

There was no national medical care.

There was no system of social security or pensions for the elderly.

In short, it was every man for himself.

The Chinese people were on their own.

And for the first time in their long, benighted history, they showed signs of no longer tolerating the bad with the good. Too many were being trampled underfoot by the headlong rush to economic primacy. Each day found public demonstrations taking place in one part of the country or another. Some were confined to villages, but others numbered hundreds, if not thousands, of angry souls. A month earlier, 50,000 people had filled the streets of Shenzhen to complain about government corruption. Before that, 25,000 had marched in Beijing. Unrest was no longer the exception but the norm. The first ripples of discontent were rapidly rising into a tsunami.

Yet despite all this, Astor knew that all would be forgiven so long as the nation's economy was thriving.

In China, there was one rule and one rule only: make money and get rich.

There was a knock on the door, and a receptionist entered bearing a tray of mineral water, espresso, and biscotti. Astor added three sugars and knocked back his espresso in a single draft. His heart responded nicely. He sat a little taller. "So we're agreed. Chinese exports are under pressure. If exports keep tanking, so will GDP. If GDP tanks, civil unrest will explode."

"The country is in dire straits," said Goodchild. "Credit is drying up.

Real estate prices have collapsed. Factories are shuttering up and down the coast. The PMI numbers are bogus. So is the GDP. The only way out is to pump up exports, and the only way to do that is to devalue."

Longfellow nodded. "The only way China can contain unrest is to stoke the economy. It goes back to the first rule. Make money. Get rich."

While everyone in the world was certain the Chinese would accede to U.S. demands to increase the value of the yuan, Astor saw things differently. The Chinese would devalue.

If the Central Committee of the Chinese Communist Party wanted to quell unrest, the government must return GDP to more than 11 percent. The only means to boost GDP to that level was to boost exports, and the only way to boost exports was to keep the costs of those exports as low as possible. Ergo, devalue.

QED.

No shit, Sherlock.

And so he'd bet against the yuan.

But there was another reason.

After the meeting, Astor retreated to his private apartment. He checked his watch to make sure it was a reasonable time over there and used a landline to dial a fourteen-digit number. He had waited long enough.

"Hello, Bobby."

"Just what the hell is going on?"

"A momentary disagreement in Beijing."

"A disagreement? Sounds like anything but. Our trade rep said you're continuing your policy of revaluing the yuan to the tune of an additional three percent this year."

"He had to, didn't he?"

"You tell me."

Astor was pleased to hear his friend's calm voice. They had known each other for ten years, dating to an investment conference in Hong Kong where they had both been featured speakers. At the time China was not actively investing abroad, but his friend had a plan to change that. The plan was the China Investment Corporation, the country's first sovereign wealth fund, and it turned out to be a bigger success than anyone could have imagined. Since then, the men had met once or twice a year in New York, Beijing, Hong Kong, and even Paris. They shared opinions about their countries' respective economies and the world at large. Each had been correct more times than not.

"You promised me your country was going to devalue," said Astor.

"And so it will."

"This is America, not China. We're not known for our long attention span. We don't like journeys of a thousand steps. More like ten."

"Things will change soon."

"How soon?"

"Friday at the latest."

"What makes you so sure?"

"Trust me," said Magnus Lee. "I've heard that something dramatic is going to happen."

43

Magnus Lee called his plan Troy.

First because like the Trojan horse of legend, it required gaining the enemy's trust to enter a fortified inner sanctum. And second because of the modern meaning attached to the term, a Trojan horse being a piece of corrupted software, or malware, inserted into a foreign or enemy operating system with the goal of taking control of it or exploiting it for one's own purpose.

Unlike Odysseus, however, Lee did not have to build a giant wooden horse or construct any other elaborate ruse. All that he needed to mount his deception could be found within the walls of the China Investment Corporation.

Troy was CIC's evil twin.

CIC was public. Troy was private.

CIC invested in minority stakes. Troy, through its surrogates, insisted on majority stakes.

CIC did not influence management. Troy wanted complete control.

The two shared one characteristic. They invested across a broad spectrum of industries: energy, consumer products, finance, airlines, automobiles, and, of course, technology.

"The time is upon us."

Magnus Lee looked at each of the five men seated with him at the round table. There was a general from the army and an admiral. Two more came from the highest rank of his country's intelligence apparatus. They were party members all. Lee would not forget them when he joined the Standing Committee. But even these four with their rank and power were not enough for Lee to have embarked upon such a risk-fraught plan. And so there was a fifth man. The man who had given him his blessing all those years ago. The premier.

"And so, gentlemen," said Lee, "we must decide."

For a moment no one spoke. The men stared back. He sensed their eagerness, their ambition, as well as their trepidation.

"How can we go forward after what happened in Washington?" asked the general.

"How can we not?" countered Lee. "Have we come this far only to stop at the first headwind?"

"Once we have executed our plan, there will be nothing they can do," added the admiral, who had always been the most belligerent among them.

"It is surprising that they do not already know," said the man from domestic intelligence.

"Not so," said Lee. "It is often the objects that are closest to you which are the most difficult to see."

"Astor, Hughes, and Gelman may be dead, but that leaves the person or organization who alerted them," said the general. "Palantir."

"I am working on that as we speak," said Lee. "He cannot hide forever. If he had any real power, he would have gone to the president himself. Whoever he is, he is not to be trusted. His actions say as much."

"Do we know if Edward Astor alerted anyone else?"

"For the moment, no," lied Magnus Lee. He did not want the others to know about the final text sent to Robert Astor. He was more than capable of resolving the matter himself. "All is going according to plan."

"Everyone is in place?"

Lee nodded. "They are crossing the border even now."

"So many men. I am worried."

"Do not be," said Lee. "The borders are poorly guarded. Entry was my first concern those many years ago. Through our hard work, we have seen to it that the crossing will be as risk-free as possible."

"The timetable remains the same?" asked the premier.

"As ever," said Lee. "I see no reason to alter it."

"Very good," said the premier. "We have waited in the shadows long enough."

Magnus Lee stood. "All in favor?"

44

J an, it's Alex."

"You've been gone twelve hours. What is it?"

"The French ID'd him. His name is Luc Lambert. We were right about the tat. He served in the French Foreign Legion for nine years, then worked as a mercenary afterward."

"Great news. Pass it on to Bill Barnes."

"I already e-mailed him the particulars. But listen, Jan, there's more." Alex explained about Lambert's participation in the failed Comoros coup and his ties to Executive Outcomes, the private military company that had acted as a recruiter for the effort. "The way I see it, the same group may know why Lambert was in the States."

"Executive Outcomes . . . never heard of them."

"I did some checking. They went out of business after the failed coup. The owner was a guy named James Salt, former SAS officer, decorated soldier, all that. Salt started another business soon afterward called GRAIL."

"Slow down, Alex. I'm not getting all of this."

"G–R–A–I–L. Global Response, Analysis, Intelligence, and Logistics. They don't call themselves a 'private military company' anymore. These days they go by 'security consultants,' and they trawl for contracts providing protection and security services in Iraq and Afghanistan, that kind of thing. Their website lists their address in London. I want to fly over and meet with them."

"When? In a few days?"

"Today. I'll need a jet." McVeigh said nothing. Silence was not the response Alex wanted. "It's our chance to break this thing wide open," she continued. "If GRAIL recruited him, we can find out on whose behalf."

"Those are some big ifs. Client confidentiality is a cornerstone of that business. I doubt they'd say a word without a court order."

"We can go in with our friends at Five," said Alex, referring to MI5, the British domestic security service and sister agency of the FBI. "Have a heart-to-heart. I don't think any firm would want to be identified as being a backer of a shoot and scoot on U.S. soil."

"If that's what we're looking at."

"Even if it's not, the least we're talking is international weapons smuggling and multiple homicide."

"Have Bill call our legate at the embassy over there. He can pursue the matter."

"I think I can make this happen more quickly."

"It's not your decision. I'm not laying on a jet for you to go on a wild-goose chase when we have a network in place that can get us the answers we need."

Alex had rehearsed her arguments in advance. She had initiated the surveillance on Windermere Street. It was her legwork that had led to the discovery of Lambert. She had experience working with Scotland Yard and MI5. By the tone of McVeigh's voice, she knew that none would work.

"I'll convey our concerns that this needs to happen fast," McVeigh went on. "But from here on out, talk to Bill. I know what you're feeling. You think that what happened at Windermere is your fault and that it's up to you to make things right. But I respect the chain of command more. This is Bill's show. End of story. Are we clear?"

Alex didn't answer. McVeigh repeated her question angrily.

"Yes," said Alex. "We're clear."

"Goodbye."

Alex hung up. She called Bill Barnes, and in the interests of honesty and future working relations relayed her conversation with McVeigh. Barnes said much too politely that he'd make the call to their man at the London embassy and promised to keep Alex in the loop. "The second anything happens, I'm on the horn to you. You have my word."

Alex was underwhelmed by his sincerity. She entered the kitchen and made herself a pot of coffee. She knew in advance how Barnes's request would play out. First the legate in London would call his opposite at MI5. A meeting would be scheduled later that afternoon at the earliest, but more probably for Wednesday. MI5 likely would have some connections at GRAIL. A call would be made. A luncheon would be arranged. All very formal. Very by the book. Very British. Thursday would roll around, and then . . .

Alex slammed her mug on the counter, spilling coffee everywhere. Thursday was too late.

45

Team Two landed at Waterloo International Airport on the outskirts of the twin cities of Kitchener-Waterloo, 100 miles east of Toronto, at 8:05 a.m. local time. Kitchener-Waterloo, or KW, as it was more commonly called, was known as a beacon of the Canadian high-tech industry. The cities boasted two universities renowned for their electrical engineering and information technology programs and were home to several multinational corporations, including a world leader in the development and manufacture of smartphones and a smaller but highly respected developer of microchips.

The seven men and women who deplaned walked solemnly across the tarmac and into the customs and immigrations hall. No other planes were due in until noon, and a single officer of the Royal Canadian Immigration Services manned the arrivals booth. The officer smiled and welcomed the visiting Portuguese executives to his country. He assumed they had come to visit their Canadian colleagues at one software enterprise or another. None of the arrivals said anything more than "Good morning" or "Hello." If they appeared too tan and too fit for men and women who made their living banging out software code for hours on end and subsisting on a diet of Red Bull and Skittles, the official did not mention a word. Nor did he remark upon the absence of baggage. It was hardly strange for professionals in the IT industry to make day trips to company headquarters. Besides, he was preoccupied with another matter: a glitch in the airport security surveillance systems.

Ten minutes before the plane landed, the airport's entire video grid had gone dead. Sixteen cameras providing real-time views of every square foot of the 20-acre airport complex went black. Despite ongoing feverish efforts, the airport's technicians could not find the cause. It was as if, one of them said, "someone had unplugged the entire system." Nothing they tried made a whit of difference.

The team boarded a van parked at the curb. They drove twenty minutes through lush countryside, past cows grazing in the sun and farmers rolling hay. Inside the van, a stillness settled on the team. All present knew that the run in was as important as the operation itself. They were on foreign soil. At any moment something could go awry, and their every sense was attuned to the possibility. When the van slowed suddenly, all heads looked to the fore. But it was only an Amish man driving his horse and buggy down the center of the road.

They had numbered thirty when they had gathered in Namibia one month earlier. The continent of Africa was in as much a state of turmoil as ever in its tumultuous history. Machinations of every variety ran high from Morocco to Mozambique, from Togo to Tanzania, and everywhere in between. The source of tensions was not land but what lay under it. If the late eighteenth century had witnessed the last great land grab, the early twenty-first was seeing the great minerals derby. Countries around the globe were scrambling to lock up rights to oil fields, mineral deposits, and precious metals. First and foremost among them was China. Private contractors crowded flights to every major capital. Some were miners, others engineers, and others colonialism's old favorite, mercenaries.

The training site was a 20,000-acre tract of land five hours north of Windhoek. Selection began upon arrival. All thirty men and women underwent an in-depth physical followed by a battery of psychological tests. The final stage was a grueling series of fitness tests culminating in a ten-hour overland march covering 40 miles while carrying an 80-pound pack.

Twenty-four people passed. All were assigned aliases and given accompanying documents. True identities were not to be revealed, on pain of dismissal. The rule went out the window after a week. The rigorous daily training quickly built camaraderie. As the course progressed from timed 10-mile runs, hour-long calisthenics routines, and evolutions on an obstacle course to more sophisticated team-building exercises, the recruits abandoned aliases for real names. There was a good possibility a few would die on the mission. Most preferred to hear their true Christian name before going to their Maker.

They were a diverse lot.

There was Sandy Beaufoy, the former South African commando nicknamed Skinner. There was Berndt from Stockholm, who'd done NATO duty in Afghanistan and had been asked to leave the service when he continued to request repeat tours. There was Peter from Kiev, who'd made a name for himself as a sniper in Grozny. His mates in the Red Army had christened him "the Widow-maker," and at the shooting range he proved that his talents hadn't diminished one iota. There was Rachel, a veteran of the Israeli Defense Force who had grown a bit too angry with the Palestinians. And Brigitta, a former Berlin policewoman who enjoyed knocking heads too much for her pacifistic superiors. There was Miguel from Colombia, and Jacques from France, and Billy, Bobby, and Ian from England. All were of a type. Aggressive, disciplined, organized, sociopathic, and to a large degree fearless. And all possessed a chip on their shoulder the size of Ayers Rock, which made it impossible for them to lead a quiet, ordered, rule-abiding life.

For the job, each would earn a fee of $1 million, $200,000 having been paid upon completion of the selection course and the remaining $800,000 due upon completion of the operation.

And, of course, surviving.

Their destination that morning in Kitchener-Waterloo was the headquarters of Silicon Solutions. Silicon Solutions was not as large a company as Intel or National Semi or Advanced Micro Devices. The company occupied a specialized niche in the telecommunications industry. It was its chip that was used in three-quarters of the world's cellular phones.

The van drove to an enclosed hangar at the rear of the factory grounds. Here the members alighted and strolled up and down the poured concrete floor. Those who so chose smoked cigarettes. Several performed calisthenics to relieve tension and to burn off the excess energy that builds before a hazardous operation. Most, however, simply paced back and forth and made small talk.

After an hour the hangar doors opened and a truck entered. It was not an eighteen-wheeler but a simple delivery truck painted with Silicon Solutions' bright, hopeful logo. The driver lifted the rear door. The cargo compartment was filled floor to ceiling with boxes of finished microchips. One row, however, was not filled, leaving a path for the men and women to enter. One by one, they climbed into the truck and filed to the front of the cargo area, where a bench had been installed for their comfort. Once inside, they rearranged the boxes so that the compartment appeared full and their presence was suitably camouflaged.

At eleven o'clock the truck pulled out of the hangar and left company grounds. It required two hours' driving to reach the border crossing in Buffalo, where the truck was waved through after a cursory check of its manifest. The driver had been making the run for fifteen years and knew the inspector personally. They traded comments about last night's baseball game between the Toronto Blue Jays and the New York Yankees. To the inspector's chagrin, the Yankees had won on a ninth-inning home run blast by A-Rod. The inspector tore off his copy of the manifest without casting so much as a look and handed the remaining sheets back to the driver. The exchange was over, start to finish, in forty-five seconds.

Forty-five seconds after that, the Silicon Solutions truck crossed the border into the Empire State.

Team Two was on American soil.

46

The madness began minutes after Astor ended his call with Magnus Lee.

"Bobby, it's Jay Cantrell."

Jay Cantrell ran the prime direct division at another of Comstock's lenders. He was Texas royalty, scion of an oil baron who owned half of Houston. Cantrell had lived in New York for thirty years, but his twang was still as strong as the day he arrived.

"I'm guessing this isn't a social call."

"Wish it was. Just wanted to give you a heads-up that if the rates hold, we're looking at a margin call of one hundred fifty million this afternoon."

"I'm aware of that."

"I know you are," said Cantrell. "And I know we don't have to worry about Comstock one little bit."

"You don't, Jay. The dollar's going to rally versus the yuan."

Cantrell cleared his throat, and when he spoke his twang had lost some of that down-home sweetness. "That's not what I meant."

"I know what you meant, Jay."

"And?"

"I'll talk to you after the close."

"Now hold on a sec there, Bobby," said Cantrell, one good ole boy to another. "A buck fifty's a nice pile of change. I'd like to be able to give my boys a heads-up that everything's hunky-dory down your way."

"Couldn't be better, Jay. And I thank you for asking."

"So I can tell 'em—"

"You can tell 'em that I'll speak with you after the close."

Astor hung up. His eyes had been glued to the monitor for the length of the conversation, checking the slightest fluctuations in the position. Every tick up or down of a hundredth of a cent translated into a gain or loss of millions of dollars. With every tick, he felt a vein in his temple throb.

A second later his phone rang again. "Sam Bloch on line one," said his assistant.

Bloch was another lender, one of the two people at the clambake on Sunday night whom Astor had counted as a friend. Bloch was old-school. They had always kept one rule between them: no bullshit.

"Yeah, Sam."

"You fucked up, Bobby."

"Give me some time."

"You've got six hours till the close. And twenty-four after that to make good."

"What are we out to you?"

"Couple hundred. You got it?"

"Let me check my pockets."

"No one's in the mood to laugh today, buddy. This is real. No sign the rates are softening. I saw that press conference last night, too. You're not the only one sweating this. What the hell were you thinking?"

Astor grimaced. Win big or lose big, it was the same question. Only the tone differed. Admiration or condemnation. Right now, he was damned if he had an answer. "I'll talk to you after the close, Sam."

"I can't be your rabbi on this one. Rules are rules. Lots of people are watching. You know how it is."

"Yeah, I know how it is. And Sam . . . thanks." Astor hung up.

The pain in his temple increased.

The phone rang again. "Who is it now?" he asked his assistant.

"Adam Weinstein from the *Times*."

Weinstein wrote the "Deal of the Day" column for the paper. He was Wall Street's Hedda Hopper, and just about as warm and fuzzy, with a reputation for breaking the big story. Astor couldn't trust himself to dish out the requisite bullshit this morning. Telling a newspaper the truth was like handing the hangman a rope. Astor had no illusions. Weinstein was an executioner. Astor knew just the person to shut him down. "Give him to Marv."

Another light was blinking. Astor ignored it. Instead, he called Sully and asked him to bring the car around to the front of the building. He placed one last call. "Get me Septimus Reventlow."

"One second."

The call went through a moment later. "Hello, Bobby. Why aren't you calling on your private number?"

"Phone issues. Hello, Septimus. Have a minute?"

"I should ask you the same question after the reception I received yesterday. I don't have to ask why you're calling."

"Markets move up and down."

"Should I feel reassured, or should I be demanding to withdraw my family's money from your fund?"

"Time will tell. We're standing behind the position."

"And the Chinese announcement?"

"Posturing ahead of the election this Friday."

"Can one election change so much?"

"Absolutely. The new members elected to the Standing Committee will signal which direction the country is heading in."

"And you think they will backtrack on their promises to your government?"

"They don't have a choice. It's hard enough to govern a country of a billion and a half people when the economy is booming. Right now the economy's in the tank. The Chinese prize stability above all else. You do the math."

"Tell me, Bobby, are they still building too many motorcycles?"

Astor chuckled. During their first meeting, three months earlier, he'd told Reventlow a story that illustrated the economic quandary the Chinese found themselves in. There was a government-owned motorcycle factory in Dalian that turned out two hundred beautiful bikes a day. The motorcycles were picture-perfect knockoffs of Harley-Davidsons but at half the price, and for years they'd sold like hotcakes to countries such as Malaysia, Mexico, and Brazil. But as the yuan grew stronger and the wages of the skilled Chinese workers who assembled them also increased, the motorcycles grew more and more expensive. Clients in expanding nations were price-sensitive. Sales faltered. Soon the factory was turning out two hundred bikes a day but selling only one hundred fifty. The unsold bikes quickly piled up in the freight yard. The government was faced with a dilemma. It could either cut production and fire 30 percent of the workers or continue manufacturing motorcycles that no one wanted to buy. The first alternative would result in the layoff of a thousand workers, a steep decline in the local economy, and certain unrest. The second alternative would result in contented employees, growing losses for the company, and eventual bankruptcy. The Chinese, being ever nimble and ever frightened at calling a spade a spade, chose a third course. It continued making the motorcycles, then created a new company to purchase the motorcycles, take them apart, and sell the metal as scrap. Problem solved. Or at least put off to another day.

To Astor's mind, that day was today.

"Yes, Septimus," he replied. "I believe they are."

"Then there is hope," said Septimus Reventlow. "What can I do for you?"

"Show your faith."

"Let's see how the market closes. I need to talk to my family members before I make a decision. Shall we continue this discussion tomorrow?"

Astor knew better than to push. A commitment from Reventlow to invest the $300 million he'd promised would go a long way toward meeting a margin call and restoring the marketplace's faith in the firm. "That will be fine."

Astor hung up and started toward the door, only to walk into Marv Shank.

"You're not leaving, Bobby. Not today."

"Marv, please."

"I know that your dad is important to you, but Comstock is more important."

"There's nothing I can do to fix the position," said Astor. "Unless you want me to start liquidating the fund right now."

"Our guys need to know you're here. A captain doesn't abandon a sinking ship."

"This isn't the *Titanic*."

"Right now it feels like it." Shank shut the door. "Here's how it is, Bobby. I'm forty-one. Everything I've earned is in that fund. I don't have a cattle ranch in Wyoming or an apartment building in Chelsea or a freakin' French masterpiece, and if I did I wouldn't cart the thing around Manhattan as if I were carrying a six-pack of Bud Light. I've got fifteen years of blood, sweat, and tears with you. Fifteen years working seven to seven inside this glass tower. I know it's my fault that I forgot to grab a wife on the way up. It's always just been about work for me. You're my friend, Bobby. Pretty much my only one. I'm asking you. Stay."

Astor put his hands on Shank's shoulders. "Here's how it is, Marv. You're my friend, too. But you're not my father. And about all the other stuff—the ranch, the apartment—pretty much everything I have is pledged to the firm. We go under, I go under. You can write your ticket at any other firm on the street. Me, I'm fish food."

Shank didn't budge. "That isn't good enough. There are people you can call. Chips you can cash in."

"I'll see what I can do if and when the time comes. Now come on, out of the way."

Still Shank didn't move. "What about your father's estate?"

The pounding in Astor's head intensified. "Excuse me?"

"Your old man was loaded. He sold his company for a billion ten years back, and that's not counting how much he earned before. You're his only heir, right? I mean, your mom's dead. You don't have any brothers or sisters. Who else was he going to leave it to? Call his attorneys. Ask them to read the will immediately. They can pledge something. I know a banker who'll front you the dough."

Calm down, Astor told himself. *He's just scared. He has no idea what he's saying.* "You do?"

"Yeah."

Astor looked away, hoping his anger would recede. When he spoke, it was in a whisper. "Don't ever tell me what I can or can't do. I'm leaving now. And Marv . . . don't ever bring up my father again."

47

Michael Grillo did not like to be kept waiting. The time was ten past nine. He stood beneath the awning of a deli at the corner of 61st and Third Avenue, enjoying the shade. He had a rule about this kind of thing: never smoke more than three cigarettes while waiting for a contact. Staying in one place too long put you in jeopardy of being spotted. Just as dangerous, it signaled desperation to your contact. Grillo dropped cigarette number two and ground it beneath his heel.

He gazed up the block to the corner of 62nd Street, his eyes focusing on the entry to a steel pier and glass office building. His contact worked on the tenth floor of the building, behind a door bearing the words *Johnson, Higby, and Mather, Attorneys at Law*. His contact was not a lawyer. The names on the door were a front. His contact was a twenty-five-year man with the Central Intelligence Agency's Directorate of Operations, and the offices of Johnson, Higby, and Mather housed an Agency collections office engaged in the analysis of foreign intelligence.

Grillo checked his watch for the third time in ten minutes. He felt for his Shermans. Instead, he took out his phone and looked at his e-mail. Nothing new had arrived since his contact at the credit bureau had put him onto Edward Astor's scent an hour before.

"Astor has a credit score of seven sixty-one," the contact had reported.

"Won't do him much good now," said Grillo. "Just tell me what cards he carried."

"Visa, MasterCard, American Express, the usual. Pays off his balance every month."

"His salary is listed at five million a year. He can afford it. Just forward me the card numbers."

After receiving the information, Grillo phoned the credit card companies, specifically the individuals who headed the companies' anti-fraud departments. As with the nation's phone carriers, he had spent considerable time and effort cultivating contacts. Unauthorized sharing of customer records was a felonious offense punishable by hefty fines and prison time. His approaches were made in person and with discretion. On occasion he'd been forced to call on a person's patriotism, meaning that he'd misrepresented himself as an agent for a United States government law enforcement agency. If his requests were denied he had alternate means at his disposal, namely a crafty, cunning, and completely amoral band of hackers based in Shanghai. But they were a last resort, and not to be trusted.

Copies of Edward Astor's charges began landing in Grillo's secure servers soon afterward. By noon he would possess a comprehensive record of all charges the late CEO of the New York Stock Exchange had made over the past ninety days. Grillo was interested not in what he had purchased but in studying the location of his charges to track Astor's movements.

Grillo's phone rumbled in his pocket. He looked at the caller ID and answered. "That was quick."

"You told me to impress you," said the female executive at the nation's largest phone carrier. "Check your mail. Just sent over his last three months of calls, including correspondents' names and addresses."

"I'm impressed."

"Prove it."

Grillo brought up the message on his screen as they spoke. It was apparent that Edward Astor had spent an enormous amount of time on the phone. Page after page was filled with numbers and the names of the individuals or corporations to whom the numbers were registered. He scrolled to the last entries, detailing calls made to and from Edward Astor's phone on Friday, Saturday, and Sunday. He recognized a few names as belonging to well-known corporate supremos. His eye fixed immediately on a call placed to Edward Astor on Friday morning at 9:18. Duration, seventeen seconds. The caller had no name and no address. To Grillo's eye, that meant the call had probably been made from a throwaway, a cell phone purchased from any corner vendor with a prepaid number of minutes. It might even be from Palantir.

"I don't suppose the usual will do," he said.

"I don't suppose it will."

"Double, then."

"Deal."

Grillo hung up. He accessed his banking app and transferred

$10,000 from his work fund to the woman's numbered account at a discreet Dutch bank in the Cayman Islands. He sent a copy to a secure address he'd set up for Bobby Astor.

Grillo fished out his third Sherman. As he flicked the Zippo and brought the flame toward the cigarette, he saw his contact emerge from the building. He replaced the unlit cigarette in its box, entered the deli, and headed to the refrigerated foods section in the rear. A minute later a portly, bald African-American dressed in khakis, button-down shirt, and club tie sidled up next to him.

"America's greatest hope," said Grillo.

"Fuckin' A," said Jeb Washburn. "Bring it."

"There is such a thing as dry cleaning."

"I appreciate that coming from a man who's wearing my annual salary. Those Ferragamos you got on?"

"You noticed."

"I noticed they run six bills in the Bloomingdale's shoe department."

"That's why I left our government's service."

Washburn picked up a package of sliced ham and pretended to look for the sell-by date. "You better be careful, or you're not going to be around to enjoy those fancy Eyetalian loafers, Mr. Grill-O. You're barking up some very dangerous trees."

"What can you tell me?"

Washburn put down the ham. "About Palantir? A little and that's already too much. Let's get out of here. I don't like being penned in like this."

Grillo and Washburn left the deli and headed down 61st. Foot traffic was light, and the steady stream of cars passing enabled them to speak without fear of being overheard.

"Like I said," Washburn began, "I only know a little, and that's all I want to know. Don't suppose you want to tell me what this is about?"

Grillo shook his head.

"Fair enough," said Washburn. "All right then, here it is. Palantir's some kind of far-out software platform that collects information from about a trillion sources off the Internet and analyzes it for possible threat scenarios."

"Sounds like a straightforward data-collection tool."

"Nothing straightforward about it. It started as one of the crazy-assed projects financed by DARPA, but at some point the government lost control of it."

DARPA. The Defense Advanced Research Projects Agency. "Did DARPA cut the funding?"

"On the contrary. They wanted to double-down. It was better than anything they expected."

"Better?"

"More powerful. It was too good at what it did."

"And that is?"

"Predict future events. A real-life Eight Ball. You remember that thing you shake and wait for the answer?" Washburn stopped and pulled Grillo into a doorway. "It was Afghanistan that did it. Palantir's mandate was to upload and integrate all our intel over there and see if it could tell us what was going to happen. We're talking everything from combat after-action reports to local police chiefs' threat assessments, provincial reconstruction team reports, Agency intel—everything. Palantir just vacuumed everything up."

"And?"

"It worked," said Washburn. "That was the problem."

"I don't follow."

"It started predicting when and where attacks would take place, the probability of Afghan troops rebelling against us, transport choke points. It was too much."

Grillo had served a ten-month tour in the AfPak theater as a company commander with the Fifth Marines. Hellmand Province. It had been a bloody summer. "We could have used something like that."

"Don't you see, man? Palantir wasn't just looking at today and tomorrow. It was looking at next month, next year—*and it told us we were going to lose.* That did not go over well at the Pentagon. No siree, Bob. The four-stars over in Virginia were not keen on a top-secret, multimillion-dollar experimental software platform that predicted that the United States of America didn't have an ice cube's chance in hell of winning that conflict. They had serious blood and treasure invested."

"But you said DARPA wanted to double-down."

"Sure, DARPA did. They're a bunch of mad scientists. Not a soldier in the lot. It was the men with the scrambled eggs on their covers who wanted to shut it down."

"What happened?"

"That was the end. Goodbye, Palantir. Whoever created Palantir disappeared. Went off the grid."

"And that's it? No one's heard from him since?"

"You expecting him to make contact after we dumped him?" Washburn gave him a look. "Sounds like you've been talking to him more recently than we have."

Grillo pulled a grimace. It meant "No comment."

Washburn gave him a thump on the shoulder. "I'm outta here. Any of my bosses see me talking to a rich-ass boy like yourself, they'll think I'm pulling an Aldrich Ames."

"In this case, I'd say it's the opposite. You're helping the good guys."

"Good guys?" said Washburn. "Who are they?"

"You know who they are."

"Maybe I do. You're one of 'em, Grill-O. That's the only reason I'm here."

The two men reached the corner of Fifth Avenue and stopped before crossing, allowing the pedestrians to stream around them.

"Look, Jeb, my client would like to thank you for your services."

"No way," said Washburn in horror. "I do this for God and country."

"Maybe I'll buy you a pair of shoes. Ferragamos."

"Buy my wife a pair. Size seven. Don't ask me how I know."

"You got it, Jeb."

Washburn turned and looked Grillo in the eye. "You still smokin' those nasty cigarettes?"

"Shermans? Yeah. Want one?"

"Hell, no. Just wondering why a smart, suave motherfucker like you wants to kill himself." Washburn laughed. "Cigarettes ain't bad enough, now you go asking about Palantir. Tell you something for free, Grill-O. Your days are numbered."

48

The CH-53 Super Stallion carrying the eight members of Team Three approached the Tamondo oil rig from the south and touched down on the landing platform at 8:20 local time. The rig was a hive of activity. The night crew had four hours remaining on their shift, and the roustabouts and roughnecks could be seen scrambling among the rig's catwalks, tending to the giant drill that turned twenty-four hours a day, bringing heavy crude to the surface. Nearly half of the sixty-five-man shift worked in confined environs deep inside the rig, where temperatures routinely hit 100 degrees and the mechanical noise was deafening. Only a few people noted the helicopter's arrival, and they were quick to turn their heads and quicker to forget that the bird had ever arrived. Word had spread about a group of visitors inbound from Mexico. Word said to keep your eyes closed and your mouth shut. None of the crew had a problem with that. Roughnecks knew how to follow orders.

The members of Team Three jumped onto the deck. A supervisor in a hard hat and sunglasses led them to a private dining room adjacent to the chow hall. A regal spread awaited. Pancakes, eggs, bacon, sausage, fresh fruit, baked goods, and a variety of juices filled the buffet table. The mercenaries loaded their plates and ate quickly and without comment. They had been given instructions, too. Eat. Get in. Get out. And shut the hell up.

Thirty minutes after touching down, they returned to the landing platform and boarded the refueled helicopter. At two minutes past nine the helicopter took off and banked north toward the coast of the United States of America. At no point had anyone checked their travel documents, though technically they had arrived from a foreign country. Nor had anyone made an official notation of their presence. For all intents and purposes, Team Three had never set foot on the Tamondo rig.

Two hours later, the CH-53 landed at the Noble Energy compound in Houma, Louisiana. Team Three hit the tarmac and walked to a waiting van. Again, no travel documents were checked. No customs officials were present. What was the point? To watching eyes, the team was just another crew happy to be back on dry land after their two-week stint at sea.

Team Three was on American soil.

49

Where we headed?" asked John Sullivan.

"Cherry Hill." Settling into the backseat, Astor caught Sullivan's look of surprise. "You heard me. And step on it."

"Yes, sir."

Sullivan navigated north to Delancey Street and crossed the East River on the Williamsburg Bridge before merging onto the Brooklyn Queens Expressway. At 10:15, traffic was light, and the vehicle made good time driving north, reaching I-495 in just fifteen minutes.

"Got your wheatgrass if you're interested," said Sullivan when the ride had smoothed.

"Screw my wheatgrass."

Astor stared out the window glumly. How quickly they deserted the cause. At the first signs of adversity, they all fled like rats from a sinking ship. Marv had likened the firm to the *Titanic*. If he was right, the rats were the smart ones, and Astor was the fool rushing around the deck mustering the band to play one last waltz. He felt a blackness nipping at his heels. It wasn't fear. It was doubt, which was more ill-defined and thus more dangerous.

On an early trip to Paris with Alex, he had visited the sculpture garden decorated with many larger-than-life artworks by Rodin. One black marble piece showed a powerful, confident man poised in reflection, his countenance gripped by a terrible uncertainty. Gripped by doubt. It wasn't audacity that killed a trader. It was doubt. Doubt led to indecision, and only the decisive survived on the Street.

Astor played back the conversation with Longfellow and Goodchild. Their reasoning was sound. China was posturing. Some sort of political gamesmanship was occurring, but in the end Astor was right. And Magnus Lee had confirmed it.

Screw doubt.

"I know it," said Astor aloud, banging his fist on the armrest.

"Everything okay, boss?"

"What?" Astor shook himself back to the real world. Leaning forward, he clutched his driver's shoulder and gave it a friendly squeeze. "Yeah, Sully. Never better."

Cherry Hill sat on top of a broad grassy knoll overlooking the expanse of Oyster Bay. It was an old Victorian pile built in the 1880s, when the Roosevelt family had lived nearby on Sagamore Hill. Over the years each owner had added on a room or a terrace or a porch until it resembled a sprawling hotel more than a home. The Astors had purchased it in 1950 for the then astounding sum of $175,000. Following in the tradition of their predecessors, they'd expanded the kitchen, built a sauna on the second floor, and added a gymnasium on the third for Edward, then a boy.

A paved road wound up the slope and emerged from an orchard onto an immense lawn that collared the estate and made Cherry Hill look like a frosted white decoration atop a wedding cake.

Sullivan spotted the striped tape stretched across the front door first. "We're late," he said. "The feds have already been by to have a look."

Astor opened the car door before the Audi came to a halt. He was out and striding across the gravel forecourt as Sullivan hurried to join him.

"Tampering with evidence is a felony. Be careful what you touch."

Astor stopped at the top of the front stairs. "It's my house. I have every right to go in. Besides, who you going to tell?"

Sullivan reached his side. "Have it your way. But let me take a look first. We don't want any surprises."

Astor noted that the alarm system was disarmed and the door locked. He fished in his pocket for his old key. It worked like a charm. "You're the only one who knows I'm here," he said, ducking under the tape as he pushed the door open. "Be my guest."

Sullivan passed beneath the tape and entered the foyer, his pistol held in front of him. "Wait here. I'm going to do a quick walk-through."

"Knock yourself out," said Astor.

Sullivan padded down the stairs five minutes later. "All yours. Looks like the feds took a look around and left everything here. I'd count on them being back anytime. They'll be taking another look now that Penelope Evans is dead, too."

From his vantage point in the orchard, the warrior monk fashioned his plan.

A car was parked in the gravel drive, a large silver SUV. The front door of the house stood open, a band of yellow-and-black tape strung across the entry. The stocky white-haired man with the florid cheeks paced back and forth on the porch. Astor must be inside.

Kill him, his brother had said.

The warrior monk revered family above all. He would not disappoint him.

Bobby Astor walked into the house and time stood still. Ten years had passed since he'd last set foot inside. The occasion had been Thanksgiving or Christmas. It had been a happy time. Katie was five or six. Alex's career with the Bureau was starting to hum. Comstock was doing well, and his father had just sold his own firm to one of the big boys for an ungodly sum.

It was a time before their falling-out.

A time before Astor had confronted his father about the events of his childhood.

The black belt.

Three words, and they conjured up an immediate and unsettling terror that after thirty years had lost none of its ability to paralyze him.

Astor pushed away the words, pretending he did not hear them. *Pretending that nothing had happened.* He turned a circle on the parquet floor, studying the vaulted two-story entryway. It was more a minstrel's gallery than a family foyer. His eye ran up the staircase, past the stodgy oil portraits of his father and his grandfather, Edward and Frederick Astor, respectively. Why was it ever the dream of first-generation immigrants to emulate the immigrants who had come before them?

Of course Astor wasn't his family's real name. He had discovered his true lineage when he was thirteen and home on break from prep school. Having pilfered two of his father's Cohibas, he and a buddy were searching for matches to light them. The first place to look was his father's desk. There, stashed away in his top drawer, was a stiff, yellowing envelope marked *Private* in archaic, curling script. Astor was a born snoop. He could have asked for no better invitation. He opened the envelope at once. It contained his grandfather's immigration papers, naming him not Frederick Emile Astor but Feodor Itzhak Yastrovic of Lvov, Poland. Stunned, Astor replaced the document and fled from the room. Bobby Astor was not an itinerant Polish Jew. He was an American blueblood born on the Upper East Side of Manhattan, educated at the Horace Mann School, and confirmed at All Saints Episcopal Church in Oyster Bay, New York. He never looked at the envelope again.

Astor tucked away the memory. There were other secrets within these walls, other lies that best remained concealed.

The black belt.

Astor climbed the stairs slowly. He held the piece of blue stationery with the word *Cassandra99* in his hand. The stationery came from one place and one place only. The top right drawer of his father's desk. He did not stop to admire his father's portrait. Nor did he marvel at the Swarovski crystal chandelier made a century earlier for his Imperial Majesty, Charles I, the last Emperor of Austria. His pace quickened with each step, so that when he reached the first-floor landing and started down the hall, he was moving briskly and passed his father's bedroom without peeking in.

Later, he told himself. There would be time after he searched the office.

Astor stopped in his tracks.

There was no later.

Edward Astor was dead. He would never have the chance to explain. He would never have an opportunity to reconcile with his only son. The time for that was gone. Astor would have to reconcile for both of them. He was done running.

He retraced his steps until he stood at the doorway to the bedroom and peered inside. The room was as he remembered it: the vast bed with the white bedspread, the maple furniture that might have served a founding father, the windows looking over the orchard and the expanse of Oyster Bay.

He stepped inside the room like a man mounting the gallows.

The black belt.

The punishments always took place here in his parents' bedroom, and in the early evening. There was a strict protocol about them, a procedure that never varied. It began with a summons, his father's operatic baritone trumpeting his name from upstairs.

Master Robert Frederick Astor.

Always the full name. Always uttered without a trace of malice or anger.

Come.

Astor had only vague memories of the actual crimes. Once he had played with his father's double-edged razor blades and cut himself. When asked about the gash on his finger, he had lied and said he caught his hand in the medicine cabinet. The evidence was discovered lurking at the bottom of his parents' toilet, where he'd tried valiantly to flush it away. Astor was mischievous by nature. Fibbing came easily. Even then he had courted trouble. At some point, boyish dares hardened into adolescent transgressions. The sentences were never unjust.

With dread he would climb the stairs. (It was years before he'd learned to camouflage fear with arrogance, bravado, or confrontation.) Trembling, he waited at the bedroom door, palms sweating, stomach sick with anxiety.

Enter.

There stood his father, Edward Everett Astor, Wall Street supremo, chairman of the school board, pillar of society, a man of untarnished rectitude. He was not a tall man, but broad across the shoulders and barrel-chested. He wore his hair slicked back with pomade. At day's end, a few strands hung loose and he had the rough, capable air of an accomplished seaman. He had removed his jacket and tie and stood with his white shirt unbuttoned. In his hand he gripped his black crocodile belt, folded double, and in the manner of Bligh on the *Bounty*, he tapped it threateningly on his thigh.

How do you plead, Master Astor?

Guilty, sir.

Astor had learned early on never to proffer excuses. Excuses were an extension of the crime and merited further beating.

The punishment is ten lashes.

Astor advanced to the bed. He lowered his trousers, then his underwear, and bent over, hands scrubbed, trimmed fingernails clutching the bedspread. A final indignity demanded that he himself signal the punishment.

Please begin, sir.

The strokes were administered crisply and with brute force. The punishment was meted out in full.

One.

Astor heard the snap of leather against flesh and jolted in his shoes. He was breathing hard, the paper in his hand crumpled into a ball. He looked around the room, half expecting to find his father still there, belt in hand. He met only his reflection in the mirror. He stared at himself, remarking on how much son resembled father.

Astor sat down on the bed. Carefully he flattened out the stationery. He felt lighter, somehow freed of a burden. The past had no claim on him. From here on out, his actions were his own. He was not assisting his father out of guilt or fear or some long-repressed need to repent for sins either real or imagined. He was helping him for another reason.

Because it was the right thing to do.

The monk circled the home to the rear. When he was sure the older man could not see him, he dashed across the lawn and mounted a short flight of stairs to the raised back porch. He peered in a window. The kitchen was as large as his childhood home. The door was locked. So were the three windows nearest him. He needed only three seconds to climb the drainpipe and hop onto the roof that skirted half the second floor. He ran to the wall and pushed his body against it. He paused, finding his center, then peeked into the window to his right. The room inside held two single beds. The door to the interior hall was closed. He tried the window and found it locked, too. The next window was locked as well. A wraparound terrace met the corner of the roof. He hopped the railing and landed on the decking. He waited again, allowing his heart to slow, his senses to come to life. He had no idea where in the house Astor might be, or if he was alone. The Audi had already been parked in front when he had arrived. It had become necessary to use other means to ascertain Astor's whereabouts and intentions since he had destroyed his phone.

The monk peered inside the window. Astor was seated on the bed inside, his back facing him. The monk continued to watch, hoping to catch a glimpse of a second person if there was one. He placed a hand against the wall, feeling for vibrations within the home. All was quiet.

This close he could sense Astor's energy. The man was strong, aggressive. A fighter, but too arrogant and headstrong for his own good. Still, it was a powerful energy, and the monk would find pleasure in defeating a formidable adversary. He looked more closely into the room, drawn by Astor's spirit. It was then that he observed the mirror and noted the dark triangle in the lower quadrant that was his face and hair.

A moment later Astor saw it, too, and jumped to his feet.

50

Astor broke out of his reverie, his attention caught by a flash in the mirror. Warily he walked to the window behind him. He looked outside and saw nothing. And yet he sensed something. A presence. He opened the door to the terrace, stepped outside, and walked the length of the deck, unsure what he was looking for. Below, in the gravel drive, Sully stood by the car, taking a call.

"Sully, you see anything out here?"

John Sullivan lowered the phone. "Like what?"

Astor looked to either direction. It had been a bird, he decided. Something that had landed on the railing and flown away. "Forget it."

"Find anything?"

"Not yet."

"Don't take too long. I don't like this."

Astor reentered the bedroom, taking in everything with an investigator's eye. It was immaculate and showed no sign of a rushed departure. He guessed that Penelope Evans had stayed behind when his father traveled to Washington, D.C., and that she had cleaned up after him.

He walked into the bathroom. It, too, was neat and orderly. Shaving cream, aftershave, and deodorant were missing from the medicine cabinet. It had been an overnight trip. On the top shelf were prescriptions for Lipitor and Viagra. Astor smiled. Dad was getting some.

Astor entered the closet. One wall was taken up by suits. Dark gray, light gray, gray pinstripes, gray Prince de Galles, summer weight, winter weight . . . but gray. He turned, expecting to find the opposite wall similarly racked with clothing. Instead he found himself looking at dozens of framed photographs, laminated articles, and mementos running from floor to ceiling. It was the trophy wall Astor had never given himself. There were photos of Bobby as a preteen, playing baseball and football, and older, skiing in Colorado and the Alps, and of Bobby in high school at the beach in Martha's Vineyard and the Hamptons.

There were plenty of more recent photographs, too, nearly all of him arm-in-arm with Alex or playing with Katie.

And then there were the articles, taken from numerous newspapers and magazines, chronicling his rise to the top. Astor smiled, seeing the front-page piece from the *Wall Street Journal* with the stipple-pen portrait that made him look like a leering zealot. There was even a framed invitation from his first clambake, which his father had neither attended nor acknowledged.

Everything about *him*.

Astor felt his throat tighten. Confusion and comprehension battled. He stared at his life in pictures, and he knew, maybe for the first time, that his father had loved him.

Astor turned away. It was too much. A distraction. Emotion merited no place today.

A dresser stood at the far end of the closet. He opened the top drawer. A polished wooden box with the word *Beretta* engraved on a corner sat on the jumble of socks. The name jarred him back to reality. He set the box on the dresser and flipped open the lid. A stainless steel pistol lay cradled on a bed of black velvet inside. It was a 9mm with a tapered snout and a crosshatched grip. He freed the pistol. It was heavier than he expected, and he noted that the magazine was in and the safety was on. Sully had taught him more than he ever wanted to know about firearms. He racked the slide. A copper-nosed round lay in the chamber.

Ready to fire.

Astor regarded the pistol. His father had been a fire-breathing liberal and no friend of the NRA. Imagining him with a gun was like picturing Mother Teresa brandishing an M-16. There was only one reason for him to possess any kind of weapon. Edward Astor was frightened for his life.

Astor slipped the pistol into his belt. If his father had needed a weapon, so did he. And Penelope Evans? Nothing could have protected her against an assailant so stealthy he could get within an inch of her in broad daylight without her knowing.

Astor left the bedroom. If he were to find answers, he would find them in his father's office.

The monk leaped the railing, retreated across the roof, and slid down the drainpipe to the back porch. A check around the corner confirmed that the driver remained next to the car. Astor called out from the second floor, asking if the driver had seen anything. The driver responded that he had not. The monk heard Astor cross the terrace, then retrace his steps and reenter the bedroom. Content in his knowledge that Astor was on the second floor and confident that he had not been seen, the monk used a penknife to jimmy a kitchen window and climbed inside the house. A block of cooking knives sat on the counter. He selected a short, slim instrument, ideal for jabbing. Despite its size, the knife had heft. He swung it back and forth, gaining a feel for it. He ran his tongue delicately across the blade and tasted blood. The knife would do.

He left the kitchen and climbed the back stairs. He emerged in a dark, narrow corridor. To his left, the stairs continued up another flight. He walked to the door and gripped the knob firmly. He turned it slowly, feeling the metal components brush against one another, begging to squeak. The knob reached its apex and he opened the door a sliver. He was standing at the rear corner of a landing running around the perimeter of the two-story foyer. Diagonally across the open foyer, the door to the bedroom where the monk had seen Astor stood ajar. The monk placed a hand on the floor. A vibration reached his fingers. One footstep. Another. Slow. Measured. The sound of a man searching intently, without hurry. He saw no shadows in the bedroom. Instinct told him to wait.

The tempo of the footsteps increased. A shadow approached the open doorway. Astor emerged from the bedroom and disappeared down the hall. The monk sprang from his hiding place and glided across the landing, using Astor's footsteps to conceal his own. He gained the hall and peered around the corner in time to see Astor enter a room at its far end.

The monk paused. He heard a chair scoot across the floor. There was the sound of papers being examined, objects being moved from one place to another, then a soft but definite thud, indicating that Astor had sat down.

The monk advanced down the corridor with patience. He held the knife in front of him, his wrist pronated so the blade faced up, in the killing position.

The noises from within the room grew louder. The clack of a keyboard told him that Astor was at a computer. The monk slowed, allowing his victim a moment to be drawn deeper into his research. There was no risk of his stopping Older Brother's plan. Anything Astor learned in the next few minutes, he would keep to himself forever.

The monk peered around the doorway. Astor was seated in front of the computer, engrossed in his research. The monk entered the office. He walked with excruciating calm, closing the distance to his victim. He noted something change on the computer screen. There was the sound of a dial tone. A black box opened.

"Who are you?" asked a man's voice.

The warrior monk froze.

He made the decision not to attack but to listen.

Astor reached a hand inside the top drawer of his father's desk. The sepia envelope was where it had been twenty-seven years ago. He removed it gingerly and slipped Feodor Itzhak Yastrovic's immigration papers onto the desk. His past no longer frightened him. What was in a name, anyway? Astor or Yastrovic? Episcopalian or Jew? The ease with which his family slipped between the two showed how little weight a label carried. If his name stood for anything, it was honesty, integrity, and success. If Comstock failed, he would tarnish all those words.

Astor replaced the document in the envelope and set it on the desk, laying the pistol on top. Next to the computer rested the stationery and the fountain pen Penelope Evans had used to write *Cassandra99*. A Hermès scarf lay draped over a chair nearby. On the table next to it stood a glass vase filled with a summer bouquet, the flowers still fresh. Yet something was missing. There hadn't always been a vase full of flowers on the table. Astor remembered there being a pair of crystal decanters filled with amber liquid in that place. He thought back to his father's bedroom. He hadn't seen any liquor there either, yet his father had always kept something close by for a late-night drink.

She'd done it, he realized. She'd broken the old bastard of his habit. Edward Astor had died a teetotaler.

Astor hit Return and the screen lit up. He pulled down the bar for Recent Items. The first application listed was Skype, the Internet phone service. He clicked on the sky-blue icon to launch the program. Astor selected History from the menu. Edward Astor and Penelope Evans had called a single person repeatedly over the past several days.

Cassandra99

Astor opened the correspondent's details. Snatching the fountain pen, he noted the web address: Cassandra99@donetsk.ru.

Ru for Russia.

The last call had been placed on Saturday at 2 p.m.

Astor moved the cursor to the Connect icon and clicked. A window opened at the center of the monitor, but it was black. No one was visible. A second smaller window displayed his own face, captured by the camera embedded in the computer frame. He looked drawn and tired.

"Who are you?" asked a male voice.

Friend or foe? Astor had no time to deliberate. "Robert Astor. Who are you?"

The man ignored the question. "What do you want?"

"I'm sure you know."

"I know that you're Edward Astor's son. That doesn't explain your presence at his home."

"My father texted me a message before he was killed. I believe it had something to do with the reason for his meeting with Gelman and Hughes that night."

"What did he text you?"

"I need to know who you are first."

"I'm the person who alerted your father to the problem in the first place."

"Look," said Astor, "I'm tired of talking in circles. If you're not going to tell me your name, at least tell me what this is all about."

But again the man refused to answer. "What did your father text you?"

"One word. Palantir. I told Penelope Evans, and she seemed to know what I was talking about. Now she's dead."

"So you spoke with Penelope?"

"Briefly. She wouldn't tell me anything over the phone. She said that *they* were listening and that *they* knew everything I did."

"Did you believe her?"

"Not at first."

"And now?"

"Yes."

"What changed your mind?"

"When I learned that she had been working with my father, I contacted her to see if we might meet. She told me to come to her house. She asked me to hurry. The only way anyone could have known I was going there was to have hacked my phone and used it as a microphone to listen in on my conversation. I didn't know that was possible until last night."

"What convinced you?"

Astor explained about the doctored voice mail luring him to his garage and his near fall into the elevator shaft. "If they could do that, they could easily use my phone as a mike."

"They're getting desperate. An incursion like that will leave tracks a mile long. It must be happening soon."

White noise mottled the screen.

"Is that them?" asked Astor.

"They're trying to listen even now." The voice had lost its natural timbre. It sounded robotic, the words strangely modulated.

"What's happening soon?" demanded Astor. "Who are they? Why did they kill my father?" He had too many questions, and Cassandra99 offered too few answers.

"They killed your father because he knew. I'd venture to say the same about Penelope Evans. I told her to leave. I'm not responsible for her death, too."

"She was packing a suitcase. She was waiting to speak with me."

"I told her to leave this alone. I'm telling you the same. It's too big for you. Do as I say. Leave the premises now and forget anything your father told you."

"I can't do that."

"I won't be responsible for you, too."

"I'm a big boy," said Astor. "I can look after myself. Tell me why Penelope Evans was looking into Silicon Solutions and Britium." Astor listed the names of the other companies whose reports he'd discovered at Evans's home.

"It's too late, Mr. Astor. No one will listen to you anyway."

"But you know?"

"That's my job."

"Who killed my father? What are they planning?"

It was then that Astor saw the reflection in the monitor.

A man was standing three feet behind him.

"Go home, Mr. Astor," the voice on the computer went on. "You were brave to check on Miss Evans and braver to come to your father's house after the attempt on your life. If you want to live, leave now, go back to work, and forget about this matter entirely."

The man in the reflection came closer. It was him, Astor knew. It was the phantom who had killed Penelope Evans. Astor willed himself not to look over his shoulder. To look was to die.

"You can't just let it happen," he said. "I'm his son. I deserve to know."

"Oh, you'll know soon enough. We all will."

"But—"

A door slammed inside the house. Footsteps pounded up the stairs, echoing through the foyer.

"Bobby!" shouted a female voice. "You in there? It's me."

51

Astor spun in the chair, raising an arm in an effort to protect himself. "Alex," he shouted, "run!"

A sharp pain radiated from his forearm to his shoulder. His eyes rested on the man standing a few feet away. He was slim and menacing, a dark forelock falling across almond eyes colored a robin's-egg blue. He wore black pants and a tan T-shirt that revealed arms corded with muscle. The blue eyes were not on Astor but on the knife protruding from his forearm.

"Bobby!"

The man darted a glance over his shoulder. Astor ignored the knife and lunged for the pistol. Something struck him in the solar plexus. A blow delivered so quickly he had not seen it. A phantom's blow. The pistol dropped to the floor. Astor could not breathe. He could not move.

The phantom advanced on him, hands and arms extended in a classic martial arts pose.

Footsteps bounded across the landing.

Astor tensed for the blow.

And then the man was gone, running from the room with a speed Astor had never before witnessed or thought possible.

"Freeze!" came Alex's voice.

Gunfire. One shot. Two.

Astor still could not move. He sat as if entombed, listening.

"Stop!" shouted Alex. "FBI!"

Another shot.

Alex, he wanted to cry out. *Careful.*

The warrior monk ran down the hall. He could hear the woman approaching. He did not need to feel her energy to know she was a force and dangerous. Her voice told him these things and more. He turned the corner to the landing and she was there, 10 feet away, running at him with a pistol in her hand.

"Freeze!" she called.

The monk ran straight ahead. Toward the railing. Toward the expanse of the two-story entry. He heard the gunfire, felt something strike his body, spinning him slightly. Still he kept running. He leapt as if hurdling. His foot landed squarely on the railing, and he propelled himself across the void, his head brushing the chandelier's crystal prisms. There was no question of making the stairs. He focused on the balustrade, bringing up his hands, lunging for the width of wood. He caught it, his chest slamming into the railing. A rib cracked, but he held on. A breath to find his center, and he flung himself over the balustrade and rushed down the steps, leaping three at a time.

The old man was rushing to the house, struggling to pull a gun from his jacket. The monk leveled him with a forearm to the chest, sending the man sprawling onto his back. The monk didn't slow. Eyes focused ahead, he charted a path through the orchard and down the hill. He felt a tear in his side, his muscles fighting him. He had been shot. The discomfort was considerable, but he had known worse.

A bullet whizzed past his head. A second clipped a branch nearby.

The monk ran faster.

And then he was out of range, dashing down the slope.

He reached the car minutes later.

"Brother," he said, when his heart had calmed and he had driven a safe distance from the home. "I found him."

"Who?"

"The cause of our problems."

Only then did the monk lift his shirt to study the wound. He saw a bloody track across his side where the bullet had grazed him. Another millimeter and it would have entered his chest and killed him. The wound hurt, but no worse than many other pains he had suffered. He would live.

Alex knelt beside Astor, regarding the knife in his arm. "How is it?"

Astor could speak again. "Bad."

Alex took the arm gingerly in her hands. "Impaled on the bone. Guess you move pretty fast."

"I saw him behind me in the monitor."

Alex removed a handkerchief from her pocket and unfolded it. "Hey," she said. "Can you see Sully from there?"

"Where?" Astor turned his head, squinting at the bright light. Alex grasped his arm and yanked the blade free. He cried out as she clamped a handkerchief on top of the wound. "Just breathe," she said.

Astor sank down into his chair, the pain reduced to a manageable level.

Alex settled down onto the couch. "I shot the son of a bitch and it didn't slow him a step."

"You're sure you got him?"

"He was six feet away. I got him."

John Sullivan limped into the room. "Prick knocked me down," he said, resting against the doorway. "I got off a couple shots, but I never had a chance. Friggin' jackrabbit." And then he saw Astor's arm. "What happened to you?"

"I got to be his pincushion."

Alex held the knife by her fingernails. "He's a very lucky boy."

"I thought you said fast."

"Fast and lucky." Alex set the knife on the desk. "We just might find out who he was."

"It's him," said Astor. "From Penelope Evans's house."

"You think?" asked Sullivan.

"I'm sure of it."

"He wasn't inside earlier. I'd swear it."

"Don't sweat it, Sully." Astor wanted to say more, but his throat was tight and he was shaken. "Give us a minute."

Sully nodded and stepped outside.

Astor picked up the gun off the floor.

"And whose is that?" asked Alex.

"Dad's. I found it in his bedroom."

Alex gently pushed the muzzle toward the ground. "You want to give it to me."

Astor handed his ex-wife the gun. "Why are you here?" he asked.

"Forget why I'm here. I want to know why you crossed police tape to come inside here and who it was that jumped over this railing like Superman leaping a building in a single bound."

"He's a killer, actually," said Astor.

"Excuse me?"

"I'm pretty sure he's the man who killed Penelope Evans."

"I'm sorry," said Alex. "But you're losing me. Who is Penelope Evans?"

"My father's assistant at the Exchange. She was murdered yesterday in her home in Greenwich. It was all over the news."

"I've been busy with a few things."

Drawing a breath, Astor related the actions he'd taken since receiving the text from his father two nights before, beginning with his visit to the New York Stock Exchange and the theft of his father's agenda and culminating with the certainty that the man he had seen standing close behind him was Penelope Evans's killer.

"And Sully? He just let you traipse off without calling the police?"

"Leave Sully out of it."

"He's a cop. He knows better."

"He *was* a cop. He works for me now. He was looking out for my best interests."

Alex's eyes narrowed. She knew about Bobby's interests. She didn't like them one bit.

"The killer got a knife into her heart before she even knew he was there."

"Maybe more lucky than fast." Alex put a hand on his leg, and her touch sent a jolt of electricity through him. She smiled, and for a moment he felt as if everything were okay between them. He knew it was her training. He was the victim. She was there to provide succor. As quickly, the smile faded. Her game face returned.

"My ex, the private eye. You must be doing something right if the bad guys send a contract man to kill you. Why didn't you call me when you got the text in the first place?"

"You'd just been at the house. You said it wasn't your case. I didn't know what *Palantir* meant or if it would lead anywhere."

Alex sat straighter, her shoulders tightening. "You knew it meant something yesterday afternoon when you found Penelope Evans dead in her house. It ends now. The amateur gumshoeing. The son tracking down his father's killer. All that bullshit. You're going straight to Janet McVeigh and tell her everything you just told me." She paused, appraising her former husband, trying to sense whether he was hiding something. With Bobby, there was always another angle. "And if you leave anything out—I mean *anything*—I'm going to hold you responsible for whatever it is that's going on here."

Astor nodded. He'd been honest so far . . . to a point. He saw no reason for her or anyone else to know about Mike Grillo. "I understand."

Alex shot him her "for real" glance, and Astor nodded solemnly. She relaxed. "You actually fell into your elevator shaft?"

Astor nodded. "Caught the cable. When the elevator came up, I let myself down onto its roof and managed to open the emergency hatch."

"And if you hadn't? Or if that knife had missed your arm and gone into your chest? Your daughter loses her father for no good reason."

"I'm close to figuring out who killed Dad, Gelman, and Hughes. They were visiting the president for a reason, Alex. They'd discovered something. Some kind of plot. Something about an attack. Whoever is behind it was able to take control of their car, just like those people hijacked my elevator. They hear everything. They listen." Astor stopped short, realizing he was issuing the same warning that Penelope Evans had given him.

"Who are 'they'? What kind of attack? Where? When?"

"I don't know."

"He's certainly closer than your colleagues," said the mechanized voice.

Alex shifted on the couch, peering around the office. "Who said that?"

"I did," came the voice from the computer. "I believe Mr. Astor deserves some credit. After all, he found me before the vaunted Federal Bureau of Incompetence did."

"He stole evidence that would have led them to the same place."

"But Ms. Forza, your colleagues were here yesterday."

Alex stood and approached the computer. "Who are you and how do you know my name?"

"He contacted Dad in the first place," said Astor, coming to her side. "He warned him."

"About what?"

"He hasn't said." Astor beckoned to the monitor. "If you won't tell me, tell her. She can take care of herself. I can promise you that."

"My relationship with the government ended years ago. Messily, I'm afraid. I've had enough of leading a horse to water and getting kicked in the groin for my efforts."

"Whatever may have happened in the past, I can promise the Bureau's full cooperation in this matter," said Alex.

"I don't want the Bureau's full cooperation," said the unidentified voice. "Otherwise I would have contacted it myself. The Bureau isn't safe."

"What do you mean it isn't safe?" asked Alex.

"It has been penetrated."

"By a mole? Is that the information Edward Astor was trying to give the president?"

"Not by a spy per se. But it's been penetrated nonetheless. Weren't you listening to your husband when he told you that someone had been listening in on him and Penelope Evans?"

"You're saying they're listening to the FBI, too?"

"Why not?"

Alex looked at Astor. "Exactly who's listening in on whom? How do you know this isn't the asshole causing all the problems?"

"Alex, please. Calm down." He turned back toward the computer. "You know why my father was taking Gelman and Hughes to visit the president. What's stopping you from telling us?"

"Nothing is stopping me. As a matter of fact, I've decided to take matters into my own hands. You see, I've finally realized that the only way I'm going to get any respect is if I prove to the government that I'm right."

"So you're going to help us," said Astor.

"On the contrary. I'm not going to do a thing."

"Why should we care what you say anyway?" demanded Alex.

"I'd have thought that was obvious."

"What? That you're a hacker—some kind of creep with a bone to pick with the government? Take a number."

"Because I'm the one you're looking for. I'm—"

White noise filled the screen. Cassandra99's words were garbled and unintelligible.

"What did you say?" asked Alex.

The screen cleared. The audio was as crisp as ever.

"I am Palantir."

52

For a few minutes neither of them spoke. Too much had happened. Each needed time to make sense of it. Alex went to the bathroom and returned with warm towels to wrap Bobby's wound. She told him he needed to get to a hospital, and he said he felt all right for the time being. She gave him her look, and he promised he would go immediately.

Seized by a need to do something—anything—Astor stood and sorted through the papers on his father's desk. He was looking for something similar to what he'd found at Penelope Evans's home. There were letters from member firms, invitations to galas, memos from his father's office. All appeared related to Edward Astor's day-to-day responsibilities, both public and private. If his father had been concerned about unwanted attention the investigation might bring, it made sense that he'd conducted his research at Penelope Evans's home. She was his cover.

"Don't take anything," said Alex.

"I'm just looking," said Astor. "Besides, it's my house."

"It's your father's house. You have no legal right to be here. Technically, you're trespassing."

Astor stopped and faced her. "So?" he said. "You want to tell me what you're doing here?"

"I need the jet. The G4. For work. I didn't think you'd say yes on the phone."

"You guys have jets."

"Officially, I'm supposed to be taking a couple days off. Getting over Malloy and the others."

"But you can't?"

Alex shook her head. She almost smiled. "Of course not."

"So what gives?"

"It has to do with what went down on Windermere Street yesterday. Something bad is about to happen. I can't go into it."

"Like what 'something bad'?" The question was not driven by idle curiosity. The kinds of bad things Alex dealt with might adversely affect the market, and hence his funds. The fact that she was requesting a jet did little to settle his nerves.

"I'm not at liberty to say."

"Can you tell me where you're going?"

"London."

"That's twenty grand, fuel and pilot there and back. If you hustle, you can pack and still be able to make a commercial flight out of JFK."

"Too tight. I can't chance missing it." Alex brushed hair off her forehead. "Twenty grand isn't very much to prevent an attack that might take a lot of lives."

"Now you're scaring me."

"That's the idea."

"You still didn't answer me."

"I don't have to. I'm asking a favor. Just tell me yes or no and let's cut the horse trading."

"You're serious? An attack . . . where?"

Alex ran a finger over her teeth, tapping them, shaking her head. "Sometimes I think you're in the wrong job. They could have used you down at Gitmo. You could talk the nuclear codes out of the president. Where's the attack? Here. New York. Or somewhere close by. At least, that's my guess."

"Soon?"

Alex nodded.

"You stop to think it could have something to do with my dad? The guy—Palantir—said something about an attack, too. He talked about their being desperate, whoever they are."

"This isn't financial. We're talking a real physical assault."

"Something took control of the car my father was in and made it appear as if it were a threat to the White House. If that isn't physical, I don't know what is."

"You can't be sure of that."

"I am. The same people screwed with my elevator."

"I'm not willing to make that connection. Your elevator could have malfunctioned on its own. A woman was killed in midtown just last year when an elevator went haywire."

"This isn't a coincidence."

"Bobby, the guys I'm looking for aren't desperate. They're well organized and well financed and well armed. I've seen nothing that suggests these two incidents are tied together."

"What are we talking then, another 9/11? A nuke? I don't know what kind of stuff you guys come up against every day."

"I'm thinking Mumbai."

"That's not good." Astor knew all about the attack. Alex had called it a shoot and scoot and had been one of the team sent to Mumbai to work with the Indian police to analyze the event, with a view to formulating plans to improve their response. Astor also knew that she had been part of a task force to train the NYPD in how to deal with such an emergency if it took place in Manhattan. "If this thing is going down in New York, why are you so keen on taking the jet to London?"

"Jesus, Bobby, stop hounding me. I have to go to London. That's all there is to it. Tell me yes or no."

Astor sat on the edge of the desk. "Yesterday when Sully told me about the shooting out on Long Island, there was a second there when I didn't know who had been killed. I thought about you—about us."

"There is no us, Bobby."

"That was your decision, not mine."

"That's bullshit and you know it," Alex flared before catching herself. "We hadn't been getting along for years. Don't act like it was all my fault."

"You stopped talking. You stopped wanting to be near me. You stopped . . . well, you stopped everything."

"Yes, I did, Bobby. You know why? 'Cause you were half in the bag every time I was near you. You weren't exactly a romantic yourself. When was the last time you tried to make an effort?"

"From my exile in the guest bedroom? Getting into the bedroom was like breaking into Alcatraz."

"I don't sleep with drunks," Alex said.

The word hit Astor like a hammer. She'd never called him that before. He rose and walked to the far side of the room. "I was never a drunk."

"Maybe not. But it got bad all the same."

"It did," he said. "And I'm sorry."

Alex met his gaze. For once, she didn't challenge him. Something in her face softened.

"Really?"

"I wonder if I'd done something differently . . ."

"It wasn't just the drinking. It was your business. It never ended. The first thing you did when you got up and the last thing you did before you went to bed was check the markets. Last couple of years, you even slept with a phone under your pillow so you could look at your positions if you woke up. That's not a job, Bobby. That's an addiction."

"Were you always this harsh?"

"Were you always this sentimental?"

Astor shrugged. "Something about nearly being killed, I guess. I do know that I'm ready to give it another try."

"That's not going to happen."

"You meet someone?"

"No." Alex shook her head, angry at letting herself be drawn into this kind of conversation. "It's none of your business. Leave it alone."

Astor came closer. It was difficult not to touch her. "We had something good."

"This is not the time or the place."

"I'm not going to get another chance. Not if you go to London." He saw her eyes light up as she realized that she would get the jet. "Just think about it."

Alex cocked her head. "That's your best shot?"

"I had more planned, but I can't have you thinking I'm too sappy." He took a breath, and when he looked at her, he was looking at the same headstrong, beautiful girl he'd met all those years ago. "I'm still the man you married."

"I liked that man."

"Later," said Astor. "After all this."

Alex didn't answer. Not at once. She held his gaze longer than he had imagined, hitting him with her inquisitor's eyes. "Maybe," she said.

That was as good as he was likely to get, today or any other day. He had a chance. It was all he could ask for.

He looked at his ex-wife, her eyes steadfast, jaw raised, all of her battle-ready. Her dedication to her job was the quality he admired most, and the one he found most maddening. In his world of masters of the universe and big swinging dicks and London whales, not one of his competitors had balls half the size of hers. He couldn't fathom what she'd gone through the past two days, losing three colleagues in a gun battle—one of whom was a close friend—not to mention being shot at herself at close range. Yet here she was, driving out to Oyster Bay, not resting, not quitting, but going strong, maybe even gathering steam.

"You're sure about the jet?" she asked.

"I'll call the FBO now and get everything set up."

Alex smiled tentatively. She gently pulled his hand away from his arm and studied the cut. "That's deep. Emergency room. Pronto."

"You care," he said sarcastically.

"I ought to cuff you and take you downtown. That'd show you how much I care. Now come on. Let's get out of here. I don't want some of my people showing up and finding you in here."

"And finding you?"

"Yes, Bobby, and finding me."

"When are you back?"

"I hope it'll be a day trip."

"Good thing you came to ask."

"Guess it worked out for both of us." Alex walked out of the office, pausing at the doorway to wait for him. "By the way, what's up with your phone? I couldn't reach you."

"I thought you said you came out here because you thought I'd say no on the phone."

"I lied."

"It was hacked. I'm going to buy a new one when I get back to the city. I'll call you with the number."

"Do that. I need to be able to reach you."

Alex ducked into the corridor.

Astor took a last look at the desk. It was then that he observed a splotch of red under a corner of the leather desk pad. Quickly he freed the piece of paper. It was a set of driving directions from MapQuest. The address was in Reston, Virginia. Something clicked. He'd recently read something about Reston. He scanned the header and saw that the directions had been printed on Saturday morning. He looked more closely, and his heart jumped a beat.

Britium Technologies.

It was the company mentioned in the article Penelope Evans had been reading prior to her death.

"Coming?"

Astor folded up the paper and stuffed it into his pants pocket. He caught up to Alex on the landing. "Let's go."

Alex said yes, and they walked down the stairs together. They paused to say their goodbyes on the front porch.

"From here," she said, "you're going to get your arm taken care of, then go to Jan McVeigh and tell her everything you've learned."

"Are you going to say you found me here?"

"I'm going to say you phoned me when you realized that you were in over your head and that this was a matter for the federal authorities."

"I'm a civilian. I just say 'the cops.'"

"Say whatever you want. Just get your butt down there. Ask for protection. Sully's a little past his sell-by date."

"I trust him."

"I trust him, too, but whoever wants you dead got past him going in and going out." Alex ran her fingers along the lapel of his jacket. "They've missed you twice. Three's a charm."

Astor lowered his head to kiss her, but she saw it coming a mile away and ducked her head.

"I said maybe."

53

Magnus Lee stood on the balcony of his private office, hands on his hips like a conquering field marshal, marveling at the Eiffel Tower. The original structure had been built more than a century earlier, yet its design remained contemporary and its engineering continued to astound. It was a masterpiece.

Lee looked down upon the Champ de Mars, the wide grass field that led from the Invalides to the Eiffel Tower. Apartments built in the Haussmann style ran for four city blocks on either side. The detail was exact, down to the mansard roofs blue with verdigris, shutters that actually closed, and molded cast iron railings on every balcony. Inside, the apartments boasted hardwood floors, Poggenpohl kitchens, and Sonichi express elevators that opened to the foyers.

Magnus Lee knew this because it was he who had built the apartments and the Eiffel Tower. Like all government officials, he had a second career, one dedicated to making as much money as humanly possible. His salary at the China Investment Corporation was the equivalent of $5,000 a year. His salary running a real estate development company ran to $5 million. Or rather, it had until recently.

Still, it was not his sudden drop in salary that troubled him. It was something else. Magnus Lee had not used his own money to fund his building projects. If he had, he would not be in such a bind. He had used money entrusted to him.

Lee had built other developments, too. The developments had names like St. Mark's, Belgravia, and even St. Tropez. Like Paris, they resembled the architecture of their namesakes. Of late, however, the market for single-family homes and apartments had not been faring well. In fact, it had been in the shitter.

Lee returned to his desk and fell into his chair, contemplating his fate.

At that moment there was a commotion in the outer office. Miss May's high voice could be heard uttering supplications. Lee's door swung open, and a frail old man shuffled into his office. He was not wearing a Western business suit but traditional silk trousers and a high-collared jacket and soft shoes. He was bald and stooped, and his skin had the texture of rice paper.

"Elder Chen," said Lee, catapulting to his feet. "As always, a great pleasure."

"Do not get up on my account," said the old man.

"Come in. Come in. Your presence brightens my day."

Elder Chen, whose full name was Chen Ka-Ting and whose age Lee could only guess at, stopped on a dime. "Does it need brightening?" he asked sternly. Before Lee could respond, Chen broke into an avuncular grin. "It is enjoyable for a worthless old man to tease such a famous financial genius."

Lee smiled, too. "You are too kind. I am certainly no genius."

"Yes, yes," said Elder Chen, patting Lee on the arm. "Why else would the wise men in Beijing allow you to invest the country's funds? We were wise to elect you Big Mountain and entrust you with the society's funds."

Magnus Lee's rise in finance was matched only by his ascendance in the Purple Dragon, Beijing's most revered triad. Triads were secret societies founded in the last century to help support and protect communities from the tyrannies and injustices of government. They provided financing to local businessmen, helped ensure that police or petty government officials did not interfere with their activities, and engaged in other, less proper businesses, such as prostitution, drug trafficking, and extortion. In the end, a triad was a business, and like all businesses, it was required to earn a profit.

The head man in a triad was called Mountain Master. The member in charge of finances was Big Mountain.

Lee's cheeks ached from smiling. The purpose of the visit was clear. No one had ever accused Elder Chen of being subtle. "Thank you, Elder Chen. May I offer you tea—or coffee, perhaps?"

"Coffee, yuck! Never! A Western calamity. Tea. Red Lip, if by chance you happen to have some in your cupboard. My liver is troubling me."

"Of course." Lee wrapped an arm around his visitor and guided him to a chair. "But first you must sit."

The rumor was that Elder Chen was suffering from cancer and ate only two-turtle soup. When you looked at him, it was hard to determine whether he was healthy or ill. He weighed little more than 100 pounds and his walk was so unsteady that a child's whisper might blow him over.

Lee called in Miss May and relayed the order for tea. Elder Chen insisted on taking her hand and stroking it for far too long, all the while complimenting her on her beauty. Miss May was a smart, tireless worker, but she possessed the face of a pug. Poor girl, thought Magnus Lee. It wasn't two-turtle soup that kept the old devil alive. It was the mighty blue pill.

Miss May freed herself and returned with hot tea. The two men drank in silence. Abruptly, Elder Chen set down his cup and stood. "It is a lovely day. Let us walk."

Lee glanced out the window. The sky was a dense cloud of putrid yellow, no trace of blue to be seen. Emissions from the region's factories lay trapped beneath a strong inversion layer, blanketing the city with a noxious sulfur monoxide cloud. "A fine idea. It is always nice to get outside."

The two men left the building and walked along the Champ de Mars. Elder Chen's bodyguards followed ten steps behind.

"Your work is marvelous," said Chen, waving an arm in admiration at the buildings on either side of them. "I feel like I really am in Paris."

"You are. Paris, Beijing prefecture. I officially adopted the name. Buyers appreciate authenticity." Lee stooped to pick a flower. "See? French tulips imported from Grasse, in the South of France."

They walked in silence until they reached the base of the Eiffel Tower. Lee's model was one-quarter the size of the original, approximately 100 feet tall. This morning the smog was so thick he was unable to see the French tricolor waving from the tower's summit.

"Stunning," said Chen.

"We even built a restaurant on the mezzanine level. Three stars. It is called the Jules Verne."

"After the famous chef?" inquired Elder Chen.

"Ah," said Magnus Lee, wagging a finger at the old man. "It is you who is clever, Elder Chen."

"Ayee-yah," said Elder Chen. "Has something died?" Chen gazed down upon the River Seine. The riverbed was dry except for a trickle of raw sewage snaking down its center. The smell provoked an immedi-

ate desire to vomit. Lee noticed that the bodyguards had put handker-
chiefs to their noses.

"A problem with the water authority," he explained. "A flaw in the
local pumping station."

Chen turned and started back toward the office. "It is all very
impressive, Big Mountain. I am pleased. I'm certain that I may
pass along news to the society that you have sold all the apartments."

"Not yet."

"Ninety percent?"

"Soon, Elder Chen."

"How many?"

"Two."

"Two percent?"

"Two units. A bit less than one percent."

Elder Chen showed no reaction. "And the society's investment?"

"It is safe, as you can see."

Chen turned, his ugly face contorted with anger. "I see buildings
with no occupants. Streets without automobiles. A river that smells
like beetle dung. I see a city with no citizens. What do you see?"

"All will change when I get to Beijing and assume the vice premier-
ship."

"If you get to Beijing."

"The leaders know my policies. They know I advocate for a more
competitive yuan. That is why they have summoned me."

"And those who wish to keep our currency strong?"

"They are capitalist puppets and will be exposed as such."

"But the American influence is considerable. They wish us to buy
their products and to develop a middle class. They have many allies in
the party."

"In due time we shall follow their example. But not now. Not when
factories are closing and people are without work and food. Not
when our banks are facing mountainous debts from unsold buildings. Not when people save their last pennies out of fear for the
future."

"You speak wisely, but—"

"As soon as we act, the economy will improve. Our exports will
become cheaper. Our businesses will thrive. People will not be afraid
to spend. Trust me, Elder Chen."

"I trust you. You have always been like a son to me. Others I cannot vouch for. They are worried about the society's money."

"Silly."

"One billion dollars is not silly."

"In time we will have four times that amount. I have taken measures."

Elder Chen had been a criminal for too long to miss the conspiracy in Lee's words. "Oh?"

"Something will happen soon that will give our country all the power it needs to resist the Americans."

Chen smiled a toothless smile. "May I inquire what?"

"Patience, Elder Chen. I can tell you one thing. When it does happen, you will not miss it. Nor will anyone in the world. Especially our American friends."

"I will relay your message. In the meantime, may I tell them that you will at least be able to repay their investment in your company?"

"You may assure them that their money is safe."

The men had reached Chen's Rolls-Royce. A bodyguard held a door open. Miss May sat in the back seat, eyes wide. Lee could see that she was trembling. Elder Chen slid into the car with the ease of a man half his age and placed himself close to the young woman. He looked at Lee.

"One billion dollars, Vice Premier Lee. Shall I tell them Monday?"

54

Michael Grillo was making progress.

It was four-thirty in the afternoon and Grillo sat at a back table in BLT Steak at 57th and Park. Finishing his coffee, he cast an eye about the room. The lighting was dim, and a few diners were seated here and there. Jeb Washburn's words about Palantir's being a software program that accurately forecast future events stuck with him. Predictability was out. He would return to Balthazar when the job was over and done. Until then, he would alter his routine to make it unrecognizable—and unpredictable—to him, to Palantir, and to anyone else who might be watching. Satisfied that none of the remaining patrons was paying him any mind, he returned to his work. He was safe . . . for the moment.

Every investigation required a premise, a hypothesis around which you marshaled your evidence and built your case. Grillo's premise was that the person who called himself Palantir had phoned Edward Astor on Friday morning. And further, that Astor had left the Exchange to take possession of some type of evidence—either written or other—from Palantir pertaining to his investigation.

And now the evidence.

Grillo examined the agenda in reverse chronology, beginning the past Friday and going back week by week. He pinned July 8, the Monday after the Independence Day weekend, as the date their investigation had begun. Prior to that date, Edward Astor met with Penelope Evans no more than three times a week. After the eighth, the two met at least seven times a week. Something was up.

Working on his smartphone, Grillo drew up the file he had obtained from his contact at the country's largest phone carrier, listing all calls Edward Astor had placed and received over the past ninety days. He downloaded the file into an app he had developed himself that used a simple algorithm to analyze which numbers were called most and least frequently. In this instance, he was interested in a number that appeared for the first and perhaps only time on July 5 or 6.

The app kicked out three numbers. Two were for mobile phones in the New York area and the third for a landline in Miami. Grillo was disappointed to learn that none matched the number that had called Edward Astor last Friday morning.

The Miami number was registered to a medical products corporation in Key Biscayne. The call had lasted nine minutes. Grillo checked the firm's website, confirming that it did in fact exist, then phoned the number. He was surprised when the firm's CEO answered. Grillo represented himself as an FBI agent and established that the executive had met Astor at a business function and had called to learn the listing requirements for his firm. Grillo struck the number from his list.

The New York numbers belonged to a private individual named Anthony Vanzetti, with an address at 910 Fifth Avenue, and an entity titled Melsen Inc., billing address at 46th Street and Ninth Avenue. Grillo placed 922 Fifth somewhere near 73rd Street, which put it among some of the most expensive real estate in the city. He noted that the call had lasted three minutes. A Google search showed that Vanzetti was a big-shot i-banker who had been appointed on July 1 to the NYSE's board of directors. While it was possible that Vanzetti might have launched Edward Astor on his investigation, it was more likely that he had called Astor simply to get acquainted. He certainly didn't fit Jeb Washburn's description of Palantir as a brilliant scientist who had done work for DARPA.

Grillo graded Vanzetti "doubtful."

The last number appeared suspect from the outset. He found no mention of Melsen Inc. on the Net. Moreover, the billing address belonged to a UPS store, indicating the use of a rented mailbox. The call had lasted only twenty seconds, so short that it might have been a wrong number. Grillo dialed the number. A woman answered.

"Hi, this is Kristy."

"Hello, this is John Stewart from the New York Stock Exchange. I'm calling in reference to Edward Astor."

"Who?"

"Edward Astor. The former chief executive of the Exchange."

"I think you have the wrong number. I don't know anyone by that name."

"I apologize, but our records indicate that someone from your company phoned Mr. Astor on July sixth of this year."

"That's impossible," said the woman. "I only got this phone a week ago. Who is this again?"

"Never mind. The mistake is ours. Goodbye."

Grillo wrote himself a memo to call his contact at the phone company and obtain more information about Melsen Inc. While carriers recycled numbers as a matter of necessity, it was common practice for them to wait at least six months before reassigning them.

Grillo slid back his chair and loosened his necktie. There were only two diners remaining, and the staff was preparing the tables for the evening rush. The room was too quiet. He needed noise to think. He preferred the constant activity and chatter that infused Balthazar with such brio.

The next order of business was to examine Astor's credit card bills. Astor had used his Visa card most frequently. Grillo focused on the past Friday. There were charges to Yellow Cab for $10, Starbucks at Broadway and 42nd for $12, Bobby Van's Steakhouse for $65, and Barnes and Noble on Fifth for $200. A $10 cab ride from the Stock Exchange would have taken him no more than 2 miles in any direction. The $12 at Starbucks was most likely for two people; likewise the meal at Bobby Van's.

Grillo put together a picture of Astor leaving the Exchange at 9:30 a.m., taking a cab to meet Palantir at a Starbucks in Times Square, then returning to the Exchange to brief Penelope Evans over lunch at Bobby Van's. It was something, but not enough.

The final charge of the day was for $225 at a restaurant in Oyster Bay. Astor appeared to have laid low all Saturday, making only one credit card purchase: a round-trip air ticket to Washington, D.C., departing the following morning.

Grillo called his contact at the credit card company and requested that he drill down on Astor's Friday charges and supply the exact times the card had been used. He put down his phone and fished in his pocket for a cigarette. He had a feeling about the phone registered to Melsen Inc. The short duration of the call combined with the use of the UPS dropbox and his inability to find the number's previous owner appealed to his instinct for larceny. He called his contact at the phone company.

"One more thing," he said.

"Isn't it always?"

Grillo read off the number and requested all relevant information about the owner, the mode of payment, the date of first service, and, most important, a list of all calls made to and from the number in the past three months.

"That's going to cost extra."

"I already doubled the price. This one's on the house."

"No, babe, it isn't."

Grillo caught a note of anxiety in the woman's voice. "Something you want to tell me?"

Her answer was a whisper. "You're not the only one interested in this number. Some of the big boys were snooping around before you."

"The Bureau?"

"Bigger. The NSA put a priority warrant on this number a year ago."

Jeb Washburn had mentioned that Palantir had worked with the National Security Agency. It was standard practice for the agency to monitor calls made by contractors and employees. A priority warrant was something else, reserved for a select list of high-value targets.

"You win," he said. "Two grand do the trick?"

"Only because I like you."

"I need it in an hour."

"Already on the way, babe. And Mike," she added, "don't call back."

Grillo hung up the phone. A minute later the message was in his secure e-mail and he was perusing a long list of phone numbers, names, and addresses.

He drank the rest of his coffee and breathed a sigh of relief.

Now they were getting somewhere.

55

"What the hell happened to you?"

As always, Marv Shank seemed to intuit the exact moment of Astor's arrival. He stood by reception and flanked Astor as he walked down the corridor.

"Don't ask."

Shank grabbed his arm to stop his progress. "I'm asking."

Astor wrenched himself free. "I saw the close. What have we got?"

Shank clenched his jaw, his eyes looking this way and that, anger oozing from every sweaty inch of him. "Lawyers in conference room one," he managed after a painful second. "Brad Zarek's in conference room two and he's about to have a coronary."

"Did he bring his mitt?"

"What mitt?"

"Forget it. What about Reventlow?"

"In your office."

"And?"

"He's smiling like the cat who swallowed the canary."

Astor stopped short of the end of the corridor and stepped into the CFO's office. "Give me the lowdown."

Comstock's chief financial officer was a blond, whippet-thin woman named Mandy Price who had forsaken a husband and family for a career and running marathons. A chart on her wall showed that so far she'd run eight races that year, and it was still July. "Total exposure is six hundred million."

"Cash on hand?"

"Fifty."

"So we're five-fifty short."

"That's correct. There's three billion left in the fund—all long equities—but most positions are negative or treading water. If you sell, you'll take a hit."

"How bad?"

"On top of the two billion you lost on the yuan contracts and the five-fifty to meet the margin requirements? Does it matter?"

Astor did the math in his head. He'd be down to two billion and change out of five in the space of one afternoon. A loss of over 50 percent. He smiled. "Thanks for the news. You had me worried for a second."

Astor left the office and crossed the trading floor. He made a point not to look at anyone. From the corner of his eye, he noted Goodchild and Longfellow flying out of their chairs, already mouthing explanations. He raised a hand in their direction. His expression said the rest. *Don't even think of getting any closer.* The two Brits wisely retreated to the safety of the trading desk.

Astor slowed before entering his office. After leaving Cherry Hill, he'd stopped first at his physician's office. The knife had missed all major veins but had taken a chunk out of his bone and possibly damaged the muscle. The doctor wanted him to check into a hospital for surgery then and there. Astor settled for twenty stitches, a shot of Demerol, and a promise to reconsider if the pain became too severe. Afterward he'd passed by his home for a shower and a fresh set of clothes. He did not once consider visiting Janet McVeigh. If Alex felt it was so important, she could tell her herself.

Astor checked that his necktie was knotted satisfactorily. He was sweating and in discomfort, and he'd barely slept in two days. It was not how he would have preferred to go into the most important meeting in his company's history. Check that. The most important meeting in his career.

He glanced to his right. The conference rooms stood adjacent to his office, and he glimpsed his lawyer from Skadden seated calmly at a table. In the next room, Brad Zarek was pacing back and forth, his cell phone pressed to his ear as if sustaining his life's breath. Both could wait.

Astor entered his office. "Septimus. Good of you to come."

"I'm surprised you let me in, let alone called," said Septimus Reventlow.

Reventlow's grip was dry and too loose, his perpetual smile saying that he was anything but bothered both to have been so rudely dismissed the day before and to have been called back on such short notice.

"So, Bobby, interesting times." Reventlow's habit was to speak softly to draw the other man into his sphere, force him to listen closely.

"Keeps the heart beating nicely."

Reventlow laughed.

"Let's sit," said Astor.

"Your arm. Do tell."

"Accident at home. Nothing serious. Anyway, thanks for coming on such short notice. I wanted to revisit your investment in our Comstock Astor fund."

"You declined."

"I'd like you to reconsider."

"Yesterday you wouldn't touch my money with a ten-foot pole."

"The situation has changed since then."

"The piece in the *Times* suggests your position in the yuan is dangerously overexposed."

"Time will tell if we're overexposed. It's not a question of if the Chinese will devalue, but when."

"Unfortunately, it's the when that concerns me now. I already have a hundred million in the fund. If you're underwater, I'd like to know it before committing anything further."

"We are facing a margin call, but that's nothing new. We have the means to meet our requirement, but rather than liquidate any of the fund's other positions, we want to seek an injection of capital that will allow us, *and you*, to profit when the yuan changes course."

"If it changes course."

"*When* it changes course."

"How much additional capital were you seeking?"

"You were proposing three hundred million. On top of that, I'll guarantee your participation in all of our future funds."

"I have another idea."

Astor kept a tight smile on his face. "I'm listening."

"Three hundred million for a twenty percent ownership stake in your firm. You can use the money as you see fit. Meet the margin call or even start another fund."

"The firm isn't for sale."

"Let's not be hasty."

"I'm not. The first rule I made when I started Comstock was to run it alone. No partners. Ever."

"I'm prepared to go higher. Five hundred."

"You flatter me. But as I said, the firm isn't for sale. I'm looking for additional investors, that's all."

A shadow crossed Reventlow's face. The perpetual smile hardened to a frown. He stood and took a step toward the door. "To be honest, Bobby, word on the street is that without a lifeline, you're going under. I don't think you're in any position to turn me down. In fact, I think your lawyers might say that you have a fiduciary responsibility to your investors to take the money. To do otherwise would be criminal."

"Is that a threat?"

The shadow left Reventlow's face. He laughed. The perpetual smile returned, and once more he was the picture of the urbane, cosmopolitan gentleman. "You are a funny guy," he said. "I'll think about the investment. I need to ask around. We wouldn't want to put three hundred million dollars into your fund only to lose it all a few days later."

"Call me whenever you're ready."

"I believe you need an answer by three p.m. tomorrow. After that, a wire wouldn't hit your account before the market closes at four-thirty. Comstock would be in default. Technically, you'd be bankrupt." Reventlow seemed to find the idea amusing, though it would cost him all or part of the $100 million already invested. "I'll see myself out."

Astor walked with him to the door and wished him goodbye. Shank was in conference room one with the firm's attorney, Frank Arcano. Astor joined them but did not sit at the table.

"And so?" asked Shank.

"He wants to buy a piece of the firm."

"What did you tell him?"

"The firm isn't for sale. Not now or ever."

"So we're screwed."

"He's considering his investment."

"What kind of idiot would put his money into the fund now?" asked Shank.

"I would," said Astor.

Shank sank in his chair. "I work for a crazy man."

56

"If McVeigh asks where I am, just say I'm not feeling well. Make up something about the incident hitting me harder than I'd thought. You know the drill."

Alex sat inside Barry Mintz's Ford at the highway rest stop 5 miles from Teterboro Airport, where Bobby kept the jet.

"I know the drill," said Mintz. "The question is if Jan will buy it."

"Let's hope so, or else it may not be such a happy homecoming." Alex looked over at Mintz, who was retrieving a black mesh bag from the back seat. "You got everything I asked for?"

"I want to live, don't I?" Mintz unzipped the bag and took out the items one by one for her examination. "One zinc-powered microtransmitter, one in-ear receiver, one extra battery."

"And the other thing?" asked Alex after she'd handed each back.

"And the other thing," said Mintz.

It was wiser not to discuss the "other thing," a next-generation information gathering apparatus. Suffice it to say that possession of said device constituted an infraction of the legal code for both civilians and law enforcement professionals. Alex called it "the vacuum."

She zipped up the bag and opened the door. "I'll let you know what gives as soon as I learn something. I should be back late tomorrow night or early Thursday morning."

Mintz tried on an encouraging smile. "You're hanging it out there pretty far on this one—I mean, even for you."

"Yeah, well, you know what they say. Act first, apologize later."

"I'll keep that in mind."

"Just keep an eye on Bill Barnes for me. If you learn anything, I want to know it before he does."

Alex climbed into the Charger with renewed purpose. She had the plane. She had her toys. Now she just needed to find her source. Someone in London knew who had hired Luc Lambert. She wasn't coming home until she knew as well.

She covered the 5 miles to Teterboro in three minutes flat. She dropped the speed from 110 to 85 (to be safe) when she turned into the airport entrance and found a convenient space in the parking lot adjacent to the Jet Source fixed-base operation, or FBO. Before leaving the car, she tucked Mintz's bag of goodies into her overnight bag.

Alerted to her arrival, a steward in livery waited at the curb. "May I take your bag, ma'am?"

Alex continued past him directly into the modern terminal. "Just get me to the plane."

The protocol for flying internationally on private jets was similar to that for commercial air travel, she noted, but without the lines, bad attitudes, fussy children, and, most important, the chance of a tardy departure. Five minutes after checking in, she was crossing the tarmac to the G4. The sleek black aircraft was gassed up and ready to go.

The copilot stood alongside the stairs and offered a hand as she mounted the first step. "Good afternoon, Mrs. Astor," he said.

Alex stopped cold, staring at the man. She started to dress him down, but her anger deserted her. "Good afternoon."

"Watch your head."

Alex ducked to enter the cabin, but once inside, she found she could stand to her full height. The aircraft was designed to accommodate twelve passengers comfortably. There were six oversized leather chairs facing each other on either side of the cabin, a desk to the right, and a couch running along the back left wall.

Alex collapsed into a chair and went to work. Unzipping her bag, she removed her notebooks and set them on a folding table. The notebooks contained everything she'd downloaded concerning Executive Outcomes, the private military company that had recruited Luc Lambert for the ill-fated coup in West Africa, and the company's successor, Global Research Analysis and Intelligence, or GRAIL.

The steward offered her a warm towel and set a bowl of roasted almonds in front of her. He informed her that the dinner en route would be roast duck à l'orange with wild rice and braised Brussels sprouts. Should madam wish a hot lava cake for dessert, she should say so now so that it could follow her meal promptly and allow madam time to enjoy a restful night's sleep. Madam declined the dessert and an offer of champagne, asking instead for an espresso and some peace and quiet, thank you very much.

At 5:12 the aircraft's wheels left the runway. Alex was airborne. Flying time was six hours and ten minutes, with landing previewed at 5:22 a.m. Greenwich Mean Time. If she wished to arrive earlier, she had only to ask the captain. Fuel was no object. He could shave fifteen minutes off their time. Alex said it wouldn't be necessary. The company she planned on visiting did not open before nine-thirty. She had more than enough time to take the Underground into central London and even give herself a proper English breakfast.

She stared out the window for a few minutes, before lowering the window shade and turning her attention to work. She had surprisingly little to go on besides open-source information—newspaper and magazine articles she'd found on the Net and a Wikipedia brief. The Bureau had no information on either company. Private military companies and security consultants fell under the CIA's purview, and she hadn't had time to reach out to her contacts at Langley. She had tried to reach a colleague at MI5 en route to the airport, but it was late in the U.K. and he hadn't responded. She settled for leaving a message.

One thing was clear. GRAIL had grown and prospered in the years since its founding. Articles mentioned contracts with the United States and British governments totaling tens of millions of dollars. A download from the company's website offered its mission statement:

To provide a highly professional and confidential military advisory service to legitimate governments.

To provide sound military and strategic advice.

To provide the most professional military training packages currently available to armed forces, covering aspects related to sea, air, and land warfare.

To provide advice to armed forces on weapon and weapon platform selection.

To provide a totally apolitical service based on confidentiality, professionalism, and dedication.

Alex put down the paper. GRAIL could call itself an international security consultant all it wanted, but as far as she was concerned, it was still a private military company, or as they used to say in the Old West, a gun for hire.

She leafed through the remaining newspaper articles discussing the firm, but the reports failed to hold her interest. Instead she found herself thinking about Bobby. The burst of sentimentality she'd been witness to at Cherry Hill wasn't like him. Was it because his life had been threatened, or had he really changed? She chastised herself for considering the possibility. Maybe she was the sappy one. In her experience, people rarely changed. If anything, their dominant personality traits grew stronger, and more dominant, as they aged. In Bobby's case, those traits counted as arrogance, stubbornness, overconfidence, and, she had to admit, generosity.

Alex forced Bobby from her mind. Sitting straighter, she tried once again to read the documents. Air travel made her tired, and the words quickly grew fuzzy. A dozen espressos couldn't stop her eyelids from drooping. Bobby came to her thoughts again. She imagined his touch on her skin, the texture of his cheek against hers . . .

With an effort, Alex fought off sleep. Her memories frightened her. Every relationship had its good times. Why were they always so much easier to remember than the bad times? The plane banked and flew due east. Darkness enveloped the aircraft. Her last thought as she drifted off to sleep was not about work but about him.

Bobby.

Did he really mean it about giving things another go?

57

"D id you find him?"

Astor slammed the door closed and slid across the back seat. "He's waiting now."

"And you didn't use your phone?"

"I found the last pay phone in the city and said exactly what you told me."

"All right. Floor it. I have to be at Central Park West at seven."

Sullivan put the Audi into gear and started the drive uptown.

Astor leaned his face against the window, watching the city go by. He was thinking about Septimus Reventlow and wondering what kind of game he was playing. It was understandable that he might want to put more money into the fund yesterday . . . but today? Shank had been right when he'd called Astor a crazy man. And what to make of Reventlow's tepid attempt to purchase a share of the firm? Maybe the man had better contacts in China than he did. Time would tell. Anyhow, Astor wasn't planning on waiting until tomorrow at three to line up the funds he needed.

The Audi hit a pothole, jolting Astor and sending a twinge of pain through his arm. The anesthetic had worn off an hour ago and the wound ached intensely. He felt for the bottle of pain relievers in his pocket. Vicodin. Strong stuff. He dropped it back into his pocket. Instead, he used the pain to focus his attention on his current predicament.

Astor was not one for deep thought. He did not hold with Frost and the "life unexamined" nonsense. Or was it Socrates? Another fault of his truncated education. He preferred to read military histories and biographies of generals and decorated soldiers. He knew that a good general leads from the front. He liked to think that he lived from the front, with his eyes locked on the horizon. Yet if there was ever a time to stop the tanks, to take a long look back and ask how he had gotten here, this was it.

It seemed like yesterday that he was turning the keys in the door of his first office, at 21st and Madison, in some leftover space he leased from First Boston, and taking his first step up the ladder. He had no lofty goals, either monetary or social. He never once said, "I want to make a million dollars a year" or "ten million," or "I want to be worth one hundred million by the time I'm forty." He simply went to work each day at the appointed hour and dedicated himself to his job, which meant analyzing annual reports, watching the market, and picking stocks better than the next guy. The secret came in the repetition of this cycle, day in, day out, year in and year out, without fail. Was he ever the best at picking stocks? Of course not. But on some days he was better than average, and when you added those days together they were enough to enable him to rise to the top of his profession.

It had been so much simpler in the beginning. No possessions. No family. No money. There was just the job. But as the years passed, all that changed. He married. He had a child. He hired employees. He earned money. He hired more employees. He earned more money. He bought a home. His name appeared in the paper. He began to have status and he enjoyed it.

Wash. Rinse. Repeat.

Until *voilà!* One day, here he was. He was the same Bobby Astor who'd started his business on a wing and a prayer and the fifty grand he'd made at poker tables around the city. Yet there was no denying he'd grown into someone different. Someone bigger. Someone more substantial. It was as if success, responsibility, fatherhood, and philanthropy had fused to create a new Bobby Astor, and that Bobby Astor demanded a larger physical portion of the world. He'd started out a gecko and grown into Godzilla. And goddammit, he liked it. He liked it a lot. No apology necessary.

And then came the descent.

The estrangement from his father.

The separation from Alex, and then the divorce.

And now the bet on the yuan.

From the heights of Olympus to the edge of the abyss. What had taken twenty years to create, he stood to lose within twenty-four hours.

Astor looked in the mirror. Fighting eyes glared back.

58

Astor spotted Grillo seated at the end of the bar.

"This public enough?" asked the investigator.

It was six, and the Oak Bar in the Plaza Hotel was packed. Tourists with red faces and sweat-moistened shirts mingled with executives in pressed suits and polished shoes. Drawn blinds shaded the dark, wood-paneled room in permanent air-conditioned gloom. It was a place for making deals and plotting takeovers and planning divorces.

"It should do," said Astor, though he was by no means certain.

Grillo smiled his gambler's smile, then took a sip of his drink. Astor looked at the rivulets of water sliding down the highball glass. He could smell the sour-mash whiskey, the happy hint of sweet vermouth. A manhattan, then.

"Drink?"

Astor could feel the cooled blend coating the inside of his mouth, soothing his throat, soothing his life. "Sure."

Grillo signaled the bartender.

Astor swallowed, waiting, deciding. The bartender arrived.

"Pellegrino with lime. Highball glass. Big lime." He saw Grillo give him the look. He waited for the drink, and when it came he drank half of it straightaway.

"I talked to him," said Astor.

"Who?"

"Palantir."

Grillo lost the smile. "How's that?"

"Skype. At my dad's place in Oyster Bay. My father was in touch with him online. Palantir was helping with the investigation. In fact, he said he was the one who had contacted my father in the first place."

"About?"

"He didn't get that far."

"Slow down."

"All I know is that they're listening. That's why I had Sully call you on the pay phone."

"Not to me, they're not. I take precautions." Grillo had taken his Zippo lighter from his pocket and was flipping the cover open and closed with his thumb. "Give it to me slow. Start from the beginning and don't leave anything out. I'm a good listener."

Astor relayed the events of the past thirty-six hours just as he had to Alex, beginning with his visit to Penelope Evans's house in Greenwich and continuing through the trip to Cherry Hill. Grillo didn't ask why he hadn't been more forthcoming when they'd met the day before. Astor knew he'd been right not to tell. He pulled back the sleeve of his jacket and revealed the bandage. "The guy stuck me and took off," he said in conclusion. "So here we are."

"Did you get a good look at him?" asked Grillo.

"He was as close to me as you are."

"A description might help. Tell me after. Once more about the companies."

Astor went back over the annual reports he'd found at Evans's house and his belief that the key could be found in the companies' common tie to private equity firms.

"But different sponsors invested in each," said Grillo.

"Five of them. Two sponsors invested in more than one of the companies."

"And the companies themselves aren't in any way related."

"No, but still . . ." Astor's argument slipped away like sand through his fingers.

"Tell me more about the company your father visited."

"Might have visited." Astor handed him the article he'd found and pointed out the mention of Britium. "Mean anything?"

"Not to me, but I'll ask around." Grillo slid his lighter back into his pocket. "One last thing. Did you get the web address of the man who said he was Palantir?"

"Cassandra99.donetsk.ru."

"Russia. Figures."

"Can you find him?"

"With a Skype handle? Not likely. But it'll help. Every little bit gets us a little closer."

"And you?" asked Astor. "Find anything?"

"Palantir's the real thing. I can tell you that. Did some work for the Pentagon. Very hush-hush stuff. Didn't earn many friends along the way. We can assume that's why he didn't want to bring in the FBI on this."

"Did his work have anything to do with Britium or something that tied in with the companies my father was looking into?"

"Wouldn't know." Grillo leaned closer, so Astor could smell his cologne and see how his wrinkles carved canyons around his eyes. "All I can say is that whatever it was he and your father were investigating, some very powerful people don't want them—or anyone else—to find out."

"The man who tried to kill me was Asian, but he had these strange blue eyes."

"Asian, eh?"

Astor provided a detailed description of his dress.

"Speak English?"

"We didn't get a chance to talk."

Grillo entered Palantir's Skype address into his smartphone, then stood. "Do you need protection?"

"I have Sully."

"Don't go home. Stay where people can see you. You still got that apartment in your office? That might be okay." Grillo squinted and shook his head. "Actually, scratch that. Go to a friend's. Maybe a hotel."

"I'll be careful."

"Good. You never know where these guys are going to turn up."

59

The operations center was as busy as Grand Central during morning rush. Forming the Joint Terrorism Task Force, over thirty law enforcement agencies kept representatives in the FBI's New York counterterrorism office. Normally their varied duties combined to keep nearly all of them out of the office at any one time. Not today. As Barry Mintz hurried across the room, he counted off agents from police, fire, DEA, ATF, Port Authority, parks and wildlife, nuclear regulatory, and everything in between.

Alex wanted an investigation. She got one.

"Mintz. Hold up."

Mintz stopped a foot shy of being clear of the room. "Hi, Bill."

Bill Barnes was in his media best: blue suit, white shirt, red tie with the American flag prominently displayed. "Where you been?"

"Out running down some more info on Luc Lambert."

"Who? Oh, Shepherd. That's right. I forgot his real name for a second. Who you talk to?"

"The Agency."

Barnes shook his head. "Take forever."

"Had to try."

"'Course you did." Barnes tucked a file beneath his arm and took up position a bad breath away. "What's Alex up to?"

"Guess she's at home. Resting."

"I've tried her phone a bunch of times. Keeps going to voice mail. She won't answer my texts, either."

"She's probably sleeping."

Barnes raised an eyebrow. "We talking about the same Alex?" He leaned closer, as if they were two buddies sharing a secret. "Come on, Mintz. You can tell me. What's she doing? No way she's at home sleeping. What's that Alex is always saying? She'll sleep when she's dead?"

Mintz met his gaze and winced, hating to say what he was about to say. "Between you and me, she's not doing so hot. Losing Malloy knocked the wind out of her sails. I think she needed a couple drinks."

Barnes smiled cruelly. "Figures. She talks a good game with that crazy picture of Hoover and the battering ram on the floor, but in the end she's still a woman. I knew she'd buckle." He chuckled. "Maybe you should take her some chicken soup."

"I'm sure she'll be okay," said Mintz. "Anything new here?"

"Got a lead on those AKs. Shipped originally to China, then exported to their great ally, Venezuela. No idea how they got here." A call came in on Barnes's phone. He gave Mintz a thumbs-up. "Good talking, Bar. Keep up the fine work. Don't count on Langley. Bunch of hard-ons." He began his conversation, then stopped abruptly. "If you do talk to Alex, tell her I phoned London. They're checking up on those firms right away. Should have an answer by Friday. Monday latest."

Mintz gave a thumbs-up in return and continued toward his desk, making sure to close the door to Alex's office before he sat down so he wouldn't have to work with J. Edgar Hoover's damning gaze aimed at his shoulders. Barnes was right about the picture. It was weird.

The phone rang. It was Alex's line. "Mintz speaking."

"I'm looking for SSA Forza."

"She's not in right now. Can I help?"

"Am I speaking to Barry Mintz, tall, red-haired geek? Couldn't get laid if he was starring in a porn movie?"

Mintz slumped. "That would be me."

"It's Neil Donovan. How the hell are you?"

Mintz bucked up. Donovan had run the Bureau's organized crime unit out of 26 Federal Plaza as well as heading up the SWAT team before leaving a year ago. He was a bona fide stud and everything Mintz aspired to be. "I thought you retired."

"Me? Never. I'm in Mexico now. Running intel ops down here. Dangerous as all get-out, but damned interesting all the same. You got a sec?"

"Sure thing."

"I got a call I thought I should pass along to you guys. I already communicated with headquarters, but I wanted to get it into your hands stat. Might be something, might be nothing. Got a pen?"

"Shoot."

"One of my contacts at Juárez Airport touched base last night. Said he had some interesting folks passing through passport control. About twenty or so men and women arriving from South America, all of them carrying brand-new Portuguese passports."

"Portuguese? You're sure?"

"Dead sure. Apparently they were young, fit, and a couple were real tough guys. Funny thing was that none of them were speaking Portuguese."

"No? What, then?"

"English. But not American English. Foreigners' English. Not only that, these guys were met at the gate by two big shots. One was a general in the Federales and the other some kind of spook from the DFS, the Mexican security service. Real scary types. Anyway, they were crowing about the group being a team of athletes."

"Athletes," repeated Mintz, writing down Donovan's words verbatim. "From Portugal."

"Small problem, though," Donovan went on. "None of the passports had an entry visa for Venezuela or any kind of stamps. We're talking virgin travel docs. My guy's a smart guy. He takes notice and memorizes a couple of the passport numbers. I ran them through the Portuguese embassy down our way. Turns out the passports were stolen from the consulate in Macao a month ago."

"Macao . . . near Hong Kong?"

"Former Portuguese colony, now a gambling mecca. That's the one."

Mintz read his notes, then asked, "Did your guy get an exact count on the number of passengers with these stolen passports?"

"Think so—let me check. Yeah, he did. Twenty-three."

Mintz grabbed his inventory of equipment seized at Windermere. Halfway down the list was an item, "New York City Maps 18–24." Scratch Luc Lambert. "Twenty-three. You sure on that?"

"Yeah."

"And where exactly did they fly in from?"

"Air Mexicana Flight 388 from Caracas."

Mintz underlined the name of the city. Then he wrote one word next to it: *Venezuela*.

60

O ne last shot.

Jack Steinmetz, owner of the Steinmetz Fund, with over $30 billion under management, billionaire ten times over, poster boy for Wall Street excess, lived in the famed San Remo Apartments on Central Park West. His place in the city was one of his smaller residences. Four floors and 15,000 square feet overlooking the park. The elevator opened. Steinmetz stood waiting, arms open, smile on his face. Sixty, trim, and tanned, he looked like everyone's favorite uncle. Looks were deceiving. Jack Steinmetz, or Jack the Ripper, as he preferred to be called, was not a nice man, and he had four failed marriages, five kids in rehab or recovery, and six former business partners, all of whom were engaged in litigation against him, to prove it.

"Bobby, it's been too long."

"Jack, good to see you."

Steinmetz drew him close for an embrace as if they were long-lost brothers. "Tough times. Sorry about the bad news."

"It's all right. My father and I weren't close."

"I wasn't talking about your father. I meant your fund. Word on the street is that you're going belly-up. Yeah, and about your father—just imagine I said all the usual things. Condolences, sorry, whatever. What the hell happened, anyway?"

"I know about as much as the next guy. The investigation is ongoing."

"I'd thought you'd have a direct line to the scene, what with Alice being an agent."

"Alex."

"Whatever. She's a good-looking piece, ain't she? Wouldn't have minded a little of that myself. You're divorced, right? I'm not stepping on any toes. I'm getting a little sick of Miss Russia. Had to leave her up in Jackson Hole with Sumner and Larry. Give her a chance to find the next meal ticket."

Astor ignored Steinmetz's comments. He'd been the same loud-mouth twenty years ago when Astor was starting out and Steinmetz was being feted in the press as "king of the LBO."

"It's not Alex's show," Astor said, nonplussed. "The Bureau's serious about keeping things locked down."

"TV says the car went berserk, like that thing Hasselhoff used to drive—"

"KITT."

"That's the one. Me, I think it was the driver. The Secret Service guy went postal." Steinmetz laughed at his joke. "Well, it's not all bad. Maybe we'll get a Fed chair who knows what he's doing. Charlie Hughes had his head so far up his ass he could tickle his tonsils. Always calling for higher capital requirements. The problem isn't too much leverage, it's not enough. I used to put down three billion and buy a company for thirty. Now I need to pump in eight or nine up front. I don't have to tell you what that does for returns. Of course, I'm not hanging it out there in the wind like you."

"It's worked so far."

"Yeah?" said Steinmetz, thrusting his chin out. "That why you're here? Tell me how rosy things are at Comstock. Paint me a nice little picture."

"You were happy enough with how your other investments turned out."

"Past history. Made it. Spent it. Now I'm looking to make more. Don't ask me to thank you for doing your job."

"Wouldn't dream of it." Astor walked behind Steinmetz into the living room. A two-story floor-to-ceiling window looked over Central Park. The waning light gilded the trees with a warm orange glow. Stare at it long enough and it would hypnotize you. *Everything's all right. Everything's all right.* Astor looked away.

He'd been here once before. The occasion was Jack Steinmetz's fiftieth birthday, and he and his Russian wife had turned the place into a re-creation of Studio 54 during its heyday in the late 1970s, complete with a white horse parading down the stairs. That was ten years back, but Astor still had a hard time erasing the image of Steinmetz wearing silver lamé pants, a silk shirt unbuttoned to his navel, and a gold coke spoon around his neck.

"Hear about my latest deal? Vodka?" Steinmetz sauntered to his bar and selected a strangely shaped bottle holding a clear liquid. "It's Lenin," he said, catching Astor's curious glance. "They took the cast from his face in Red Square. I bought the distillery last month. Fifty million lock, stock, and barrel. Forget those other ones from France and Sweden. Real vodka should be Russian. Try it. Goes down like water."

"No, thanks," said Bobby. "I've got work to do."

"Suit yourself." Steinmetz made a show of pulling back his sleeve and checking the time. His gold wristwatch was as large as a deep-sea diver's helmet. "Okay, Astor, enough of this bullshitting. Spit it out."

"We're facing a margin call on the flagship fund. We're short yuan. The market moved against us."

"You're short yuan?" gasped Steinmetz, spraying a little vodka in Astor's face. "And here I was, all these years thinking you were one of the smart ones. The deputy trade minister stood up on TV last night and confirmed his country's policy of allowing the currency to appreciate."

"We think it's going the other way."

"*You think.* And you want me to bail you out so you can hang on and see if you're right."

"I want to give you the chance to get in at a good price."

"Bargain basement, no doubt. And?"

"And what?"

"And what's the kicker? You expect me to get in line with the rest of the schmendricks you already conned?"

"I can't give you any preferential treatment. That's illegal."

"Now that we have it on record that you're an honest businessman, let's talk turkey. What are you looking for?"

"Three hundred."

"That it?"

"Lock, stock, and barrel."

"Forget it. I'm not interested in your fund. Too risky. You do get points, however, for having the balls to put it to me like you did. You got big ones, that's for sure. Tell you what—I'll loan you the money if it can be secured by your other funds."

"Fair enough," said Astor. "I can give you six percent for ninety days."

"Come again? I thought you said six percent."

"Six for ninety. That's twenty-four percent annualized."

"I can do the math, thank you. Here's what I'm thinking. Ten percent for thirty days."

"Thirty million for a month. That's a hundred and twenty percent annualized."

"What do you care? You're the genius who's going to make a fortune when the Chinese surprise the entire world and decide to depreciate the yuan."

Astor smiled to himself. Loan-sharking was alive and well and operating in plain daylight on Central Park West. "Can you have the funds in my account by three tomorrow?"

"I can have them there at nine in the morning."

Astor extended a hand. "Deal."

Steinmetz regarded him. He smiled cagily, and Astor thought, *I knew this was too easy.* "One more thing. I'd like you to ask nice."

"I just did."

Steinmetz knocked back the rest of the vodka. "You call that nice? I'm thinking you take a knee."

"Pardon?"

"Hit the carpet." Steinmetz teetered, and Astor realized that he was drunk.

"That's enough, Jack. Do we have a deal or don't we?"

"Actually, two knees. I want to see you grovel."

"Be serious."

Steinmetz threw his hands on Astor's shoulders and tried to force him down. "Grovel."

Astor hit him. He didn't know where the fist came from, but his knuckles ached and Steinmetz lay sprawled on his couch, blood trickling from his mouth.

"That's assault," sputtered Steinmetz, struggling to get to his feet.

"Actually, it's battery. Arrest me."

Steinmetz came at him and Astor chucked him aside, sending the older man toppling onto a coffee table. Astor bent down to help him up, but Steinmetz refused his help. "Where you going to go now? I was giving you a bargain. You're toast, Astor. Hear me? Toast."

"Yeah, I know," said Astor. *French fried, with maple syrup.*

He left before he decided to hit Steinmetz again.

61

C*lick.*

Mike Grillo stood across the street from the office building on Third Avenue, his eyes on the revolving doors. It was eight o'clock. The evening exodus was long over. Men and women trickled out intermittently alone and in pairs. Grillo marked each departure with a flip of the Zippo's cover.

Click.

He considered himself a reasonable man. He knew the world was a complicated place. Rarely was an issue black or white. Too often, gray was the palette of choice. He realized that everyone, himself included, had to make bargains from time to time. Compromises. Settlements not entirely to their liking. Still, there were a few lines he didn't cross. He did not steal from clients. He did not engage in activities that might cause harm to come to a person. He did not lie to his friends. So when one of his friends lied to him, he was upset. He wanted to put that person's head through a plate-glass window.

Click.

A shadow approached the revolving door. Even through the tinted glass, he recognized the shambling gait, the air of world-weary fatigue. A moment later, an African-American man wearing a rumpled blazer, khaki pants, and crappy loafers emerged from the building and walked north. Grillo dropped the Zippo into his pocket and checked his watch. Eight-oh-three. He couldn't fault his friend for shortchanging the American taxpayer.

Grillo set off up the sidewalk, following from across the street. The man turned west on 70th Street. The light was with Grillo and he crossed, walking faster now. The sidewalk was crowded. He saw his moment.

"Hello, Jeb," he said when he reached the man's shoulder. "Funny running into you again."

Jeb Washburn barely turned his head to answer. "You smooth, Grill-O. Didn't see you coming for a sec."

"You should know that I've got a piece on you right now. A little PPK aimed right at your kidney. It's got one of those Czech silencers we used to use. Don't work for shit, but in this traffic, it'll do." Grillo nudged him with the barrel.

"Guess you're serious."

"You didn't tell me he contacted you."

"You didn't ask. You asked if I knew who he was. The answer is still no."

It was there in the file Grillo had received from the phone company, as plain as day. The list of calls placed to and from the phone Palantir had used to contact Edward Astor showed that Palantir had spoken with Jeb Washburn on six occasions between June 10 and June 30.

"I'm waiting."

"He called in June to say that he had something for us. Proof about a cyberattack to be initiated by a foreign power against our national infrastructure. At first he was all over the place. Could be against the power grid, air traffic control, the Net. Then he narrowed it down to the financial infrastructure. Even so, he was vague. Wouldn't name the country involved or the place. Didn't have a firm date. The only thing he knew for sure was that the financial industry was the target. There was something else."

"Oh yeah?"

"He said it was a game changer."

"What does that mean?"

"Ask him. Whatever, it can't be good."

"So what'd you do?"

"What I was trained to do. I evaluated the intake and passed it up the chain of command."

"And that's it? Didn't talk to him again? Done?"

Washburn shook his head slowly, as if bemused. "Grill-O, this is way above your pay grade."

"I'm private sector now, bro. I don't have a pay grade. That's why I can afford my seven-hundred-dollar Italian loafers and you're wearing resoled Weejuns. By the way, are you the preppiest black man on the planet?"

"In my blood. What can I say?" Washburn gave him a smile.

Grillo didn't bite. "Ever meet with him in person?"

"Negative. Last contact I had was end of June. He wanted a paycheck before he'd play ball. Said something about DARPA still owing him for work he did a few years back."

"So DARPA must have his name."

"If they do, they didn't say. Wouldn't even admit they'd ever heard of the software program."

"One of those, eh?"

"One of those."

"And so you gave his number to the NSA to see if they could track him down."

"They looking for him, too?" Washburn curled his mouth in distaste. "Figures."

"The NSA put a Code Black priority on his number on June eleventh."

"I wouldn't know about that. That's the problem with the intelligence business in this country. Right hand doesn't know what the left hand is doing. Except in this case there are more like a hundred hands. All of 'em are looking for something to do and no one wants to say jack about it."

"And you give me your word you didn't know the NSA was trying to track him down?"

Washburn shook his head. "As you recall, our shop is not allowed to operate on home soil. If we do get info about something going down, we pass it along to the proper domestic agency."

"Just what is it you do these days?"

"Threat mitigation. You were on offense. Me, I play defense. You got something you want to pass along to me, Grill-O? For example, just why in the world you are so interested in Palantir? And don't give me that client confidentiality crap. We are way beyond that."

"Palantir contacted Edward Astor in early July. I'm guessing that whoever you passed the information along to declined to pay him for his services. Anyway, Astor wasn't so cheap. He probably saw himself as a patriot endeavoring to do some good for his country. The way I see it, Palantir delivered the goods last Friday. Astor left work early and headed to midtown, I'm guessing to meet with Palantir. He went home, digested the material, and—"

"And set up the meet with Hughes and Gellman?" Washburn suggested.

"Not right away. First he contacted a company in Reston. Britium. Looks like he paid the place a visit."

"Britium, eh? Never heard of it."

"My guess is that he had to check out whether Palantir was on the money before taking the whole thing upstairs."

"It appears he was."

"Yes, it does."

Washburn's eyes dropped to Grillo's jacket. "You going to put away that gun now?"

"Someone's killing off anyone with an interest in Palantir. I'd rather play it safe."

Washburn laughed gently. "You're safe with me, Grill-O. We're all after the same thing."

"Not exactly. I'm only being paid to find him. Interdiction, arrest, sanction—all the messy shit is up to you."

"You got something to take us all another step down the road?"

There it was. The offer of the deal Grillo had been working toward. You scratch my back, I'll scratch yours.

"Couple things," he said. "My client spoke to Palantir today. Apparently whatever he was warning everyone about is set to go down soon. He was cagey, wouldn't give any details. Sounds like he has a real hard-on for the government. I can give you his Skype address and a number he used to call Edward Astor Friday morning. Give the information to your friends, have them put it in their magic box and shake it around a little. If they're as good as they're always bragging, we should have a name, address, Social Security number, and favorite brand of condom."

"I'll do my best," said Washburn.

"Screw your best. Just get me an answer."

Washburn buttoned his jacket. "Say, Mike, that's not really a gun in your pocket, is it?"

Grillo withdrew his hand, his fingers shaped in the form of a pistol. "Bang."

Washburn shook his head. "Been behind a desk way too long."

62

A firm hand awoke Alex from her sleep.

"Ms. Forza. I'm sorry to disturb you."

Alex opened her eyes. The pilot stood above her. "Yes," she said. "I must have dozed off. I'm sorry . . . what time is it?"

"Just after nine p.m. New York time. Three in London. Someone wants to talk to you. A Special Agent Mintz. He's patched through to the cockpit. He says it's urgent."

Alex threw off her blanket and moved forward through the cabin. The copilot handed her a headset. "Yeah, this is Alex."

"It's Barry. Got some news that you need to know about right away. Looks like our shooters came through Mexico City last night."

"How do you know?"

"This group was coming out of Caracas traveling on virgin Portuguese passports that had been stolen from the embassy in Macao."

"Lambert's passport was Portuguese."

"Exactly. And you'll never guess how many."

"Twenty-three."

"Bingo. Same as on those city maps. And they weren't speaking Portuguese. All of them were speaking English."

"Do we still have a bead on them?"

"All we know is that they climbed into a couple of vans and drove away. Two big shots from the Federales greased their arrival. Neil Donovan is trying to locate them now, see if he can sweat them."

"Not likely," said Alex.

"Turns out you were right, boss."

"About what?" asked Alex.

"The groceries in the cupboard at Windermere Street. If the shooters hit Mexico last night, there's no reason that they couldn't already be here."

"Did you tell Barnes?"

"Of course."

"And?"

"He's presenting it to the mayor, the police commissioner, and Homeland Security in the morning. Says he needs more info before hitting the panic button."

"In the morning? That could be too late."

"Alex?"

"What?"

"Hurry."

63

Midnight on the Jersey Turnpike.

Astor sat in the passenger seat of the Sprinter, peering out the window at the rotting hulk of industrial America. Newark, Trenton, New Brunswick. All were beaten down by time, neglect, and obsolescence. Rusted factories and abandoned plants loomed in the distance, specters of a hopeful, prosperous past. Astor was no doomsayer. He believed that the American dream was alive and well. He just didn't understand why no one cared that it had been snuffed out here.

"Everything feel okay?" he asked Sullivan. "No problems steering or anything like that?"

"You mean am I driving it myself and not some asshole with a remote control a thousand miles away?"

"Something like that."

"So far, so good. First sign of the body snatchers, I'll let you know. Till then, why don't you get some sleep? You don't look so hot."

"I'm good."

"You want, I can pull over and let you climb in the back. The bed's nice."

"You've tried it?"

"Sneaked in one night after I'd had a few too many. Knew the Mrs. would kill me and I didn't want to shell out for a room at the Athletic Club."

"Cheapskate."

"You try bringing up four kids on a cop's salary."

"What did you make your best year?"

"A hundred, maybe one-oh-five with overtime. 'Bout what you dump in a month."

"That's about right. Tough raising a kid on my salary."

"With all due respect, fuck you."

"Get in line, Sully. Get in line. But seriously, how much did you put away?"

"The wife was good about saving. Her brother was a broker. We handed him the nest egg. He wasn't so good about investing."

"Lose it all?"

"Not all, but in dribs and drabs. He was always putting us in the next hot stock. Me, I'm a Mick from Queens. What do I know?"

"How much you got with me?"

"Everything I got left."

"Nothing in the bank?"

"And what, earn one percent per year? I hear what you and your buddies are pulling down. I figure I'll stay with the master. What did that magazine call you? 'The prince of risk'?"

"Where are you now?"

"We started at two twenty-five. Think you got us up to four and a quarter. Thank you."

"That's something."

"Not like I can stop working. I'm sixty-seven. I'm feeling pretty good. Who knows how long before I crap out?"

Astor saw a shadow pass over Sullivan's features. "Don't worry, Sully. I won't screw the pooch."

Sullivan nodded, but he didn't say anything.

Astor sat up straighter and yawned. "How long we got?"

"Two hundred miles to our destination, though I have no idea what you want to do when we get there at four in the morning."

"I'll figure something out."

Astor looked away so Sullivan couldn't read the doubt in his face. For the first time, Bobby Astor wasn't sure if he would.

64

The safe house was a large, unloved Colonial located in the rolling hills outside the town of Darien in the Connecticut countryside one hour north of New York City. The house needed paint and a new roof, but it would be just fine for the summer, provided it didn't rain too much. The leasing agent had called it a steal at $3,000 a month. The tall, vaguely Asian gentleman with the vaguely German name who signed the papers offered no comment. He didn't mind the flaking paint or the leaky roof. What interested him was the home's isolated location, the endless back yard that ran into a glade of elms, and the fact that the nearest neighbor lived 500 yards away, with a steep hill to separate them.

"A summer retreat for my family visiting from Singapore," the client had explained. "They have enough of the sea. It's land they want."

The leasing agent took one look at his suit, his shoes, and his solid gold Breguet wristwatch and didn't ask another question. Clients who paid in advance were a rare commodity—and a cashier's check to boot. Done.

Team One landed at Westchester County Airport at 7 p.m. local time. The plane taxied to the end of runway two-niner at the far end of the airfield, where a hangar blocked it from view. As the flight had originated in Harlingen, Texas, there were no customs formalities to complete or passport control to clear. An unmarked van belonging to the Sonichi Corporation waited at the designated spot. Keys were left in an envelope inside the dash.

The eight passengers deplaned at 7:09.

At 7:10, all were seated comfortably inside the van.

At 7:15, the van left the airport grounds through the east exit. A lone security guard manned the gate. She was too busy watching the New York Mets wallop the Atlanta Braves to register who was in the van, let alone which direction it traveled in.

The driver kept the speed at the legal limit and made the 48-mile trip in just under an hour. It was full dusk when the van arrived in Darien. The passengers alighted wordlessly. It had been a long day, and it was far from over.

Team Two arrived at 8 p.m. after an eight-hour drive from upstate New York. After crossing the border, the team traveled to the Silicon Solutions distribution center in Buffalo, where they traded the cramped confines of the delivery truck for the more comfortable interior of an unmarked passenger van. From there it was a straight shot east by southeast, traversing the breadth of New York State, turning north at the coast, and entering Connecticut.

Team Three landed at Tweed New Haven Airport at 8 p.m. following a three-hour flight from New Orleans aboard a Noble Energy jet. As they had no luggage, they proceeded directly through baggage claim. A van waited at the curb. As the driver signaled to pull into traffic, an airport policeman motioned for him to stop. The policeman walked up and down the van, eyeing the young men and women inside.

"Who are your passengers?" he asked.

The driver was recently arrived from Poland. His English was passable. He had no idea who his passengers were. He'd been tasked with picking up eight arriving passengers and that is what he had done. He shrugged and shook his head.

The policeman came closer.

"Here for a conference in the city," volunteered a tall blond man in the front seat who had spent five years as a noncommissioned officer attached to the SBS, or Special Boat Service, a crack commando unit of the British armed forces. "Noble Energy. We're the European sales staff. Know any places to go to find the ladies?"

The policeman was a fan of English Premier League soccer. The Brits were good people. "In New Haven? Nah. You're better off heading into Manhattan. Standard Hotel. You'll be fine there."

"Thanks, mate."

The drive to the safe house was brisk and uneventful.

Upon arrival of all three teams, the first order of business was to remove the weapons and equipment from storage and prepare it for tactical use. By now, all of the mercenaries were aware of the loss of the operation's commander, Luc Lambert, and the capture of the weapons store. Though regrettable, neither occurrence was a disaster. This was a military operation, and military operations by definition made contingencies for setbacks exactly like these. As mandated prior to their departure, Lieutenant Sandy Beaufoy, the leathery South African commando known better as Skinner, took command. His first concern was to organize the delivery of a replacement cache of weapons and supplies to the safe house. Arrangements were made for a delivery first thing in the morning.

Skinner gathered the team in the garage to draw their gear. Each member was issued a Kevlar vest, a communications belt with a virgin cell phone and a two-way military-grade radio, a Sig Sauer 9mm pistol and fifty rounds of hollow-point ammunition, a Heckler and Koch MP5 submachine gun along with fifteen clips, each of which contained twenty-seven rounds, two antipersonnel hand grenades, one white phosphorus grenade, a Camelbak hydration system, a packet of high-grade dextroamphetamine, better known as "go pills," and a KA-BAR knife and sheath.

All members received a last item: a protective plastic pouch containing one 500mg capsule of pure sodium cyanide.

The carrot was the sum of $800,000 to be paid to each member upon successful completion of the mission, on top of the $200,000 each had already banked. The stick was a life sentence without the possibility of parole, to be served at a supermax prison. There inmates spent twenty-three hours a day locked inside a 10-by-7-foot cell where the lights never went out. Exercise was taken one hour a day inside a narrow yard with walls rising 40 feet on all sides and fencing covering the sliver of daylight visible above.

Death was preferable to capture, either by a New York City policeman's bullet or by the lethal poison tablet.

The mercenaries spent the next hour getting familiar with their gear. Pistols were disassembled and put back together. Machine guns were field-stripped, examined, and modified to meet individual demands. Clips were loaded and stowed in gear bags.

Afterward, Skinner Beaufoy ordered the teams to assemble in the garage with all tactical gear. All donned their vests and commo belts with pistols and spare clips. They slung their gear bags over their shoulders and strapped their machine guns to their chests. Fully equipped, each carried a load of more than 35 pounds.

"Long day," he said, looking with pride at the group. "Lights out in an hour. Hit the rack and get as much sleep as you can. When you get up, I want you to stay inside until I recce the area and give the all-clear. We've made it this far—let's not muck it up. Thirty-six hours, lads. *Gott mit uns.*"

65

It was raining in London.

Alex stepped out of the cab at the corner of Oxford Street and Regent Street. She struggled to open her umbrella. A moment was enough for the downpour to douse her hair and soak her jacket. The fare from Gatwick was £90, nearly $140. She counted out the notes, consoling herself that at least she hadn't had to purchase an airline ticket.

The cab pulled away and Alex looked to her left and right, orienting herself. She knew the city. Shortly after separating from Bobby, she'd spent a month at Scotland Yard as part of an interagency task force on cybercrime. On weekends she'd jogged along the Embankment east to west, a distance of 9 miles, then walked back, taking hours to explore the city's neighborhoods.

Alex continued south two blocks, then turned the corner at Brook Street. Mayfair counted as the city's poshest borough, and New Bond Street was its epicenter. Art galleries, boutiques, and local outposts of the world's most elegant fashion labels lined either side of the street. In the midst of them, she found 200 New Bond Street. Instead of a show window, there was a two-story wall of milky green glass. Five stainless steel letters placed at eye level on the right-hand side of the building announced the inhabitants. GRAIL. Entry was through a brushed steel door at the end of a recessed doorway. She pressed the buzzer and lifted her head so the security camera could get a good look at her. There was no speaker visible, and no disembodied voice asked her name. The softest of clicks sounded as the lock disengaged. She pushed open the door and entered a dimly lit foyer.

Carpeted stairs led to a first-floor reception area. There was a desk with no one behind it. Smoked glass walls blocked her view of the rest of the office. She could see shadows moving behind them. A glass panel swung open and a trim blond woman dressed in a pale gray two-piece suit approached, hand outstretched. "Chris Rees-Jones," she said crisply. "Nice to meet you."

"Alex Forza. You're kind to see me."

"One likes to keep one's friends at Five happy."

"Future employees?"

"Something like that," said Rees-Jones, with a Cheshire Cat's grin. "This way."

Rees-Jones led Alex through an open warren of desks and workspaces. Occasionally a man occupied a desk. All wore fancy striped dress shirts, open at the collar, sleeves rolled up. A few read the morning paper. One was on the phone, but when he spoke his voice was so soft, it sounded like rustling velvet.

"Quiet day?"

"Not so much."

Alex could expect that half the employees were former intelligence agents of one sort or another, with time at MI5, known colloquially as Box, or at MI6, the security service. The rest would come from Scotland Yard and various branches of the British military, primary among them the SAS, or Special Air Service.

Rees-Jones passed through a doorway into an airy, spartan office. The desk was frosted glass with polished steel legs. There was a phone, a blotter, framed black-and-white photographs of stark landscapes, and not much else. "Please sit. Tea?"

"I'm fine," said Alex, setting her shoulder bag on the floor as she took her place.

Rees-Jones dropped into a low-backed chair. "Good flight over? Private travel makes things so much easier."

Alex had said nothing to her contact at Five about using Bobby's jet, which meant that Chris Rees-Jones had contacts of her own. "I was expecting Major Salt."

"Major Salt no longer works here."

"I wasn't aware of that. A recent change?"

"Three months now. Clients are always surprised to learn that a woman took his place. I see you are, too."

"A little," said Alex. It was a lie. She was very surprised. Women might be prominent in law enforcement in the States, and increasingly in Western Europe, but she hadn't known them to have entered the preserve of private combat arms.

"I'll take that as a compliment." Rees-Jones gazed at her boldly. Her eyes were blue, her skin as smooth as alabaster, and her hair the platinum blond that only the most expensive colorist can guarantee. Alex put her at fifty, give or take. She also had her down as a spy put out to pasture. She was too smooth, too polished to be a police officer.

"You're wrong," said the Englishwoman, as if reading her mind. "Not a spook. That's what they all think. Not Scotland Yard either. I did my training at the LSE, the London School of Economics. I'm a banker. Or I was. Private equity. My firm bought the place three months back. Military privatization's a growing market."

"And Major Salt?"

"He was never much of a numbers man. Still likes to get some mud on his boots, if you get my drift."

"Mud or blood?" asked Alex.

"Probably both." Rees-Jones smiled politely. "Major Salt sits on our board. He consults."

Alex nodded, her hopes for getting any information about Lambert fading by the second.

"This is all rather unorthodox," said Rees-Jones. "Of course, we're used to visits from our colleagues on the other side."

"I thought we were on the same side."

"I meant the public sector."

"Excuse me," said Alex. "I thought we were talking law enforcement."

"We help when possible, but we do like some warning. Don't you have legates and that sort to arrange these things?"

"There wasn't time to go through the usual channels."

Rees-Jones took this in. "So," she said finally. "What's up?"

"We're interested in a man with ties to your company. Luc Lambert."

"Go on."

"Lambert's ex–Foreign Legion. He signed on with Trevor Manning a few years back on the Comoros deal. Major Salt was a part of that, if I'm not mistaken. It's open knowledge that your office helped recruit the soldiers."

"That was the old company. Before my time. And if it were not, I still couldn't comment. It's policy not to discuss our clients. Ironclad, I'm afraid." Now that that was settled, Rees-Jones placed her hands on the table and smiled. "What's this Lambert done, anyway?"

"He's dead. I thought that given the circumstances, you might wish to make an exception."

"And the circumstances are?"

"We believe that Lambert figured as part of a larger group planning an imminent attack on U.S. soil."

Rees-Jones leaned forward, the blue eyes colder. "How imminent?"

"Today, tomorrow, Friday—a week at most."

"That's quite a statement."

Alex explained the events of the past forty-eight hours, beginning with the stakeout in Queens, the shootout with Lambert, and the deaths of the three Bureau men and culminating with the discovery of the weapons cache. "Luc Lambert wasn't in New York on vacation. He was there to do a job. If we're right, twenty-three others are either already there or arriving soon to join him."

"Sounds rather frightening. Why aren't you putting out the alarm?"

"Not enough to go on yet. We can't go around causing panic. For the moment, it's all still strictly internal. We also have rules about sharing information, but in this case we have to make an exception."

"Special Agent Forza, discretion is the currency of our trade. If word spread that we'd revealed our client list or in any way discussed our business with the authorities, we'd be shuttering the premises within the day. Besides, as I said, that was years ago. Technically a different company altogether."

"I thought you'd say that."

"Yet you came all this way."

"I hoped I might be able to convince Major Salt. He's a soldier. I can't imagine he'd want one of his own going to the dark side."

"I'm sure you're right."

"I know that GRAIL would never have anything to do with this kind of operation. If word got out that your company recruited mercenaries to mount a Mumbai-style terrorist attack in New York City, the authorities would close it down in a heartbeat. The directors would be lucky if they got off with a long spell in jail. If they lived that long. Israelis aren't the only ones pursuing a policy of targeted assassinations these days."

"Are you threatening me?" asked Rees-Jones angrily.

Alex kept her voice as flat as water. "Do you feel threatened?"

Rees-Jones considered this before conjuring a laugh and a winning smile. "Look, we're not as bad as all that. I'm sorry if I came off as brusque, but we deal with some pretty rough types. Nature of the beast, I suppose. We do have firm principles, and they are absolutely necessary if we wish to maintain our position in a competitive global market." Rees-Jones sighed, placed both hands on her glass tabletop, and stood. "Wait here. Let me check our database. If Lambert was a part of Colonel Mann's expedition, we may still have record of it. Don't sic the Israelis on me just yet."

Rees-Jones left the office. Alex opened the black mesh bag and took out a compact and lipstick to reapply her makeup. She traded lipstick for mascara, and sighed when she dropped the mascara on the floor. Her fingers scooped up the mascara but made a detour on the way back, slipping beneath the arm of the chair to attach a listening device.

Rees-Jones returned as Alex finished putting away the mesh bag.

"Not much, but something," said the Englishwoman as she sat. "This is in no way an admission that we've ever had contact with Mr. Lambert. I do, however, have an address for a man by that name who lived in Paris. The address is seven years old, but the French postal authority should be able to help."

"No French social insurance number? Phones? Next of kin? Anyone we can reach out to."

"I'm sorry."

"And there's been no contact since?"

"None. We rather got out of that line of work after the Comoros fiasco."

"Probably smart," said Alex, smiling for the first time.

"Indeed."

Alex looked at the paper. "It's a start. I'll get on to the French at once." She stood. "Thank you for your time. And it was I who was brusque. I lost a close friend the other day. I apologize."

"No need. If there's nothing further . . ." Rees-Jones placed her palms on the table, stood, and led Alex to the entry, where she wished her goodbye.

Back on the street, Alex opened her umbrella and set off up the block. The rain was coming down hard as ever and a corner of her umbrella immediately sagged, ladling water onto her shoulder. She barely noticed. In her mind, she had an image of Chris Rees-Jones's glass desk and the two damp palm prints visible on its otherwise immaculate surface. A few minutes earlier, the woman's hands had been as dry as chalk. Something had made her nervous.

Very nervous indeed.

66

The Starbucks at the corner of New Bond Street possessed an unobstructed line of sight less than 100 yards from GRAIL. Alex set her venti latte with a triple espresso shot on a table near the entrance. Digging into her pocket, she retrieved a nubbin-sized receiver and fitted it inside her right ear, taking care to activate it with a flick of her thumbnail. A burst of static gave way to silence, then the sound of someone ticking a pencil against a glass desk. "Jonathan," came Chris Rees-Jones's voice. "Cancel my appointments for the rest of the day. Something's come up. And see if the solicitors are free this afternoon. Tell them it's urgent."

"Yes, ma'am."

A door closed. Alex could hear footsteps receding down the hall outside Rees-Jones's office. The zinc-powered microtransmitter she'd placed beneath the arm of her chair was working better than she had dared dream. It was only a matter of waiting. She had every confidence that the dime would drop at any minute.

Alex opened a copy of the *Times* and feigned reading. In her ear came the sounds of a drawer opening and closing, papers being arranged, a woman clearing her throat. Alex drank half the latte. The espresso hit her like a thousand volts and she put down the cup. Enough of that. She was already jacked enough.

Rees-Jones dropped something metallic on her desk. "Come on," she whispered angrily. "Pick up the phone, you bloody prick."

Alex smiled inwardly. The prey was running. Rees-Jones was making the call. The "bloody prick" was Major James Salt.

"Hello, Jim . . . Never mind how I am. I just had an unexpected visit from the FBI. The agent was interested in an old mate of yours, a Frenchman named Luc Lambert . . . What do you mean, you don't remember? He was one of your boys on that Comoros debacle . . . I thought you would . . . 'Lucky Luke'—cute. Well, he ran out of luck. He was killed in a raid outside New York City the day before yesterday . . . I don't know where . . . Queens or something, the woman said . . . Her name was Forza . . . Counterterrorism. New York office."

Alex stared hard at the newspaper, but in her mind's eye she was inside Rees-Jones's office, standing in the corner and watching the slick executive sweat.

"Lambert killed three agents . . . Three, did you hear? . . . You said this was a Third World operation. Training in Namibia. No damage to Britain or its allies. Another of your far-flung get-rich schemes designed to make you chief headshrinker of Booga-Booga Land. You didn't say America . . . Bullshit, you didn't know . . . This is totally unacceptable. Your boys have machine guns, grenades, and an antitank weapon. For fuck's sake, Jim, what the hell is going on? . . . Well, then find out . . . New York City, are you out of your mind? The last time someone attacked the city the Americans invaded two countries . . . Just how much whiskey are you drinking these days? . . . Are you that fucking broke? . . . No, I won't calm down. In fact, I'm just getting started . . . Of course there are links between us. Our honorarium came from your client, didn't it? . . . Their bank may be in Liechtenstein, but ours is in Mayfair. It's called Citibank, and in case you don't recall, it is American. I don't think it will have any qualms about turning over our account information to the FBI . . . Stop telling me to relax. This Forza woman is a bulldog . . . How do I know? Because she's a hard little bitch like me . . . All right, call me back. But soon. If I don't hear from you in an hour, I'm going to our solicitors."

The call ended.

Alex drank the rest of her coffee. On her pad, she'd written the words *Namibia* and *Liechtenstein bank* and *Citibank/Mayfair branch*, and finally, in block letters, *SALT*. She only wished she could have heard the other side of the conversation.

She checked her watch. It was after eleven, about 5 a.m. in the States. She wondered how Katie was doing. Her daughter had always loved the outdoors, camping, canoeing, cooking dinner over a bonfire or, more likely, a gas burner. It seemed odd to be thinking about her daughter away in New Hampshire when she was in London trying to stop a terrorist attack from taking place on U.S. soil.

During the next forty minutes, Rees-Jones took a call from a Middle Eastern sheikh and agreed to provide a cadre of bodyguards for his upcoming trip to London. The sheikh wanted only former SAS men, and Rees-Jones gave him her word. A second call dealt with a failed kidnapping negotiation in Colombia. The victim's company had agreed to pay $2 million. The kidnappers had wanted $5 million. The victim was now dead and his family was threatening to sue GRAIL.

Major James Salt called back at high noon. It quickly became clear that he'd been doing some checking on his own.

"You're sure she's on her own?" said Rees-Jones. "So what? It doesn't matter whether New York sent her or not. She's here and she knows about Lambert's ties to you . . . No, I don't know where she went . . . She arrived this morning on a private jet . . . Gatwick . . . no, I don't know what kind . . . wait, it was a Gulfstream . . . a description . . . brown hair, shoulder length, rather pretty, athletic. Clothes . . . why? . . . We bloody well do have a choice . . . I won't be party to that . . . I won't and that's final . . . Do I have to be afraid, Jim? *Jim? Are you there?* . . . Bastard."

Alex placed Chris Rees-Jones's business card on the table and dialed the company's main number.

"GRAIL. How may I direct your call?" The operator was a man, and his accent pegged him as working-class, probably from northern England.

"This is Jane Greenhill from the U.S. embassy for Major Salt."

"Major Salt no longer works on the premises. May I direct you to a voice mailbox?"

"My apologies. I forgot about the shakeup. Do you have his direct number? The ambassador would like to speak to him on an urgent matter."

"Of course, Mrs. Greenhill. I do note, however, that you're not calling on the embassy's main line."

"I'm sorry. We're in a bit of a tizzy here this morning. I'm not at my desk. Would you prefer if I call you back?"

There was a pause, and Alex assumed that the operator was checking the embassy directory for a Jane Greenhill, who was in fact the ambassador's secretary, and a friend of hers.

"That won't be necessary, Mrs. Greenhill. I'm happy to let you know where to reach Major Salt."

Alex jotted the number onto her pad. "Is that his home, office, or mobile? As I said, it's regarding an urgent matter."

"His home. I'm not permitted to give out another number."

"Do you happen to know if he's there at this hour?"

"Major Salt usually begins the day at his club."

"The Royal Automobile Club?"

"Good God, no. White's, on St. James's Street."

"Know him well, do you?"

"I served under him in the regiment, yes, ma'am."

"Major Salt is a good man. The ambassador likes him very much. Thank you, Mr. . . ."

"Nolan."

"Mr. Nolan. Goodbye."

Alex folded the newspaper, slipped it into her bag, and was on her feet ten seconds later. The rain had stopped, and once on the street, she hurried to the curb to hail a taxi.

"Where to, ma'am?" asked the cabbie.

"White's." Alex jumped into the back seat. "And an extra fiver if you can get me there in ten minutes."

67

"Pull over."

Alex spotted him standing under the awning at the entrance to White's. He was tall and trim and rigid, with sandy hair going to gray and a jaw that could break through walls. Reports put his age at fifty, but Alex thought he looked ten years younger. Dressed in a blazer, gray slacks, and a crisp white shirt, Major James Salt was still every inch the officer.

"He's a friend," she said. "I want to surprise him."

The cabbie caught her gaze. "If that's the way you look at friends, I'd hate to think how you look at your enemies."

Salt handed a ticket to a car attendant and stepped to the curb.

"I'd like you to follow him for a few blocks," said Alex.

"Your coin, ma'am. I'll follow him all the way to Glasgow if you like."

Alex sat back, her eyes never leaving Salt. It was her first break, and she was grateful for it. A navy Aston Martin came out of the car park and halted in front of the club. Salt clapped a banknote into the attendant's hand and slid into the driver's seat. The Aston Martin roared from the curb. The cabbie took the sports car's speed as an insult and pressed his foot to the floor. The taxi shook and shuddered as it picked up speed. Piccadilly was a long, straight road, and Alex counted only two more traffic lights ahead before it passed Hyde Park. After that, she wouldn't have a chance.

Ahead the first light turned yellow. The Aston Martin didn't slow for an instant.

"Go," said Alex.

The cabbie kept his foot on the pedal, sliding through as the light went to red. He could do nothing to keep up with the Aston Martin. Alex balled her hands into fists, her jaw clenched so tight she thought she might crack a tooth. The sports car widened the distance. Alex stared at the final signal. Beyond it, Salt would open up the engine and let fly (exactly as she would). Any opportunity to confront him would be gone.

"Can't you go any faster?" she asked.

"Trying, ma'am. Only have four cylinders. Your friend's got twelve. Not a fair fight."

The light turned yellow, then red. The Aston Martin didn't slow. Alex waited to see its brake lights bloom, praying for Salt to stop at the signal.

A flash of red.

Salt came to a stop. Ten seconds later, the taxi drew to a halt two cars behind him. Alex thrust her fist through the transom in the partition. "Here's twenty."

"But—"

Alex was out the door, running up the street, passing one car, then the next, her eyes on the traffic signal, ordering it not even to think of changing. The Aston Martin was still a stride away when the light turned green. Alex lunged for the door. Her fingers grasped the handle and she flung open the door as the car began to gain speed. With a last effort, she pulled herself into the car as the Aston Martin barreled through the intersection.

"What the hell?" said Major James Salt. "What do you think you're doing?"

"You know who I am," said Alex. "Keep going."

Major James Salt looked askance at her. "She said you were a hard little bitch."

"She was right."

"I could shoot you here and now and be within my rights."

Alex didn't detect a gun on Salt's person, but that didn't mean there wasn't one close by. "I don't need a gun, and I couldn't give a shit about rights. Just drive."

Salt hit the accelerator. "What the hell do you want?" he asked.

"Everything. Names. Targets. Timing. Mostly I want to know who's behind it."

"Don't know what you're talking about."

"I think you do."

"How did you find me?"

"I'd prefer it if I ask the questions."

"You're interrogating me in my own car?"

"Major Salt, you're in serious trouble. I'd say cooperating is your best bet."

"Your office didn't even send you. So what if Lambert served under me once? That was years ago. You're on nothing but a wild-goose chase."

"I know you recruited Lambert. I know he was sent to Namibia for training. I know that you paid GRAIL a fee to help you. I think we're way past a wild-goose chase."

"You listening in?"

"And it's all on tape."

"No court of law will ever admit it," said Salt. "You can take your tape and shove it up your cute little ass. Why the hell should I talk to you?"

Alex twisted in her seat, reached out her hand, and took firm, unremitting grip of Salt's unmentionables, giving a salutary squeeze to make sure the good major got the message. "Because if you don't," she said, "I'm going to rip your balls off right here and now."

Salt's eyes widened. The car swerved wildly.

"Steady," said Alex. "Eyes on the road. We're going to have a full and frank discussion. All right?"

Salt nodded. His face was very red. He turned the vehicle into Hyde Park. Traffic was sparse.

"If you think you can hide behind a lawyer on this one, you're wrong. Your ex-messmate Sergeant Lambert killed one of my dearest friends. I am here on his behalf, his wife's, and his two baby daughters'. I don't give a fuck about a warrant, a lawyer, or whether the Bureau sent me here or not. This is between you and me. Are we clear?"

"Just let go," said Salt. "Please."

Alex clenched her fingers viciously, then released her grip. Salt exhaled and slid lower in his seat. "Bloody hell. Let me pull over. Do that again and you'll get us both killed."

"Talk," said Alex. "Who contracted you to find Lambert and the rest of them?"

"Yeah, yeah," said Salt. "I'll tell you. Just let me get off the road."

The car crossed Serpentine Bridge. Ahead and to the right was a small parking lot. Alex noted that there were only a few cars, probably due to the earlier rain.

Salt looked over his shoulder to signal. Reflexively, Alex looked, too. She realized her mistake a split second too late. She saw only a

THE PRINCE OF RISK

flash from the corner of her eye before Salt's forearm clubbed her head, slamming her face against the window. She saw stars. Salt hit her again, this time with his fist, his curled knuckles crunching her cheekbone.

Vaguely, she observed Salt pounding his hand into the dashboard, the compartment falling open, Salt reaching for something black and bulky, and she knew it was a pistol, a Glock like the one she carried. He freed the weapon from the compartment, and she knew that he would use it, that no soldier draws a weapon for show. A bolt of adrenaline returned her faculties. As Salt swung his arm to her head and brought the pistol to bear, she grasped his shooting hand and forced it high and away. The gun fired inches from her face, and Alex felt the powder burn her cheek. The gun fired again. She was deaf and blind, her head clamoring with a terrific ringing, her sight a wall of blackness.

She was at Windermere, lying flat on her back, powerless to stop Lambert from shooting Jimmy Malloy.

Not again.

She blinked and her sight returned. Salt was driving on the wrong side of the road. A great grille of gleaming silver bore down on them.

"Watch out!" she cried.

The truck careened out of their path, the blare of its horn only barely audible over the ringing in her ears. Salt threw the wheel to the left and regained their lane. At that moment Alex rose in her seat, took hold of his upper arm with her left hand, and twisted her torso, wrenching the forearm down across her knee, snapping the arm.

Salt screamed. The pistol fell onto the floor. Alex scooped it up and pressed the snout to Salt's temple. "Stop the car," she said.

The Aston Martin turned into the parking lot, still traveling at high speed. Salt braked too hard, and the car fishtailed before shuddering to a halt.

"You bloody bitch. You broke my arm."

"I want a name," said Alex. "Or I promise you I'll break the other one, too."

"I don't know his name," said Salt, cradling his arm. "He contacted me three months ago. Something about assembling a team for a job overseas. A coup. Dangerous business. Promised to pay me a fortune. I'm broke. I needed the money. He never said anything about America."

"How much did he pay?"

"A million. Pounds, not dollars."

"Who were the others?"

"Chaps I've worked with before. Some from the regiment, some from the legion, like Lambert. There were others from all over. Belgium. Sweden. Women, too."

"Women?"

"He insisted. Had to blend in."

"Blend in where?"

"I don't know."

"How many?"

"A few. Ten. Maybe twelve."

"Bullshit." Alex tapped the fractured limb. "How many?"

"Thirty. Sent them all to Namibia. They had a ranch out there. A training facility or something. Six washed out." Salt winced. "I've got to get to a hospital. Feels like a compound fracture."

Alex felt the arm, and Salt shuddered. "No bleeding," she said. "You can stand a little discomfort."

"Discomfort? This is bloody agony."

"What do you call him?"

"I don't. He calls himself my old friend."

Alex detected hesitation in his response. Salt was lying. No one went to that length to recruit thirty men and women without knowing the name of his employer. She tapped the pistol against Salt's broken arm. "Don't lie to me. I want a name."

Salt gnashed his teeth. "Screw yourself."

"I want a name!"

And in that instant his other arm rose from his side. Alex saw the flash of silver gleaming between his fingers. She fired the gun twice into Salt's chest. He fell against the door, and she observed the thrusting knife in his hand, the stubby, razor-sharp blade protruding between his middle and ring fingers.

Salt regarded himself. "Shite."

"Who paid you?" asked Alex. "Who's your 'old friend'?"

"You're too late anyway," he said.

"When is it happening? Today? Tomorrow?"

Salt grimaced as a tremor shook his body.

"Please," said Alex. "Save your friends' lives at least."

"Sod off."

Salt coughed. Blood flowed over his lips. He died.

68

Alex climbed out of the car, stumbling and unsteady. A few deep breaths restored her strength but did little to lessen the pounding in her skull. She had a concussion. Her cheek was tender to the touch, and she could feel her eye swelling. She needed distance, room to make sense of her predicament.

She took stock of her surroundings. Rain had given way to scattered clouds and sun. She counted three other cars in the lot. All were parked a ways away. For the time being, she saw no one nearby, but that would change soon. A truck rattled along the main road, and then she was alone, with only the whipping wind and her own labored breathing to keep her company.

Alex looked back at the car. Salt sat slumped at the wheel. He was very bloody, and she knew she must think fast in case a policeman drove past. There was no question of running. She'd killed a man. She was a law enforcement officer. On or off duty, she wouldn't try to escape her actions.

Alex returned to the car.

There was no running, but there was still work to be done.

She slid into the passenger seat and searched Salt's person. She found his wallet in his coat pocket. In three minutes she'd made a note of every credit card he possessed, as well as his driver's license number and social insurance card. He carried £500 in cash. No pictures. Only a few old business cards listing him as founder/CEO of GRAIL.

Salt kept his phone in his trouser pocket. She scrolled through his recent calls, eager to learn who he'd contacted after receiving the tip-off from Chris Rees-Jones. Salt was nothing if not efficient. Each call was listed for her. The call from GRAIL was followed by a call to the U.S. embassy. The call lasted three minutes. Salt was canny. He was smart enough to use the main number and have the call forwarded to his contact. Still, it would be no problem to learn that person's name.

Alex was more interested in finding out who Salt's source at the embassy had phoned at the FBI at 5:15 a.m. New York time. She reasoned it had to be someone close to her, maybe even someone in CT.

The next call was to his solicitor. The third was to someone named Skinner. No last name attached. Duration, fourteen minutes. Some weighty matters to discuss, no doubt. It took her a moment to recognize the country code. South Africa.

And then a call to Jerry at Olympic Travel. Duration, three minutes. She could hear Salt's gruff voice in her head: "Get me out of here, now." It made sense that he had an exit strategy on the shelf. Alex guessed that Brazil, with its flimsy extradition regulations, would be Salt's refuge of choice. Or was it South Africa? A visit to his friend Skinner?

She opened the e-mail application. One unread message from Olympic Travel. A first-class seat on a flight to Rio de Janeiro for nine that evening, booked under the name George Penrose. Alex was right about Brazil.

Several innocuous messages followed from friends, confirming a golf date, dinner at the club, and then a missive from a woman named Regina asking if he'd been "a naughty boy and required punishment from his mum." To which Salt had replied, "Very naughty."

Alex rolled her eyes. Englishmen.

And then an e-mail from "BeaufoySLT." The message ran to one line. It was at once familiar and cryptic. "The Eagle Has Landed. *Gott mit uns.*"

The full address was BeaufoySLT@orange.sa. "Sa" for South Africa. Message sent at 3:33 Greenwich Mean Time, 9:33 Eastern Standard Time.

Was BeaufoySLT from South Africa Salt's friend Skinner?

Alex looked away, the hackles on her neck standing at attention. She needed no translation to know what the message meant. *The Eagle Has Landed. Gott mit uns.* The bad guys were in the States.

This was happening now.

The phone rang. The incoming call was from C. Rees-Jones. Alex knew better than to answer. It was imperative that the woman know nothing about Salt's death. She let the call roll to voice mail. She waited until the message was complete, then listened.

"Jim. It's me. You've really got us scared. We've decided to go to our solicitors this afternoon. We have to get in front of this. Whoever you're working with, I am pleading with you to call it off. Do you hear? You've lost your mind. Call me. Now."

Alex listened to the message again. Rees-Jones was right to be flipping out. Her business, not to mention her life as a free woman, was at stake. She was smart to be proactive. She wasn't so smart to have worked with James Salt.

Opening her purse, Alex snatched the mesh bag holding her electronic toys and plucked out the small rectangular unit she called the vacuum. She freed the SIM card from Salt's phone and inserted it into the vacuum's slot. Thirty seconds later the vacuum had copied the SIM card's data to its own internal memory. Alex returned the SIM card to Salt's phone, then slipped the phone back into Salt's pocket. She wouldn't want anyone accusing her of tampering with the evidence.

Alex popped the trunk. Inside was a beautiful set of golf clubs and, tucked to one side, an even more beautiful calfskin briefcase. The case was locked, so she borrowed Salt's thrusting knife and broke it open. So much for tampering with evidence. Inside it were files and more files. A vial of cocaine. Condoms. A container of barbiturates. Salt wasn't lying. He really had been a naughty boy.

And there beneath a legal pad, one crisp white envelope addressed to Mr. George Penrose from the Bank of Vaduz, Liechtenstein. Against every rule, she removed the letter with her bare hands. It was a computer-generated confirmation of deposit into his account in the amount of one million British pounds paid by Excelsior Holdings of Curaçao N.V.

The smoking gun.

And the map leading to Salt's "old friend."

Alex closed the trunk, then placed the briefcase on the passenger seat. She checked her watch. It was one-thirty. Seven-thirty at home. She grabbed her cell phone, mustering her courage. Where was her picture of J. Edgar Hoover when she needed it? She counted to three, then placed the call.

"You're up early," said Janet McVeigh.

"Actually, I've been up quite a while," said Alex.

"Can't sleep?"

"Not exactly. I'm in London."

A period of silence followed. For once Alex appreciated McVeigh's ability to hold her temper. "Go ahead," she said finally.

"I know I broke the rules. You can fire me later. Right now there's a lot you need to know. I was right about Lambert's ties to GRAIL. The company was involved in hiring him and twenty-nine others. Not directly, but it provided introductions to Major James Salt, the officer who ran Executive Outcomes alongside Trevor Manning. Salt also played a large part in the Comoros raid. I'm e-mailing you a recording between Salt and Chris Rees-Jones, GRAIL's director. This conversation took place ten minutes after I met with Rees-Jones and asked her about Lambert. I bugged her office during our meeting, so there's only one side to the conversation, but it's enough."

McVeigh's diplomacy deserted her. "How did you—"

"Let me finish. As I said, Salt hired thirty men and women and sent them to a training compound in Namibia. Six of the recruits washed out. Lambert's dead. That leaves twenty-three. It's my guess they were the ones who came through Mexico City two nights ago."

"So you spoke with Salt, too?" McVeigh's anger was laced with a grudging admiration.

"I tracked him down to his club in London and interrogated him in his vehicle."

"Voluntary or coerced?"

"Somewhere in between. I asked him a few questions. He tried to kill me. I shot him. He's dead."

Alex looked at her reflection in the window. Her hair was disheveled. She was bleeding from the nose, and her eye was starting to look like an eggplant. "Jan? You there?"

"You killed Salt?"

"Yes."

"Let me get this clear—and I'm talking to you as your supervisor and as AD of the New York office, not as a fellow investigator. You disobeyed my express orders not to return to work. Also against my express orders, you traveled to London. I imagine I should be thankful that you didn't hijack one of the Bureau's jets. You conducted an illegal surveillance operation in a foreign country, then you killed a person of interest during the course of a hostile interrogation."

"He pulled a gun and discharged his weapon twice in an effort to kill me. When I disarmed him, he attempted to stab me instead."

"Are you all right?"

"Except for a black eye, yes. Thank you for asking."

"You're in trouble, Alex. You know that?"

"Yes."

"All right, then. We'll deal with that side of things when you get back. Did you get any useful information out of this escapade at all?"

"A confirmation of deposit from Salt's account at the Bank of Vaduz, Liechtenstein, in the amount of one million pounds from an Excelsior Holdings of Curaçao. My guess is that that's who is bankrolling this whole thing. Find out who's behind Excelsior and we find out who's pulling all the strings."

"Good luck with that. Between Liechtenstein and Curaçao, we'll be lucky to have a call returned three months from now."

Alex had other ideas, but kept them to herself. "There was also an e-mail on his phone sent last night at nine your time from someone named Beaufoy. South African e-mail address. It read, 'The Eagle Has Landed. *Gott mitt uns.*'"

"And that means?"

"You know what it means."

"No, I don't. And neither do you."

"Bullshit. You'll know when you hear the tape. I'm going to contact a friend of mine at Five and tell him what happened. I don't want to end up in jail for the next week. You might want to brief the director. I imagine the shit's going to hit the fan pretty good."

"Alex—"

"Listen to the tape." Alex hung up before McVeigh could scream at her. She felt faint and paced back and forth until the blood returned to her head. The concussion was worse than she thought. She crossed her fingers that McVeigh would see things her way and vote with her badge instead of her rulebook.

Alex called her colleague at MI-5 and explained about her visit to GRAIL and the interrogation of James Salt. He told her to drive Salt's car to an address in Kensington not far from Five's headquarters on the River Thames.

"What about Scotland Yard?" she asked.

"*Who?* Now move it."

Alex checked the surroundings. She noted a couple walking beneath some trees fifty yards away. She turned full-circle. No one else was nearby.

Corpses were heavy and ungainly. It required all of her strength to shift Salt to the passenger seat. When she slid behind the wheel, she noted that her clothing was matted with Salt's blood. She buttoned her blazer and raised the collar to camouflage as much of it as possible.

Alex fired the engine, then spun the car in a one-eighty and left the park.

McVeigh called back five minutes later. "You haven't contacted GRAIL again, have you?"

The anger was gone from her voice. It was operational McVeigh speaking. Alex had her reprieve. "Chris Rees-Jones called Salt a few minutes ago, but I didn't answer. I listened to the message. Apparently she's considering going to the company's solicitors to admit her part in this thing before it blows up even further."

"Good. I've spoken to Five. They've agreed to take your evidence to a magistrate straightaway. Between what's happened on our turf and what happened over there, he should be able to obtain a warrant to storm GRAIL's offices and Salt's home."

"Nice," said Alex. The British didn't mess around when it came to thwarting terrorist attacks. If a corner needed to be cut, so be it. They'd glue it back in place afterward.

"We're pulling the director out of a breakfast meeting on Capitol Hill to deal with this," continued McVeigh. "It's clear he'll have to go to the British PM. That means the president will have to be read in. You're really putting the special relationship to the test."

"Jan, I need a favor. About that South African e-mail address. Salt called someone named Skinner with a South African phone number immediately after talking to GRAIL." Alex read off the number. "Give that to the boys in Tech. See if they can ping it, find out where Mr. Skinner is. If my hunch is correct, we're not going to like the answer."

"We'll need a warrant for that."

"The tape should do the trick."

"You're pushing things, kid."

"Salt has a contact in the embassy here. He knew I wasn't in England on official assignment." Alex read off Salt's number and gave the exact time of the call. "Trace it and let's find out who he has on the payroll at the embassy and who his contact called in the Bureau."

"Any ideas?"

"Someone in our office. Guarantee it."

69

The house in McLean, Virginia, was a large two-story redbrick with black shutters and a lawn jockey out front to greet the guests. Astor held the knocker in his hand and waited until precisely 7:30 to rap three times. A man in the throes of dressing for work answered almost immediately. "Yes?"

"Mr. Nossey. I'm Bobby Astor. Sorry to disturb you so early, but I believe my father came by to see you on Sunday. May I come in?"

Nossey was slim and olive-skinned, with hair cut to the scalp and deep-set brown eyes. He wore khaki pants and a company polo shirt with *Britium* sewn above the left breast. Astor was in the right place.

"I've been expecting somebody," said Nossey. "But I thought it would be the FBI or the police."

"No law enforcement agents have been by?"

"Just you. I take it you're not an agent or anything."

"I'm a hedge fund manager. I live in New York."

A light went on behind Nossey's eyes. "Comstock?"

"That's me."

Nossey sipped from a coffee mug with the words U.S.S. DALLAS on its side. "Come in. I'm just about to shove off for work."

"That your ship?" asked Astor, pointing to the mug.

"Sub, actually. I put in ten years aboard a nuke. In this house, a door's a hatch, the floor's the deck, and the bathroom is the head. Wife hates it. Kids think it's fun as all get-out." Nossey looked over Astor's shoulder at the Sprinter parked at the curb. "Yours?"

"Yeah."

"It's bigger than some of the boats I served on. There a driver somewhere in there?"

"There is."

"Why don't you drive with me to the office? We can talk on the way. I have a call at nine I can't miss. The new owners." Nossey rolled his eyes.

"Sure thing."

It took Nossey another ten minutes to finish his coffee, kiss his three children goodbye, and pat his golden retriever. Astor stood at the kitchen door, witnessing the daily ritual. He thought of his own daughter, Katie, currently vacationing in New Hampshire. He couldn't remember the last time he'd seen her in the morning before he went to work, or for that matter when he came home. The office was his wife, mistress, and child, rolled into one. He wouldn't apologize for it, but he could at least give her a call to say hi and tell her that he loved her.

After this meeting, he told himself.

Promise.

Astor and Nossey sat in the front of a Ford Explorer cruising at 70 miles per hour along the George Washington Parkway. The Potomac flowed to their right, green and lazy. The Sprinter followed behind, more of a bodyguard than Sullivan would ever be.

"You look like him."

"I'm taller," said Astor.

"I'm sorry about what happened. Any news?"

"Not that I've heard. I'm trying to look into what happened myself. I found your address in my father's home. He had several articles about Britium, too. You're not planning on listing on the New York Stock Exchange anytime soon?"

"We just got bought up by Watersmark. You must know that."

Astor nodded. "So my dad was here on other business."

Nossey took his cue. "He surprised me, too. I mean, he didn't call or anything. He just showed up Sunday morning on my doorstep."

"We have our reasons for showing up unannounced."

Nossey waited, but Astor didn't elaborate. "Anyway," Nossey continued, "he was eager to learn about the company. He said he wanted to hear everything about us, A to Z. I tried to put him off. It was Sunday and the kids had a baseball game. He didn't care. I figured if he'd come all the way down here, it must be important. I sent the kids off with my wife. He came inside and I told him."

Astor listened intently as Nossey gave his CEO's speech. Britium had started out ten years earlier writing application control software, code that automated infrastructure technology, translating varying computer protocols into a common, easily understood language.

"In English, please," said Astor.

"Sorry. You Wall Street guys are pretty wonky. You usually get off on the lingo."

"Layman's terms will be fine."

"In a nutshell, we write software that allows a person or a business to control and operate any kind of electronic device, anywhere in the world, via the Internet."

"Exactly what kind of electronic device?"

"Anything. We can help a power grid monitor the temperature of all its turbines and control their speed. Or allow a supervisor to check out a security system from a remote location, to adjust lighting in a building, to control air-conditioning, check out a company's phone system. You name it."

"Can it control an elevator?"

"An elevator? Sure. It can control anything. And the beauty of it is that it can be done from an easy-to-use interface, kind of like a universal remote control. Take, for example, a hospital. You have all kinds of independent systems running in there. One computer system controls the security system—alarms, cameras, all that. Another runs the employee timekeeping and access system. Still another governs the heating and plumbing. And so on. The problem is that each runs on its own protocol, or language. It's important for one person to be able to control all of those separate and independent systems from a single location. Our software translates the differing protocols into a common language. Think of it as controlling your TV, Blu-ray, and DVR via a single device from your armchair."

"And this is popular?"

"God, yeah. We call our software the Empire Platform. Right now, Empire controls eleven million devices in fifty-two countries."

"Like who?"

"Hospitals, power plants, airports, jails, government offices. Even the FBI and the CIA use our stuff."

"The FBI? What for?"

"Same as any other large organization that needs to keep track of its employees and manage its infrastructure."

"Is there anyone who doesn't use it?"

"Not that I can think of."

"Impressive."

"Watersmark thought so."

Nossey left the highway and negotiated the busy streets of Reston, Virginia. He pulled into a lot fronting a five-story glass office tower and parked, then he took Astor to his office on the top floor. "Take a seat."

Astor slid into a chair, pausing to look at a set of architectural plans on the table. Nossey stood beside him. "It's going to be the tallest building in the world. Empire will control all the building's critical functions." The Britium CEO smiled. "Including the elevators."

A secretary entered, and Nossey told him to bring coffee and doughnuts. He checked his watch for as long as it took to be rude, then returned his attention to Astor. "Five minutes," he said, pointing to a clock on the wall.

"What was my father interested in?"

"He already knew pretty much everything we did, but he wanted to know if we worked with firms on Wall Street. I said, 'Of course.' Every major bank uses Empire technology."

"Does the Stock Exchange use the Empire Platform?"

"Your father asked me the same question. I had to check, but yes, it does."

"For what?"

"Security. Access control. HVAC. Elevators. Telecom."

"Why telecom? Shouldn't that be the phone companies' job?"

"Once a call leaves the building, sure. But before it leaves the building we have to make sure all the computers are properly hooked up to the Net. Orders are placed on the floor but are executed off-site. The information has to go out and come back without any interference."

"How did he feel about the fact that the NYSE uses your platform?"

"Tell you the truth, he didn't seem too happy about any of it, but he was specifically interested in knowing whether Empire was in place before July 2011."

July 2011. Astor had no problem recollecting the date. It was around that time that the Flash Crash had occurred, the mysterious breakdown in trading that resulted in the Dow Jones Industrial Average plummeting a thousand points in minutes, only to regain two-thirds of the amount within an hour and the rest a day later. Its cause still offered fertile ground for debate. Hence the articles in his father's office at Cherry Hill.

Astor remembered the annual reports he'd found at Penelope Evans's house. One by one he named the companies, and one by one Nossey confirmed that all used the Empire Platform. Astor began to see Britium and the Empire Platform in a different light. "I hope this isn't rude," he said, "but how secure is Empire? It seems that a lot of critical industries use it to control their operations in one way or another. Have there ever been any instances of hacking or cyberattacks against Empire?"

"Not a single one. The Empire Platform is equipped with its own firewall to stop unwanted incursions dead."

"So no one has ever hacked one of your clients and messed with their controls? Not once?"

The question made Nossey nervous. "I'm not at liberty to discuss security issues. I can direct you to Mr. Hong. He handles queries dealing with product integrity and litigation."

Astor raised his hands and smiled. "No need to use the *L* word. I'm just trying to learn as much as I can about your company."

"You can't be too careful."

"I do have one question. Can the Empire Platform be used to control an automobile?"

Nossey laughed, before realizing the intent of the question. "No, it can't. Only a driver can control a car." He rose suddenly. "I'm sorry to kick you out, but my master awaits."

Astor stood. "You mentioned that my father was interested in your new owner."

"Watersmark? Yes, he was curious about management practices. He wanted to know just how involved they were in our day-to-day operations."

"And?"

"Of course they spent lots of time with us during the due diligence process and for the first six months after completing the acquisition. They studied all our internal systems—accounting, payroll, reporting, things like that. After that, they let us run things our way."

"So you'd say things are pretty much the same as before?"

"Sure, Mr. Hong doesn't bother us at all."

That was the second time Nossey had mentioned the name. "Who is Mr. Hong?"

"Watersmark put him in and pays his salary. He gathers all the data they want. Looks after the bigger issues. Smart guy. MIT. Stanford. And he's an engineer. He totally gets what we do."

The secretary announced the conference call over the loudspeaker.

"It's been fun," said Nossey. "Hope I helped."

"Tremendously," said Astor, though he wasn't entirely sure. "I appreciate your time."

Nossey walked him to the door. "Mr. Astor," he said, his face a mask of concern, "you don't really think Britium had anything to do with your father's death?"

"You mean my question about the car? I was just curious after you talked about Empire being like a universal remote control."

"Empire can't control a car. You'd have to hack the GPS, and of course you would have had to install a remote steering system." Nossey's demeanor brightened. The nuclear engineer turned software entrepreneur had scented a challenge. "Just maybe . . ."

70

They arrived in two cars, quietly and without pretense. Alex rode in the first with her colleague from MI5, Colonel Charles Graves. Three officers followed in the car behind. A second team had assembled in London outside the offices of GRAIL. It would be a synchronized entry.

"All right then," said Graves. "Shall we?" He was blond, blue-eyed, and sandy-haired, handsome except for his permanent frown.

"Let's go earn our beer," said Alex.

"Guinness, I hope?"

"Bud."

"Crikey." Graves called his counterpart in London. "We're a go." He turned into the drive and accelerated up a long driveway. Trees shaded the path. There was a pasture with horses and a pond with a dock and rowboat. They rounded the bend and Major James Salt's home came into view. It was a modest Georgian country house, a fat square slab of pale sandstone. The Bennett sisters would call it a big step up. Mr. Darcy would consider it a bigger step down. The road widened as it entered a crushed-gravel forecourt. Graves stopped the car next to a wheezing fountain and climbed out. Alex beat him to the door by a step.

"By all means," said Graves, motioning to the doorbell.

"You're too kind." A call to the house ten minutes earlier had established that Salt's wife was at home. Five's dossier on Salt said the wife was not involved in his activities. Alex punched it with her index finger.

Inside, footsteps approached. A stout, matronly woman with messy ginger hair and a cleaning dress opened the door. "Yes?"

Graves gave his work name and presented matching credentials. "We have a warrant that allows us to search the premises. Any interference will be regarded as a crime against the Crown. We would, however, welcome your help."

"Is this about James?"

"I'm afraid we can't answer any questions, ma'am. Now, if you'll be so kind."

Mrs. Salt stood aside to let the search party enter. "Where is he?" she asked. "I keep calling and he's not answering."

"In custody," said Graves.

"But he's a hero," Mrs. Salt protested.

"Not today," said Alex.

Mrs. Salt caught the American accent and took a closer look at Alex. Her mouth tightened in distaste at the sight of her swollen eye. "You all right?"

"Fine."

"Why is there blood on your trousers then?"

Alex glanced at her slacks and noted a patch of crusted blood on her knee, visible despite the dark wool. Graves had provided a fresh blouse. There hadn't been time to pop by Selfridges for a new suit. "Accident."

"Is it James?"

Alex glared at the woman. Mrs. Salt was an accomplice by association. She merited no sympathy. Alex brushed past her into the small, musty foyer. There was a grandfather clock and a throw rug and a tapestry on the wall that was not quite from Bayonne. But the home was immaculate. The major might be broke, but the missus had her pride.

Graves offered a rare smile. "Might we inquire where your husband's office is?"

"Upstairs. Second door on the left. Clean it up while you're there. He won't let me touch a thing. He's retired, you know. He sold his business a few months ago."

Alex started up the stairs, Graves and two more officers close behind. One stayed with Mrs. Salt. Behind them, they heard the woman inquiring in increasingly desperate tones, "What have you done with him? Why isn't he answering?"

Alex opened the door to Salt's office.

It was a room from the nineteenth century, all dark wood and heavy furniture, with grimy oils of British sailing ships covering the walls and velvet curtains obscuring a view to the back garden. An oak desk with feet of lion paws held pride of place. A new Mac sat on the desk, and near it an ashtray overflowing with cigar butts. Papers covered every other square inch of the surface, with several stacks piled taller than Alex.

"Do you mind?" she asked, pulling out the chair.

"Be my guest," said Graves.

"This may take a while." Alex sat and opened the first folder she saw. It was a personnel file, and clipped to the paperwork was a color photograph of a handsome soldier in the uniform of the French Foreign Legion. She recognized him at once. It was Luc Lambert, a.k.a. Randall Shepherd. "Then again, maybe not."

In the end it took two hours.

Major James Salt was as meticulous in his cataloguing of information pertaining to the project he had named Excelsior as he was careless in keeping it secret. Alex divided the information into three stacks: Personnel, Materiel, and Logistics.

Personnel contained dossiers on every one of the thirty mercenaries—twenty-two men and eight women—who were originally to take part in the coming action. Each dossier held a photograph, a handwritten employment application, medical records, an employment contract, and a reference to a bank where all fees were to be wired. Each member was to be paid $200,000 up front with a further $800,000 upon completion of the assignment. Graves was quick to point out that such salaries were far above normal compensation and hinted at an assignment with abnormally high risk.

"For that money, I give 'em fifty-fifty odds of getting back," he said. "It's their last payday and they know it. Make it out alive and retire to a white sand beach far, far away."

"Twenty-four shooters earning a million apiece," said Alex. "And it was supposed to be thirty. Who's got that kind of dough?"

"Want my answer?" said Graves. "State-sponsored."

Alex nodded. But which state? Only a rogue nation would go outside its own intelligence bureau to mount such a large operation.

One personnel dossier especially interested her. It belonged to an Alexander "Sandy" Beaufoy, age forty, former lieutenant in the South African Army and, like Lambert and Salt, a participant in the ill-fated Comoros coup. Under the section marked "Past Experience," she noted that Beaufoy's nickname was Skinner. It was Beaufoy who had sent Salt the ominous message stating "The Eagle Has Landed. *Gott mitt uns*" and with whom Salt had spoken for fourteen minutes shortly after GRAIL had alerted him to Alex's visit.

It was imperative to ping the phone.

Materiel provided a combined how-to manual and road map of international arms smuggling. There were names of dealers, ports of loading and unloading, false bills of lading, contacts at three U.S. ports of entry, including JFK, Philadelphia Port Authority, and Houston. The list of weapons purchased corresponded to a T with the armaments found at Windermere. Except for one difference: there was more than three times the amount.

Last, and to Alex's mind most important, came Logistics. The stack held flight details to and from Namibia, then onward to Caracas via Angola (which she noted was a former Portuguese territory). There were names of contact people at each stop, including phone numbers and e-mail addresses. There were names of hotels, along with confirmation numbers and prepaid vouchers. Alex was especially interested in the hotel in Mexico City where two nights earlier twelve rooms had been reserved under the name Excelsior Holdings. There was the name of the transportation company contracted to pick up "a party of twenty-five" from Benito Juárez International Airport, including details of the arriving flight. There was even the name of one General Jaime Fortuno of the Mexican Federales, who had agreed to meet the passengers and ease their passage through immigration, along with the general's banking details. A handwritten note on top of Fortuno's file stated, "Paid $10,000 cash. 15 July."

The funding, it seemed, was unlimited. But the trail ended there. There was no further mention of Excelsior or of the Bank of Vaduz. Nothing at all to lead them to Salt's "old friend."

Alex was frustrated. She had all the evidence any prosecutor would need to put away the bad guys for a hundred life sentences after the fact. But the trove of information brought her no closer to the essentials of the plot: where, when, how. Like all her fellow agents, she was conscious of the FBI's less-than-stellar record at stopping acts of terror before they occurred. When she'd assumed command of CT-26, she'd sworn that she would be the one to spot the attack *before*, and not the one who responded *after.* Yet once again she, and by extension the Bureau, found herself facing a brick wall. She needed actionable intelligence to get her people in place to foil the attack.

"You missed these," said Graves, dropping another stack of folders on the desk. "Fell behind the radiator."

"What are they?"

"Something you'll find interesting."

Alex picked up the folder. "Arrivals/USA." She looked at Graves. "Salt knew all along."

She opened the folder and read. Three groups. The first entering through Matamoros. The second via an oil rig off the Gulf Coast. And the third through Canada. All under the guise of being corporate employees. All slated for arrival in the greater New York metropolitan area yesterday evening.

The Eagle Has Landed. *Gott mitt uns.*

But where were they staying? She shuffled through the papers looking for any mention of a safe house, a place where the group would hole up and get their bearings prior to the attack. There was nothing about Windermere or anywhere else. She took that to mean one thing: the operation had a contact already in place in America.

It was as she reread the papers that she caught the name. The address for the drop-off in Matamoros belonged to a large supermarket chain called Pecos. The oil rig was owned by Noble Energy. And the drop-off in Canada was at the Silicon Solutions plant in Kitchener-Waterloo.

Pecos. Noble Energy. Silicon Solutions.

Alex dropped the file onto the desk. "Oh, no."

"What is it?" asked Graves.

"He was right," she said.

"Who?"

"Bobby."

71

Hello, Marv."
Astor poked his head out of the elevator and peered around the landing. *"Marv?"*

He saw no one. For once, Shank wasn't there to greet him.

Astor entered his office. The trading floor was surprisingly quiet. No one glanced up as he passed the desk. Even Longfellow and Goodchild had their faces buried in their computer screens. The calm disturbed him. It was like the silence before an execution. He reached his office and looked inside. No Shank there, either. Conference room one was packed with lawyers. They were sharply dressed, straight-backed, and disciplined to look at. He recognized Frank Arcano from Skadden, who would be leading the charge to grant him more time to meet the margin requirements. They were the good lawyers.

Conference room two was packed with more lawyers. They wore baggy suits and had their neckties undone and shaggy haircuts. He didn't recognize any of them and he knew they hailed from the CFTC, the Commodity Futures Trading Commission, the body that regulated foreign currency transactions. They were the bad lawyers.

He craned his head toward conference room three. He half expected to see a camera crew from CNBC setting up camp and the Money Honey herself getting made up in preparation for an interview with the latest victim of Wall Street hubris. Enter Robert Astor. Thankfully, conference room three was empty.

Astor retraced his steps toward the reception desk. He knocked at the CFO's door, then opened it. The boss didn't require an invitation. Marv Shank sat across the desk from Mandy Price.

"Look who decided to come to his own funeral," said Shank.

"Rumors of my death are greatly exaggerated." Astor pulled up a chair. "What have we got?"

"Per your instructions, we're liquidating all equities in Comstock Astor showing a profit," said Price. "So far we've sold a hundred million."

"That's a start."

"We have another five hundred million in equities that are more or less where we bought them."

"And the rest?"

"Losers."

"At the moment," said Astor.

"That's all that matters today," said Shank.

Astor buried his head in his hands. "The goddamned position."

"And our contact?"

"Lee? He says wait till Friday."

"There's still Reventlow," said Shank. "You call him?"

"The ball's in his court."

Shank looked at Astor with disgust. He started to speak, then settled for shaking his head and sighing.

The clock on the wall read 2:40. Astor was not optimistic.

He returned to his office. He sat down and darkened the blinds. His arm ached. He opened his drawer and took out the bottle of painkillers his doctor had prescribed. He shook one loose, then thought better of it, if only because he needed to have his wits about him.

Closing his eyes, he once more ran through everything he knew about his father's special project.

In early July, Edward Astor was tipped to some type of imminent plot by Palantir. The plot involved at least seven companies that were now or had been owned by a private equity firm. Each company was a client of Britium's and used the Empire Platform to manage its products. The industries included computers, software, satellites, engineering, and energy.

Astor concluded that it was their common tie to Britium that had most frightened his father and that his visit to Britium's CEO was for the sole purpose of confirming or disproving Palantir's accusations. He further concluded that since his father had inquired about whether Britium was in place before July 2011—the time of the Flash Crash—he had viewed Empire as responsible. Astor's own experience with the elevator in his home testified to the fact that Empire was vulnerable to hacking. If systems controlling the New York Stock Exchange and his

own home could be hacked, then so could any other system that relied
on the Empire Platform, including the FBI's and the CIA's. No wonder
his father had convinced Charles Hughes and Martin Gelman to join
him in waking the president.

According to Palantir, *"They were getting desperate."*

"And so?" Astor said aloud. "Who are 'they'? What in the world are
they planning?"

Astor was sure he possessed all the information he needed to find
the answer, yet he felt as far away from understanding the forces he was
up against as when he had first decided to look into his father's cryptic
message.

He stood too quickly, knocking his arm against the desk. He
clutched his injured limb, grimacing until the pain subsided.

Who?

Astor spun to face the computer. He brought up Google and typed
every relevant keyword he could think of into the query bar. First
he listed the seven companies whose annual reports he had found in
Penelope Evans's house. To those he added the names of the five private
equity firms. Finally he wrote, "Britium." He hit Return.

He had an answer in .0025 seconds.

The first link was to an article titled "Watersmark Welcomes New
Investor." Astor read on. "Watersmark LLC, the New York–based private equity firm, today announced the sale of a thirty percent stake in
the firm to the China Investment Corporation for three billion dollars.
Watersmark chairman Duncan Newman stated, 'We welcome CIC's
participation and look forward to working with them to make exciting
investments in the future.' Newman added that several of the Chinese
sovereign wealth fund's executives would take up residence in Watersmark's New York office to gain firsthand experience of the private
equity business and to offer a Pacific perspective."

The China Investment Corporation. It couldn't be.

And then Astor read the last line and the floor dropped from the
gallows. "CIC Chairman Magnus Lee commented, 'Of course, our participation is limited to a minority interest, but we hope to learn very
much from our American business partners.'"

Magnus Lee. His special contact. The man whose advice he had
summoned to place the biggest investment in his firm's history.

Astor blinked, not quite believing his eyes—maybe not wanting to believe them. He stood, his feet as heavy as if they were embedded in concrete.

Lee was the connection.

Lee was the man behind his father's death.

Astor forced himself back to his desk. He landed in his chair with a thud.

The next link read, "Oak Leaf Ventures Sells Twenty-five Percent Stake in Firm to China Investment Corporation." It went on to say that the CIC would send three of its executives to Oak Leaf's offices in Chicago. Again Magnus Lee was quoted as being "thrilled" with the investment while pointing out that CIC's participation would be strictly as a silent partner.

Lies. Lies. More lies.

For ten minutes Astor continued reading link after link.

The China Investment Corporation had invested billions of dollars in each of the private equity firms involved with the corporations his father had been investigating. Lee always made the point that the investments were passive, but in every case the CIC had placed a few executives at the private equity firms as "executives in training."

Read "spies."

Astor remembered the Asian man with the keen blue eyes who had tried to kill him yesterday. Eyes the color of Magnus Lee's.

Astor pulled up Watersmark's web page. He searched under its list of executives and was not surprised to find a familiar name: "Herbert Hong. PhD Stanford, MIT . . . born in China." Hong was one of the CIC execs implanted in Watersmark, who had then gone on to work at Britium.

Suddenly it was clear to him. The CIC used its power as a minority partner in Watersmark and Oak Leaf and all the others to gain influence over certain key companies in the funds' portfolios—companies involved in critical sectors of the nation's economy: computers, energy, satellites, missiles. But to what end?

Control.

Until now, Lee's actions—and by extension his country's—had been hidden behind the cloak of everyday corporate activity. But Astor knew that time was coming to an end. Lee was no longer content to spy.

He had something else in mind. Something terrible was brewing. His father had had knowledge of it and it had cost him his life. Palantir knew it, too.

"They're getting desperate."

Lee himself had told him to wait until Friday.

Whatever it was, it was happening now.

Astor took out his phone to call Alex. He'd gone as far as he could. He felt no satisfaction from his efforts, only horror. It was up to the FBI. As he dialed, his secretary's voice came over the speaker. "Call for you, Bobby. Septimus Reventlow."

Astor looked at the clock. It was one minute before three. One and a half hours until the funds to meet the margin call were due. One and a half hours to bankruptcy.

Astor hung up the cell and picked up the landline.

"Hello, Septimus."

72

Phone pressed to her ear, Alex Forza stared out the window at the shadowy contours of the passing English countryside. It was after nine. The late European dusk was turning to night. Charles Graves sat beside her at the wheel, driving hell-bent for Gatwick Airport. He promised to have her there in an hour. She told him she could make it in forty minutes. They settled for "as bloody fast as possible."

"I don't have his new number," Alex said to Bobby's secretary. "It's important that I reach him."

"He left five minutes ago to see a client. Septimus Reventlow. I believe Mr. Sullivan is driving him. Perhaps you can try him."

Alex hung up and called Sully's number. No one answered, and the call rolled to voice mail. "Sully, this is Alex. Tell Bobby to call me right away. It's urgent."

Alex tried again, thinking it was the lousy New York City cellphone reception. Again the call rolled to voice mail. *Damn you, Sully,* she cursed silently, wanting to attribute the failure to him.

There'd been no love lost between them when they'd worked on the JTTF, and her faith in him had taken a further hit after his failure to protect Bobby at Cherry Hill. To her mind, Sully was a slacker. He'd taken a bullet early in his career and coasted on it for thirty years. He wasn't a bad cop. He was just an average one. To Alex, the two were synonymous.

She hung up and called McVeigh to relate the discoveries made at Salt's house.

"Hi, Jan. I'm calling to talk to you about Bobby."

"What about him?"

"He called you yesterday, right?"

"No. What did he need to discuss with the FBI?"

"No?" Alex pressed the phone against her leg for a second, so McVeigh wouldn't hear her swear. She drew a calming breath, then related as best she could everything she knew about Bobby's investigation into his father's death and the links to it she'd found at Salt's home.

"So you're saying that Luc Lambert and the weapons we found at Windermere are tied to the deaths of Edward Astor, Charles Hughes, and Martin Gelman?"

"It would appear so. Prior to his death, Edward Astor was looking into the same corporations, which either wittingly or unwittingly helped smuggle the shooters into the States. I don't think that's a coincidence."

"I should say it isn't. Why didn't you relay this to me earlier?"

"My bad. I was counting on Bobby to tell you in person so you could sit him down and grill him. Frankly, I didn't think there was much to go on."

"This Palantir—all you have is his Skype handle?"

"That's correct."

"I'll see what I can do. In the meantime, write up the deets and e-mail them to headquarters."

"Do they have anything new?"

"One thing. The forensic team discovered a device attached to the steering column and throttle of the Secret Service vehicle Astor and the others were riding in. There isn't much of it left, but the smart money is saying it's some type of receiver that enables a third party to operate the car."

"Like a remote control?"

"Exactly."

"So we can write off the rogue Secret Service agent?"

"Maybe. There are lots of other questions about how anyone could hijack a vehicle. And we still don't know why Astor insisted on meeting Hughes and Gelman on Sunday and what they planned to tell the president. I'll pass on your info to the director right away. He'll be happy to have something to go on."

"Did we ping the phone?"

"We're waiting on the phone carrier in South Africa."

"And the bank?"

"Forget the bank. We'll never have that information in time. And Alex, tell Bobby to get his butt into my office pronto or else I'm going to send a team to bring him in. And I'll make sure it isn't a warm and fuzzy encounter."

"Yes, ma'am. I'm getting on a plane in an hour or so. I'll see you in the morning. Am I still on the bricks?"

"I'll decide that tomorrow."

Alex found Graves staring at her when she ended the call. "What?"

"Sounds like you're in hot water."

"You know what they say. Act now. Apologize later."

"Brave girl."

"Either that or stupid."

Alex walked with Charles Graves across the tarmac. A light rain fell, and the weather was forecast to worsen in the next hour. The captain stood at the base of the stairs to Bobby's jet, motioning for her to hurry. "There's an active storm cell moving in. We've got to get this bird into the air or we'll be stuck on the ground for hours."

Alex shook Graves's hand. "I imagine I'll be back to give evidence about Major Salt."

"We'll see if we can help you avoid that unpleasant piece of business," said Graves. "Right now, just worry about getting home and stopping the bad guys."

"I can't thank you enough for your help."

"Godspeed."

Alex climbed aboard and settled into a seat. From her window, she watched a bolt of lightning rip the sky. She counted slowly, waiting for the rumble of thunder. It came on three, cracking loudly enough to make her jump in her seat. She tightened the belt an extra inch and said a prayer. Not for a safe flight, but for luck in pinging Sandy Beaufoy's number. It was a long shot. The Bureau would have to contact his phone service provider in South Africa and have them access their records. Johannesburg was an hour ahead of London. She didn't think there were many telecom executives awake at midnight.

As the plane picked up speed and rolled down the runway, she tried to give John Sullivan one more call. Reception was poor, and the call didn't go through.

Bobby, she thought to herself. *Why aren't you calling me back?*

73

Astor arrived at Septimus Reventlow's office at 49th and Park at 3:30 sharp. Sully kept the Sprinter circling the block. Astor promised it would be a short meeting. He entered the building and checked the tenant board. RCH, or Reventlow Consolidated Holdings, was listed at 3810. He decided to put on a necktie to make up for his rude behavior. He wasn't sure whether it was an admission of victory or defeat. He used the glass as a mirror. Knotting his double Windsor, he saw that a familiar name was also a tenant of the building and also on the thirty-eighth floor. What were the odds? He decided to stop in for a surprise visit before his meeting with Reventlow and ask some questions.

The elevator arrived. Astor paused before stepping inside. A woman held the door, and finally he entered. The ride was mercifully quick, making only a single intermediary stop. Astor exited on thirty-eight. Room 3810 was to his left. He turned right, walking down the hall until he came to a double-doored entry. Raised letters gave the name of the tenant. *China Investment Corporation.* He put his hand on the doorknob and considered entering. What would he say? Who could he speak to? The sovereign wealth fund undoubtedly made its decisions in Beijing, not New York. He retraced his steps and continued to the end of the corridor. The door to Reventlow's office had the same standard lettering. He opened the door and stepped inside. The reception area was empty. No secretary. No assistants. The office was as quiet as the grave. Astor had the impression that few people visited.

"Septimus," he called. "I'm here."

"Come on back. You can't miss me."

Astor walked to the end of a short corridor, where an open door admitted a stream of light. Reventlow sat behind an unassuming desk. There was a bookshelf behind him and a small table to one side. A window looked over the roof of St. Patrick's Cathedral.

"Glad you could make it," said Reventlow. "Sorry to make you come so far uptown this time of day."

"Cutting it close," said Astor.

"I have your account details in my system. My banker is expecting my call. Any change in the position?"

"No."

"So you're amenable to taking the full three hundred million dollars?"

"We don't need quite that much to meet the margin call, but we'll take it for a cushion. You sure you want to do this?"

"Are you sure the yuan is going to depreciate?"

Astor stood up and walked around the room. He didn't answer Reventlow. The truth was that he wasn't sure about anything anymore, least of all whether the Chinese government was going to devalue its currency, as Magnus Lee had promised. If the China Investment Corporation did in fact have something to do with his father's death, and therefore with the attack that Palantir (and Edward Astor) believed was imminent—whatever it was—Lee could not be trusted. For the first time, Bobby Astor had come to see himself as part of the plan. He didn't know how or why. He only knew that there was a degree of interconnectivity that defied coincidence or happenstance. His malaise was only compounded by Septimus Reventlow's continued desire to invest $300 million in Comstock.

"You know," said Astor, "you never told me where the Reventlow family earned its money."

"A long story," said Reventlow. "Past history. No time to go into it now. Did you bring the paperwork?"

"In my briefcase," said Astor. "I just need a few signatures. Did the money come from Germany?"

"Partly, but from before Germany became Germany. You might call it Prussian with a dash of White Russian. Berlin by way of Kiev. Dynasties long since dismantled and consigned to the scrap heap."

"I didn't realize it was only you running things here. No secretary?"

"I prefer to see to all administrative details." Reventlow motioned toward his phone. "I think I should make the call."

Astor stopped pacing. It came to him that Reventlow was the more nervous of the two. His normally ashen countenance was flushed.

Despite the air-conditioning, perspiration dampened his forehead. Then again, thought Astor, he stood to lose quite a bit of money if Comstock went belly-up.

The shelves behind Reventlow were decorated with a dozen Lucite tombstones, mostly small mounted mementos of completed financial transactions. Astor studied them, interested to learn what other investments Reventlow had made, besides pouring $300 million into a wobbly hedge fund. His eye stopped on the third tombstone. For the second time in an hour, he felt as if he'd been struck in the chest by a baseball bat.

"What do you know about these guys?" he asked.

Reventlow took the tombstone that commemorated the purchase of Britium Technologies by Watersmark Partners. "I have a substantial investment in Watersmark. They send me one for every deal."

"Every one?"

"Yes."

"What about Silicon Solutions? Watersmark was involved with that transaction, too, weren't they?" Astor found the tombstone buried among the others. Before he could comment, his phone vibrated against his leg. "Excuse me, I need to check this." The message from Marv Shank read, "Getting our money? Hey, two FBI agents just came in looking for you. Janet McVeigh wants you to report to her at 26 Federal Plaza by five or else she's going to issue a warrant for your arrest. Call me when you leave RCH."

"Important news?"

"Nothing that can't wait."

Astor set down the tombstone. "You work with Oak Leaf Ventures, too?"

"Sit down, Bobby."

Astor took a seat.

Reventlow steepled his fingers. "What is it you think you know?"

"First off, that I don't need your money."

"That's too bad. You're going to accept it."

"So you're in on this?"

"Yes, Bobby. I'm in on this. And so were you, the moment you accepted our money."

"Why did you kill my father?"

"I had nothing to do with it. The Secret Service killed him, and no one will ever prove otherwise."

"Because of Britium?"

"Not because of Britium—with Britium's help. The Empire Platform is the greatest weapon that has ever been invented. Forget the nuclear bomb. Why wipe out a city when we can take over an entire country without anyone's even knowing it?"

"Who's 'we'?"

"If you know about Watersmark and Oak Leaf, you already have the answer."

"It isn't a coincidence that the China Investment Corporation is on the same floor."

"No."

"And you . . . you're not Chinese."

"In fact I am. I wasn't lying about the Russian ties. My grandfather was Count Radzinsky. He went to Shanghai to escape the purges after the White Russian army was defeated in the revolution. I inherited more of his genes than I would have liked. When it was decided that I would come to America, I had surgery to help things along."

"Ray Nossey told me that the Empire Platform was invulnerable to hacking."

"For the most part it is. That's why we like it so much."

"But then . . ."

"How do we manipulate it? Through people like you and your friends at Watersmark and Oak Leaf. You know already that the CIC owns between thirty and forty-five percent of both, as well as several other private equity firms. Enough to exert some control inside the boardroom. Not enough to be visible outside it. We influence Watersmark or Oak Leaf or the others to purchase companies whose products and technology use Britium's products, especially the Empire Platform. Once we take control of the company, we use our insider status to legitimately gain access to the source code controlling the products. Buying Britium itself was the pièce de résistance."

"And then?"

Reventlow smiled, as if he'd escaped a simple ploy.

"I take it Mr. Hong is a friend?" said Astor.

"Herbert? A brilliant man. On the record, he works for Watersmark.

But each day he goes to work in Britium's office. Each day he has free, unfettered access to every system using Britium's technology."

"Like giving a thief the keys to your house."

Astor thought about the companies whose annual reports he'd found at Penelope Evans's home. Between them, they manufactured power plants, communications satellites, missiles used by the navy and air force, and much, much more. He'd been right to suspect that the private equity firms were the common factor, just in a different way than he had imagined.

"The Flash Crash back in July of 2011—was that you?"

"A test to see if our theory was viable. It was. Frighteningly so. We had to scramble to patch things up and cover our tracks. We certainly didn't want a full-scale meltdown—then."

"Was Feudal you, too?" Astor was referring to a recent incident involving Feudal Trading, a bank that had lost over $500 million in the course of three hours when it accidentally uploaded a faulty algorithm into its trading software.

"No comment."

"And now? Why are you getting so desperate?"

"Desperate? Are we? Is that what your father said, or perhaps this Palantir? You'll find out soon enough."

"Why the investment in Comstock?"

"This really is a family office. You see, we believe the yuan is going to lose a fair bit of its value, too. If you fail to meet your margin call, we'll be out a good deal of money." Reventlow picked up the phone. "Hello, Rajeev. It's me. Please make the transfer to Comstock. Immediately. Thank you." He hung up. "Your turn. Call your CFO and instruct her to use the funds to meet the margin calls."

"If I don't?"

"You remember that capable man you met yesterday at your father's home? Blue eyes. Fast as lightning. He's my youngest brother. He was trained at the Shaolin Temple as a warrior monk. Unfortunately, he enjoyed practicing his skills a little too much. We were able to get him out of the country before the police jailed him. He particularly liked harming young women. You have a daughter, don't you? Katie, isn't it? Sixteen years old. A student at the Horace Mann School. Lives at—"

"Hand me the phone."

"Do as you're told and everything will turn out fine. The yuan will depreciate. Comstock will make a killing. You'll be the new Soros. Isn't that what you want?"

"How do you know the yuan will depreciate?"

"My brother assures me of it."

Astor nodded, his stomach sick with worry. "Who is your brother?"

"Magnus Lee. The future vice premier of China."

74

B uilding Six.
Zero hour.

Magnus Lee hurried along the corridor on the fifteenth floor (below-ground) of the secret installation. There were no company signs hanging from the ceiling. There was only one room, and it was designated with a *T*, for *Troy*. Two guards stood outside. Seeing Lee, they snapped to attention. Their reward was a perfunctory nod and a grunt.

Lee entered the operations center. Only four men were present. They sat side by side in front of computers and monitors. Each man held advanced degrees in computer science, mathematics, and statistics. They were the best of the best, the smartest of the smart, spotted by watchers at the country's finest universities and snatched away to work on behalf of their people. There was no greater honor. They had other skills, too, and these skills were not taught at universities. They were the nation's best hackers, and therefore the world's.

Lee sat down in a chair at the rear of the room. There was a word for people who possessed the ability to do so much with so little. That word was *super-empowered*. Lee liked the sound of it. Of course, it helped if you had the might and the resources of an entire country behind you.

A digital clock broadcast the time in minutes and seconds on one wall. Less than eighteen hours remained before the key was inserted. A giant screen covered the wall facing him.

Lee watched as a simulation of the attack was broadcast. The first target had never been a subject of debate. As Troy had come into being and Lee and his assistants at Watersmark and Oak Leaf and all the other sponsors had begun to acquire stakes in so many companies across so many industries, it was always clear that the U.S. financial system would be their mark. In no other area did the Americans hold such a vast superiority to China. China's heavy industry was the equal of

America's, as was its energy sector, its computer sector, its transportation, and soon even its military. But as a financial center, China lagged far behind. Daily, the world followed the fluctuations of the Dow Jones Industrial Average, the NASDAQ, even the VIX, with bated breath. No one gave two hoots about the Shanghai Exchange. Shanghai was a second-rate market, fit for gamblers who burned joss and said a prayer while closing their eyes and throwing a dart at the stocks page.

It was not enough for China to succeed—America must fail.

And so tomorrow, when the key was inserted and the door finally opened, America would fail.

First to fall would be the New York Stock Exchange, or more specifically, its proprietary trading platform. The Flash Crash had been a taste of the chaos to come. For years i3 had been secretly decrypting the trading strategies employed by America's most important investment banks. All were clients of the Exchange. All traded hundreds of millions of shares each day. Lee would use this knowledge to corrupt these strategies. Once the firewall was breached, a virus would infect the Exchange's trading software, causing a wholesale meltdown the likes of which had never been seen.

An order to buy a thousand shares would read as an order to buy a hundred thousand. An order to sell fifty thousand shares at $40 would read as fifty thousand at $35. The discrepancy would trigger complex program trading orders to buy or sell hundreds of thousands of shares at a time. Perplexed, the software would no longer know how to match proper buy and sell orders. Order imbalances would multiply. The Dow Jones index would fall five thousand points in minutes, and when the Exchange's built-in circuit breakers failed to arrest the decline, the index would fall further, until trading would be shut down altogether. London, Paris, Frankfurt, Milan, and Tokyo would follow. No trading platform was safe. For all the exchanges were interconnected. Once the virus infected one, it would naturally seek out another and another. Pandemonium would ensue.

From the Exchange, the virus would seek out the giant data centers where records of every trade and transaction completed were stored on state-of-the-art servers. The New York Stock Exchange had recently built a new, ultrasecure facility in Mahwah, New Jersey, but it kept backups in Ohio and England. What crippled Mahwah would cripple

Ohio and London. All would be compromised in seconds. Data would be erased wholesale. Efforts to reconstruct an accurate financial picture *ante cyberbellum* would be met and neutralized.

That was only the beginning.

From the data centers, the virus would travel to clients of the Exchange themselves. To banks, insurance companies, trading houses, credit card companies, and then to their clients. Everywhere, the virus would seek out data and destroy it.

The permutations were endless. For the virus was written to move continually upstream. To use the first target to find the second, and so on ad infinitum.

All would know that the crash was the result of an error in the trading platform. No matter. Trust would be compromised. Billions of dollars lost. Within hours, all commerce would cease. Economic Armageddon would ensue.

Still, it would not be enough.

On top of all this would be the physical attack. The ordinary citizen did not understand cyberwar. A computer virus was not tangible. It was a concept, ethereal by nature. It meant nothing.

Ordinary citizens needed blood and guts and bombs and rubble to know they were under attack. They needed to see the faces of the dead, the anguish of the survivors, the rage of the violated, and the tears of orphans. They needed to feel unsafe, insecure and at risk.

They needed to feel in danger.

Only then would they understand.

9/11 was a good beginning, but it did not go far enough. Stock prices plummeted. The Exchange closed for a week. But when it reopened trading continued as if nothing had happened. America was bruised, but came back stronger than ever. Tomorrow, China would land the decisive blow and complete the mission to dethrone the United States as the financial and economic capital of the world.

It was not enough for China to succeed—America must fail.

All this Magnus Lee saw played upon the screens in front of him. Step by step, victim by victim, country by country.

And when the virus had done its worst and all seemed lost, Lee himself would call the American president. He would volunteer China's services to locate the virus, kill it, and restore the lost financial records. For no one had a safer, more secure, more stable platform than the Chinese. No one had foreseen such an attack and taken preemptive measures. No one had guessed its adversaries' motives, means, and methods.

No one except the Chinese.

America's "old friend."

There would be no calls for the yuan to be revalued. If the Chinese preferred a weak yuan to bolster their export sector, they were welcome to it. If Chinese-made products resembled those of their American competitors a bit too much, nothing would be said. If a breach of a defense contractor's most sophisticated weapons systems was traced to a Chinese computer, the discussion would be made behind doors and without acrimony.

America knew how to be grateful.

The attack wasn't about bringing down America permanently.

It was about control.

75

Astor knew Reventlow was lying. Everything would not turn out fine. He and his brother, Magnus Lee, would not put this behind them. All who knew about the CIC and its plan to exercise control over key components of the country's financial and national security infrastructure had to be eliminated. There would be no handshake and promise to keep it all a secret. Astor possessed information vital to his nation's defense; in fact, every bit as vital as the pictures from on high showing Soviet missiles being installed on Cuban soil in 1962. As Reventlow had said, why wipe out a city when you can control an entire country without anyone's even knowing it?

Astor called his CFO and told her to expect an incoming wire any minute and to call each of Comstock's lenders and inform them that Comstock would meet its margin call. He handed over the papers for Reventlow to sign, then replaced them in his briefcase.

"Are we done?"

"For now. But don't be in a hurry to leave. I can't let you go just yet."

"I need to get back to the office. My lawyers are expecting me."

"I'm sure they will celebrate their reprieve just fine without you. I'm afraid I do need to ask you some more questions. It's important for us to learn how much you know about our affairs. My brother told me you were speaking with someone on your father's computer who was involved in his investigation. Does Cassandra99 ring a bell?"

"That was Palantir. He might have helped my father earlier, but he refused to help me."

"I wish I could believe you. We also have a record of your call to a Michael Grillo, a corporate investigator. We weren't able to listen to his calls, so we must rely on you to tell us what you were discussing."

"It had nothing to do with this. Grillo does other work for my company." Astor picked up his briefcase and turned to leave. Standing in the doorway was the man from Cherry Hill. The warrior monk. Alex had said she was sure she had shot him, but he appeared to be in good health.

"May I introduce my brother Daniel," said Reventlow. "He's going to escort you to a private spot where we all can chat."

"Hello, Mr. Astor," said Daniel, his English unaccented, essentially an American's.

"Hello," said Astor. "And by the way, my arm's fine."

During the entire meeting, Astor had felt his father's Beretta pressing against his spine. He measured the distance between him and the monk as 15 feet. Four long strides, to be sure. "All right," he said. "I'm ready to go."

Septimus Reventlow rose and offered his hand. Astor regarded it, the man's insincere smile, his patrician demeanor, as a grotesquerie. He extended his hand as if to shake, then drew the pistol from his belt. Before he could bring it to bear, a blow paralyzed his wrist. Daniel, the warrior monk, stood inches away, holding the pistol by the barrel. "Very slow."

Astor dropped his briefcase and clutched his hand. It hurt badly. "Yeah," he said. "Looks that way."

Reventlow came around the desk, picked up the briefcase, and handed it to Astor. "If you make a sound on the way downstairs, he will kill you," he said. "No one will see him crush your larynx. My advice is to cooperate. And one more thing. If I might have your phone . . ."

Astor regarded Daniel, and handed Reventlow the phone he'd purchased earlier in the day.

"The FBI," said Reventlow, reading the last text. "Shall I call them to cancel on your behalf?" He gave Astor an avuncular pat on the shoulder. "We'll have lots to talk about."

"After you," said Daniel.

Astor walked with him to the elevator. They descended to the ground floor and passed through the turnstiles. Crossing the lobby, he spotted Sully double-parked at the curb. It was a little after four, and the lobby was busy but not crowded. Daniel walked at his side. Three officers manned the security desk. Two were fat and uninterested, the third trim and alert.

Astor saw a chance. "Which way?"

"Straight ahead," said Daniel.

It was the answer Astor wanted to hear. "You have a car waiting?"

"I'll show you when we get outside."

Astor passed through the door. A uniformed policeman stood immediately to his right. The sidewalk was bustling. A horn blared. Astor looked at the Sprinter and caught Sully's eye.

It was now or never.

"Hey!" shouted Astor, wanting to draw the cop's attention. He dropped the briefcase and ran. "Sully!"

Astor dodged the pedestrians, weaving this way and that. Sully saw him coming and opened the rear door. Astor jumped inside and slammed it shut. He had made it. "Get out of here. Floor it."

Astor threw himself into the recliner, grasping the armrests in anticipation of accelerating. The car stayed where it was. "Sully. What are you doing? Go!"

John Sullivan did not start the ignition. The side door opened. Daniel climbed in and placed the briefcase on the floor, then closed the door behind him. He looked at Astor, then toward the driver's seat. "Thank you for waiting, Mr. Sullivan."

Astor leaned forward. "Sully, what's going on?"

John Sullivan turned in his chair and fixed Astor with a vengeful gaze. "No way I'm letting you fuck up my retirement."

And with that he turned around, put the Sprinter into drive, and joined the late afternoon traffic.

76

Marv Shank announced the news of Reventlow's investment in Comstock on the trading floor. As one, every man and woman present rose and cheered.

"The boss did it," he said, shaking with pride. "He saved our asses."

Shank walked the length of the desk, shaking hands and exchanging high fives. After a few minutes he retreated to his office and called Astor. There was no answer. He texted, "U da man! Troops over the moon. Comstock lives to fight another day!"

He kept the phone in his hand, waiting for a reply. Astor was always quick to respond to good news. There was no answer, but he had little time to think about it. His phone began ringing, and it didn't stop for an hour. First there were the lending institutions, which wanted to thank Astor but settled for Shank in his place.

"Never doubted you for a second," said Brad Zarek from Standard Financial. "Now that we're all square, the credit committee would like to increase your line of credit. Bobby mentioned another hundred million the other day. It's yours for the asking. And at Libor plus a quarter. Of course we'll beat any competitive bid."

Shank was tempted to hang up. For once he erred on the side of diplomacy, thanking Zarek as nicely as he knew how, which basically meant he didn't tell him to go screw himself.

Following the banks came the journalists. There were calls from the *New York Times*, the *Wall Street Journal*, even *Der Spiegel*. The only thing better than a big shot getting his ass handed to him was a miracle recovery.

By six the office was pretty much deserted. The last-minute miracle had sent even the die-hard grinds to the local watering holes to toast Bobby Astor. Shank walked to Astor's office and peered inside. He checked his phone again, even though he knew that Bobby hadn't replied to his call or his text. Shank decided he must be tied up at the FBI. He called Sully, but Sully didn't answer either.

A quiver of unease passed through his body. He felt certain something was wrong.

"Marv, good night. Turn off the lights on your way out." It was Mandy Price, the chief financial officer. He saw that she was wearing her running clothes, probably off for a quick 10-miler to celebrate. Maniac.

Shank smiled and waved. "Good night. We live to fight another day!"

He stood like that for another minute, gazing around the empty office. He made a slow tour from front to back, taking his time, reminiscing about deals done, about trading strategies that had worked and those that hadn't, about the pile of money he'd made. He ended where he had started, standing in the middle of the trading floor. He didn't think he'd ever seen it so quiet.

He looked at his watch and wondered what to do.

He had nowhere to go.

77

A t first he was scared.
After an hour he grew restless.
Now Astor was bored.

He sat on a wooden chair in the center of a vacant two-car garage.
He had no idea where he was. There were no windows to look out. The
garage door was locked, as was the only other entrance, a single door
leading to the house he'd been led through. He looked around. There
was a lawn mower, trash cans, a rake. He could hear crickets sawing
outside, and the smell of cut grass was rich in the air. He took a sip
of water from a liter bottle Daniel had left him. He was hungry, so he
knew it was after seven o'clock, which was the hour he ate dinner.

Leaving Manhattan, Daniel had placed a hood over his head. No
one spoke during the ride. Left alone with his thoughts, Astor had tried
to map his journey by the landmarks he passed. One bridge. One tunnel. A long spell on a highway. But which bridge? Which tunnel? And
which highway?

Once more he made a tour of his prison, banging on the garage door,
shouting "Help!" as loudly as he could, and repeatedly kicking the door
to the house. Sully's betrayal provided his anger with ample fuel. It did
no good. The only result was a ruined shoe and a bruised heel.

He gave a last kick for good measure. Regaining his balance, he saw
the doorknob turn. The door opened and John Sullivan walked in, followed by Daniel and Septimus Reventlow.

"Take a seat," said Reventlow.

Astor sat down. He observed that Sully was limping and that his
face was swollen and inflamed, as if he'd been crying. Sully looked at
him and offered a sad, weary smile. "I'm sor—"

A gunshot cut off the word. Sullivan dropped to the concrete floor,
dead.

"Jesus," said Astor, cringing. The boredom was gone. He was scared.
"Why did you . . . what the . . . but he was helping you."

Daniel slipped the Beretta into his waistband. He approached and knelt in front of Astor. The placid blue eyes looked into his. "Give me your hand."

"Why?"

"Please."

Astor extended his left hand warily, and Daniel laid it palm down across his own, gently splaying the fingers. Astor didn't see him insert the sliver of bamboo beneath his fingernail. A flame traveled through the finger up his arm and into his neck. He screamed, and as quickly the sliver was gone and the monk was patting his hand, holding a cloth to absorb the blood.

Astor looked from Daniel to Reventlow. "You didn't ask me anything."

"The questions will come," said Reventlow. "Daniel needs to soften you up first. By the time he's done, you'll be begging to tell me everything you know."

78

The intel started arriving when Alex was halfway across the Atlantic. First came the download of James Salt's phone's internal memory and SIM card. There were a slew of phone numbers, in fact a list of every call placed or received, some six thousand in all. The phone also provided access to Salt's e-mails for the better part of the past two years. Many contained cc's to other parties, giving the Bureau and MI5 a plethora of leads. There was less luck with texts, as the phone deleted these, and it was necessary to obtain them from the service provider.

Alex spent the flight crouched in the cockpit, listening as Barry Mintz relayed the information. She was interested in two things: where the bad guys were hiding and what was to be their target, or targets, plural, God help us every man. But even as she guessed at their plans, she kept in mind Jean Eyraud's words about Lambert and his fellow mercenaries. They were not terrorists. They were professional soldiers who wanted to survive, which meant they had an exit strategy mapped out and memorized.

"Have they pinged that phone yet?" she asked.

"Still waiting on the South Africans."

"Time frame?"

"Any minute now."

"You said that an hour ago." Alex was beside herself with frustration. Trapped in the plane, she could do nothing but monitor progress being made by others. "And Bobby?"

"We can't reach him anywhere. He's not answering his cell or home phone. Neither is his driver."

"What about the office?"

"Closed for the day."

"Call Marv Shank. He's Bobby's best friend. He'll know where he is."

"Will do," said Mintz. "There's something else. Jan sent him a text ordering him to 26 Federal Plaza at five. He didn't show."

Alex was worried. Bobby might disobey her command to get his butt down to Federal Plaza. He would not disobey Janet McVeigh's. If his meeting had run long, he would have called to explain his tardiness. She tapped the captain on the shoulder. "What's our ETA?"

"Two hours, but we have a problem. A line of thunderstorms is coming down the Hudson Valley toward the city."

"How bad?"

"Bad. It extends all the way into western Pennsylvania. The forecast is calling for four to six inches of rain. The storm could shut down every airport in the vicinity until dawn."

Alex squinted to read the flight instruments. "You got any more juice left in this bird?"

"We're pushing 500 knots and that's with a headwind."

"My Charger goes faster than that."

"I can get you another fifty knots. Any more than that and we'll be landing on fumes."

"Step on it."

79

I'm not here," said Jeb Washburn.

"Definitely not," said Mike Grillo.

"I am way off the reservation."

"Different county entirely."

"County? I need to be in a different *country*. I work for the Central Intelligence Agency. Anyone finds out I'm helping you, Grill-O, I am done."

"You can come work for me."

"Lord help us both, then."

The men were parked in Washburn's car at the corner of 44th and Eleventh across from a Ray's Pizza. Washburn had exchanged his blazer and flannels for jeans and a bowling shirt that nicely hid his .45 but couldn't quite make his paunch disappear. Grillo had dressed as casually as he would allow himself, in pressed slacks, a navy polo shirt, and deck shoes. The Shermans were gone, too, replaced by a cigar clenched in the corner of his mouth. He always smoked Cubans on ops.

Grillo glanced down the street, focusing on a three-story brick building a third of the way along. It was a neighborhood of row houses and tenements, one built next to the other. Number 3415 was more run-down than its neighbors, with concrete stairs leading to a glass-paned entry. Among the thirty or so men, women, and children who called it home was a man named Paul Lawrence Tiernan. Grillo preferred to think of him as Palantir.

"You ready to roll?"

Washburn shook his head. "I can't believe I am doing this for you."

"'Cause I'm one of the good guys, remember?"

"Better not forget those shoes."

"Size seven."

Washburn slipped his gun free and put it on the center console. "You going to recognize him?"

"You think there are other guys like him in there?"

"Wouldn't doubt it, all the boys that got hurt over there."

"Amen," said Grillo. "Let's roll."

Washburn put the car into gear and slowly cruised down the block. It was 10 p.m. and the sky was black with clouds, the air buzzing as it does before a storm. A few people walked along the sidewalk, heading toward Times Square.

"Hey, man," said Grillo. "Whichever way it goes, thanks."

A fist bump between friends.

It had required all the pieces of the puzzle to locate Palantir. The agenda, the credit card bills, the phone records, and finally the Skype address that had tied it all together. It was not, as it turned out, the first time the NSA had seen Cassandra99.ru. The same address had turned up in a search a few years earlier in a request from DARPA asking to investigate a cyberattack against its server. At that time two phone numbers were associated with a credit card used to pay for the Skype account. One of the numbers matched a phone Palantir had used to contact Edward Astor. By means of triangulation, the NSA had narrowed down Cassandra99's location to one of two areas. Using Edward Astor's credit card receipts from last Friday morning, when he had ventured to midtown to meet Palantir, Grillo was able to offer an educated guess as to which location was more likely to be Palantir's home. The triangulation was accurate to 10 feet as far as latitude and longitude were concerned. It did not, however, offer much help in terms of altitude. Number 3415 was a three-story tenement. It required a human's gumshoeing to find out who lived inside the building. In this case, Grillo had slipped the postman a twenty to let him look at the names of all those receiving mail at the address. Paul Lawrence Tiernan fit the bill. The military records Grillo obtained afterward confirmed that he had his man, as well as the probable reasons for Palantir's grudge against the United States government.

Washburn stopped the car in front of the scruffy building. Grillo climbed out and jogged across the street, checking that the tail of his shirt was loose and covering his pistol, a slim Smith & Wesson with a nine-shot clip. The front hall was clogged with bicycles chained to a radiator, bags of trash, and empty beer cans. Salsa music drifted from an open door upstairs. Tiernan's apartment was at the back of the first floor. Grillo knocked twice and stepped back. He noted that there were two spyglasses built into the door, one at eye level, the other at his waist. He knocked again and the door opened.

Mike Grillo looked at the legless man in the wheelchair. "Gotcha."

"Good guy or bad guy?"

"You're still breathing, aren't you?"

"You win." Paul Lawrence Tiernan rolled his chair back to allow Grillo to enter. "Name?"

"Grillo, Michael T. That would be Captain to you. Fifth Marines. Seventh Battalion."

"Semper fi," said Tiernan without conviction. He was a handsome man with short black hair parted neatly, blue eyes, and a reliable set to his jaw. "You a fed these days? DOD? FBI? What?"

"Strictly private sector. I work for Bobby Astor."

"Do I need to be scared?"

"Not if you help me out."

Tiernan motioned for Grillo to come in. "It was the Skype, wasn't it?"

"And some other stuff. Hard to stay hidden when so many people are looking for you."

In contrast to the ramshackle foyer, Tiernan's apartment was spotless, if sparsely furnished to provide ample space to move about. A bookshelf held pictures of Tiernan during his time as a United States Marine. He'd served for ten years and been in line for a second rocker when he was hit.

"I was over there, too," said Grillo. "Helmand. Kandahar. I was lucky."

"I wasn't."

"You've got a right to be bitter. You don't have a right to hide information that weighs on the security of the country."

"I'm not hiding anything," said Tiernan. "I offered it to the Agency. They didn't want to pay. They said I owed it to the country to tell them. Edward Astor forked over fifty grand without batting an eye. Now I have a rail in my bathroom so I can use the head easier. Next week they're coming to install a bigger shower so I can roll all the way in. There might even be enough cash left to buy me a van I can drive myself."

"I'm glad for you. I'm going to need a copy of the report you prepared for Astor—whatever it was you gave him last Friday morning. Where'd you meet him? Starbucks on 42nd and Broadway?"

"You're good."

Grillo shrugged. "The thing about being on my side of things, I don't have to worry about breaking laws. You're lucky I got here first. Penelope Evans wasn't."

"I saw that."

"So who's after you?"

"A big shot in the Chinese government named Magnus Lee. Runs some kind of gigantic investment fund. He uses his fund to buy into companies that manufacture or control critical infrastructure in the U.S. and Europe, South America. We're talking microchips, satellites, power plants, that kind of thing. Afterward, he puts his people into key positions in those companies, where they can install software to give him control of it."

"That's what got Edward Astor so worked up?"

"Only half of it. Lee is planning to sabotage a critical financial system in the States. He's using the attack to advance his chances to get elected to the Standing Committee of the Chinese Communist Party. He wants to be a vice premier."

"What financial system are you talking about?"

"That I don't know. But something that requires a new hardware complex. It's all in the report. Wait here." Tiernan spun a one-eighty in his chair and rolled down a hallway. He returned with a folder on his lap. "Have at it."

Grillo picked up the slim folder. The summary alone made for scary reading. "Edward Astor owe you any more money?"

"We're square."

"If things go south, there're going to be some people want to speak with you."

"Maybe they'll offer me a job."

Grillo shook his head. It was amazing how smart people could be so dumb. "If they do, it'll be one you can do from a prison cell."

80

Pain, the purifier.

Astor had lost the first fingernail an hour before. He did not know how he was still conscious, or why he was actually alert and seated in the chair, his eyes locked on the sadistic blue-eyed monk's. The index finger was ruined. So was the middle finger. They hung limp, as bloody and lifeless as John Sullivan.

Astor watched as the monk's hand darted forward, as fast as a cobra's tongue, and the bamboo shoot disappeared into his nail bed. He winced but made no noise. He was done with that. He had already cried for them to stop. He had begged. He'd pleaded to be shot. He'd surrendered his dignity and more.

It was only then that Reventlow had begun his questions.

"How long had you been working with your father? How did you learn about Penelope Evans? Tell me everything you found in her home. What did you tell your ex-wife?" And finally, "Who is Palantir?"

Astor told the truth. He knew nothing more than they did. If anything, he talked too much. He provided Reventlow with more information than he needed. He offered his own theories about Magnus Lee's plans. He adopted the strategy to lengthen the periods between his torture. A second of respite was worth infinite cunning. But quickly he discovered that his fevered guesses provoked telling responses about the plot, and that by process of elimination he was closing in on what the target really was.

"Why was your father interested in the Flash Crash? Did you know of any safeguards taken to protect the Exchange? Tell me again which companies your father suspected of being infiltrated. Wasn't he interested in other companies?"

And here Reventlow threw out five or six names, and Astor knew that he was interested in only one of them, so he made himself commit them all to memory.

"Who is this Michael Grillo?"

They had finally arrived at the subject he knew he must lie about.

"A corporate investigator."

"Why did you hire him?"

"I work with him all the time. He was helping me gather information on a rival fund that I suspected was poaching clients."

"You're lying."

"Ask him. Ask Grillo."

"That's the thing. We can't find him. Tell us what Grillo knows."

"Nothing. He isn't involved in this."

The shoot shot forth.

It was more pain than he had known. More than the first foray beneath his fingernail. This time the shoot probed more deeply into the flesh, finding a fresh bed of nerves to upset. Reventlow repeated his question, but Astor didn't stray from his story. He had found a new source of strength. It came from his private storehouse of terrible memories. He saw himself standing at his parents' bed at Cherry Hill, and he recalled the terror he knew as he anticipated the black belt's first blow. The boy had survived. And so the man would survive, too.

The shoot dug in.

No noise. Not a whimper. When pain consumed you, it lost its ability to frighten. It became a new reality, and a known reality could be endured.

"How can we find Grillo?"

Every minute he delayed was a minute Mike Grillo gained. He would find Palantir, and when he did, he would make him talk. Grillo didn't need a sharpened bamboo shoot.

"I had his number on my other phone," said Astor. "I called him. I don't know where he lives."

"Where is Grillo?"

"I told you, he's not involved in this. You're wasting your time."

Astor closed his eyes, readying himself for the agony. But the bamboo shoot did not come.

After a moment he looked around and saw Reventlow studying a phone. It was Astor's phone. "Ha!" he said, a surprised outburst. "His name is Paul Lawrence Tiernan. Palantir. Clever." He looked up. "It seems Mr. Grillo has done our work for us. He writes that he has found Palantir and is in possession of the report he prepared for your father.

He'd like to know where to meet so he can turn it over to you." Reventlow pondered the matter. "I think he should stay put. After all, you do want to meet the man who was working with your father, don't you, Bobby? I would."

Astor said nothing. It was done, then. Game over.

Reventlow texted back a message, then spoke to Daniel in Chinese. The monk stood and walked to the door. Reventlow patted Astor on the shoulder. "We shouldn't be long. When we get back, we'll put an end to this charade."

Reventlow and Daniel left.

Astor dropped his head. His hand was a mess and hurt too much to contemplate. He stood, walked to the garage door, and put his ear against the wood. He heard a car start and drive away. He tried the other door. Locked. He waited a few minutes, expecting one of them to return. A little time passed. No one came.

They were gone.

Astor looked around the garage. At the lawn mower, the rake, the trash barrels. At the cinder-block walls. He noted that the door had been ripped off its rail and that wood blocks nailed it shut. He had an hour, maybe a little more, to free himself.

81

LaGuardia air traffic control is denying us permission to land," reported the captain of the Gulfstream G4 to Alex. "The wind across the runway is gusting to sixty knots."

"I have an agent waiting for me on the tarmac."

"I don't care if the president of the United States is waiting for you. A gust hits this plane when we're about to touch down and it will flip us over like a tiddlywink."

Alex squeezed herself in between the pilot and the copilot. "You heard what's going on," she said. "This is a matter of national security. We are hours away from an attack on the city. Put us down."

The captain consulted with the copilot. "Get strapped in. We're going to have to go in like a Zero at Midway. I hope you're used to hard landings."

Alex hurried to her seat and pulled the safety belt tight against her stomach. A minute later the nose dipped, then dipped some more. Her bag slipped from beneath her chair and slid the length of the cabin. She didn't think of retrieving it. The plane hit an air pocket and bounced noisily. She gripped the armrests harder.

"Oh, Father," she said to herself, "help me through this."

She wasn't sure whether she was praying to Hoover or to the Lord above.

And then the plane began to rock and roll.

Barry Mintz stood on the tarmac at the base of the stairs. More than ever he looked like a rumpled teenager, all gangly limbs and a head of red hair standing on end in the driving wind.

Alex walked past without acknowledging him. She kneeled to kiss the runway, rose, walked 10 feet away, and vomited.

"A little rough coming in," said the pilot, standing with arms crossed in the doorframe.

"She okay?" asked Mintz.

"She'll be fine. She's one tough customer."

"Tell me about it," said Mintz.

The clouds that had threatened since early evening rolled overhead, dark and ominous. A few drops of rain fell. Alex returned, wiping her mouth with her sleeve. Screw it. The suit was still soiled with Salt's blood and she was fresh out of hankies. A little puke wouldn't hurt. A man from Customs and Border Protection stood nearby. Passport formalities were handled quickly. Alex accepted her passport back and turned to Mintz.

"Good news, please." It was an order.

"We got him," said Mintz. "The South Africans pinged Beaufoy's phone to a home in Darien. We rousted the real estate agent out of bed. He leased the residence to a foreign gentleman from Singapore who paid with a cashier's check for a three-month period. Same MO as at Windermere."

"Name on the lease?"

"An alias. We ran it and got nothing."

Alex picked up her bag and started toward the car. "Call SWAT and the local police. Tell Jan McVeigh."

"Um, Alex . . . hold it. You're not even supposed to be working the case. Bill Barnes is already out there. He's leading the SWAT team in. He said he's going to be breacher."

"Are you in contact with him?"

"He sent a two-man probe team. They have ten heat signatures inside the house."

"Any sightings?"

"Not sure."

Alex considered this. Her motion sickness had disappeared the moment she puked, but now a new, more troubling nausea threatened to take its place. "Are you telling me that there are ten bad guys inside the safe house fourteen hours after Salt called Beaufoy to give him a heads-up that I was on the trail? No chance."

The door to Mintz's Ford opened. A portly, disheveled man with a five o'clock shadow got out. "Hey, Alex, long time."

"Marv," she said. "What are you doing here?"

"We can't find Bobby. He isn't answering his phone. He's not at home. I'm worried that something's happened to him. You know—what with his looking into his father's death. I called looking for you and got put in touch with Special Agent Mintz."

"Mintz, did he ever go see Jan?"

"Negative."

Alex checked her own phone and saw that Bobby hadn't called back. He never failed to return a message promptly. "Where was he last?"

"He left the office at three to visit a client named Septimus Reventlow at 49th and Park," said Shank. "Reventlow says the meeting was over quickly and Bobby left a little after four."

"Who is this Reventlow?"

"An investor. He has a lot of money in one of our funds. The thing is, Bobby was in a pickle. He had a big bet that went south on him. Reventlow put in three hundred million to help us meet a margin call. Essentially, it saved the company. There's no way Bobby would not call me to talk about it."

"He didn't say a word? Not even a text?"

"He talked to our CFO to tell her to expect an incoming wire transfer. That's the last we heard."

"And that was at four?"

"More or less."

Alex weighed the information. If Bobby left Reventlow's office at four, he would have had plenty of time to make it downtown for his appointment with Janet McVeigh. "What about Sully? I left two messages for him."

"Nothing. I tried his home, too. Nada. Don the doorman hasn't seen Bobby either. It's like the two of them have disappeared."

Mintz took a call. "Barnes is suiting up. They have the place surrounded. If we want to make it out there, we have to go now."

A drop of rain hit Alex's cheek. She gazed up at the sky. Any minute, it was going to dump buckets. She looked at Marv Shank, then back at Mintz.

"What was Sully driving?" she asked.

"The Sprinter," said Shank.

"Get in. Let's go find my husband."

Alex's first assignment upon joining the Bureau had been bank robbery. The work was fast and exciting, and there were plenty of arrests.

She was shot at twice (both misses), and she herself shot and wounded three assailants. Good times. Bank robbers, she learned, were not the smartest guys in the room. Most were druggies, drinkers, your basic street-level perp in need of a quick five grand and too stupid to consider that ten years of hard time were too steep an interest to pay on the money. Many used stolen cars in the commission of their crimes, thinking that a hot vehicle would offer an anonymous getaway. Nine out of ten forgot that nearly all late-model automobiles come equipped with LoJack, a location finder/radio transmitter hidden in the rear tire well of an automobile. If the car was stolen, the LoJack office nearby would activate that car's transmitter and immediately receive a ten-digit GPS location, pinpointing the car to a 2-square-foot patch of planet Earth. It could also, if desired, disable the car's engine.

Bobby's half-million-dollar Sprinter had the same kind of LoJack as any Nissan or Hyundai, except that Mercedes-Benz charged $5,000 for it instead of $500. Alex needed two calls to get a mark on the Sprinter; the first to the insurance company to get Bobby's license number and the second to LoJack to ask the company to turn on its transmitter. In three minutes she had the location of Bobby's Sprinter.

"It's at 27 Foxhollow Road, New Canaan," she announced after hanging up.

"Sully lives in New Canaan," said Shank.

"I know."

"That doesn't make sense," Shank went on. "Sully never drives the Sprinter home. It's Bobby's car."

"Well, it's there now, and it's not moving a muscle," said Alex. "The engine has been disabled."

Shank remained unsatisfied. "But if Sully's at home, why isn't he answering his phone?"

The drive to New Canaan took forty minutes. Alex shooed Mintz aside and took the wheel. She was done with being a passenger. The winding country roads were her own private racetrack. If her aggressive driving bothered anyone, no one dared admit it.

Sully lived outside the city, and she needed her onboard navigation to steer her through the country roads. She abandoned the GPS when she turned onto Foxhollow Road. She had an easier beacon to follow. Directly ahead, a wall of flame rose into the sky. Cresting a rise, she saw a platoon of fire trucks pulled up in front of John Sullivan's home. The Sprinter was parked a few yards away. Alex slid in behind an EMT's truck and got out of the car. The firefighters were only just arriving and were running to attach a hose to a hydrant. The chief stood by the main engine, establishing his battle plan.

Alex flashed her identification and introduced herself. "Is anyone inside the home?"

"Too hot to go in," the chief responded. "The place could collapse at any second. We're going to spray down the roof with water and retardant, then send a team in the front door."

Alex ran as close to the entry as the flames would allow and called Bobby's name. No reply came. The heat was ferocious, battling her back. She called again, but there was no response. A firefighter tugged her sleeve and told her to retreat from the flames. Alex shook her arm free and stayed where she was. "Bobby!"

The flames were growing rapidly, the crackling of timber and popping of the dry shingles lending the blaze an explosive, hazardous character. She looked for ways to get closer, if only to be able to hear her ex-husband's cries. If he was alive, she wanted to know it.

Then she saw something. On the ground, inches from the garage door, lay a small, colorful card.

"Give me a pole," she said.

A young fireman handed her a long pole with a rubber grip that was normally used to move fallen power lines. She approached the blazing garage door with caution. When she was 10 feet away, she used the pole to retrieve the card.

"What did you find?" asked Mintz.

"He's inside." Alex handed him Bobby's driver's license and broke into a run.

"Where're you going? Alex!"

Alex climbed into Mintz's car and circled the fire engines, navigating a path through them until the Ford sat at the head of the driveway. The fire chief pounded on her window and yelled for her to move the car away. She ignored him. She hit the horn three times, then floored it, driving the Ford straight through the garage door, sending flaming wood and cinders in all directions.

Bobby crouched in the center of the garage, fire licking at him from the ceiling. There was a snapping sound and a timber fell from the roof and landed on the car's hood. Bobby opened the passenger door and got in. Alex threw the car into reverse. Her eye fell on another body, this one prone and motionless, a crust of blood forming a halo around its head. "Sully?"

"Dead."

A second timber fell, striking the car. Alex reversed through the flames. In seconds they were in the driveway, safe. Bobby pointed to her face. "Your eye," he said. "What happened?"

"The job. It's nothing." Alex looked at the bloody towel wrapping his hand. "What did they do to you?"

"Asked me some questions. I told them what they already knew. Look, we have to get out of here. He's going after Mike."

"Slow down. Who's Mike?"

"Michael Grillo. A PI who does some work for me. I hired him to find Palantir. Paul Lawrence Tiernan. That's his name. I mean, Palantir's name. Grillo sent a text saying he'd found him and had the report. Reventlow's going there now."

"Septimus Reventlow? Where?"

"I don't know, but it can't be too far. He said he'd be back."

Alex called over Barry Mintz and gave him Palantir's name. "Look for an address in the tristate area."

"Right away," said Mintz.

Alex took the swathed hand and unwrapped the towel. "Oh, Bobby."

"Looks worse than it is." Emotion overcame him, and he sobbed. He banged his good fist on the dashboard. "The bastard," he said, gathering himself. "He didn't even blink an eye. He liked doing it."

"Who did this, Bobby? Was it Reventlow?"

"Septimus Reventlow and his brother Daniel. Just so you know, Reventlow isn't their last name. It's Lee. They're from China."

Alex couldn't take her eyes from her ex-husband's ruined fingers. Three were missing fingernails, and the flesh underneath hung in tatters. As gently as she could manage, she replaced the towel. Bobby winced but said nothing. He was in shock.

"Calm down," she said. "You can tell me what happened in a second. Right now, there's someone here who wants to see you."

Astor got out of the car. Marv Shank hit him like a linebacker com-

ing on an all-out blitz, wrapping his arms around him and hugging him
tight.

"Easy, Marv."

"Sorry." Shank released him and Astor saw that he was crying, too.
"If you want a friend . . ."

"Buy a dog," they said in unison.

"Had me worried," said Astor. "For a minute there, I thought you
were getting soft on me."

"Thought you had a heartbeat."

"Never."

Astor hugged Shank, then said he needed to talk to Alex. "Sure
thing," said Shank.

Astor walked to the end of the drive with Alex. He told her about
everything that had happened since she had left. She, in turn, related
her discovery that her investigation into the arms cache at Windermere
was in fact linked to his father's death. Sadly, she had no information
about Reventlow's and Salt's ultimate target.

"And they lit the fire to burn you to death?" asked Alex.

"I lit it myself. I figured it was the only way I could get out. I thought
if someone saw the flames, they'd call the fire department and that
would be that. Things got a little out of control."

"How did you do it?"

"There was a lawn mower in the garage that had a little gasoline in
the tank. I looked around and found some Hornet Coils and a box of
Ohio Blue Tips. I piled some dry leaves and tinder that Sully had put
in the trash on top to get the fire going. I think I may have put a little
too much."

Barry Mintz jogged over to them. "715 West 44th Street," he said.
"Paul Lawrence Tiernan's address."

"That's it," said Astor. "Grillo had him pegged to be somewhere in
midtown. We need to hurry."

"The only place you're going is to the hospital," said Alex.

"No chance. I need to see Palantir's report. I can go after."

Mintz pulled Alex aside. "I just got off the horn with Jan," he said
quietly. "Bill Barnes is going in."

"No way Beaufoy and his men are still there. Salt tipped them off
fourteen hours ago that we were on their trail. Let me talk to him."

"Too late. D.C. gave the green light. Barnes isn't talking to anybody anymore."

Alex turned away, not sure whether she was angrier because Barnes was risking his men's lives on a fool's errand or because she wasn't there to go along. She looked at Bobby. "Okay," she said. "Get in the car. Let's go find your friend Mr. Grillo."

82

Supervisory Special Agent Bill Barnes, head of intelligence for the FBI's New York counterterrorism division, former leader of its SWAT team, crouched at the foot of the driveway. Twelve men dressed in assault gear, faces blackened with night grease, stood in an arc around him, the rain sluicing off their helmets like so many waterfalls.

"Normally this would be Jimmy Malloy's slot," said Barnes. "We all know what happened to him. I'm taking his position and it's an honor. Okay, then, it's a long run up to the house. We're exposed the entire way, but the weather is on our side. If we skirt the tree line, no one will see us until we're already on top of them. We break into two teams. I'll take my guys through the front. The rest of you take the back. We go in hot. Whoever is inside, they are not nice guys. Shoot first, ask questions later. These are the animals that took out Jimmy, Terry, and Jason. Take them down hard. If you can, try to leave one or two alive so we can ask them what they have planned. I want the place cleared inside of thirty seconds."

Barnes extended a gloved hand. Twelve others covered it. "Fidelity. Bravery. Integrity."

He broke formation, put on his helmet, and started up the drive. He jogged along a grass berm that bordered the driveway and ran alongside the forest. He glanced over his shoulder. His men were shadows. He rounded a bend and the home came into view. It was an old, rambling, one-story place with a shingled roof and two chimneys. Lights burned in the front window. He had the floor plan etched into his memory. Four bedrooms, three baths, living room, den, library, and kitchen. A 4,200-square-foot maze with low ceilings and two back doors. He couldn't have picked a worse house.

Barnes gripped his pistol tightly. The rain had picked up in the last minute and the grass was soft and slick. He kept his eye on the front door. The probe team sent three hours earlier had scanned the residence with an infrared heat detector and come up with ten separate heat blooms. Jan McVeigh had relayed Alex's view that the mercenaries had decamped long before. Maybe. Maybe not. Something was creating the heat blooms. Either someone was growing pot with heat lamps or there were ten bad guys inside.

Barnes raised a fist. Behind him, his men halted. The front door stood 50 feet away across an expanse of lawn. No protection there. They had no choice but to run, a difficult task when you were wearing 35 pounds of body armor and equipment. New York's FBI office did not possess an armored vehicle to plow down the front door. He and his men would have to do things the old-fashioned way. They would have to put their lives on the line.

Barnes directed two fingers at the house. His men sprinted across the lawn, lining up in single file at the front door. Barnes hit the side of the house, breathing hard. He wiped the rain out of his eyes and gave the signal to go.

A man ran ahead and broke open the door with a battering ram. Barnes was breacher, which meant that he was first man in. He turned on his pistol's laser sight and flashlight and stormed into the house, tossing in a flashbang to say hello.

The stun grenade exploded. He heard the second team come through the back door. Another grenade. His men ran past him, securing each room. Cries of "Clear!" sounded through the house.

Barnes's boot knocked something over. It was a tin bucket. He bent to pick it up but pulled his hand away when he noted that it was glowing with heat. Next to the bucket was a Sterno can—a solid-fuel canister used to heat food. It was apparent that the bucket had been placed atop the Sterno can for hours. Hence the glow. Hence the heat blooms. He ran through the house and found nine similar setups.

Barnes returned to the front door. The smoke was clearing now, and he switched on the lights. There were no bad guys. The FBI had been played. It was then that he saw the black wire stretched against the wall. He followed it toward the door, where it lay on the ground, snapped in two by his own careless feet.

"Out! Out! Out!" he shouted. "The place is booby-trapped."

He stood by the door, counting his men as they ran past. The last man brushed by.

Barnes turned to leave.

He never made it.

Twenty-nine seconds after he had entered the house, a 10-pound charge of C4 plastic explosive wrapped in a bed sheet filled with cutlery, candelabra, and cooking ware and hidden in the dresser 2 feet away detonated.

Supervisory Special Agent Bill Barnes was vaporized.

Miraculously, no other member of the SWAT team was seriously injured.

83

Michael Grillo took a long, satisfying draw from his cigar. Jeb Washburn sat next to him, enjoying one of his own. The men were talking to Paul Lawrence Tiernan about his Palantir software and how it had spotted the coming attack.

"I first noticed the pattern a year ago. I use the program to trend stock market activity. I noted that a lot of investments were being made in corporations with high national security quotients. Power plants, oil, satellites, microchips, Net hardware. Companies you'd never allow a foreigner to own, especially someone who wasn't an ally. I ran a regression analysis to see if I could find a common thread. Bingo! There it was. All the purchases were run through private equity firms. But then I thought, no way. Each firm can't be making its decision independently. It's statistically impossible for that kind of activity to be random. There has to be some kind of correlation, something that ties them together. I dug deeper, and that's when I hit on the CIC, the China Investment Corporation, which had made large investments in all the private equity firms. Still, I thought the connection might be benign. There are a lot of sovereign wealth funds and it's their job to invest all around the world. I decided to do some dirty work. Those sly bastards in Shanghai aren't the only ones who can hack at will." Tiernan took a sip of Coke and grinned.

"You know the best way into a closed system? Photocopiers. They're all linked to the Net and they have virtually no defense at all. I got into the CIC's internal system and everything kept feeding up the ladder to Magnus Lee. He wasn't just running the CIC. He also headed up a covert organization called i3, the Institute for Investment Initiative, which he created to steal every industrial secret in the United States, Japan, and Europe. The Chinese are not just making fake Rolexes anymore. We're talking stealing the latest car designs from General Motors, microchip architecture from Intel, stealth technology from Northrop. I don't know how, but they have eyes and ears everywhere. This is government-sanctioned piracy." Tiernan looked from one man to the other. "That's when things got scary and I reached out to Mr. Washburn here. I know when I'm out of my depth. When his supervisors didn't want to remunerate me for my considerable investment in time and money, I thought about who else might be interested in getting their hands on this information. I saw that Edward Astor sat on the CIC's international board of advisers. No way he knew about this. He's a hard-ass. Boy, I thought, would he be pissed if he learned about all this."

"You still haven't said anything about the target," said Grillo.

"In China, everything is about face. Dignity. Standing. How people regard you. Lee's goal is to elevate the reputation of China as an international financial center. He's up for a slot as vice premier of finance. No better way of getting it than bringing mighty America down a notch or two. Right now New York, London, and Tokyo are the world's financial centers. Shanghai is way down on the list. He wants to change that."

"How?" asked Washburn.

"Not sure. Edward Astor thought they had had a hand in the Flash Crash a few years back and in that Feudal Trading debacle, where that company lost a billion dollars of its own money in thirty minutes, supposedly by entering the wrong algorithm. I don't know whether they did or they didn't. What I do know is that Lee has everything he needs to bring our financial infrastructure to its knees. The last company Watersmark bought built the hardware that runs the New York Stock Exchange's brand-new trading platform. That ought to tell you something."

"So the Exchange is the target?" asked Washburn. "I've got to make a call."

There was a knock on the door. "That's Mr. Astor," said Grillo.

Grillo rose and put his eye to the peephole. He saw the back of Astor's head, a dark T-shirt.

"Come on in," he said, opening the door.

A fist drove into his solar plexus. Another smashed his cheek. He collapsed on the floor as a slim Asian man stepped over him. A taller, imperious man followed, slamming the door behind him.

Washburn dropped his phone and stood, struggling to free his gun. The Asian launched a flying roundhouse that snapped Washburn's jaw and sent him sprawling. The pistol fell to the floor. Washburn reached for it, but the Asian scooped it up, stepping on Washburn's wrist and breaking it with an audible snap.

Grillo rose to a knee. He had a glimpse of Tiernan turning and wheeling himself down the hall before a heel struck him flush across the face, slamming his head into the floor. Grillo lay on his back, stunned and hurting. His nose was broken, and he suspected that his sternum was bruised. Worse, his pistol was missing. There came the sound of a scuffle, of furniture being violently rearranged. Then a truncated scream. The Asian dragged Tiernan into the room by a dislocated arm.

"You're Grillo?" the tall man asked the corporate investigator.

"That's me."

"Well done. Or perhaps I should say thank you. Paul Lawrence Tiernan. *Pal-an-tir.* Clever."

"I thought you guys were the ones listening in on everyone," said Grillo.

"We found you, didn't we? Just a little late."

"Where's Mr. Astor?"

"Safe and cooperating with us."

"I'm not buying that."

"At this point, I don't care what you buy." The tall man addressed Tiernan, who despite his injured arm had pushed himself up against the couch. "The report, please."

"On the desk," said Grillo.

"I'd like all the copies."

"That's the only hard copy," said Tiernan. "The original is on my computer."

"Really. I thought you of all people would know better than to store it in such a vulnerable location, so easy for people like . . . well, like you and me to find. I'm guessing you store your research somewhere safer, say on a flash drive."

"Don't give it to him," said Washburn.

"And you are?"

"None of your damned business."

"If you're not Grillo and you're not Mr. Tiernan, then I really don't care who you are." The tall man looked at the Asian. "Daniel."

Washburn tried to get to his feet, but the Asian was ungodly fast. A curled fist struck Washburn's throat, crushing his larynx. The CIA agent dropped to his knees, clutching at his fractured windpipe. The Asian locked his arms around his neck and snapped his spine.

"Okay," said Tiernan. "You can have it. It's on the flash on the desk next to my computer. I swear that's the only copy."

"Show me."

"Can you get me my chair . . . please."

The Asian retrieved the wheelchair and lifted Tiernan into it. The tall man rolled him to his office. Grillo busied himself with his nose, groaning, making it appear that he was in too much agony to be aware of what was going on around him. There was quite a bit of blood. The Asian lost interest and walked around the apartment.

The tall, pale man returned with Tiernan five minutes later. He held a flash drive in his palm. "I believe we're done. Of course, there is one other place you have the report." He tapped his forehead. "I'm afraid I can't take you with me. Goodbye, gentlemen."

The tall man left.

The Asian looked at Grillo, who was still recumbent, then picked up a pillow from the couch and approached Tiernan.

"No, man . . . no," said Palantir, doing his best to wheel himself backward with his one functioning arm. "Please!"

The Asian put the pillow to Tiernan's face, buried the pistol in its folds, and fired three times. The muffled gunshots sounded no louder than heavy footsteps.

By then Grillo was up off the floor. All this time he had been marshaling his resources, gathering his strength for one charge. He knew a little about martial arts, too. He'd earned black belts in Brazilian jujitsu and full-contact karate. He'd also spent six months learning Krav Maga with the Israeli Defense Force. The sum of his experience, aided by the vicious blows he'd received, told him that the Asian was a superior fighter. In a prolonged bout, Grillo didn't stand a chance. It would have to be fast, ugly, and with deadly force.

As the Asian turned, Grillo was on him, landing a frontal kick. His foot struck the intruder's chest, sending him sprawling over Tiernan's body and upending the wheelchair. The Asian turned his fall into a back somersault and rose unhurt, hands in a fighting position, eyes seeking advantage.

The pistol lay on the floor between them.

Grillo launched a roundhouse kick to the jaw. He was slow. The

Asian saw it coming and dropped to the floor, sweeping his foot and knocking his opponent's legs out from under him. Grillo hit the floor hard. The Asian lunged for the pistol. Grillo locked his legs around the Asian's neck and twisted his torso, and then brought his knees together to crush the man's larynx. The Asian was strong. Inch by inch, he pulled himself toward the pistol. And then he had it. He threw his arm behind him and fired wildly, the shots bracketing Grillo's head. The third shot struck Grillo's shoulder. He bucked, trying to create a whiplash to snap the Asian's neck. The gun dropped from the Asian's hand and slid across the floor, stopping inches from Grillo. Close, but not close enough. The Asian arched his back and pried Grillo's legs apart. He was pulling free. Grillo stretched an arm toward the weapon. His fingers brushed the grip. His assailant turned on his side, and Grillo knew he was losing him.

Grillo unlocked his legs and hurled himself at the pistol.

He saw a shadow from the corner of his eye. A form descended on him. A knee dug into his back. Hands gripped his neck, arching his spine as if it were a bow. Grillo searched for something to latch on to to gain leverage. His hand found the solid ashtray. Not leverage, but maybe just as effective. He lashed out behind him, throwing blows over his shoulder. Again and again the ashtray struck the intruder's head, but there was no lessening of pressure. A verterbra snapped. A current sizzled along his spine and into his neck. Grillo lost sensation in his fingertips. The hands tightened around his neck, fingers crushing his throat. Grillo found Jeb Washburn's dead eyes staring at him. They offered neither hope nor encouragement, only resignation. Grillo struck out again. The grip weakened. Again. And then he was free, rolling to his side.

He looked up to find the Asian aiming the pistol at him.

A gunshot cracked the air.

Grillo felt nothing.

The Asian lowered his gun. Blood trickled from a perfect hole in his forehead. He pitched forward onto the floor.

Grillo turned. A gangly redheaded man stood in the doorway, a wisp of smoke rising from his pistol. An athletic, dark-haired woman stood behind him. Her eye was swollen and she looked like hell.

Alex Forza tapped Barry Mintz on the shoulder. "Nice shot, Deadeye."

84

It was his last run.

Sandy "Skinner" Beaufoy hurried up Tenth Avenue, carrying a tray of coffee and doughnuts. It was nine, and the storms that had pounded the city all night had stopped. Here in Chelsea, the sidewalks teemed with pedestrians. The sight was a relief. The more people out and about, the better. Police were trained never to shoot into a crowd. He suffered from no such reluctance.

Beaufoy turned into one of the commuter lots near the Holland Tunnel. The excursion onto the city streets wasn't just for refreshments but to monitor for heightened police activity. He sought out police at several street corners and lingered nearby long enough to pick up an indication that they were on alert. He noted nothing out of the ordinary.

Beaufoy hurried up the ramp to the second level. He was forty going on sixty, with a decent patch in the South African Army behind him, followed by less decent patches chasing a paycheck in hellholes across Africa, the Middle East, and Asia. There was always work to be had if you were handy with a gun, knew how to take orders, and kept your cool under fire. But Beaufoy had escaped too many times. Even a cat only has nine lives, and he reckoned he'd used up a fair number more than that. He'd taken a bullet in the lung in Liberia and escaped an IED by a whisker in Baghdad, though he still suffered migraines from the explosion. The capper was the six-month stint in Black Beach prison, a cold, damp pit that had robbed him of his teeth and left him shivering even when it was 90 degrees outside. There were no two ways about it. He was played out.

The two hundred grand he'd been paid up front was tucked away in a numbered account in Vanuatu, which was the last truly safe banking haven, even if he couldn't spell it correctly, or for that matter find it on a map. It was an island somewhere in the South Pacific, and that was good enough for him. After this, he planned on going somewhere warmer, where he could bake in the sun until his skin was tanned as black as that of the Kaffirs in the Transvaal and the last bit of cold was burned out of his bones.

As for his nickname, it wasn't what people thought. He wasn't some savage who enjoyed skinning his enemies alive. It came from his first posting in the army, as a mule skinner with the 10th Mountain Cavalry. No one knew animals like he did. So it would have to be an island with plenty of grass for his horses to eat, and of course with no extradition treaties to the U.S. or Britain or wherever the hell he might end up behind bars. He'd made himself one promise going in: no more prison.

Beaufoy spotted the van at the rear of the lot. He climbed in and distributed the coffee and doughnuts to his team. Because of the rushed departure, there hadn't been time for a last hot meal. The six men and two women seated behind him were dressed in civilian clothes. Loose, slightly oversized shirts covered their Kevlar vests and communications equipment. Athletic bags at their feet concealed their automatic weapons. They looked like a young, healthy, clean-cut bunch.

Beaufoy placed a call on one of the operational phones. "Checking for any last-minute details," he said.

"There have been no compromises," replied Septimus Reventlow. "Everything is a go."

Beaufoy hung up and checked his watch again.

"If anyone needs a little pick-me-up, now's the time." Beaufoy popped a go pill. At his age, he needed everything he could get to maintain his edge. He looked from person to person, receiving a committed nod from each.

Beaufoy started the engine. *"Gott mit uns."*

85

Magnus Lee studied his collection of neckties. He needed something elegant yet modest. A tie that would suit a future member of the Standing Committee of the People's Republic of China. Blue, not black. God forbid red. He took a step to his right and ran a thumb across his navy ties. He selected a midnight-blue Dior and held it against his white shirt. Perfect.

Lee finished dressing and walked into his bedroom. His manservant waited on his knees, ready to apply a coat of polish to his shoes. John Lobb. Custom made in London. A future vice premier had to look the part. The Chinese people did not want their leaders dressed like peasants.

Lee took the elevator to the lobby. His chauffeur held open the door to the Mercedes and Lee slipped into the back seat. Traffic on Dongguan Avenue was light, and he arrived at the Peninsula Beijing, 3 miles from his home, in forty minutes. In the Huang Ting Restaurant, he was shown to a favored table. The premier arrived soon after. The men ate an expansive dinner of dim sum, shark's fin soup, fresh grouper, and Peking duck, followed by a plate of fresh fruit and snifters of Hennessy cognac.

"Word from New York?" the premier asked finally, his cheeks reddened by the spirits.

"Any minute," said Lee.

"If all goes well, you will be on the Standing Committee tomorrow, Vice Premier Lee."

"I have every confidence that Troy will succeed."

The premier wiped his mouth, suppressing a mean smile. "It's not enough that we succeed," he whispered. "The West must fail."

Lee nodded.

The premier held his arm as the men descended the stairs to their separate automobiles. A photographer from the *Beijing Times* took their picture. In a few hours, it would be posted on the newspaper's website.

Tomorrow morning it would appear on the front page of every paper across the land. Word would spread that his election was assured. Magnus Lee, vice premier of finance. The yuan would drop like a stone. His investment with Bobby Astor would bear fruit and he would repay Elder Chen.

It was all so close now.

Lee checked his watch.

Any minute.

86

Thirty minutes before the opening, the floor of the New York Stock Exchange was a scene of ordered pandemonium. The floor was spread over three cavernous high-ceilinged rooms covering a total of 40,000 square feet, with electronic trading posts situated in a rambling fashion like bumpers on a pinball machine. A balcony encircling the floor provided tight quarters for media outlets such as CNN, Fox News, CNBC, and others that maintained mini broadcast studios and kept reporters on call from dawn to dusk. Overlooking it all was the terrace where dignitaries stood to ring the opening bell.

Alex stood restlessly at one of the two main entries to the floor, from which she could see outside the building to Exchange Place and the old headquarters of J. P. Morgan across the street. "Mintz," she said into her lapel microphone. "Come back."

To protect against the bad guys listening in, she'd demanded access to a military bandwidth reserved for national emergencies. It wasn't foolproof, but it was the best they could do at a moment's notice.

"All clear," said Mintz, his voice plumped with pride at his newfound status. He was no longer Deadeye in jest. He was the real thing.

Alex checked in with her agents who were patrolling the streets surrounding the Exchange. None had sighted any of the mercenaries whose dossiers she had found in James Salt's home, or numbers 1 to 23, as she thought of them.

She'd read Palantir's report and passed it on to Janet McVeigh, along with all she'd learned from Michael Grillo. From there the information had traveled to the police commissioner, the mayor's office, and of course FBI headquarters in Washington, D.C. There was no question that the New York Stock Exchange was the target. The mayor was adamant in his wish that the Exchange remain open for business as usual. The law enforcement authorities agreed, though their reasons had nothing to do with pride, and everything to do with tactics.

It was also decided not to publicly broadcast the nature of the threat.

A plan was fielded to block off all vehicular traffic in a 1-square-mile radius of the Exchange building. That, too, was vetoed. Alex pointed out that it was probable that a secondary target had been chosen and mapped out. The idea of an attack against a department store, a government building, or, God forbid, a school by so many heavily armed, battle-hardened mercenaries was too terrible to contemplate.

There was really only one choice, and that was to capture the terrorists. To achieve this, two hundred policemen and FBI agents, most from the local Joint Terrorism Task Force, had been called in, briefed, and assigned a sector to patrol. All wore plain clothes. They were dressed as Wall Street traders, secretaries, tourists, and city workers. All had been provided with photographs of the mercenaries. The last order was the most important: no one was to engage a suspect until being given the green light from Alex. The only visible sign of the beefed-up security was an additional Hercules brigade positioned at the corner of Wall and Broad, but this was hardly out of the ordinary. The New York Stock Exchange was a hard target in the best of times.

As Alex peered out to the street, it appeared to be a normal midweek summer morning.

What could go wrong?

87

Sandy Beaufoy drove the van down Broadway. Traffic was moving nicely. There was a police scanner on the center console. As he neared the drop-off zone, he listened to the usual litany of petty crime, larceny, and traffic mishaps that filled a big-city policeman's day, be it in Jo'burg or the Big Apple. There was no hint that the police were gearing up for something out of the ordinary. Even so, he was wary, and listened carefully for any euphemism or nuanced turn of phrase. He was almost disappointed that the police were so clueless. There was, after all, no question that the FBI and NYPD knew they were here. Not after the bomb in Darien.

There hadn't been time to remove all the weapons and munitions from the safe house, so he'd made the decision to booby-trap the place and blow it to kingdom come. The less evidence, the better. The morning radio buzzed with reports of the explosion in the Connecticut town and the death of an FBI agent. If he hadn't heard from James Salt in over twelve hours, it was to be expected. At this point, it was impossible to communicate without compromising one another. Salt's master had given him the green light. That was all that mattered. Sandy Beaufoy was a soldier. He followed orders.

The signal turned red at Zuccotti Park. Without prompting, the passenger door slid open and three men jumped out. They separated immediately. Wearing baseball caps and sunglasses, two of them carrying athletic bags, they looked like any other unthreatening Caucasian males. For all intents and purposes, they were invisible.

Beaufoy stopped again a block further on. A second three-man squad alighted in front of Trinity Church. Wall Street began to his left. Barricades prevented cars from entering. The Exchange was 200 feet down the narrow road. As such, there was always a police presence. His eye searched for reinforcements. Several uniformed policemen manned the vehicle barricades across the street. They appeared at ease—jovial, even.

If they only knew what was going to hit them, thought Beaufoy.

He had divided his remaining men into two teams, one infiltrating the target by the Number 5 line of the subway, Wall Street Station. It was common for Transit Police to search rucksacks and bags, no reason needed, so he'd ordered the team to strap their compact H&K submachine guns to their backs and tape their spare cartridges to their calves.

The other team came by car, but from the south. The plan called for the three teams to converge on the Exchange and to open fire only when they reached a distance of 20 feet from the building. From there it was a lightning strike through the entry. A hail of automatic-weapons fire, grenades, and, for the team entering on Exchange Place, a hearty hello from their TOW antitank weapon to see themselves in.

Beaufoy stopped the van a third time at the corner of Morris Street, allowing the final two mercenaries to get out. He turned right at the light and drove 200 yards, then parked illegally. He threw the keys in the sewer. He would not be back. Approaching Broadway, he made a commo check with every member of his team.

"Alpha comeback?"

"Alpha clear."

"Beta?"

Twenty-two were called. Twenty-two answered.

Beaufoy reached Broadway. He spotted three of his men fanned out along the sidewalk, crossing the street and closing on the target. If he had a shred of sanity remaining, he would be scared out of his wits. It was a suicide mission. No one paid a merc $1 million with $200,000 up front. And yet he wasn't. He was battle-bright and battle-ready. If this was to be his last day, so be it. He would have it no other way.

Gott mit uns.

Beaufoy ran across the street.

88

The yuan was dying a quick and ugly death.

"You watching the rates?" Marv Shank stood in the doorway, smiling broadly. "We're up five hundred mil. You were right all along. The Chinese are depreciating. If the yuan keeps dropping, we're going to have our best quarter ever."

Astor looked at the screen. The yuan was trading at 6.5 and rising, well above the rate at which he'd purchased his contracts. The dramatic shift had occurred an hour ago, after a picture of Magnus Lee and the Chinese premier exiting a popular restaurant in Beijing was splashed across the Web. The heir apparent had been officially anointed. Lee was outspoken in his support of an export-driven economy. It was simply a matter of putting two and two together.

"Not bad."

"'Not bad'? What, are you kidding me? We're already up a couple hundred mil. It's stellar. You da man, Bobby."

"Sure, but, it's not ours."

Shank's smile evaporated. "What do you mean, 'not ours'?"

"I informed our lenders that the wire transfers they received yesterday to cover our margin call was made in error. I asked that they wire the money back to the originating bank."

"To Septimus Reventlow's account?"

"Exactly. Technically, we stand in default of our agreements at the close yesterday. All our positions were frozen at the prevailing rate."

"The rate at which we go under?"

"That's correct."

"You're kidding, right?"

"It's done. We don't do business with terrorists."

"But . . ." Shank shook his head, searching for words. Finally, he sighed and gave up. Even he couldn't disagree with Astor.

"Sell at the open to cover what we owe. Talk to Mandy Price. See what she thinks."

"What's going to happen to Reventlow's money?"

"Nothing for the moment. First the government needs to get proof against him. So far, there's only my word he's involved in this whole thing."

"Show 'em your hand," said Shank, incensed.

"I don't think that will count for much a year from now when this thing finally gets to a court of law. And anyway, Reventlow's gone. He probably hopped a jet as soon as he figured out that his brother didn't make it. I give you even money no one sees him again."

"So tomorrow the yuan falls through the floor, we should be up two billion, we should be the toast of the town, but instead Comstock is broke, I lose my shirt, and Septimus Reventlow just gets to walk away."

"Pretty much. Unless the government presses charges against him or his family office, and we both know that isn't going to happen."

Early that morning, Astor, Alex, and Shank had been ushered into an office at 26 Federal Plaza and given a sharp talking-to by the director of the FBI himself. No word of Magnus Lee's or Septimus Reventlow's involvement in the affair could be allowed to get out, now or ever. Palantir's report was on the president's desk. A special meeting of the National Security Council was scheduled for later in the day. Were word of China's involvement in Charles Hughes's and Martin Gelman's deaths to leak, the diplomatic repercussions could be unthinkable. The assassination of government officials counted as a *casus belli*. The hawks on Capitol Hill would be calling for war.

"Fuck me," said Shank, throwing up his arms, turning and leaving the office.

Astor watched through his window as his friend moved up and down the trading floor, screaming out sell orders, scowling, berating anyone who dared ask him a single question. He was a creature of the Street. Marv Shank would live and die on the floor.

Astor called Alex. "Anything?"

"Nada."

"You think they gave up?"

"Not a chance."

"But Reventlow knows we're on to them."

"Does he? I'm not sure. And if he does, I don't know if it matters."

Astor turned and walked to the east-facing window, looking down toward Broadway and Wall Street. "So did you think about it?"

"What?"

"You know . . . *us*."

"I don't go out with men who chew their nails," said Alex.

"Very funny."

"Hold on for a sec." Alex's voice hardened, and her worried tone sent a chill down Astor's spine.

"What is it?" he asked.

There was no answer, and Astor asked again.

"They're here," said Alex.

The line went dead.

Astor put his hand to the window, his eyes finding the Exchange building.

It was happening now.

89

Two more bad guys were identified approaching up New Street from the south.

And another two after that, coming down Liberty.

One on Broadway.

Alex's earpiece bristled with reports from her agents. A template of the suspected bad guys quickly emerged. Baggy shirts. Baseball caps. Sunglasses. A few carrying athletic bags. She passed the description along and told everyone to be ready to take down their man on her order.

Ten had been spotted. Then twelve. But time was running out. The mercenaries were getting too close to the Exchange. At any moment they could open fire.

Alex walked outside. Well over two hundred people crowded the streets bordering the Exchange and sat on the stairs of Federal Hall. It would take only one machine gun to wreak havoc. She spotted Dead-eye Mintz, dressed in jeans and a T-shirt, sitting behind the statue of George Washington at the entry to Federal Hall.

A voice in her earpiece. Another sighting took the number to fourteen. Alex made her decision. "Move in," she said. "Take 'em down."

All around the Exchange, undercover FBI agents and policemen converged on their targets. Groups of three, four, and five officers swarmed each assailant. Alex was watching a violent flash mob in reverse. Instead of standing apart from the crowd, the bad guys disappeared from it, thrown to the pavement, hands pulled behind their backs and cuffed. Those law enforcement agents not tracking a suspect rushed among the bewildered pedestrians, seeking out the nine remaining assailants.

Alex ran to the security checkpoint at the corner of Broad and Wall. She eyed a woman looking much too calm in the melee erupting all around her.

Baggy shirt. *Check.*

Cap. *Check.*

Sunglasses. *Check.*

Athletic bag. *Check.*

The woman's hands delved into the bag.

Alex leaped the barricade and drew her Glock, advancing on the woman. "Freeze. Let me see your hands."

In an instant three other agents surrounded the suspect. The woman raised her hands high. Alex ripped the bag off her shoulder. Inside was a submachine gun. The other agents pushed the woman to the ground and cuffed her.

The first gunshot sounded.

Alex turned to see where it had come from and saw a man running toward Broadway. He carried a submachine gun in one hand. And then he was down, shot by one of three policemen almost before the welter of gunshots exploded.

"I'm hit," a man shouted.

Alex saw one of her agents clutching his leg. A policeman ran to his side and administered aid.

"Give me a count," she said.

"Ten down."

Alex returned to Exchange Place. She turned the corner to the main entrance as a woman screamed. A blond man held the woman to his chest and pointed a pistol at her head. A dozen officers surrounded him in seconds. Alex approached him, her pistol at her side.

"Your move," she said.

The blond mercenary looked around him. He was young and handsome, by all accounts someone who had the world before him. He smiled sadly, realizing that he was hopelessly outnumbered. He put the pistol beneath his chin. "Ah, fuck it."

It wasn't the Exchange.

Astor stood at the window of his office looking down toward the Stock Exchange. From his aerie sixty stories above the ground, all looked calm, peaceful, and orderly. It didn't make sense. Magnus Lee's and Septimus Reventlow's strategy was to buy a controlling interest in a company, place a man inside, and use the Empire Platform to see into and, when needed, control its operations. An outright Mumbai-style attack on the Stock Exchange might shut down trading for a few days, even sow doubt in investors' minds about the invincibility of the United States, but it would do nothing to enable Lee and his brother to gain control over the entire trading system. And yet Palantir and Astor's father had been sure that their target was the Exchange. This belief was reinforced by the CIC's last investment, in Matronix, the company that manufactured the servers and hardware recently installed to run the New York Stock Exchange's trading platform.

A line from Palantir's report was stuck in his mind: ". . . and though there is no question about the depth and extent of the penetration of critical national systems, the aggressor cannot use TEP to trigger a modal system-wide default until a source code is introduced."

TEP, for The Empire Platform.

But an outright physical assault wasn't enough.

Astor looked at his television. It was 9:30 a.m., and he watched as the opening bell of the New York Stock Exchange was rung by United States Navy Master Chief Ron Blackburn, a member of SEAL Team Six and the nation's most recent recipient of the Medal of Honor. Accompanying him on the dais were his wife and child, as well as the man who had replaced Edward Astor as CEO of the NYSE. After an initial surge of energy, the floor grew quiet. Each year fewer and fewer men and women were required to supervise the trades. More and more of the work was done by computers.

He left his office and hurried across the floor. By the time he reached Ivan Davidoff's office, he was running. "Ivan, you free?"

"Sure, boss," said the bespectacled IT professional.

"You familiar with a company called Matronix?"

"Of course. Their machines run the most sophisticated trading systems in the world."

"And we just bought a bunch of them—I mean, my father did."

"Yes, they're housed in New Jersey."

"No," said Astor. "I mean here in Manhattan. The ones housed at the Exchange."

"There are only a few there. Traders on the floor use remote terminals to input orders. The heart of the machinery is at the trading center in Mahwah."

"Where?"

"Mahwah, New Jersey. All trading moved there two years ago."

"So you couldn't screw with the trading platform from the floor?"

"The only place you can tinker with the system is in Mahwah."

"And you could introduce a source code there?"

"That's correct." Ivan Davidoff eyed Astor strangely. "What do you know about source codes?"

Sandy Beaufoy watched helplessly as the police took down three of his men. He glanced to his left. At the corner of Wall and Broadway, police tackled another one. Down the street, a female plainclothes officer held a pistol to the head of one of the Swedish girls. The entire area was swarming with undercover policemen.

The operation had been compromised.

"Freeze!"

Beaufoy spun and shot the policeman standing behind him in the head. Thirty feet away, another plainclothes cop charged his way, firing his gun. Beaufoy shot him, too.

Beaufoy ran into the building behind him. It was a bank. The lobby was crowded, but all activity had frozen at the sound of the first gunshot. As one, customers and employees stared at him. A security guard drew a gun. Beaufoy fired into the ceiling and the lobby devolved into chaos, every man, woman, and child for himself. Beaufoy ran through them, dodging and elbowing his way to the rear of the building. A narrow lane separated him from the Exchange. He freed his H&K, broke from the door, and charged toward the building's New Street entrance. The police saw him coming, but he opened fire first. Glass shattered. Men fell. He threw open the door and shot a man in front of him.

Beaufoy ran along the corridor. The exfil plan was as important as the attack itself. He did not want to give his life to cause a blip in trading volume. He ran down one corridor, then another. He heard voices behind him. A woman shouting for him to freeze. A bullet struck the wall above his head. Too close. He slid on his knees, turning and spraying the corridor behind him. The woman was nowhere in sight. Beaufoy stood. The hall ended dead ahead, with offshoots to the right and left.

Which way?

He started right, then remembered it was left, then down a flight of stairs to the passageway that led out from under the Exchange a full city block south, to Beaver Street. The passage had been built when gold had been stored on the premises and bank officials did not want to bring it in under full public view. Beaver Street was the exfil point. From there, the teams would divide up and lose themselves in the warren of streets and alleys that made up the southern tip of Manhattan Island.

To the left, then.

The first bullet hit him before he could cover a step. A gut shot stopped by his vest. He hardly felt it. Beaufoy lifted the H&K and swiveled to get off a shot. The second bullet struck his neck and severed his spinal cord. He dropped to the ground as if he'd been unplugged.

A woman who was much too pretty to be a cop stood above him. She had lovely brown hair and eyes the color of good whiskey. He noticed that someone had given her a nice little shiner.

"Hello, Skinner," she said.

"Like a labyrinth in here," he muttered.

Beaufoy died.

90

Six buttonwood trees lined the pathway to the entrance of the New York Stock Exchange's data center in Mahwah, New Jersey. The trees commemorated the storied buttonwood tree on Wall Street, where the first brokers of the infant United States had gathered in the late 1700s to trade shares. Septimus Reventlow thought it was a quaint touch. Ahead, a single set of doors provided entry to the building. No other doors led inside. There were no windows, either. The imposing stone structure looked more like a fortress or a monument to a modern-day pharaoh than the home of the world's most sophisticated stock trading platform.

Reventlow walked easily toward the building. He had already cleared the security checkpoints without a hitch. First there had been the tall earthen berm and ironwork fence that surrounded the complex. Then there had been the three Delta barriers, each lowered only after he'd passed over the one before. None posed any problem. Reventlow's name was on the visitors list. He was the day's guest of honor.

An official waited at the door. Reventlow gave an alias, along with a matching identification, in this case a New York driver's license. The alias matched the name of the vice president of a small investment bank that his brother had recently purchased. Like any similar institution, the bank desired to rent some space in the facility to house its own computers so they would be in close physical proximity to the computers that ran the Exchange. The proper term was *colocation*.

"All the Exchange's proprietary computers are housed in a single twenty-thousand-square-foot room, or pod," explained the official as they walked into the heavily air-conditioned building. "These machines match all buy and sell orders in the most efficient manner. We call them 'matching engines.'"

"And these matching engines run the entire Exchange?"

"Eighty percent of it, and more each day. Of course, there are specialists on the floor who handle large block trades for their clients. But we're able to assume more of that business, too. We also handle trades for the American Stock Exchange. All told, over three billion shares a day."

"Impressive," offered Reventlow.

"We'd like to put your hardware in a pod just down the hall. You'll be sharing the space with a few other banks, but rest assured that you'll be equidistant from our servers."

"I wouldn't want anything less," said Reventlow. In the day of high-frequency trading, when millions of shares changed hands in seconds, the smallest difference in the time it took for a trade to be executed was crucial. Every thousand feet away from one of the Exchange's matching engines meant an additional millionth of a second in transit time. While differences of a foot or 10 feet or even 1,000 feet conveyed no competitive disadvantage, differences of 10 miles or 100 or 1,000 miles did. Hence the need to allow banks to position their mainframes as close to the Exchange's as possible.

"Do you think I might see the matching engines?"

"I'm sorry, that's out of the question," said the official. "I hope you understand."

Reventlow reluctantly nodded. "Before I went into banking, I worked in systems design. I've heard this is a beauty."

"If I do say so myself, it is. Tell you what, I can let you see our Risk Management Gateway. It's the hardware we put in place to guarantee against any errors on your end."

"So all trades pass through it?"

"Of course," said the official, offended. "We consider it our prime competitive advantage."

The official led the way down a hallway and into a large, brightly lit room housing six mainframe computers. Reventlow smiled in appreciation even as his heart beat faster. Reaching into his pocket, he withdrew a slim envelope, concealed it in his palm, and with his thumb opened the flap.

"According to parameters you set, these machines will filter every trade to make sure it complies with SEC requirements," the official continued.

Reventlow leaned closer to a machine, raising a hand to touch the control panel.

"Please," said the official testily, gently removing his visitor's hand.

It was then that Reventlow raised the concealed envelope to his mouth and blew. A fine spray of cyanide powder flew into the official's face. He breathed in once, gasped, then collapsed. Reventlow caught him and laid him on the floor. He stepped over the writhing man and walked to the last computer in line.

From his other pocket he withdrew a small flash drive. He looked at the slim black device and a boost of adrenaline warmed his chest and shot to his fingertips. In his hand he held the end result of years of planning, of countless sums of money spent, of his family's boundless ambition and his country's most daring scheme.

It had all come down to this moment. It had come down to him.

Inside the flash drive was the source code that would give China control over every machine in the data center, and by extension every machine connected to them. These included matching engines in London, Frankfurt, Singapore, Paris, Tokyo, and, as important, the backup data centers in Basildon, England, and Cincinnati, Ohio. The code would also infect every piece of hardware that did business with the exchanges. Every bank, insurance company, and brokerage. And from there, every client who did business with them.

In short order, China would have control over every stock exchange in the world and every financial institution that did business with them.

Reventlow found the control unit. He moved his hand over the main panel, neatly flipping it open. He saw the USB slot immediately. All he needed to do was insert the flash drive and the source code would transfer immediately, and untraceably, to the mainframe and enter the Exchange's proprietary trading software. He breathed easier, knowing his job was done. No one would have the slightest idea that his family—his country—was clandestinely controlling the most powerful market in the world. The faintest of smiles pressed at his lips. It was so simple, really.

A footstep sounded nearby. Then another.

"Stop."

Reventlow spun and looked down the row at Bobby Astor. "You're too late," he said, turning his attention back to the server. Desperately he tried to insert the flash drive.

"That means now."

It was a woman's voice. Reventlow looked in the opposite direction.

A woman stood 10 feet away, her pistol aimed at his face. He made his decision. His fingers flew again to the computer. The flash drive pressed against the USB slot. Metal met metal.

The pistol fired.

Reventlow fell.

He was dead before the flash drive hit the floor.

"No," said Alex. "We're not."

91

Magnus Lee sat alone in his office at Excelsior Holdings, watching the terrible news unfold on the television. The attack on the Exchange had been foiled, intercepted before it had begun. Half the mercenaries were dead, the other half taken prisoner. Septimus was not answering his phone. Neither was Daniel. He feared the worst.

Lee's cell phone buzzed once again. It was the premier, calling for the fourth time. The chief of the army had also called, as had the director of the Ministry of State Security. He had answered none of their calls.

He stood and walked unsteadily to the balcony. The Eiffel Tower was lit top to bottom with bright yellow bulbs. In the night sky, it glowed like an electric jewel. He sighed, then tried to phone his brothers once again. Neither answered.

He was alone.

Lee returned to his desk and poured himself a measure of scotch. He drank it down and shuddered. He realized that the one thing he had forgotten to have his people copy was a decent scotch whiskey. There was still time. He could purchase a small Scottish distillery and pirate the recipe. He wondered what would be a suitable name. He thought of nothing.

It was done.

He would not be elected to the Standing Committee. He would not assume the position of vice premier. His career in the party was finished. But it would end there. He had taken pains to hide his involvement in the affair. There was no proof linking him to any of it. Not the attack on the Exchange or his brother's infiltration of the Mahwah complex. He would receive a censure, have his hands slapped, perhaps do a year in exile in some provincial backwater, but it would end there.

Lee smiled inwardly. He knew that his safety was assured. He was too valuable, making money for his country and his colleagues.

Make money and get rich.

It was the Chinese way.

Lee turned off the lights and left the building.

He was surprised to see his car and driver waiting. At least there was still one loyal retainer left.

He climbed into the back seat and shut the door.

"Hello, Magnus Lee."

Lee jumped at the sight of the old man. "Elder Chen. It is a surprise." He shifted his gaze to the front seat. It was not his driver behind the wheel but Elder Chen's chauffeur. Lee grew afraid. "To what do I owe this honor?" he asked.

It was then that Lee saw the enormous pistol in Elder Chen's frail hand. The old man shook his head. A flame spit from the snout. The gunshot was unbearably loud. Lee felt a sharp pain in his chest.

"But Elder Chen . . ." Lee wanted to explain that failure was beyond his control, that he had planned everything to propel his country to a position of pride and prestige it had never known, that he needed only a few more days to repay the society.

The words never came.

Magnus Lee slumped on the seat and died.

"Vice premier," said Elder Chen. "Never."

92

W hat do you think?"
Bobby Astor pushed open the door to his new office.

"This is it?" asked Alex, walking inside, taking a skeptical look at the shoddy surroundings.

"It's just me and Marv. Like the old days."

The office measured 1,000 square feet and was located on the seventh floor of an older building directly across the river from Battery Park in New Jersey. The carpet was worn but clean. The fluorescent lights didn't flicker too badly. And the subway was only a quarter of a mile away. They did, however, have a wonderful view of Manhattan.

"What are you calling it?" asked Alex.

"Renaissance Capital. Corny, but hey, if it fits . . ."

"I like it."

Marv Shank trundled into the office and dropped a box of office supplies on one of the two desks that made up the furnishings. He opened the box and took out a bottle of champagne and glasses. He popped the cork and poured two glasses. He handed one to Alex and lifted the other.

Astor regarded the bottle of champagne, then poured the rest of his Coke into the third glass. "To renaissance," he said.

"To new beginnings," said Alex.

"To family," said Shank.

They drank and looked at the view for a minute.

Shank set down his glass. "Which side do you want?"

Astor looked at the two desks, pressed face-to-face. "The first big corporate decision," he said. "You pick. You're the boss. I only work here."

Shank sat down at the desk on the right. "That'll be the day."

The three months following the attack had not been kind to Comstock or to Bobby Astor. It was never officially confirmed that Magnus

Lee had engineered the plot to sabotage the West's financial system, or that China had been in any way involved in the failed assault on the New York Stock Exchange. All the same, the yuan made a sudden and abrupt about-face and not only retraced its earlier appreciation but surpassed it, making a historical high against the dollar.

Unofficially, someone knew.

The revaluation resulted in a $600 million loss. Astor was ruined. He'd been telling the truth when he said that he had everything tied to the fund. It was all gone now. The house in the Hamptons, the ranch in Wyoming, the ski cabin in Aspen. He'd even sold his duplex in Chelsea to repay investors.

As for his father's estate, Edward Astor had bequeathed the entire amount to Helping Hands.

Bobby Astor was broke. Almost.

Shank looked at Astor, then at Alex. "So what's this vibe I've been getting the last few weeks? You kids going to give it another try?"

Astor regarded his ex-wife. Alex was dressed in a natty blue suit, her hair cut so that it touched her shoulders. She looked much too coiffed, a little too mature, and way too responsible.

"If she slows down," he said. "After all, we're looking at the new assistant director for the New York office."

"If he gives it a rest," said Alex. "No more fourteen-hour days."

"Hey," said Astor. "We're just starting up."

Shank looked between the two. "Is that a yes or a no?"

Astor faced Alex. "That's a yes. Definitely."

Alex crossed her arms and gave Bobby her most intimidating glare. She looked back at Shank. "All right," she said finally, before breaking into a grin. "That's a yes."

Just then her phone buzzed. She checked the screen. "Gotta go, boys. Duty calls."

Astor kissed her. "See you at home."

"Carbonara for supper?" asked Alex.

"You got it. With extra bacon, just like you like it."

She kissed him again and then turned to Shank. "Have him home by six."

Alex left the office.

Shank looked at Astor, horrified. "You're the cook?"

Astor walked to the door and made sure Alex was gone. "For now."

Shank made a tour of the small office. "So, buddy, you figure how much cash we're starting with?"

"I've got fifty grand in my account," Astor said. "What about you?"

"A little more. I didn't put everything in Comstock."

Astor smiled guiltily. "Actually, neither did I." He opened a large moving-box sitting in the corner and pulled out the package wrapped in brown paper. With care, he peeled back a corner and looked at the painting.

Shank screwed up his face. "God, that is ugly," he said. "Who did that?"

"Picasso."

"What'd you pay?"

"Two. But that was ten years ago."

Shank offered the painting a more appreciative gaze. "And now?"

"I showed it to Sotheby's. They made me an offer."

"Yeah? More than two?"

"A little." Astor showed him the e-mail from the famed auction house. Shank's eyes opened wide. "For real?"

"Give or take five million."

Shank did a little jig, then picked up Astor and held him in a bear hug.

"Easy, Marv," Astor groaned.

"Sorry." Shank released him. "I know, I know. If you want a friend—"

"Hold it," said Astor.

"What?"

"I do want a friend. We're going to do it differently this time." Astor put out his hand.

Shank looked at it uncertainly. "We are?"

"Yes, we are," said Astor. "I want a friend . . . and a partner."

Shank took Astor's hand and shook it. For once, he was speechless. After a moment he walked to the window. He stood there for a long time, staring across the water at the greatest city in the world.

Astor walked to the other desk and sat down. He hit a button on the keyboard and the flatscreen monitors came to life. He moved his chair closer, studying the columns of symbols and numbers, the dozens of figures ticking up and down that spoke to him in their own secret language. The markets were open and working as efficiently as ever.

A current of electricity ran up his spine.

Sit down. Buckle up. And plug in.

Astor smiled.

He was back.

Acknowledgments

It is my great pleasure to thank the following individuals for their assistance in the writing of this book: Jonathan Knee of Evercore Partners, David Ballard and Robert Sloan of S3 Partners, Drew Nordlicht of Hightower Partners, Nate Hughes at Stratfor, Stan Scheufler, Phil Trubey, Dr. Jon Shafqat, Doug Fischer, and Ted Janus.

I owe a debt of gratitude to Special Agent Anne Beagan of the FBI and her colleagues at the New York Counterterrorism Division and Joint Terrorism Task Force.

At Doubleday, I would like to thank my talented and energetic publishing team: Bill Thomas, Todd Doughty, John Pitts, Alison Rich, Rob Bloom, Bette Alexander, and, of course, my editor and good friend, Jason Kaufman.

Finally, I can't say thank you enough to my incredible team at Inkwell Management: Michael Carlisle, Kim Witherspoon, David Hale Smith, Lyndsey Blessing, Alexis Hurley, Charlie Olsen, Eliza Rothstein, and, most of all, my agent, Richard Pine.

A Note About the Author

Christopher Reich is the *New York Times* bestselling author of *Rules of Deception, Rules of Vengeance, Rules of Betrayal, Numbered Account, The Devil's Banker,* and many others. His novel *The Patriots Club* won the International Thriller Writers Award for Best Novel in 2006. He lives in Encinitas, California.